MIMI MALLOY, AT LAST!

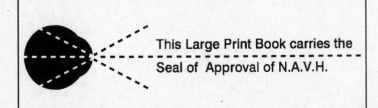

This Large Print Book carries the Seal of Approval of N.A.V.H.

MIMI MALLOY, AT LAST!

JULIA MACDONNELL

THORNDIKE PRESS
A part of Gale, Cengage Learning

GALE
CENGAGE Learning·

Farmington Hills, Mich • San Francisco • New York • Waterville, Maine
Meriden, Conn • Mason, Ohio • Chicago

GALE
CENGAGE Learning·

LIBRARY OF CONGRESS CATALOGING-IN-PUBLICATION DATA

MacDonnell, Julia.
  Mimi Malloy, at last / by Julia MacDonnell. — Large print edition.
    pages ; cm. — (Thorndike Press large print core)
    ISBN 978-1-4104-7102-4 (hardcover) — ISBN 1-4104-7102-0 (hardcover)
    1. Retirement—Fiction. 2. Life change events—Fiction. 3. Memories—
Fiction. 4. Family life—Fiction. 5. Large type books. 6. Domestic fiction.
I. Title.
PS3563.A29142M56 2014b
813'.54—dc23   2014012588

Published in 2014 by arrangement with Picador, an imprint of Farrar, Straus, and Giroux, LLC.

Printed in Mexico
1 2 3 4 5 6 7 18 17 16 15 14

In memory of
Meg Felice, Veronica, Denise
Wondrous women who left too soon

ONE:
TOO CLOSE FOR COMFORT

I'm at my table by the window, watching, without wanting to, other tenants rush off to work, bundled up against the frigid morning — running to catch the T, or starting their cars, warming them up in the parking lot before they take off for offices, stores, banks, schools, hospitals, wherever, just the way I used to, not so long ago. The only work I'm doing now is on my first cup, Maxwell House Master Blend, and a True Blue, lit with the last match from a splint book picked up at Grab & Go. I'm enjoying the first drag, if not the scenery, when, like an alarm, my phone rings. I check the time. Just past eight. I let it ring a few more times. It's got to be Cassandra, my firstborn. This time of day, she works on her to-do list, at the top of which is my name, my life, her plans to make it better scribbled underneath.

"Mimi, there's an open house tomorrow

at that new seniors' complex, Squantum River Living." She's breathing hard, like she's just won the Powerball, but me, I could spit fire.

"Squantum River Living," I echo. Just read about it in the *Patriot-Ledger,* in a special senior living section. Plus she already sent me a brochure.

"It's a great new place for seniors, subsidized too."

I swear, at times like this Cassandra's voice works on me like a dental drill.

"Let's go. It'll be fun."

"I already know all I want to know about that place."

Squantum River Living, an environmentally friendly low-rise development with three wings and solar panels on the roof. Three wings. What kind of creature has three wings? One wing is for the so-called active, independent living; the next is for transitional living, meaning one foot in the grave; and the last is an assisted living part, meaning they're only too happy to help you put the other foot in. After that, I figure, they can dump you into the river that runs through the property. Squantum River. No fuss, no muss. If you're lucky, you'll just float away.

"Squantum River Dying, that's what they

ought to call it."

"You're so negative."

"Am not!"

Evicting Mimi from her home: a pot boiling on Cassandra's front burner ever since I lost my federal civil service position over at the VA Hospital in Jamaica Plain. Since I began living on a fixed income, fixed just above the poverty line — enough so you can survive, but not enough to have much fun — Cassandra's been trying to get me out of here.

"You're going to be broke in a couple of years."

"My money situation's not your problem."

"It will be when you don't have any."

"MYOB," I say, louder than I intended, but maybe the high volume will get through to her.

Instead, she starts sniffling. I made her cry. I'm so cruel to her, one of my many sins, my shortcomings. Not that my apartment is so great. Just three rooms — not enough space for many visitors and certainly not enough for a family party. But it's in a sweet garden apartment complex called Centennial Square, near downtown Quincy. I'm on the lower level — below grade, I think they call it — so the view isn't all that great, but the rent is cheaper. Plenty of

9

windows, though. Those in the living room are level with my chest. Mostly what I see are my neighbors' feet when they're rushing off to work and home again. But it's mine. All mine. I don't have to share, and I don't have to take care of anyone else. The slightest little problem I have and Duffy, the super here, will come to fix it. A more reliable guy you couldn't find anywhere on the South Shore. I come and go as I please. No one criticizes me.

"Next question, baby." I'm nicer this time, certain Cassandra's got another item on her list or she'd have hung up by now.

"Did you get the questionnaire?" She's still breathing hard, as if the future of the planet depends upon my answer. "The questionnaire," she repeats, louder, like I'm deaf instead of only dumb.

"The questionnaire?"

"Oh, Mimi!" she wails in a way that tells me I've failed, yet again, to meet her standards of behavior and intelligence. "You've got a mind like a sieve."

"Do not." I picture one of those utensils, full of little holes, with a scalding liquid — soup, say — pouring through and the big chunks getting stuck. "It's just a senior moment. I'm entitled."

"Next thing you know, your senior moments will be stretching into days and you'll end up like Aunt Lillian. Anyway, you know darn well what I'm talking about, Aunt Patty's questionnaire. For the family history. The genealogy, a gift to our children. She sent it out last week."

Right, right. It comes back to me. My sister Patty, egged on by one of her grandsons, a gifted little prince — her words — came up with a plan to write our family history. Patty, of all people, who can't even write a postcard from Disney World.

"Oh, sure, the questionnaire," I say, though I haven't actually seen it. Most likely it's in the basket of mail on the table by my front door. With the ads for lube jobs and commemorative coins from the Franklin Mint, and solicitations from the Society for the Propagation of the Faith.

I've got a system: At about four each afternoon, I walk out to the foyer of my building and pick up my mail from its locked cubby. Back in my apartment, in my own little foyer, I drop it all into a basket, a pretty basket with apples printed on it. Unless I have an overwhelming urge to open something, which I rarely ever do, it goes into the trash bag on Monday night when I'm on my way out to the Dumpster. Cuts down on clutter and wasted time. The system works, as long as you remember to look for your rebates and Social Security check.

"Look in that pile by your front door." Cassie, bossy as always. She's like my ex, thinking that she, and she alone, can make the world run smoothly. "It's probably in there."

"OK, sure. If it's there, I'll call you back."

I hang up and finish my coffee and have another smoke before checking the mail. I'm in no hurry, in no mood to obey Cassandra's commands. I've got to take her in small doses, like bitter medicine for a chronic, low-grade pain. Besides, the last thing on my to-do list is Patty's genealogy. No interest in it whatsoever. I'm not the type to get all hot and bothered about the past. I look ahead, pride myself on it. Whatever might befall you, get over it, move on. That's how I've lived my life and raised my girls. Or, rather, how I've tried to raise them despite the constant undermining influence of John Francis Xavier Malloy, aka Jack, said ex.

The basket's on a table in the hallway with a mirror hanging over it, both the table and mirror left behind by the previous tenants when I moved in here fifteen years ago. I finger through the mail. A flyer for Senior

Fun Day at a local wellness center, another for golden-age tai chi classes at the Y. *Lubricate your joints! Improve your balance! Find serenity!* Oh, and that damned brochure for Squantum River Warehouse for People Past Their Use-By Date. No questionnaire. Typical Patty — a day late, a dollar short.

That's when I catch sight of myself in the mirror. Is that woman really me? A fading brunette, well padded, and well past her prime. When I flip on the hallway light, it's worse. Mimi, all alone. Mimi Malloy by herself. Then, behind the old me, I see the shapely brunette I used to be, the one with the tiny waist and the dimpled smile, the one Jack Malloy fell in love with oh so long ago. Maire Sheehan, aka Mimi. *Little Mimi, I love you so.*

The mirror whispers something I've known for ages: I'm no longer the fairest of them all. Not a by long shot. Jowls around my chin line. Love handles, but no love. When I lean in closer, I find that one long hair, a whisker, growing out of my chin on the left side, white and thick as thread. I pluck it every couple of weeks, but it grows back every time. Sometimes I forget til one of my daughters sees it, screams, and goes running for the tweezers.

I flip the light back off.

Back when my daughters were growing up, I was the envy of all the other mothers. *Oh, Mimi, how do you do it?* they raved after every one of my pregnancies. *That shape with all those little girls.*

Chasing after children, all day, every day, I used to joke. *That's my diet plan.* The truth is I didn't dare gain an ounce. Gaining weight was not an option. A month after every birth, as soon as I stopped bleeding, Jack wanted me back in my straight skirts and high heels, my white maillot if it was summer. His fantasy was that I could be mistaken for Liz Taylor. I never dared to let myself go, which is exactly what my daughters have accused me of ever since I left him. *Oh, Mimi, you've really let yourself go.*

All women lose their looks. Sooner or later. It's inevitable, like sun in morning, moon at night. No female escapes, no matter how much time or money she's got to spend on herself. Most women, though, lose their looks in bits and pieces, a wrinkle here, an extra pound or two there, then the drooping boobs, the sagging bottom, the thinning hair and thickening waist. But me, I lost them all at once — here today, gone tomorrow — the same way I once lost a good watch and then a pair of rosary beads Jack had given me, no clue about their worth until I realized they were gone for good. I was forty-nine, hadn't even started the Change, when they cut me open and scooped me out like an old fruit. My female organs, turned into medical waste, carted off in a red plastic bucket to be incinerated who knows where. It was all those babies, six, Jack wanted me to have and then left me to care for — one of whom, Malvina, the nurses held inside me, squeezing my legs together until the doctor showed up twenty minutes later. The trouble with my girl parts started then. So they tell me.

But I didn't let myself go. Never, ever let myself go. If I let myself go, what would I be left with? Nada. Instead, I was erased. No more wolf whistles when I walked along the beach. No men making way so I could get into line ahead of them at the bank or the post office, or helping me put the groceries into the car. They didn't see me anymore. I'd disappeared.

The mirror's some type of fake filigree, with gold, curly things around the edges, not my taste at all. I reach for it, wonder why I haven't thought of this before: Take the damned thing down! Who needs reminders? I'll put up a pretty picture, say of children

15

picking flowers in a meadow. I've seen some nice ones at Kmart. Or an arrangement of my grandkids' school pictures. That's it! Right here in the front hall. That would shut my daughters up, all their complaints about how I don't display the grandkids' pictures properly. That I don't show enough interest in the grandkids, don't love them enough.

I get my stepstool from the kitchen so I can grasp the mirror better. It weighs a ton. The wall behind it is pure white, the rest of the walls tinged yellow from my True Blues. "Imagine what they're doing to your lungs!" Cass would say if she were here, and then probably make a note of it to share with her sisters. I lug the mirror into my bedroom, stopping every couple of steps to catch my breath. I rest it against my bed while I look for a place to store it.

My bedroom has a big closet all along one wall. I use the closest half for my everyday things and the far half for storage, which is plenty for me. I'm not a saver or a keeper, not a pack rat like most of my sisters and my kids, who cannot bear to part with anything. I have a place for everything, and keep everything in its place. No skeletons in my closets, nor any dust bunnies, either, thank you very much. Crazy clean, my daughters say. I prefer to say I travel light.

I slide open the door on the far end of the closet. Click, the sensor light goes on. Love it! Plenty of room for the mirror. I'm sliding it in when a drop of water hits my head. I stand there for a minute, waiting for another, just to prove to myself that I'm not loony. Sure enough, another drop falls. This time, it hits the mirror. Splat! It slides down the glass, reflecting itself. Another hits my head, then another. *Raindrops keep falling on my head. . . .* One of my ex's favorite songs. I look up and see a wet stain in the upper corner. I look down and see the carpet's sopping wet. Good lord, we've sprung a leak! Probably in the bathroom of the upstairs apartment.

I let go of the mirror, go into the kitchen. I keep the number of our super right by the phone. Dick Duffy, a World War II combat vet, a widower and one of the nicest guys you'll ever meet. I dial him up, get the answering machine. I give him my name and my apartment number, though no doubt he knows them both by heart. "I hope you'll get here soon," I say. "I don't want to be swept out in a flood in the middle of the night."

Two:
Fly Me to the Moon

This morning, I ran out to Kmart for some plastic sheeting to cover things in the closet. Otherwise, I hung around all day, listening to the drips and waiting for Dick Duffy's call. Last night, I hardly slept, hearing the water plunking — drip, drip, drip — into the saucepan I put in the closet, on top of a couple of folded-up towels to absorb the puddle. Every couple of hours, I had to empty the pot. The leak kept getting worse. And the entire time I listened to it, I heard my daughters, one after the other, accusing me of letting myself go. I thought about broken pipes, falling plaster; about deterioration — a word my daughters have used to describe my mind, and one I've used myself when I think about my own body, full of parts that are wearing out and breaking down.

But I will not breathe a word about this leaking pipe. If I tell Cassandra, she'll declare the entire complex substandard and ramp up her campaign to get me out of here. She'll gather the others — Celestine, Ruth Ann, Siobhan, and Delilah — and incite them to riot against me. My own daughters.

Usually Duffy calls right back, though I've rarely had a problem in this place. I go outside to check his parking spot, but it's empty. It's almost dusk, so cold I can hardly catch my breath, an early dark New England night a moment or two away. Maybe he's abandoned us for good, Duffy. If so, the whole complex, the pride of our neighborhood, Callahan's Corner, would go down the tubes in a heartbeat. Complete deterioration! Inside, the drip, drip, drip continues, pushing me closer to the edge. I'll sleep out on the couch tonight.

On my way back inside, I check my mailbox, and, sure enough, it's stuffed with a big fat envelope with extra postage. The questionnaire. I squelch the urge to trash it. Cassandra would hand my head to me on a platter. Instead, I place it on the table next to the basket, beneath the empty white rectangle on my wall where the mirror used to be.

Around suppertime, I mix myself a Manhattan, straight up, and put on my favorite

CD, *The Very Good Years*. My Friday routine. My boy Frankie croons to me from the overpriced Bose Wave thingy my grandkids gave me last Christmas, all of them chipping in. Oh, but I've got to admit Frankie sounds divine, like he's right here in the room with me!

I settle onto my sofa and turn on the news, but without the sound. I like to watch it while listening to Sinatra. Nobody knows, so I don't have to explain. Though I can't help reading some of the headlines crawling along the bottom of the screen. Tonight, pedophiles were arrested in a kiddy-porn ring just north of Beantown. They're everywhere these days, those child molesters. I shut the TV off — too depressing. I try calling a couple of my daughters, first Ruth Ann in New Hampshire, then Delilah in Andover. I even think about calling Malvina, my lost child in the Bronx, but I don't have her number. We haven't spoken for years.

Then I try calling my sisters, but they, too, are out or not answering. Only four of us left, the remainders of the glorious Sheehan girls. That's what they used to call us when we were growing up, *those glorious Sheehan girls.* The way the old folks said it, their Irish accents thick as clotted cream, it sounded like a prayer.

20

So I'm stuck by myself with my Manhattan, the leak in my closet, and my thoughts about deterioration; Ol' Blue Eyes singing to me and the bad news shut inside the TV. I light up, enjoying the cigarette even more because it's forbidden fruit, my daughters and surviving sisters unified in their determination to get me to quit. Next thing you know, there's a knock of my door and, sure enough, Dick Duffy's calling through it, "Mrs. Malloy, oh, Mrs. Malloy."

I snuff out my cigarette and hide what's left of my Manhattan in the sink. Don't want Duffy to think I'm a lush, drinking alone on a Friday night. I open the door, and there he is, Dick Duffy with his nice smile and his bum leg — an old war wound, they say. He's wearing one of those jumpsuits with snaps up the front, his name stitched over the pocket on his chest. He's got a metal toolbox in one hand and a small stepladder in the other. His silver hair is slicked back nicely, and when the smell of his Old Spice gets me where I live, I realize that the Manhattan has gone straight to my head.

"Sorry I couldn't get here sooner, Mrs. Malloy," he says, his voice just above a whisper, his South Boston accent thick as chowder. "Family business. Now, let me see that leak. We'll get it fixed for you right away. If I'm not mistaken, it's the cold-water pipe in the bathroom upstairs. That's what goes through your bedroom closet."

I like Duffy's manners, the way he's always so respectful.

"Come on in," I say, sounding like a game-show host, proud of how I keep my place picture-perfect, even when I'm not expecting company. I take him into the bedroom, to the storage end of the closet. Right away, he opens his toolbox, takes out a big flashlight, and shines it up into the corner.

"Hmm, yup, there she is," he mutters.

I lean in close to him to see the big wet spot in the corner, more of a seepage than a leak, with the wall and ceiling looking as soggy as a sponge. The little drips spill down into the saucepan.

Duffy grunts and hums and hmms, then says he'll do some first aid until he can get a plumber. He climbs up on the ladder to get to work and I sit on my bed to watch. A man in my bedroom. More excitement than I've had in years. Duffy's mostly hidden, standing on the ladder with his head stuck up in the corner, while Frankie says he gets a kick out of me, then begs to be flown to the moon where we can play among the stars.

"You like Sinatra?" Duffy asks from far away.

"Oh, he's the best. He's my boy." Like Frankie's an old friend, living just around the corner, not all the way across the continent.

"Saw him once, out in Vegas."

"No kidding? Lucky devil."

"At the old Desert Inn, before they tore it down." He twists this way and that, his head and shoulders missing. "Great show. My wife, Virginia, she was already sick, but it was what she wanted more than anything. To see Sinatra in concert. So I took her. Worth every penny."

Next thing I know, the top shelf collapses, snaps in two. Cheap fiberboard. Knocks Duffy off the ladder. He stumbles backward, landing on his bottom on my floor. The shelf and its contents explode above him. I grab a big piece of shelf before it lands on his head, lose my own balance, and almost fall on top of him. I use the shelf to keep myself upright and burst out laughing. Duffy laughs too, thank God.

"You OK?" I put down the shelf and try to help him up. He doesn't need it, but he doesn't push my hands away when I grab

23

one of his arms and pull.

"My pride, Mrs. M, that's all that's hurt."

"Who needs pride anyway?"

"It's an occupational hazard. I'm used to it."

We stand looking at each other for a moment. He's grinning, but his smile doesn't quite make it all the way through his eyes. Standing closer to him than I ever have before, I see a dark layer there, an unlighted place.

"Hey, you better sit down," I say. "You really took a spill. Let me get you something to drink. How about a cup of coffee?"

"I'd love a cup."

"I could use some myself."

I lead him back into the living room, gesture to a seat at the table by my window. I go brew us up some Maxwell House and put on another Sinatra CD, *Songs for Swingin' Lovers!* Once I'm seated at the table, the two of us take out our butts. Duffy lights my True Blue with his Zippo. With Duffy, unlike when I'm with my kids, I don't feel like I'm committing a mortal sin by lighting up.

"Great coffee," he says, sipping from a yellow mug.

"It's the percolator," I say. "Takes longer than those electric drips, but it really brings

24

out the flavor."

We drink our coffee and smoke and gab a little, listening to Sinatra. *I've got you under my skin.* For the past few years, whenever we run into each other outside and the weather's nice enough, Duffy and I'll sit together on one of the benches in the courtyard and share a smoke and small talk. Duffy, with his bum leg and his big heart. That's how I've always thought of him. Sometimes, though, when I see him drag that leg around, I think he's also dragging sadness — that same sadness I glimpsed just a moment ago in his eyes, an unending sadness he can't do anything about.

"How long ago did you lose your wife?" I'm thinking he might like to talk about it, since he brought it up.

"Almost twenty-five years. But sometimes it still feels like yesterday."

"You never got over it," I say, and he looks up at me, that extra layer even darker.

"No, I never did. Had a couple of boys to raise. Me, a combat vet, but it was still rough. Two boys. Give me war any day."

"I'm the mother of six. Six girls. So I hear ya."

"Six? Mrs. Malloy's the mother of six? Wow." He shakes his head, smiling his nice

25

smile, this time his eyes bright and twinkling.

I'm a sucker for a compliment. I can't help preening a little. "One of them, Cassandra, comes by a lot. She's always trying to run my life."

"The one who drives the Bimmer? Well put-together?"

"The very same."

"I've got one of those too," he says. "The run-your-life type. My oldest. Always coming up with a better way for me to live. Wants me to move up to Vermont, near him, but I figure it's cold enough here. Besides, we're near the water."

"Yes, the water." One of the big attractions of the South Shore: the Atlantic, just a couple of blocks away, plus countless bays and inlets here and there, the Fore River, the Back River. When the wind's right, you can smell the nice fresh salt air. I'm out there walking every sunny day in the summer.

"And the other one, where does he live?"

"Bridgewater. Over in Bridgewater."

"A state college and a state prison," I say, but he doesn't add anything. "Hey, how about a sandwich, grilled ham and cheese?"

"Sure, Mrs. Malloy, thanks."

His smile is so sweet. I get right to work.

While I'm cooking, he goes back into the bedroom closet and does something to the leaky pipe. *You make me feel so young,* Sinatra croons, and I laugh to myself. All the years I've lived here, and all the favors Duffy's done me, and I've never had him in for a bite to eat. The sandwiches turn out great — he eats two, while I settle for one.

"Now, how about that front-hall mirror?" he asks while we're chowing down. "I'll put it back up for you?"

My turn for a funny look. "Oh, that." I feel like he's held his Zippo to my cheeks. "I'm going to put up a display of my grandkids' pictures instead. My daughters are always nagging me."

A convincing fib, I think, but the way Duffy looks at me, I can tell he's found me out. My cheeks burn hotter. "That's how I found the leak, when I was putting the mirror away."

"Well, thank God for small favors," he says, which seems to me to have at least two meanings.

Just to change the subject, I tell him about Patty's nutty plan to write our family's history. I show him the unopened envelope. "You know, a genealogy," I say, "going back to before we even came here. My sisters and my kids are all excited about it, but me, I'm

27

not one to dwell on the past. Water under the dam."

"The bridge, Mrs. Malloy."

He looks at me like maybe he hasn't seen me before or is seeing something new about me — good or bad, I cannot tell. I wonder, can't help it, if I've ever really looked at him. "Water goes over the dam, under the bridge."

He moves his hands to demonstrate.

"Whatever. What's done is done, in my opinion."

"Can't argue with that," he says. "One of my sons is a Civil War nut, a reenactor. Gettysburg. For the life of me, I can't understand getting all dressed up in wool uniforms and going back there every July. Risking heat stroke to reenact a bloodbath."

"It happened, what, over a hundred and thirty years ago? The North won. Yippee. Get over it."

Duffy cracks up.

"Of course," I add, "you can't live in Quincy, the City of Presidents —"

"Or anywhere else in the Boston area," he interrupts.

"— without running into history on a daily basis. You run out to fill a script for your arthritis medication, and you pass the Josiah Quincy House, with all those plaques and such."

"The City of Presidents," Duffy repeats. "The Adamses and John Hancock born and raised here. A battle in the Revolutionary War fought where the CVS now stands. Oh, and don't forget this place. Built in 1976, and called Centennial Square." He laughs and lights up. "Every building named for a Revolutionary War hero."

"To think, I've been living in Paul Revere for better than a decade."

"Patrick Henry for me. Since the complex opened."

"And don't forget Dunks," I throw in. "The City of Presidents is also the birth-place of Dunkin' Donuts."

"And Howard Johnson's."

"Wow, that's right. How could I forget Ho-Jo's? But that's honest-to-goodness his-tory." I light up too. "Not the kind my sisters love gabbing about, the goings-on in some long-gone branch of the family. The Sheehan sisters, with the exception of yours truly, are charter members of what I call the Yik Yak Club. Whenever they call it into session, they get all hot and bothered. And now they plan to write it all down, preserve it for posterity."

Duffy grins.

"I kid you not," I tell him. "And a couple

of my daughters can't wait to join."

Duffy's chuckles, then grinds out his cigarette.

"That was swell, Mrs. Malloy," he says. Maybe it's my imagination, but there seems to be a little extra sparkle in his eyes. I see him to the door.

Once I've opened it, he steps right through, like he's in a rush. He makes his way down the hall, with his ladder and his toolbox, listing to the right due to that old war wound.

"I'm sure glad you weren't swept out on a flood in the middle of the night, Mrs. Malloy," he calls, not looking back.

My bedroom's a disaster, stuff from the broken shelf scattered everywhere. Gotta clean up right away, that's just how I am. Won't sleep a wink unless it's done. Going through the mess, I come across photo albums of family events from years and years ago. I'll pass them on to my girls, since I never look at them. Stacks of summer clothes and purses. You'd think I'd recognize everything, but I don't. Everything looks different, out of place. A golf visor decorated with pink flowers in puff paint, though I've never golfed, and I've got no plans to do so. A school craft project from one of my grandkids. I toss it into the trash. A lacy Victoria's Secret thong, XL, given to me by Delilah when I lost my job, like I'd retired by choice. "You're a free woman now," she said. "Go have some fun." Ha-ha-ha. I wouldn't be caught dead in that thing, with the string between your cheeks, your girl parts barely covered. The price tag's still on, $15.99 for a tiny scrap of silk. That, too, goes in the trash. I'd be too embarrassed to send it to Goodwill. Most puzzling of all is a little velvet pouch near the closet door. I pick it up, open it. Inside is a pendant, a large and clear blue pendant set in filigreed silver. You could pin it on a collar, or hang it from a chain. It looks really old, just the type of thing I wouldn't save, and it knocks me onto my butt — I follow Duffy's route straight down. A beautiful blue pendant. No idea where it came from. When I go to bed, I set it on top of its pouch and place it on my bedside table.

THREE:
I GOTTA RIGHT TO
SING THE BLUES

They say birth, death, and taxes are the only certain things in life, but in my case, you can add one more thing to the list: Cassandra, calling up and butting in; I'm shocked that she hasn't called already. It's gotten worse since I was "riffed." Yes, the federal civil service came up with this new word to use when they started firing people, a euphemism for the massive "reduction in (labor) force" that happened when the president was on his way out the door — his promise to create a kinder, gentler nation out the door with him, a lame duck if ever there was one.

"Enjoy your retirement," the HR supervisor told me with her anchorwoman smile, her blond bob all neat and shiny, and her Volvo in a reserved spot just outside the door. "You've earned it."

Yeah, right, I thought. What would you know about my life and what I have or haven't earned?

"Do some volunteer work," she suggested, volunteer work being so good for the soul. "You could be one of the president's thousands of points of light, shining out there in the darkness," she said.

"I prefer a paycheck," I told her.

I never missed work. I was never late. I was promoted five times in fifteen years and earned many federal civil service citations for my diligence. I took pride in my work. Then, all of a sudden, I was out — knowing that if I were young and built, I'd still have a paycheck. But I didn't have the means to fight it. You've got to pick and choose your battles. Learned that long ago.

For the first time in my life, I had time on my hands, and I hated it. I couldn't wrap my mind around the concept of not working anymore, me, a divorcée and an empty-nester, with no more kids at home to worry about 24/7. How would I fill up my days? I filled out an application for Kmart and another to work at the Hallmark card store down the street. God knows I could use the income, not to mention the employee discounts for all the gifts I have to buy. I've heard it's even better than my senior discount.

But when Kmart called me to work the

Christmas season, I turned them down. Decided it wasn't worth the aggravation, not for minimum wage at my age. I don't like driving on the highways anymore, or facing so many people every day. Quincy's surrounded now, Routes 128, 3, 3A, 93, and I-95 all twisting and looping around one another, merging and splitting away, clogged with SUVs and tractor trailers and nobody yielding. Terrible traffic, all hours of the day and night. Too many cars and too many people driving them too fast, many of them with these car phones stuck to their ears, blabbering away, paying no attention to the road, and then there's me, a nervous nanny in a Dodge Shadow. I couldn't keep up and I knew it. So I said thanks but no thanks to Kmart, and now I'm stuck here without enough to do, Cassie and her sidekicks forever scheming and butting in.

Sure enough, I'm no sooner settled into my La-Z-Boy recliner with another cup of coffee, holding that mysterious blue pendant I found last night, when she calls.

"Such a nice day," she says. "What are you up to?" Nosy, as always. And I can guess what's coming next — she's trying to set me up with a fitness routine.

"Same old."

"You ought to get out, go for a walk," she

says. "Get your exercise."

"You know my exercise, honey, getting up out of bed; heaving myself off the sofa to go get a snack."

"Very funny, Mimi. You know what the doctor said. Have you been taking your blood-pressure medication?"

"Check." I hate being at the top of her to-do list, and also, at times, the victim of her mood swings, up one day and down the next.

"Let's go for a walk by the water. Maybe Wollaston?"

"OK, sure, why not," I say, because I can't figure out how to say no fast enough. And I do enjoy walking by the water.

Waiting for Cass to come get me, I recall bits and pieces of a dream from the night before, that two of my late sisters, Eden and Alberta — the top of the line, they used to joke — sneaked into my bedroom and left that sapphire pendant on the floor, right where they knew I'd find it. My old sweet-hearts. It was crazy, the day I moved in here — my sisters and my daughters, at least half a dozen of them, helping. Mass confusion with everyone running around, shoving stuff here and there. No doubt some things slipped through without me seeing them, like the little pouch holding the blue pendant. That part's a no-brainer. And I know that my dearly departeds, Eden and Alberta, didn't leave it in the middle of the night. I'm not that far gone yet. But how did I get the thing in the first place? That's the real question. As I sit there looking at it, I get this feeling that it must be part of me, a deep part, though I don't have a clue about it. And when I realize I don't have a clue, and wouldn't know where to find one, I want to cry, a feeling I haven't had for years. Not since Malvina said good-bye and really meant it. Not since Dr. Jack F. X. Malloy flew down to Santo Domingo and divorced me, then married the bookkeeper in his office, the blonde I call Miss Piggy, and the two of them honeymooned in Punta Cana on some all-inclusive deal at an oceanside resort. Not since I found out my two youngest, Siobhan and Delilah, had forged my signature on several legal documents, helping Jack hide our assets during the divorce so I wouldn't get my fair share. The urge to cry, something on the inside pushing to get out, but not a single tear.

Mimi with her heart of stone. That's what my sisters and my kids call me because of all the weddings, graduations, baptisms, and First Communions I've been to without shedding a tear, as well as my generally even temperament throughout the rest of life's ups and downs. Mimi with her iron constitution, her heart of stone. But sometimes I'd like nothing better than a good cry. Maybe I cried myself out when I was growing up, no more tears left inside.

Cass shows up in two-hundred-dollar sneakers and some kind of jogging suit that shines and rustles when she moves. Her blond hair shines too, but not as brightly as the diamond studs on her earlobes, swag from her ex before she kicked him out.

"Mimi!" she yells when I open my apartment door, like my presence here is a big surprise. She takes in my workout uniform: mail-order pull-on pants; Rockport walkers; a sweatshirt from Middlebury, one of the grandkids' colleges; and a baseball cap from Georgetown, where another one of them goes. I watch her looking at me with her sharp, appraising eyes and wonder if she's willing to be seen with me. I wait for a crack she does not make.

"Well, OK, let's hit it," she says, and we're off to the beach on a cold and sunny winter day. We take her BMW, which beats my Shadow any day, on any highway, and I'm just about asleep in the heated seat when Cassie pulls into the Wollaston beach parking lot — empty now, the water stretching out before us, blending into the sky at the horizon, with flocks of seagulls wheeling and gliding and squawking overhead.

"Daddy's in San Diego with Miss Piggy, at the Del Coronado," Cassie says as we head down the stairs to the sand and the water's edge. Her words cut neat and clean, like a Swiss Army knife. Then I see the two of them, Jack and Miss Piggy, eating breakfast in an oceanfront dining room set with linen and real silver. He's feeding her a bit of cantaloupe on a silver fork, his hair slicked back neat and shiny like the big bandleader he's always longed to be.

"Doing what?" Like I care.

"A conference of some kind. They're staying a couple of extra days, then going up to Santa Barbara."

"Santa Barbara," I repeat, but she doesn't hear me. The nicest place Jack ever took me to was a cottage on Craigville Beach with all six of our girls in tow, a place with an outdoor shower where I got to cook in a kitchen even smaller than my own. While he swam and built sandcastles with the girls.

Cassandra's up ahead, trying to set the pace. Santa Barbara. Good for them! Jack showing off the young blonde on his arm — young enough so that by the time she loses her looks, he'll be long gone. He won't have to trade her in for a new one.

The tide's low, and the sand along its edge is firm, so that's where Cassie leads me. Wouldn't you know she's got one of those pedometer thingies strapped to her ankle to measure just how far we've gone, and she keeps dragging me farther, while I keep pointing out that however far we go, we're only halfway done because we've got to turn around and get back to the Bimmer. At one point she stops, and insists I take my heart rate, my fingers pressing on the pulse point at my throat. She counts ten seconds with her watch.

"Time's up. What's your pulse? I'm seventeen, which is just about my target."

"Zero. No pulse. Guess I'm a goner."

"Oh, Mimi," she says, dripping irritation along with sweat, "you're pressing the wrong spot."

Mimi, what Cassandra's always called me, her first word. I tried to teach her Mammy like our Irish forebears used to say, then Mommy, but she refused to learn it. Instead, she imitated Jack, Mimi this and Mimi that. Our other daughters copied her. Not Mammy or Mommy, Ma, Mom, but Mimi. After a while, I figured, close enough. One vowel sound just wasn't worth a fight.

We walk some more, picking up the pace, and when we check our pulse again, she presses my neck for me. Feels like she wants to wring it. "Your pulse is racing," she says. "We better slow down. Your heart rate's, like, twenty-three or twenty-four. Way too fast, even for a woman your age."

"Let's go back, baby," I say after a few. I'm not feeling so great. Out of breath, but also something underneath that, something I can't explain. She set the pace too fast, but I can't tell her, or she'll recite her litany of concerns about my health and haul me off to the doctor's. Or to that warehouse for oldies. This time, she agrees without a word.

We turn around and when we do, I see in the distance the Fore River Shipyard where my father, my sisters and I, and my ex-husband worked. Not to mention countless other relatives and friends. Owned first by Bethlehem Steel and afterward by General Dynamics, but always called Fore River — one of the world's busiest and most versatile shipyards beginning in 1883, and lasting for a century. It's why the ancestors left Belfast and headed here. When I was a kid, I thought Bethlehem meant the town where Jesus had been born. I loved the sound of it. Bethlehem Steel.

The shipyard, shuttered and abandoned

since 1986, and struggling for years before that; its Goliath crane, the second largest in the world, still punctuating the skyline, eye-catching but useless. Its vast structures — the building bays, that useless crane, the enormous brick building where I met Jack — are rusted and forlorn, but still in place, like they might come back to life at any moment. So many types of vessels built here: battleships, aircraft carriers, landing ships, heavy cruisers, light cruisers, destroyer escorts, ammunition ships, supply ships, high-speed transports, antiaircraft cruisers — each with its own complex specifications. The first nuclear subs were built here too. And just beyond the shipyard, across the water — out of sight, but present nonetheless — is the little house we lived in when we first got married, the house Jack built for me. I feel a stabbing pain, but one that isn't physical, despite my shortness of breath. A Weymouth cop lives there now.

"You OK?" Cass asks.

"Of course," I lie. She takes my arm and we slow down.

"We used to live there," I say, pointing into the distance. "Your father built that house for me. For us." She nods. No big deal for Cass, just a stepping stone on life's journey.

"I pass it most every day," she says. "Can't believe how small it is. I can't believe we really lived there." She laughs her typical ha-ha-ha.

We trudge back to the Bimmer, beneath the beautiful empty sky, the wintry sun. Even now, after all this time, it hurts to say my marriage was a failure. I'm the one who left. After thirty years. I'd had enough after finding out about the third or fourth or fifth young girlfriend — which Jack insisted were not girlfriends, but mentees. What on earth is a mentee? I asked. Some type of bird that can balance on one leg? Or a marine mammal? Mentees. Whatever. Lipstick on your collar isn't just a song. So I left him in a fit and went to stay with Patty, thinking he'd come after me and beg me to return. But while I waited at Patty's, he flew to Santo Domingo and divorced me. On the grounds that I'd abandoned him. Right after that, he married the new one. It was like we'd been playing bridge and he trumped me. I'd walked out on him, after all, and our two teenage daughters, Siobhan and Delilah, who were still at home.

Of course they — my ex and my youngest daughters — said that I was crazy, leaving behind a beautiful home and all inside it; a late-model luxury sedan; the security of

42

Jack's income and his pension; my only job seeing to it that his life went smoothly. What could have possessed me? I was nutty; I'd lost it. That's the excuse Jack used during our divorce when he recruited Siobhan and Delilah to help him hide our assets. He sneaked stuff into various new accounts that the two of them had authorized, forging my name. Convinced them I couldn't handle money, stocks, bonds, mutual funds, whatever. Said I'd squander them in a heartbeat, and they, my babies, they went along with him. *You won't inherit a thing,* Jack told them, and they believed him. Even now, they gather evidence against me about my instability, and, lately, my memory lapses. Sometimes, though, I just don't feel like paying close attention anymore.

Jack believed I was so dimwitted that I wouldn't notice that our assets had suddenly disappeared. Against the advice of my lawyer and my sisters, I settled for twenty grand and my walking papers. Less than a thousand bucks a year for all that aggravation. I was too worn out to fight. But the truth is, I didn't care. And I still wouldn't give a rat's ass for Jack F. X. Malloy's money. They can have it. And may they spend it well. I only wanted peace. Serenity, like it says on the flyer for golden-age tai chi. The betrayal by my daughters, however, remains a deep, unhealing wound.

We reach the car and Cassie helps me in. Unlike yours truly, Cassie took care of herself and her son before she dumped her husband, a CPA. She'd been miserable for years but waited until he made partner before she cut him loose. Hired a killer lawyer. Got child support and alimony and the house, a Georgian colonial, in one of the South Shore's richest towns. She works because she wants to, for Hallmark, going around to malls and shopping strips to set up and maintain their displays. Cassandra loves greeting cards and is always sending them, even when there's no occasion. *Hang in there,* said one she sent to me last month. A scared kitten clung to the high branch of a tree. The Gay Divorcée is what I call Cassandra, although, unlike Ginger Rogers in that movie, her gaiety is less evident with each passing year.

"Working out gets easier after a while," Cassie says, offering me a quick, encouraging smile, then pulling out and heading back to Paul Revere. "You've just got to keep at it."

As usual, the traffic's awful, but it doesn't matter. I'm stuck on Memory Lane with Jack. All those years we were together, my husband was a holy roller, R.C.-style: God forbid you should miss Mass on Sunday, eat meat on Friday, or forget to fast before Communion. He knew the Catholic rule-book by heart, and felt it was his moral obligation to enforce it. Even after Vatican II, Jack stuck to the old ways, attending outlawed Latin Masses. He fooled me for ages. Until I realized he was a card-carrying hypocrite who beat his breast in the confessional on Saturday afternoons, then went out and screwed anyone he could.

After he got back from the Dominican Republic, he tried to have our marriage annulled, too — this time on the grounds that I was crazy. So that he and the bimbo could be officially married in the Church and still go to Communion. He wrote an affidavit, listing all of my many failings, in order to demonstrate that I had been a nut job back when we got married, thus the marriage was invalid, and our daughters were illegitimate. Bastard daughters, all six of them. He expected me to sign it. Who's the wacko here? I wondered. Despite pressure from several of my daughters, I refused to co-operate.

But leave it to Jack Malloy. He went and found a long-haired, sandal-wearing priest to perform the marriage, a priest who has also been giving them Communion and Absolution ever since. After supper every night, Jack and Miss Piggy say novenas together, kneeling on the living-room floor. Hardwood, no carpet. That's what I hear through the grapevine, anyway. The grapevine being Ruth Ann, Del, and Cassandra. Maybe it's a form of foreplay.

Once in a while, I'll pluck a real juicy one from the grapevine. Like that Jack has to send his shirts out if he wants a clean one anytime soon. Or that if he wants a balanced meal, he's got to order it from Boston Chicken. Or that the house is filthy. Dust and scum; trash piled everywhere. They say Miss Piggy's a shopaholic with more shoes than Imelda. Del's old bedroom, I hear, is now stacked floor-to-ceiling with the unused bargains — watches, bed linens, sweaters, umbrellas, underwear — that Miss Piggy couldn't leave behind. Hah! It tickles me, I can't help it, to think of the two of them, wallowing in squalor, and Jack blowing a gasket every time she walks in the front door with another loaded shopping bag. I'd love it if just once, just a single time during his marriage to the young blonde, while he's peeing into a scummy toilet or trying to balance his checkbook, that he realizes all I did for him, and thanks me in his heart. Fat chance.

"Women who exercise vigorously three or more times a week substantially cut their risk of breast cancer and heart failure. Not to mention osteoporosis."

I turn to look at Cass, whose unasked-for opinion shoves me back into Quincy traffic. We're stopped at a light and she's drumming her manicured nails on the steering wheel.

"I'll be your support," she says. "I'll support you."

"You'll support me? You mean like an undergarment? A panty girdle? I used to hate those things. Never needed one." I look out at the landscape of banks, bars, and triple-decker houses, the sidewalks thronged with people.

"Oh, Mimi," she says, accelerating with the changing light. "I mean the people who love you and want to help you achieve your weight-loss goals."

I don't answer, don't even look at her.

"Want to drive by the old place?" she asks, like this might make me happy.

I shake my head no, and she shuts up. Every time I think about our homes — we moved every few years, following Jack's whims, always to a bigger house in a better neighborhood — a clot fills up my throat and I have trouble seeing clearly. What I wanted, all I ever longed for, really, was to stay put in that first house, that little Cape Cod cottage on the bluff above the Fore River. The house Jack built for me, for us, a cottage with big windows on all sides where no one else had ever lived. Where, on sunny days, the light shined like sequins on the water.

"We can add on. We can push up and out," I kept telling him. I went so far as to make drawings of the plans, crude drawings that he, a naval architect, squashed in his fist and dropped into the nearest waste-basket. He kept wanting to buy up. And up and up. He couldn't stop. He had to show the world what a big shot he was. And I kept getting what I didn't want: gloomy old Tudors and Victorians, full of nooks and crannies, gables, stained glass, closets, attics, cellars, shadows. More space for me to clean. More dark places for me to get scared in.

"Like it or lump it," Jack told me once when I complained. I guess I lumped it. I was his handmaiden. Yes, me, Maire. Behold, a handmaiden of the Lord! Until that last place, where I finally went on strike. The washer and dryer were in the cellar, a creepy place with cobwebs, dirt, no light, no windows, and an old coal bin to one side. I refused to go down there by myself — I couldn't, which is the part he didn't get. At last he broke down and built a new laundry room right off the kitchen. Too little, too late.

"You should feel really good about this, Mimi," says Cassie when we pull up to my apartment. Then, God bless her, she blows me a kiss out her open window and promises to take me for another walk on the next nice day.

Four:
I'm Gonna Live Till I Die

At last, some peace and quiet. Time to think, which I've had more than enough of since I got laid off. Thinking, my new hobby. Cheap and easy. I get the blue pendant from my bedroom, sit with it in my recliner. I stare hard at the beautiful blue stone, like it's trying to tell me something, but in a voice so faraway, I can't quite make out the words. A piece of jewelry talking to me. If my daughters only knew. I call Patty, the great historian.

"What's doing?" she asks, and I tell her all about the leaky pipe and Duffy's spill, and then finding the velvet pouch on the floor with the blue pendant inside.

"It was Mam's." Patty laughs like I'm kidding her. "It was Mam's aquamarine. I've always wondered what happened to it. A big blue pendant, set in silver."

"That's it, but what's it doing in my closet?"

"Daddy gave it to her when they got married. I know that much. You do too, Mimi. You've just forgotten. Maybe Daddy gave it to you. I didn't know any of us still had it."

"Me neither."

Patty laughs again. "Can't wait to see it. Show us next time we go to brunch. Oh, and I mailed out the questionnaires. You should be getting yours any day now."

"Got it yesterday."

"Great," she says. "It's going to be a gift to our children, something they'll always treasure." Then she gabs on and on about her kids and her kids' kids until I just about can't stand it anymore.

FIVE:
ME AND MY SHADOW

I'm about to nuke a Lean Cuisine, eggplant rollatini, whatever that is, when Cassie shows up. "Mimi!" she hollers when I open the door. Her usual greeting, like it's been ages, and a big surprise that I'm still here. She's wearing a lime green suit and matching pumps. "I brought you something really good."

What? I'm wondering as she puts the goodies on my counter, cold cooked lobster out of the shell, some kind of fancy salad with asparagus and sundried tomatoes, bakery rolls, and a couple of bottles of Chardonnay. I can read her like a book: she wants something from me. She plans to ply me with wine, and the kind of food I can't afford, and then get me to do something against my better judgment.

"Hope you have a corkscrew." A little wail. "You're always drinking wine from those screw-top bottles."

"Am not. I buy my wine in boxes now. Stays fresher that way."

She gives me a look.

"You keep it in the fridge and just hold your glass up to the spigot." I hand her my corkscrew. "Only trouble is, you can't see when you're running out. You have to shake the box."

I pull out a couple of wineglasses, Lenox crystal she gave me one Christmas, and watch her work the corkscrew on the dark-green bottle. Her manicured fingernails, recently done, make me think of small, sweet fruit — the kind with a hard shell you can't ever break.

"Well, this is really good stuff." She pours each of us a healthy measure.

"I could get two or three boxes of blush for what you paid for that."

"Wait til you taste." We clink glasses and I swallow. OK, the pricey corked wine, whatever it was, some name in a language I couldn't read, beats Wine in a Box handsdown. Still, as we sit feasting at my table by the window, watching the sun set outside, I know she's up to something.

I'm swallowing my last yummy bit of lobster when she says, "Tell me a story." Her cheeks are flushed and she's breathing fast, like my sisters do when the Yik Yak

Club's in session. Or maybe it's the sulfites in the wine.

"A story?" I think of *The Runaway Bunny* or *The Poky Little Puppy,* books I read to my girls when they were kids. I recall the gist but not the exact details.

"Tell me something about your family, about what it was like when you were growing up. You never talk about it."

She taps her shiny fingernails on my table. In my mind's eye, I try to see a story from my childhood, from happy times back in the day, but all I see are lines and shadows, like I do on TV when the cable's out.

"Everybody remembers something about growing up. Unless they're mentally defective." Sometimes her tone reminds me of my ex's.

"Thanks a lot." I take another swallow of wine, trying to cool down the hot buttons she keeps pressing.

Cassie has, to hear her tell it, done a lot of work on her inner child, and it makes her feel superior to the rest of us when it comes to family matters. She's spent years in therapy and insists on sharing every grim detail with me, blabbing about her dysfunctional family, and I always wondered, was it the same one I'd been living in all those years? "You just don't get it," she's told me a million times or more, and she's right, I don't get it. Not even for a hot second have I ever understood Cassandra's anger, her mood swings, her loneliness, her lapses into despair.

She had a great childhood, one most kids would envy. Jack and I saw to that. She had a real mother, an honest-to-goodness mother on call 24/7. She grew up with every possible advantage, three square meals a day and endless snacks in between, a closet full of pretty dresses, and new shoes for every holiday. Not to mention the fine homes, and me, always there to make sure things ran smoothly. She got dancing lessons and violin lessons and a new gown for the prom. No hand-me-downs for my girls. Jack wouldn't allow it. She even had her own room with a pink canopy bed. I sewed the damned canopy myself, out of dotted Swiss.

During all those years of what Cassie called her recovery, she carried around this little white stuffed teddy bear that she would cuddle. The bear held a plastic ice-cream cone — chocolate — between his paws. Cassie called him Sweet Stuff.

Sweet Stuff got dumped for good soon after Cassie's "rebirth," and not long after that, her husband got dumped too. Cassandra found some nut called a rebirther and paid her damned good money so she could be born again — in the actual, not the Christian, sense. She spent a day on the floor of a dark room — lit with scented candles — wriggling through a tunnel made up of the arms of the rebirther and her pals. This was supposed to wipe out any lingering effects of the trauma she went through when she was wriggling out of me. I didn't get it, but didn't ask. Pretended it didn't bother me, my firstborn feeling the need to be rebirthed.

Now that we're full of lobster and loopy from the Chardonnay, Cass takes a copy of the questionnaire out of her Coach bag and smooths it out on my table. She holds a pen, Cross, gold-plated, or maybe the real thing. That's what she's after: answers for the genealogy.

"What was your mother like? Start there." She holds her pen over the paper.

"Hmmm, stump the stars," I joke, stalling for time because Cassie's question draws a blank. I have no memories of Mother, not a one and, hence, no stories, either.

"Come on, Mimi. She was your own mother."

"What do you want from me? She died when I was a kid, a little kid." I count back to myself. "I was seven when she passed." A fact I've lived with all my life. "She died before I had any memories." Cassandra looks at me, cheeks pink, eyes bright blue. She doesn't believe me, but it's true.

"I don't remember anything about her. Right before I left your father, I went to a shrink," I hear myself tell Cassandra, against my better judgment. I was stuck, deep down in the dumps, and everything I looked at seemed to be filmed over with murky water or layered in smoke. "He said I had to make my way back through my childhood, step by step, like Hansel and Gretel in the forest, in order to feel whole again. Whole. Like I'd ever felt complete, or even expected to. The shrink kept asking me about my childhood and I kept telling him I couldn't remember." I see him now, plain as day. "I couldn't stand that guy, Dr. Nobody, with his black-rimmed glasses, his three chins and creepy smile."

" 'Come on, Mimi,' he said again and again. 'Everybody remembers something. You remember. You're just not telling.' " His pen and notebook at the ready.

"I got so upset, the way he kept badgering me, I got up and left and never went back. But even after I got home and tried and tried, I still couldn't remember. Then your father hollered about all the money he'd wasted, three hundred something dollars on a worthless psych evaluation. 'Take it out of my allowance,' I told him."

"Well, try again now," Cass prods, just like the shrink. I light a butt, which I usually try not to do when she's around because of her snotty attitude. But this time she seems not to notice. I crack the window on my side and exhale in that direction.

"No point. After that shrink experience, I said the hell with it. The past, I mean. What's done is done. Be grateful." And eventually, the smoke and murky water went away on their own. One day I woke up and felt like my old self again.

"That wasn't the first time you got depressed." I look at my daughter. I can't tell if this is an accusation or a question. "Right after Malvina was born."

She might as well have slapped me.

"How do you know that? You were what, five or six years old?"

"So you're not denying it," she says, her face scrunched up in a way that makes me sad, not angry. One of the deepest shames of my life, how I could not take care of Malvina after she was born. Me, still in my twenties, and she, Malvina, my fourth in six years, with a miscarriage wedged somewhere in between. I can hardly bear to think about it, even now. Patty took Malvina in for two, maybe three, months before I got myself together. And after that, nobody ever spoke of it again.

"Your aunt told you," I say, and she nods ever so slightly. "Patty, the blabbermouth."

"Aunt Patty said you could have died. Malvina, too."

"But we didn't."

"Obviously," she says, again in that snotty tone. "But I was thinking of how history repeats itself. Or almost repeats itself. Didn't your mother die in childbirth?"

"History does not repeat itself. Not in this family, anyway." I'm as certain of this as I am of my name. "History will not repeat itself."

"Well, how old was your mother when she died?"

"Thirty-four. She started her family late for those days. She'd been a teacher before she married and had us kids. She graduated from Bridgewater Normal School."

"And she died in childbirth."

"Not exactly. She gave birth just fine, but then experienced toxemia. And eclampsia."

"Toxemia? Eclampsia?"

"It happens right after you give birth, something poisons the blood. Your blood pressure spikes sky-high. You have convulsions, go blind, and then you die. Never happens anymore. At least not here, in the United States."

"With Auntie Keeley?"

I nod yes, but I feel queer.

"What was it like when she died?"

The wine and lobster bubble in my gut. My mother, Mam, gone for good, before I could even remember her. And we didn't get to say good-bye.

"You girls don't know how good you've got it nowadays." I grin, pretending I feel great. "With all the prenatal care you get, the steak and Champagne after —"

"Answer my question." Her eyes blaze the way they used to when she was about fourteen and beginning to feel her oats.

"I told you I don't remember anything about it."

"Can't or won't? You and all your secrets."

"Secrets? I don't have any secrets." Well, maybe one, not counting the blue pendant. For many years, I bowled in a church league on a team called the Angel Babies. We wore satin jackets with our names embroidered on the back, and on our ball bags. I never said a word about this to my daughters. Didn't want them gossiping about one of the most enjoyable things I'd ever done. All too soon, though, slipped disks, arthritis, high blood pressure, and macular degeneration — the other girls' problems, not mine — broke up the Angel Babies. I donated my jacket and the ball bag to St. Vincent de Paul, though I doubt there are many other bowling Mimis out there. That's my only secret.

"Your whole life is a secret, Mimi." Cass polishes off the last of the wine. "You never tell us any stories. You never have."

"Be glad," I say, though I'm not sure why, and I get up to bring our dirty dishes to the sink. Cassie follows, her high heels clicking on the tile.

"I don't even know her name."

"Mary." This word pops out by itself, four letters stuck together, no pictures attached. "I was named for her."

"Why?" She scrapes the plates and rinses them and puts them neatly into the dishwasher. In a minute, my kitchenette will be spic-and-span and she'll have a pot of coffee brewing.

"No clue," I answer, and for the first time in more than fifty years, I begin to wonder about it myself. "Nobody ever told me." All my other sisters were named for the sons my parents hoped for, even Patty, whose real name is Padraic. And Eden, whose name was Aidan.

Cassie wants the grim details, when everybody was born and when they married, how many kids they had, and when they died, all the stuff I've never cared a whit about. Leave it to Cassandra to take over the genealogy like she's the one who thought of it.

"I promised Auntie Patty," she says.

"Promised her what?"

"That I'd make you do this. She knew you'd procrastinate. Blow it off."

"Would not," I protest, but Patty's got my number. She knows exactly how I feel about ancient history.

I wrack my brain and come up with a few answers, like my mother's and my father's names. Mary and Joe. Like Jesus's parents, Cassie says, and I nod yes though I'd never thought of it before. I can more or less figure out their dates of death, though I'm not sure where my mother's buried. After she died, her parents — loathing my father — reclaimed her. At least according to the myths and legends of the Yik Yak Club.

Cassie picks and probes with her gold pen and twinkly fingernails. It's odd to see the details of my life being written out like that, names I haven't spoken or even thought about for maybe half a century. I watch the words form on the page in my daughter's lovely handwriting, all loops and curlicues — that at ten I was an orphan, though I never thought about myself that way. She writes down a true fact, that my mother died the day Keeley was born. But my sisters and I didn't even see Keeley until she was a toddler, two or three years old. After Mam died, she was sent to live with a wet nurse, but we didn't know this until she was delivered to our doorstep, already talking and walking like a Chatty Cathy doll.

"Aidan's drawing a big tree in his computer class," says Cass.

Patty's grandson. Aidan Shmaidan, I think.

"It'll have lots of little branches. We'll handwrite all this information, then scan it onto them."

"What about the broken ones?" Our family tree as I see it: an old maple suffering from blight, a tree with broken branches, some dangling from the trunk, and others, having fallen, rotting on the ground beneath it. "What's he going to do about those?"

"Oh, Mimi," says Cassandra. "There are no broken branches."

"Of course there are."

"You can't get broken off a family tree. Family's family, no matter what they do or what happens to them."

63

That's when I realize what's coming next. I look at pretty blond Cassandra, who has it all under control, and I see it coming, head-on. Realize, too, that I've known it from the first time this genealogy was mentioned. Knew exactly where we'd end up with our ancient family history.

"Even your sister Fagan."

"Fagan?" My other baby sister, gone now for almost sixty years.

"Fagan's got her own little branch on the family tree."

"Fagan?" The name burns my lips, a name never spoken, not even by the members of the Yik Yak Club. Now Cass declares it, right here in my kitchen. Fagan. After all this time.

"That's right, Fagan."

"What about her?" I can't repeat her name again. Pronouns will have to do.

"Patty and Jo told me about her, Miss Mimi Who Has No Secrets." I look away. "Somebody I never knew existed. My own aunt."

I spy a hangnail on my pinkie. I bite it off, wince from the pain.

"We can't have a family tree without including our poor little Fagan." Cassandra's voice wobbles, somewhere between rage and sorrow.

" 'Our' poor little? . . ." Fagan. The name swells inside my mouth, a lump, a malignancy. I look at Cass, my perfect eldest daughter, so smug sitting there, in her Talbots suit, clueless. "Our poor little? Our? First-person plural, like you've got some claim to her when you don't even have the right to even bring her up." My blood rises like steam in a pressure cooker just before it starts to hiss and squeal.

"She was my aunt. Or would have been if she'd lived."

"But she didn't." Hot steam shoots out my ears. My other baby sister, sent away at five years old, back to the old country, never to be heard from again. I'd like to call Patty to read her the riot act. She ought to mind her own business; let bygones be bygones.

"You should have told me, told us, all of your children. You should have told us long ago."

"Let her rest in peace, wherever she may be." It comes out soft as a prayer, and I mean it that way, I really do. *Fagan, rest in peace. Wherever you may be.* That's what we — Eden, Alberta, and I — decided way back when.

Cassandra's quiet for a minute, and for a second I believe she might actually drop the subject. Fat chance, though.

"Patty says you're the one who knows the most because you were the oldest when she got sent away. The oldest one still living now." She scribbles something in her notebook.

The oldest one still living now. That's right; that's me, Mimi, the survivor. Because we also lost Eden and Alberta along the way. The dearest friends of my youth, both gone before their time. "I don't know anything."

"When Auntie Patty told me that you girls had this other baby sister before Keeley showed up, it blew me away. And that she got sent away because your stepmother couldn't handle her. Your stepmother. I didn't know about her, either. Then you found out that Fagan had died of a wasting disease."

"You want to talk about our stepmother?" My voice is cold and quiet. I look at Cass with pity. She nods yes, all excited. She, who's so eager to march into the past, where she thinks she'll find what she's been looking for, some kind of treasure, when what's there is more along the lines of a Bouncing Betty, guaranteed to devastate.

"OK. Yes, my father did remarry. He remarried right away, another source of shock and shame for all of us. Because we thought he loved our mam as much as we did; that she couldn't ever be replaced. But no. He remarried so fast, brought home our stepmother. Her name was Flanna Flanagan. Be sure to write that down." She does.

Flanna Flanagan, my stepmother. Da's second wife. Who sent away my baby sister Fagan before the other baby, Keeley, the one we weren't even sure existed, came back to live with us. She's here now, Flanna. I see her, hovering outside over the parking lot, like Christ above the tomb on Easter morning. Flanna, resurrected, only she's charred and blackened, like she'd gone down instead of up.

"So what happened with Fagan?" Cass prods again, cold as could be. I take a few slow breaths, light another butt.

"One morning we get up and Fagan isn't there, OK? My father with the new wife gather us together and tell us they've sent her back to Cullyhanna in County Armagh, up north where we came from. My father was crying when he told us, and the new wife sat there weeping too. Fagan was going to live with somebody else's family, because our new mother couldn't handle her. 'We'll get her back, as soon as everything's under control here, girls, I promise,' my father told us. Then he raved about the beauty of the countryside in Cullyhanna, and the new wife clung to him, nodding and weeping." Cassie stops writing. She looks up at me, her eyes so familiar, so much like her father's, but now there's a different look in them, sadness maybe. "That's the last we ever heard of her."

Because nothing was ever under control again, and before we even knew where to go to look for her, Da himself passed on, and the wicked stepmother flew away on her broom. And whatever Daddy knew, he took that knowledge to his grave.

"Mimi, poor Mimi," Cassandra says. A big tear rolls down her cheek, making a track in her Mary Kay foundation.

"Here today, gone tomorrow," I tell her. "No big deal, honey. That was the world we lived in. It's how we grew up. Lots of other kids did too, back then. Our troubles were like everybody else's, common as potatoes. Nobody used the word 'trauma.' Nobody thought of things that way."

Cassandra sobs. Again I feel sad for her. Poor Cassie, almost always just off balance, and grabbing on to whatever's in reach to try to stay upright. I reach across the little table to pat her shoulder. "Ancient history," I say.

"So after Fagan was sent off, Keeley

68

showed up?"

I nod yes. "Keeley took her place, and that was that. Whatever else had happened up til then, we cremated. Scattered the ashes. We all loved Keeley, still do, right? She's the best of the bunch."

So much happiness the day Keeley appeared on our doorstep, which is how I always think of it, even though I have no actual memory of that day, nor any idea of where she'd been or why she joined our family when she did.

"What did you do after Fagan got sent away?"

"Nothing. What could we have done?" My daughter's face falls, the way it used to when I closed a book before the story ended. "We didn't do anything at all. We were kids. We were still waiting, no, hoping, I think, that our real mother would come back."

Then, maybe as the result of Cassie's disappointment, or all that pricey wine, I go get the blue pendant. I bring it back, the velvet pouch on my palm, the shiny blue stone on top. Cassandra snatches it, examines it as if it might hold the answers to all her questions.

"Where did you get this?"

"In my closet." I leave out the details

about the leak, the collapsing shelf. "I was organizing things, and there it was."

"No, I mean where did you get it? Whose was it?"

"It was my mother's. My father gave it to her when they got married."

"You never told me you had this. You never told me, Mimi, and you know how I love old things."

I shrug.

"Let me bring it to my jeweler," Cassie says, and the next thing you know, she's dropping the pouch into her purse. "He can appraise it. Maybe tell us its provenance and what it's worth."

"Its provenance?"

"Where it comes from . . . who knows . . ." The sparkle is back in my daughter's eyes, she's got something to hold on to. Then she's gone, and so is the blue pendant.

Six:
Thanks for the Memory

Flanna Flanagan. *Just off the boat* is what our grandmother, our father's mother, Nana Sheehan, said about her. She didn't mean it as a compliment. Whenever Nana said this, I saw Flanna climbing off a big boat in Quincy Harbor, one with flapping sails, and she the only passenger. She walked across the water, the last few steps to shore, her bright hair spilling from under her hat, her eyes shining like the sea beneath her feet. Da was there to meet her, the brand-new wife he called his secret rose, like in that poem by W. B. Yeats, whose words Da preferred to prayers.

Enchanting Flanna. With her flaming hair, her pink cheeks, her deep brown eyes. *She does not have to labor to be beautiful,* Da said the day he brought her home. We girls were so excited. We were getting a new mother, a beautiful new Mammy. An angel or a queen, we couldn't pick between the two.

So long ago. During the worst part of the Depression. But even so, Daddy still worked as a riveter at the shipyard, one of the few they'd kept on. Spent his days working with a welder's torch, and bore the scars to prove it. Angry red ones and pearly white ones, hieroglyphics on his fingers and forearms. No pattern, yet a complex topography, over which my sisters and I loved to run our fingers. Daddy's scars, the visible ones. Never complained, not once, no matter how much they might have hurt. So proud of the work he did, building ships.

He took the trolley there, we didn't own a car. We used to love to wait for him outside, especially on paydays, when he brought us treats — bubble gum, cookies, hair ribbons, pretty buttons. We weren't allowed to leave the yard, so we took turns running to the edge of it, trying to spot Daddy as soon as he reached the crest of the hill. Da. How he loved to tease. Like a magician, he pulled our treasures from his pockets, then hid them up his sleeve or in his hat or collar. He made the goodies disappear, then re-appear, while the bunch of us squealed and hollered. *My little bouquet of beauties.* That's what he called us until Mam died and

Flanna became our new mother.

I'm on my way downstairs to meet my sisters outside, it's almost time for Da to get home from work. I pass their open bedroom door. Mam's come back, I think for a split second. No, not Mam, but Flanna in one of our mother's best dresses, a brown silk with white pin dots. She's so beautiful. I love her, want her to love me back. She fixes herself in the big mirror, turning her head this way and that. She does not have to labor to be beautiful, that's what our father said about her. Flanna, with her dimpled smile, wearing my dead mother's dress.

In the mirror, Flanna sees me. "What're you lookin' at?" she asks, her voice as sweet as syrup but her accent so hard to understand. I try to smile but can't. "Come in, Miss Maire, Quite Contrary," she says, stabbing words. Da told her his special name for me, Contrary Maire. Flanna smiles, holding out her arms. I go, slowly, ever so slowly, my feet sinking ankle-deep into slush and ice. When I'm close enough, she smacks me. Right on my face, hard enough to snap my neck. "That'll teach you not to spy," she says.

I joined my sisters and waited for Da outside on the steps. I didn't say a word. Didn't tell my sisters anything. Pretended to myself it didn't happen, Flanna smacking

73

me in the face. She stood in the doorway at the top, her hair swept up but with curls falling all around her face, in our mother's best silk dress. Payday, but Da forgot our treats. Still, we surrounded him as Flanna sang in her sweetest voice, *"Leave him be, girls. Give the poor man some peace."* Da pushed past us, rushed up the steps to his secret rose. The two of them embraced, and then they were gone. We knew where they were going, upstairs to their room, to the bed where our mother died. They'd stay up there for ages while we girls hung around in the kitchen.

Fagan, the youngest, Keeley not yet known to us, got fussy and I soothed her, the only one who could. I held her on my lap and whispered nursery rhymes. *"Do you know the muffin man? . . ."* Fagan drifted off to sleep, but Eden, Alberta, and I could still hear them upstairs. Grunts. Cries. Laughter. We didn't get the particulars, but we knew what was going on.

Bad memories flood out the good. Destroy the good so you wonder if you ever had any, flooding in like a red tide and overwhelming the beautiful clear water that was there before. Back in the early 1970s, we had a real red tide in New England. It stretched from Cape Cod all the way up to Casco Bay in Maine, five hundred miles or more. The blue water turned red as if the earth underneath were bleeding. A stunning thing to see, terrifying until you understood what it was. Lucky for us, it happened in September, after the girls went back to school, not during summer when we went swimming every day and could have gotten poisoned by this toxic tide before it was even visible. Some type of algae, phyto-somethings, blooming like a rose garden in the salty water all along the coast, hundreds of miles, and out as far as we could see. An overgrowth of algae. That's all it really was. But it killed an entire harvest of fish and bivalves — clams, mussels, oysters, scallops. A vast destruction, the dead ones heaved onto the beaches by the tide, the stench impossible to describe. An ecological catastrophe, but also an economic one for the clammers and fishermen who earned a living off this bounty.

" 'All the waters in the river turned to blood,' " declared Jack, quoting from the Bible, the first time we saw it. All the waters have turned to blood. For those of us who lived so close it did seem biblical, the enormity of it. The red tide gave off light, and once, after dark, Jack drove me and the girls over to Nantasket to see the waves in the moonlight, glowing with this bioluminescence. A wonder in our world, beautiful if you didn't know what was really going on.

Flanna. A red tide who flooded into our lives when we were too young, too weak to hold her back, or to even understand why or how she poisoned everything. After my father died, I promised myself I'd never think of her again. I cut her from my mind the way surgeons, a few years ago, cut a melanoma out of Patty's arm. They sliced away fat and muscle all around it, leaving a crater on the upper backside of her arm. All because of a mole no bigger than a tick. Ugly as sin, but it did the trick. Destroyed the cancer. Saved Patty's life. No longer any evidence of disease. My surgery worked just as well. I cut Flanna out, along with the surrounding tissue. Didn't think of her once in almost sixty years. But now, thanks to Patty's all-important genealogy and my daughter's chronic nosiness, the red tide is coming back.

SEVEN:
IF YOU ARE BUT A DREAM

The next time Cassandra calls, before I've even recovered from all that overpriced Chardonnay, she's bounced off in another direction. Still, she's got me in her cross-hairs.

"Maybe you've got Alzheimer's," she bleats into the phone, her voice high-pitched and edgy.

"OK, so I forgot to meet you at the mall. Big deal." Thankfully, when I heard the phone ring, I remembered that she'd planned for us to do a power walk, then catch a movie — something starring Kevin Costner. Cass has the hots for him.

"It's not the first time, Mother." Mother, not Mimi. Now I'm really in it. "And Aunt Patty told me you didn't know what she was talking about when she called about the genealogy."

"Did too. She just caught me by surprise."

"You ought to get a physical and talk

about your memory lapses with your doctor."

"My 'memory lapses'? You ought to mind
your own damned business."

"It is my business," she says, snotty as
could be, but the phone's stuck between my
hand and ear. I can't hang up. "You could
end up like Aunt Lillian."

"That's not fair. I'm not anything like Lillian." Poor Lillian, my aunt. She used to be
a paralegal for a big law firm in Boston, a
real stickler for details. Lillian, the nitpicker,
and proud of it. That's what everybody said
about her. But in her later years, she forgot
entirely who she was, and even who her
children were. Lillian lost track of the most
basic things, like what happens in winter
and summer and where you sleep and where
you pee. The last straw was when her kids
— their own kids in tow — went to take her
out to Denny's for a patty melt, her favorite
meal. They found her in a neighbor's yard,
naked in the snow, insisting that she was
going to take a bath. Turned out to be her
final expedition. Her kids had her locked up
in one of those special places for "Old Tim-
ers" patients where they strap you to your
wheelchair so you can't strip and go wandering around. Lillian died within the year. Not
a minute too soon. My sisters and I had a

Mass said for her. And may perpetual light shine upon her.

"I want to plan ahead if I'm going to be changing your diapers this time next year."

"You'll never change my diapers, you brat."

"Oh, Mimi," she says, softer this time. "I don't want to fight. I only want to help. You know you need it."

Just to prove her wrong, I let her make the appointment. I'll show you, I'm thinking to myself. I'll show you who's losing her mind.

"I'll pull some strings," she says. "We'll get you in to see somebody really good, the best brain guy on the South Shore."

Much as I hate it when Cassie picks on me, she's not entirely mistaken about my memory. For some time now, it's been springing leaks, just like the pipes in Paul Revere. I've forgotten her phone number, and the Mass schedule at Our Lady Queen of Peace, both of which I know by heart. When I was playing Scrabble with my grandkids, I forgot how to spell a couple of simple words, "apple" and "pear." I got away with "pare," but not with "appel." "You're letting us win," the kids accused me, but I wasn't. "It's called a memory lapse," I told them, but they didn't understand. And the last time I tried to knit a sweater, which neither my kids nor their kids wanted anyway — not stylish enough, no corporate logo embroidered on the front — I had trouble following the pattern. I kept screwing up the knits and purls. Out of frustration, I shoved the half-finished sweater into the trash and gave up this hobby, one that I'd kept busy with for more than thirty years.

A couple of times lately I've gone to the Plaza, and when I finished shopping, I walked out to the parking lot but couldn't remember where I'd parked. Couldn't find my little white Shadow, but I couldn't tell anyone either. If I did, they'd realize I was losing it, and maybe tell my kids. So I strolled up and down the rows of cars — casually, in case anybody saw me, so that they wouldn't know I was looking for my car. I walked with my head held high, as if I knew exactly where it was, as if I were wearing the high heels I always used to love instead of Rockport Walkers.

And I knew my memory couldn't be that bad because, while I was searching, I kept thinking about all the awful things they do to old people when they can't remember anymore. I also thought about how I've always had nice legs, with thin ankles and pretty feet; how I figured these were good for life, that I'd get a lifetime guarantee on something. My ex is a confirmed leg man and he always told me that my sexy ankles drove him crazy. "Great gams," he whispered to me every now and then, in a way that turned them into Jell-O. He always wanted me in pumps, three- or four-inch heels.

All those years I was home raising our daughters, I'd bathe and change into heels by the time he came home from work and meet him at the door with a highball, as if I had nothing else to do all day except make myself sexy for him. Even after he turned me in for the newer model, I kept wearing the high heels, thinking, Ankles, don't fail me now. Maybe I'd attract a rich old man. Then the falling arches and the bunions got me. Some mornings I could hardly haul myself out of bed. Lose the heels, then some weight, the podiatrist told me, and he suggested the Rockport Walkers, genuine old-lady shoes.

Then, a week or so ago, I went to Grab & Go for my groceries, the little that I need, cranberry juice and English muffins and some Stouffer's Lean Cuisines. When I was done, I went outside, happy to see my

81

Dodge exactly where I'd parked it. Ta-da. But when I got inside, I couldn't remember what to do with the keys. For a split second, a terrible one, I looked at the dashboard not knowing what it was, and holding this sharp metal object in my hand. I might as well have been in the cockpit of a DC-10. Then it came back to me: the key goes into the hole on the steering column. It's called the ignition. Phew! Once that motor rumbled, sweetheart, I was fine. Found my way home in record time. Not that I shared this little victory with my sisters or my kids. It's strictly between me, myself, and I. So, no, my mental faculties might not exactly be in tip-top shape, but I haven't yet lost anything I can't live without.

All too soon, Cassandra calls to tell me we've got an appointment with the best brain guy on the South Shore. Again, first-person plural.

"Lucky me."

"You are lucky," she says, "darned lucky to have somebody like me looking out for your best interests."

My best interests.

Cassie calls the night before, and again the morning of, to remind me. Like I could forget an appointment with the best brain guy on the South Shore. When she picks me up, she gives my comfy sweats the evil eye, and I give her one right back, though her crisp slacks and blouse and blazer would pass muster even in the highest levels of the government. Her foot heavy on the pedal, she drives me to South Shore Neurologic and Radiologic in Braintree, a name that gives me the heebie-jeebies. It's in a new brick medical arts building just past the Plaza.

After we wait for what feels like forever, a nurse takes us to an examining room where the best brain guy, whose name I don't recall — minor lapse — asks me a million questions. He looks into my eyes and taps me here and there with a funny little hammer. Then he says he's sending us downstairs to a radiologist who'll make maps of my brain. Maps. To the tune of several thousand dollars, which Medicare will in fact cover — Cassie already checked. Just so they can find out more about what's going on inside my head than any sane person would ever want to know.

"It's totally noninvasive," the brain guy says, not looking at me, but riffling through my file, full of the notes he's been taking. "All you have to do is lie there and relax." I'd heard that advice before.

We find our way through a maze of hallways, lots of doors — all shut — until we reach Radiology, a windowless little room where, again, we wait and wait. Then a technician comes for us and brings us into a dark room. There, they make me strip and put on this thing that's misnamed a gown. Then the tech tells Cassie to stay where she is and he brings me to an even darker room and makes me lie on a narrow table. My heart's revving up, moving toward overdrive, when he leaves and presses a button from wherever he is and the table slides backward into this metal tube.

That's when I know I've bitten off way more than I could chew. This MRI device is an airless tube, steel wrapped all around you, just inches from your face, and it echoes every sound, even your own breathing. They tell me not to move a muscle, but the moment they slide me in there, I don't believe it's possible to get back out alive.

The noise is terrible — a pounding like a jackhammer wedged into my ear — and I lose it. I try to sit up and I bump my head. Can't find my way out. "Cassie, honey, get me out of here!" I holler and my voice echoes back at me, vibrating inside my skull. "Cassie, honey, I'm suffocating."

"Hold on," says the tech, even though

there's nothing to hold on to. Next thing you know, I'm sliding back out of the tube and Cassie and the tech rush in while I lie there, twitching like a victim of electric shock.

They pull me out, and Cass pats my back until a nurse shows up with a small blue pill. The tech says he'll do someone else while we wait for the pill to take effect. Sometime later, I've settled down and when they slide me back in, it's like I'm drifting on a cloud. This time they make me choose from a rack of CDs, and they give me headphones, so I go back into the tube listening to Sinatra, "Zing! Went the Strings of My Heart." They let Cassie stay with me. She sits at the end of the table and holds my ankles, the same ones that drove Jack crazy oh so long ago. Inside, I feel like I could float away, right through the metal tube, right up through the clouds. But I also feel Cassie holding on, like she's keeping me on Earth.

Cass sits there while the technician talks above the racket and Sinatra, promising me we're almost done. Just a couple of minutes more. *I still recall the thrill.* Yup, almost done. I can hear the technician breathing, his voice or maybe it's Sinatra's echoing from very far away. *I guess I always will.* "How are you doing in there, Mrs. Malloy?" he asks, and I wonder who she is.

Cassie takes me to lunch, salads at a local grill where the smell of broiling burgers drives me crazy. "No way," she says, reading the menu as if reading my thoughts. "No burgers." Due to the effects of the pill, everything happens through a gauzy curtain. My daughter orders for me, a big bowl of bitter greens, fit for a small rodent, not even a roll or cracker. "Arugula," she says, tapping her fork into my bowl, pointing out a piece. "It's loaded with micronutrients." I can hardly taste it, which is probably just as well. Next thing I know, Cassie and I are back at the brain guy's. She wouldn't miss this for the world. I want a smoke more than anything, but the signs are everywhere, the smoldering butt with the red slash through it. The brain guy's got these pictures up on a lighted board, human brains in strange bright colors. Maps. He points to the map of my brain, comparing it to the other one. That other brain's the normal one, he says. It's all swirls of greens and reds and purples inside the outline of a skull. My brain has those same colors, but they're splattered with black spots, like someone's cut it full of holes.

"Atrophy?" asks Cassie.

"Degeneration," says the brain guy, who is young enough to be my son. Degeneration. Oh, great.

"The good news," he says, "is that you don't have Alzheimer's or a brain tumor."

I turn to Cassie with a big smile, but she's staring at the maps.

"The bad news," he says, "is that you've suffered something called transient ischemic attacks, TIAs."

"Small strokes?" says Cassandra. The brain guy nods.

"You probably didn't even know they were happening," he says, a smarty-pants, just like my daughter.

I nod, but he's wrong there. A couple of times, during the past year, I'd feel my body start to tremble — nothing painful, just a queer buzz from deep inside. If I tried to write, or light a cigarette, my hand wouldn't work. Or maybe I'd try to talk but my mouth and tongue would be stiff, and I'd slur my words so people would think I'd been drinking. Once or twice, one of my legs gave way. Luckily, it happened when I was home alone so nobody saw me fall. I'd rest, and eventually the peculiar sensations would pass.

"You mean those black spots are dead?"

Cassie points.

"In my estimation, it wouldn't be inaccurate to say that," the brain guy answers.

I'm pretty sure he means yes. He makes a humming sound. He won't look me in the eye.

"And you have to stop smoking." He stares at the file, all shiny surfaces like Cassie, his skin and scalp and starched white coat. "Nicotine constricts the flow of blood and oxygen to the brain. And with your particular biology, that's very damaging." He seems to have mistaken that file for my face. Some brain guy. "You should also lose some weight and start exercising. With a change in lifestyle, you could have a long and healthy life."

"Will the black spots change color?" Cassie asks.

"What's gone is gone."

We leave the brain guy's office, but I don't think he told me everything, and I didn't know how to ask. At the same time, all of a sudden and very strongly, I feel that my brain belongs to me and what's happening inside it is nobody else's business.

As for my lifestyle, I figure, what I do or don't do is none of their business either, though I'm much too polite to say so. Butt out, pun intended. On the drive home, my daughter is silent, but I feel her gloating, a breeze rippling the still surface of the water, as she speeds me back to Centennial Square. After all, she's right, she's been proven right: I'm losing bits and pieces of my mind.

"Mimi, don't —" she starts to say when she lets me out, but I cut her off.

"Enough's enough for today," I say, and slam the door, grateful to be home and alone. At this point in my life, pushing hard on seventy, I figure I've earned the right to have a highball, a smoke, and a bowl of salted nuts whenever I want them. Give them up for what? To live a few more years? Ridiculous. So that's exactly what I do. Four Roses and ginger ale, with lots of ice. Plus a little bowl of roasted cashews, shiny with salt and oil.

EIGHT:
YOU CAN'T TAKE THAT AWAY
FROM ME

A few days later, after finishing up her greeting-card displays, Cassie stops by my apartment. This time, she shows up in a blue suit, empty-handed — no lobster or white wine. It's just about suppertime so, who knows, maybe she's in the mood for some home-cooked Lean Cuisine. I'm sipping a straight-up Manhattan, a rare treat, and having a smoke, and right away she's ticked.

"What do you think you're doing?" Her pretty face is scrunched up like a fist.

"Stay for dinner." I look at her. I can't remember ever being so young or so pretty, but that must be a normal type of forgetting. Otherwise, how could you go on?

She shakes her head no, tosses something onto my counter, like she can't wait to get it off her hands. The velvet pouch. I should've known. The pendant inside makes a soft clunk.

"It's worthless," she says, louder than necessary. My hearing's perfect. "Water and paste." She flicks the pouch toward me with her pretty fingertips. I grab it, take out the pendant. A scratch runs sideways across the stone, little fissures cut deep into it. Feels like I've been cut myself.

"It wouldn't scratch if it were real."

I look at Cassandra.

"My pendant."

"It has no value." Her eyes are harder than the stone. "So it really doesn't matter if it's scratched."

"Its value —"

She cuts me off. "Have you made your will yet?" She grabs the pendant from my hand, shakes it like a pair of dice. Her eyes bore through me, like Jack's whenever he moved in for the kill.

"What kind of question is that?"

"Have you?"

"That's for me to know and you to find out."

Her jaw drops and hangs there. "At the very least, you should consider giving me power of attorney."

"Power of attorney?"

"Over your affairs. In case you become incompetent."

"Incompetent?" I take a big swallow of

my Manhattan. It spills onto my fingers, my hand's shaking so much.

"You have the brain of an eighty-five-year-old woman." She speaks quietly and slowly. "You have an eighty-five-year-old brain and your body's only sixty-eight. That's what the doctor told me. He couldn't get over it, the way your brain looked, like the brain of a very elderly woman."

I hear her but can't say a word, not even to correct her. I'm not even sixty-eight. Not by several months, last time I checked.

"You could stroke out any day." Cassie stands there in her blue suit, and the fluorescent light in my kitchenette makes her look green and old. "The doctor said those little strokes are probably warnings that the big one is coming. You know, like those earthquakes in California. If you're lucky, he said, the big one will take you all the way instead of leaving you here paralyzed and speechless."

"I take my BP meds. My blood pressure is under control." Except when my kids and ex attack me.

"It's not your blood pressure." She shakes her head, not quite believing the imbecile she's dealing with. "It's those heart flutters, the atrial fibrillation. The doctor explained it to me. The A-fib throws off clots, and the clots can move up or down. If one moves up . . ." She snaps her fingers to signify the Big One and stares at me.

She points to my cigarette and I take a good, deep drag. "You know every time you do that, you're destroying more brain cells. And I, for one, don't think you can afford to lose any more."

Then Cassandra turns and walks out, high heels clicking, and I'm stuck, alone with my Manhattan, feeling like I've just been rabbit punched and robbed of fifteen years.

Nine:
In the Shadow of the Moon

The next morning, I'm still stewing. I take my coffee and the pendant and go sit in my La-Z-Boy. I look hard at the pendant, scratched now and declared worthless by Cass and her jeweler. Worthless, maybe, but still part of me — me with all the black spots in my brain. I hold the stone and rub the scratch, rub and rub, like maybe I can smooth it out.

The blue pendant warms in my hand. I look down at it, and the color reminds me of Daddy's eyes. Like watching a movie, I see myself one Sunday falling down the front stairs of our house. I couldn't have been more than five or so. I was sliding down the banister, roughhousing, disobeying, when I slipped and fell onto the front hall floor. I landed on my left hand. Snap. A bone cracked. It hurt so badly I retched and pain danced at the edges of my eyes. It felt like I was going blind. The rest of them,

Mam, Da, and my sisters, gathered 'round, looking at me crumpled at the bottom of the stairs.

Snapped it like a dry stick, said Daddy, examining the damage. Then he lifted me as if I were a scarf or dress that had fallen to the floor. Ran with me, cradled in his arms, all the way to the doctor's house across the railroad tracks on the far side of town, his chest heaving like a bellows. *Da,* I cried into his neck. *Oh, Da.* He squeezed me harder.

The doctor was in his garden in the backyard, kneeling, pulling weeds with his gloved hands. He looked holy, like the statue of the Blessed Virgin stepping on a snake, rising from the flowers in my nana's garden. The doctor stood up out of the tulips, peeled off his gloves, and brought us inside the house to his office, where it was dim and cool. His wife brought us lemonade in blue glasses. The doctor set my wrist, fussing for ages over the plaster cast. The pain kept dancing at the edges of my eyes but Da held me, his arms wrapped tight around me, not once letting go.

I get up from my recliner and turn on the TV, just for company. More news, all of it bad. A house fire in Roxbury, sweeping down the block, an entire family killed.

Started by a cigarette smoldering in a couch. The body of a child found in a freezer in a basement, dead for years, and nobody ever noticed she was gone. Corruption in the mayor's office. The attorney general bragging that the Commonwealth of Massachusetts has the highest conviction rate for child molesters in the United States, and the world's best facility to lock them up in, the Bridgewater Correctional Complex. I switch it off. Who needs that kind of company? I go back to my La-Z-Boy, pick up the blue pendant, hold it close. Black spots. My brain is full of them. Maybe that's where I, neatnik that I am, stashed all of my bad memories.

Fagan Sent Away. A chapter I hardly remember, though my surviving sisters insist I know more than anyone. Fagan Sent Away. These words come to me with side effects, the kind they yammer about on TV ads: cardiovascular risks, ulcers, nausea, diarrhea, tremors, and delirium. And sometime after Fagan Sent Away, the rest of us, Keeley included, went to live with our grandmother — Nana, Annie Sheehan, Daddy's mother. Life started over once we moved in with her. The past melted away, making us certain that, from then on, life would be good again. I was just ten at the time.

I look closely at the blue pendant, try to see past the scratch, but my vision wavers, shot through with shiny lines, like a migraine's coming on. Again the six of us, my sisters and me, are sitting on the front steps of our old house in Quincy, waiting for our father. Today he carries a white bag from the bakery, Hanrahan's, a cookie for each of us and an éclair for Mam. My sisters jump and dance when they see the bag, but my stomach clenches. I know what's inside: chocolate chip for Eden, Alberta, and Keeley; sugar cookies for Patty and Josephine, and caraway seed for me. Yes, I got the cookie full of bitter seeds. I only had myself to blame, but knowing that didn't make them any easier to swallow.

The first time Daddy brought those awful cookies home, he was so excited. *A real Irish treat,* he declared in his soft brogue. *The genuine article.*

Daddy loved anything to do with the old country. But when Alberta took her first bite, she spit it out and made a throw-up noise. Then Eden and the rest of them carried on, spitting out the seeds and making vomit noises. Daddy looked so sad. That's why I kept chewing mine and smiling, taking more little bites.

Look at Maire, here, he said, fluffing my hair and tickling my neck. *She knows a good thing when she tastes it.*

After that, Daddy brought my sisters their favorites, whatever they wanted, and he brought me the cookies full of bitter seeds. He did it with such love that I'd gobble them down, smiling and trying not to gag. What I would've given for a ginger snap! But I could not bring myself to tell him.

After he handed out our cookies, Mam, our real mother, called from inside the house, *Joe, you're ruining their appetites for supper, and me, slaving here, over the hot stove.* Daddy swept Keeley up onto his hip and kissed her freckled cheek. No, wait. Keeley didn't have freckles. Not a one, vain as could be about her perfect skin. Besides, Keeley was never with us when our mother was alive. Mam died giving birth to her. The memory breaks up, like pictures torn into little pieces. I struggle hard to put them back together, and I realize it's Fagan, my original baby sister. She's the one on Daddy's hip, eating a chocolate-chip cookie, ruining her appetite for dinner.

She shows up in this memory like she's been waiting for her chance, popping out from behind Keeley in a game of hide and seek. She, not Keeley, is the one who used to wait with us for Daddy. Not a shadow or a ghost, but a little girl I haven't seen since she got sent away before we had a chance to say good-bye. The sister I buried along with all the other things I didn't want to remember.

I grab Daddy's sleeve. I tug and tug. Jump up and down, tugging, begging. I want him to put Fagan down and pick me up instead. Me, a little snot-nosed kid in hand-me-downs, raggedy, just like the others, and jealous as could be. Fagan giggles from her perch on Daddy's hip. She kisses his whiskery cheek. She owns him, and she knows it. *Fay,* he calls her, *Baby Fay, my wee love.* She not only gets the chocolate chip, she gets held in Daddy's arms.

I open my eyes and look at the pendant. This time, the sky shrinks up inside it. Again, I see myself, but I'm old enough to walk down the hill to meet my father. After our mother passed, I often did this, especially if my sisters weren't around. I'd wait for Daddy and walk back up the hill with him, holding his hand. Sometimes, while I was waiting, I'd imagine him in the distance, coming toward me but not yet seeing me. My father. Daddy. Da. Thin but strong. Wiry. Tired from a long day at the shipyard, crouched in hot darkness, on the scaffolding inside the hull of a tanker or destroyer, fastening the red hot rivets that were shoved through the holes by a worker on the outside.

Nana used to complain that he — *Joey, my Joey* — didn't eat enough. *Looks like a strong wind could knock him over,* she said, a theory my sisters and I were always testing, running at him, leaping up on him. Daddy swore that whatever he ate melted off him while he worked, welding together layers of steel with rivets the size of a big man's thumb. When I was really small, that's what I imagined — fried eggs and bacon, lamb stews and mashed potatoes, melting off him and puddling on the scaffolding beneath him in the dark hull of a ship.

Today I'll run to him, slam into him, going fast as I can, but my father will not fall. No, he'll grab me, laughing. *Contrary Maire,* he'll say. *Think you're stronger than your old man, huh?* His face will be smudged with sweat and smoke and grime, and the visor of his cap will make a half-moon shadow on his face. I'll tilt back my head to see the sky spread out all around him, the exact same color as his eyes.

I wait and wait, walking down the block, way past where I'm allowed to go. I walk past all the other houses out to the corner store and the newsstand and the drugstore. Back and forth, back and forth. A million trolleys come and go. Neighbors watch me through their windows. I almost hear their whispers, *There's one of those Sheehan girls, out looking for her father.* Doesn't stop me. I couldn't care less what they think. I walk back and forth, back and forth, until long after dark, but Daddy, Da, my father, never shows.

From far, far away, I hear knocking. Who else is in trouble? "Mrs. Malloy, oh, Mrs. Malloy." The sound of Duffy's voice brings me back to my apartment; he's calling through the door. Well, dammit. Dammit all to hell. Reluctantly, I get up and open it.

Duffy's standing there with a big smile and the new shelf.

"Sorry I didn't call ahead." He's so sweet, apologetic.

"No problem," I lie through my teeth.

"Everything OK?" he asks as I lead him into the bedroom. "You look a little pale."

"I'm fine, just a little headache coming on."

"Won't be long," he says. Once he's set up, I go back to my chair and the pendant, hoping Da's showed up. Duffy drills and hammers, making a racket to wake the

dead, but my dead will not awaken. No. Da
has disappeared again, like before.

Ten:
I'm Beginning to
See the Light

I suffer through the migraine, a day and night of darkness, blurred vision, zigzags, like lightning bolts flashing behind my eyelids. But when, in the morning, it departs, the world is beautiful, bright, and sparkling. Right away I want to call Cassie, and the snotty brain guy too. I want to call them both and tell them those black spots aren't dead. Because one just broke open and inside it was my father, Joe Sheehan, the real deal, with his spiky cowlicked hair, his laughing eyes, his dimpled smile. Joe Sheehan, Daddy, Da, and stuck to him like the sticky notes I used to love at work were memories of my sisters and me, back when we were little. Even if at first I confused Keeley and Fagan, a simple mistake anyone could make.

I speed-dial Cassandra — her son Mikey set it up for me. Wouldn't you know, she's in Orlando for a greeting-card convention.

I'd forgotten until I heard the message on her machine. But as soon as I put the phone down, it rings. It's Ruth Ann, calling to remind me about her son Jared's concert tonight at the middle school. Forgot about that, too.

"I hate that drive, honey," I tell her. "I'm not up to it anymore." I think about Routes 3 and 93 and 101, and how they all merge and you've got to get yourself into the correct lane at fifty-five miles an hour or more or it's sayonara. Fighting eighteen-wheelers for every inch of highway.

"Oh, Mimi, for heaven's sake, you're what? Sixty-eight? You can handle it."

"Sixty-six."

"Sixty-seven. You're sixty-seven. Last November. You were born in 1927."

"Don't remind me." I try to make a joke of it, but I can't help but think about my ancient brain. Ruthie's getting in on Cassie's act. No mercy for Mom.

"Take the train to Nashua," Ruthie says, "and I'll drive you back to Quincy in the morning, after the kids are in school."

I can't think up an excuse fast enough. Plus, Ruthie's a good girl, and I don't want to hurt her feelings, even though she's always hurting mine. So I call Duffy and he's only too happy to drive me to the train station. Duffy's Car Service. He's got a big blue station wagon, a Caprice Classic, which he keeps in mint condition and neat as a pin, just as you'd expect from an old soldier, but with that nice tobacco smell from his Marlboros.

In the past, when I've called upon him for this favor, which he'll do for anyone who asks and a nice tip at Christmas, he's let me out at the entrance to the station. But this time he shows up at my door smelling of Old Spice, his cheeks pink and his silver hair combed wet. He walks me out to his car and then he parks and waits with me on the platform until the train pulls in. Takes my bag, even though it's one of those little ones on wheels with a handle like a telescope. A real gentleman. I keep the pendant in my pants pocket where I can feel it. I might show Ruthie, depending upon how things go, although that scratch has marred it, like a beautiful woman with a scar along her cheek.

The blood of folks living north of Boston must run thick as syrup, or maybe it's hot-fudge sauce, which we gorged on after Jared's concert. The thermostat at Ruthie's is set at fifty-five degrees when we hit the sack, Jared bunking with his brother for the night so I can sleep in his room. I crawl under layers of down that Ruthie promises will keep me toasty even if the temperature drops below zero and the boiler blows. "You'll sleep like a baby," she says. Maybe I do, but before I nod off, I think about my grandson's concert, Jared on the trumpet in the jazz ensemble. My kind of music, "Sing Sing Sing," "In the Mood," "Begin the Beguine," "Straight, No Chaser." But the truth is, I can hardly stand the sound of horns. They're painful to hear, like fingernails down a blackboard. Not that I'd dream of telling Ruthie, let alone my grandson. Like some type of parasite, the high notes crawl under my skin, linger too long. A sax, or a woodwind, is much more pleasing to my ear. Although, truth be told, Jack ruined me for clarinets.

When we got to the middle school, Ruthie wanted to sit right down in front. We'd get to see the whites of their eyes, wouldn't miss a note. We had a great view of all the darling girls and boys, all dressed in khaki pants and white polo shirts, giggling and poking at one another and trying, but failing, to act grown-up. Finally Jared was standing in the middle of the stage alone, blowing that horn, a solo part. But when he started playing, something sharp and hard stabbed me from the inside. I cringed and shivered. Ruthie grabbed my hand and squeezed.

"He's improvising," she whispered, her eyes soft and full of love. But me, I got a killer hot flash, the type I haven't had for years, where your face and neck turn scarlet and your underwear gets wet, and then you're shivering from the wet underwear. We stood up to applaud. Everyone else did too. Ruthie smiled, her cheeks shiny with tears, so proud.

Afterward, we went to Friendly's for ice-cream sundaes, my treat, with Jared still floating on Cloud Nine from the standing ovation.

"I got a standing O, Mom," he kept saying. "Didja see it? A big standing O!"

"He got his musical gift from Daddy," said Ruthie, digging into her sundae. "It must have skipped a generation, since I'm tone deaf."

"Daddy?" I echoed, my voice sharp. She was referring to Jack F. X. Malloy. My girls think that every good thing they and their kids got came by way of him. "Since when does your father have a musical gift?"

She turned to me, a fleck of hot fudge on her chin, her eyes as big as saucers, a pretty girl like all my daughters, but the only brunette. No makeup. Ruthie goes for that plain Yankee look, buys all her clothes from the L.L.Bean catalogue. It works for her.

"Oh, Mimi, did you forget he played the clarinet? Professionally? He could've had a musical career. . . ."

"Oh, honey, if he coulda, he woulda, believe me."

Jared watched us, a big spoonful of ice cream halted near his mouth. I scooped up some whipped cream and sauce. Delicious.

"You're always putting him down," she wailed, another sound that goes right through me.

"Am not." I gave Jared a big grin. "Hey, so how much do you practice every day?"

"Don't," he said, grinning back, but far more interested in our dispute than my question. "Mom's always nagging, but I hate to practice."

"No point discussing this with you, Mimi," said Ruthie, her heart shutting down. I watched it through her big blue eyes. But she was right. Because, in my opinion, Jack Malloy could play the notes, but he couldn't make the music, an opinion that enrages my daughters and results in bitter arguments.

In the morning, I wake up in the cold room surrounded by posters of soccer players and rock stars, and a band called Rage Against the Machine. What machine? I wonder. The washer? Or maybe it's the garbage disposal. Ruthie was having trouble with hers the night before. I can see my breath when I exhale, and I shut my eyes and snuggle deeper, not wanting to get out of bed, knowing that, in the cold, these old bones will creak and groan. I reach under my pillow for the pendant. I close my eyes and think about Jared's trumpet solo, the stabbing pain, and that thing inside me pushing to get out. Then it's my father I see, not my grandson, blowing on the horn. Da, standing tall, holding a shiny brass instrument. A cornet, not a trumpet, but with almost the exact same shape and sound. A hymn, "Amazing Grace." Sad notes glide and soar. I listen hard.

The sad music calls to me and my sisters, and all of us gather in the hall outside the parlor. Da's behind the closed French doors, the glass panes covered with lace curtains. We watch Da through the lace, standing, his hands around his horn, his head lifted to the ceiling. The notes slide and swirl, tickling my belly, raising goose bumps on my arms.

"Mimi!" Ruthie hollers. She bangs on my door. "Want to say good-bye to the boys?" I pretend I'm still asleep. Not my idea of fun, getting children up and dressed and fed and off to the school bus on time. Been there, done that, too many times to count.

Instead I see Da, stippled with lace shadows. His fingers press the valves of his golden horn and the notes fly up, birds we hear but cannot see. He played in an Army band in World War I; went to Europe, not for combat, but to play music for the troops. Nana always bragged about him. Told anyone who'd listen, mostly us, how good he was, playing this wonderful American instrument that nobody in Ireland had ever laid their hands on. American music on an American instrument, it didn't get any better for her. "Last call!" Ruthie shouts through the door. "Your grandsons would like to say good-bye."

Da's uniform, with its shiny buttons, its epaulettes, its embroidered patch — PFC Joseph D. Sheehan — was kept in mothballs in a chest upstairs. Once in a while, my sisters and I sneaked up to look at it, our eyes and noses stinging from the naphthalene. Now his great-grandson Jared plays first trumpet in his junior high jazz band.

When I get up, I'll show Ruthie the pendant, let her in on the mystery, how it showed up on my closet floor, and how it's helping me to remember. It's filling the black spots back in. How Jared got his musical gift from my father, not hers.

But when I walk into the kitchen, all showered and dressed and good to go, Ruthie's in a mood.

"I'm meeting Daddy for lunch. I'm going to be late."

"I'm ready, I'm all set, but I could use a cup of coffee."

"Fine. We'll go to Dunks."

Next thing we're in her minivan, making a quick stop at Dunkin' Donuts for coffee and bagels to go before heading south to Quincy. What I really want is a French cruller, or a vanilla crème in powdered sugar, but I don't have the nerve to ask. If I do, that news flash — Mimi Eating Doughnuts — will be flying through the wires all over the northeast where my daughters live. While Ruthie orders, I light up in the parking lot, thinking I'll grab a couple of puffs to hold me til I get home.

When Ruthie comes out, she gives me one of those looks to kill.

"Don't worry, I'll put it out," I tell her. "I wouldn't dream of polluting the air in your minivan."

"You were smoking in my driveway last night." She shoves the coffee into my hand.

"I counted the butts, six of them."

"Well, excuse me. Didn't know you were the smoking police."

She gives me another look.

"You really shouldn't be smoking at all," she says. "It says right on the pack, 'Hazardous to Your Health.' But to yours more than others. That's what I hear, anyway."

She's looking at my lighted cigarette, not at me.

"You've been talking to Cassandra."

"What do you expect? If you won't tell me anything important, Cassandra has to."

"She's a blabbermouth. She ought to mind her own business."

"She says you've got black spots in your brain, Mimi. Black spots. You've got an eighty-five-year-old brain, for heaven's sake."

I take my time on one last drag, then grind the butt under my Rockport Walker. Blood, thin and cold, rushes to my head.

"Cass says you could stroke out any day. She says you're not supposed to light another cigarette."

Ruthie climbs into the van and starts the ignition. I'm so mad, I'm seeing stars. "And you don't even care enough to get up and say good-bye to your own grandsons." We take our seats in the minivan, which is all nice and warm because Ruthie left it running while she ordered. She's a good, fast driver, and traffic isn't bad, but my fun is ruined. It'll be a cold day in hell before I show her the pendant, or tell her about Da's music — how Jared's following in his footsteps, not those of Jack Malloy. The highways stretch out before us, six lanes, eight lanes, where once there was only forest. Ruthie negotiates the merges like a pro, without the slightest hesitation.

Again, I see my father with his horn. When we were really young, Da played all the time. He let us in to sit with him in the front parlor, a room we hardly ever used. The same place we gathered years later, when he told us Fagan had been sent away. Way back before then, my sisters and I, including Fagan, would lounge around him on the slippery brocade couch, or sometimes on the floor. Listening, not recognizing any melodies, but loving them just the same. When Da finished, we watched him put away his instrument. He let the spit drip out into a little can, then he cleaned the inside with an old diaper and a long, thin brush. He'd take apart the valves to clean and oil them. Once he was satisfied that his cornet was spotless and dry and perfect, he wrapped it in a white linen cloth and put it inside its leather case. The outside of this case was plain black cowhide, with brass clasps. But the inside was lined with the most beautiful red velvet, and shaped exactly like his cornet. He put the cornet inside just so, smoothing out the linen covering before closing the lid. He kept it on a closet shelf where none of us could reach it.

"Cassie says you've already had some little strokes."

We've hit the long straight stretch on I-93, the subdivisions and shopping strips of Pepperell and Leominster on either side. Ruthie's tone's a little gentler now. "Those TIA things, whatever they call them. She says they left areas of atrophy in your brain."

Her sweet voice doesn't soften me.

"Is that why you had me up for a sleepover? Did Cassie put you up to it? So you could get on my case?"

"Cassie didn't put me up to it," she cries in a way that convinces me otherwise. "It was my own idea." She turns to me. "I'm really worried about you, Mimi."

"Look, Ruth Ann, you're a great girl and I love you." She turns her attention back to the highway. "Your son's a wonderful musician. I'm glad I came to visit. But we won't be talking about what's going on inside my brain. Have you got that? And you can tell your other sisters in case any of them ask."

We go the rest of the way in a loud, aching silence.

Eleven:
The Curse of an
Aching Heart

What happened to Daddy's music? That's the burning question after Ruthie leaves me off with an air kiss that's even colder than the temperature in her house at night and a promise that she'll call me soon. Not that my hug was any warmer. On her way back to the Granite State, she's stopping north of Boston for lunch with Jack F. X. Malloy. No doubt he'll take her out in his Grand Marquis, which he trades in for a new one every third year. He'll wine her and dine her at a place with linen tablecloths, servers instead of waitresses. Jack still can't resist a chance to show his daughters that he's got more money, more class, more style than their mother, the raggedy-ass orphan he lifted out of poverty.

We had some hard years, many hard years, Jack and me, but the beginning of the end didn't come until my hysterectomy, when the doctors cut me open and scooped me out. They went into that place way down below, where I'd been cut open and sewn up so many times from all those babies, it's no wonder I had trouble keeping what was inside me in, and what was outside out. And he, my husband, didn't visit because hospitals depress him.

For six weeks after that surgery, I was laid up at home, unable to cook or clean, a terrible inconvenience to him. I couldn't steam press his shirts and starch the collars, organize his socks into perfect little balls in his bureau drawers, or give him the occasional piece of tail — all out of the question in my condition.

Once I tried to tell him how I felt. "You and the girls, you take whatever you want of me, whenever you feel like it. I can't keep anything to myself, or do anything for myself. Sometimes I don't even know who I am, or who I'm supposed to be." Words deeper than the deepest prayer I'd ever prayed.

"You've never had it so good, and you know it," Jack answered, fixing me with those gorgeous blue bedroom eyes of his, eyes that had once made my heart go pitter-pat. "You've got a beautiful home, a new Ford Fairlane of your own, and six smart, healthy daughters. Whoever would have expected that from one of you Sheehan girls?" Then he walked away and my face burned as if he'd slapped me. I heard the other words he didn't say: *You Sheehan girls, raggedy-ass orphans, with the no-good drunk for a father.* Like my sisters and I were damaged goods, something from Filene's Basement after two or three markdowns.

I'm glad to be home. Glad to be alone. I love my little place. It's all mine. When I moved in, neutered by the hysterectomy, wiped out by the divorce, stung a thousand times by my daughters' swarming attitudes, the rooms were empty and I loved their emptiness. Those rooms seemed somehow holy, like the kind nuns have in a cloister. I might have left them that way, except I was too old to sleep on the floor, and my daughters would've taken it as further evidence of my craziness. So I bought some furniture, not Ethan Allen, not what Jack's house was full of — a lower grade, but good enough for me.

For the first time in my life, I had a room of my own. I could take long baths with the bathroom door open, then wander from room to room wrapped in just a towel. I had a bed all to myself. I could watch *The Late Show* whenever I felt like it. Johnny

Carson cracked me up, especially Carnac the Magnificent. What a hoot. God, I miss him, wish he hadn't retired. Leno can't hold a candle to him, and I've never warmed up to that other one, the geeky one with glasses. I'd rather sleep.

My bed is covered with the loveliest wedding-ring quilt, one that Ruthie sewed for me, in shades of yellow, pink, and green. I've got one of my own crocheted afghans, in coordinating colors, stretched out over the foot. Feather pillows, Laura Ashley sheets with little flowers, 400-thread-count cotton, found by yours truly in a clearance bin at Marshalls — a real steal. I hurried to the checkout with them, thinking they'd made a mistake and wouldn't find out if I got out of there fast enough.

I spend a couple of hours reorganizing my closet and its nice new shelf with scented shelf paper. Soon, everything's in its place, just so. I get some laundry going in the coin machines down the hall. Then I settle into the La-Z-Boy, holding the blue pendant, still wondering about Da's music. How I wish I had a photo album of our family way back when — one I could open at my leisure, lingering over the pictures. But we don't have any photos, we surviving Shee-han girls.

I think about how my father, unlike my ex, didn't just play an instrument. No, he made music, the most beautiful music. But he played less and less as the years went by, and one day he just stopped. Was it before or after Mammy died? Before or after he remarried? Before or after Fagan Sent Away? I can't remember. Not that I've thought much about it.

Then, out of nowhere, I see myself with my sisters, and we're gathered by the old black stove in the kitchen, the house around us cold and dark. My heart thumps when I see Da, sitting in a straight-backed chair, my sisters and I wrapped around him like vines, hanging off him every which way, every one of us determined to get a piece of him. I rub my cheek along his arm, the soft cotton of his shirt. He pats my hair, absent-mindedly, perhaps, but I'll take what I can get. I'm Daddy's girl, I know it, a convic-tion each of the others shared. Every one of us believed we were Da's special girl. We'd been wheedling, the bunch of us, begging him for music. *Da, Da, please. Pretty please with butter and sugar on it.* But he did not give in. Then I asked him, *Da, why don't you play your music anymore?*

Can't, he answered, making funny faces.

Why not?

120

I lost my lip. Which struck me and my sisters as the biggest joke, Da losing his lip. My sisters laughed.

You did not, I cried. *It's right there on your face.* And I grabbed his lip to prove my point.

Then Da laughed too, tugging on his lips, pulling them every which way, because they weren't lost at all but were still there, glued to his face, exactly where they were supposed to be.

But in the middle of our laughter, Da stopped; looked up as something stopped him cold. I felt it in his body, but would not turn around to look. It was Flanna. We all knew, every one of us, that it was Flanna, who could not bear to let him love us. She had to keep every last bit of him for herself. Again Da disappears before my eyes, the worst of his magic tricks.

I get up from my chair and go into the kitchen for a glass of cold water from the tap. I wipe down the counter and the stovetop even though they're already clean. I go out and move the laundry from the washer to the dryer. Things I don't quite recognize fly around me, like clothes when they're on the fluff cycle. Fear and maybe longing, stuck together, static cling. Beyond them, I see the maps of my mind up on the screen in the brain guy's office. Black spots among swirls of color. *Areas of atrophy,* he said.

I go into my bedroom looking for a project. I need something to do, gotta keep busy. I learned that from Nana, who never rested. But everything's already in its place. I open my bureau drawers and see the neat rows of bras and panties, lined up as perfectly as cars in a dealer's lot.

Of course, longing takes many forms. Even I know that. Longing to be young and thin and beautiful again. Longing for a straight-up Manhattan, so you can forget you're not. Or the sound of Sinatra singing so it doesn't matter quite as much. Longing for a bit more money so you won't have to pinch pennies, worrying every minute about how to make ends meet. Longing to take a cruise to the Caribbean, to bake half-dressed in the sun all day, and dress up every night for dinner, a dinner you haven't cooked and won't have to clean up from. With somebody who doesn't mind a little extra padding around your hips and thighs. Who loves you anyway.

Longing to be that special someone to somebody, like it always says on Cassie's greeting cards, the way it never was with

Jack. Longing for a photo album of my family back when we were kids. Longing to make it right with Malvina, my lost kid in the Bronx. A woman now, with children of her own. Longing. Longing to be loved.

Fear, on the other hand, well, it pulls tight like a fabric winding, stretching, binding even though you can't see it, can't touch it, can't wrap your mind around it. Fear of what the test results will say. Fear of what will happen when your car won't start and you don't have anyone to call. Fear of being stuck in an elevator, or locked in a dark closet. Fear of falling in the shower, breaking a hip, with nobody there to pull you out. Fear of living too long and running out of money, of becoming a burden to your children. Fear of being old, alone, and feeble. Forgotten. Fear. You can't see it; can't get a handle on it; can't contain it, but there it is: One size fits all.

It's almost dark now, so I switch on a light but don't pull down the shades. That way, if Duffy wants a cup of coffee, he'll know he can stop by. I go back to my recliner and pick up the pendant. How I wish I had Da's picture; that I could see him, handsome Joey Sheehan, just once more in his prime, with his dimples and those dreamy eyes with the thick eyelashes he hated, because the fellas at the shipyard teased that they were pretty as a girl's. Da. He had a bunch of brothers, and people used to call them those good-looking Sheehan boys. Sam, Teddy, Leo, and Joe. It was the same way, in the next generation, with me and my sisters. *Those glorious Sheehan girls.*

One of them must have an old photo of him, and I make a mental note to ask the next time we're together, though even I'll admit my mental notes are nowhere near as effective as they used to be. Not that we had any kind of family album growing up. We were too poor to have many pictures. And the ones we did own, the very few photographs of my parents and my sisters and me as babies, Flanna Flanagan tore up and burned.

Flanna, with her enchanting face for Da, another one for us — exactly alike, but not at all the same. Switched so fast you couldn't predict when it would happen. She sang and prayed in ways we didn't understand, had a garden where she grew forbidden things. There was hell to pay if we dared step into it. I never did. She would harvest those forbidden things and boil them up on the stove, stinking up the house. Old folks in the neighborhood would line up to buy them. Flanna, a Lucky Strike between her fingers, a glass of whiskey by her side. Whispering to herself, making us eat and drink the awful stuff she made when our father wasn't there.

Flanna Flanagan. *How blessed Da was to catch her, himself a widower with all those little girls to raise!* That's what everybody said. A godsend was Flanna Flanagan. But we wondered, right from the start, my sisters and me, what type of god would send someone like her our way. Somebody who was always present even when you couldn't see her.

Da said he lost his lip that night when we begged him to play music, but he didn't lose it. Flanna stole it off his face. I slip and slide into the tunnel of memory, Flanna standing over the burn can in the backyard. Smoke and flame shoot out of it. Flanna, with her face as pretty as an angel's painted on the ceiling of a church. The wind lifts bits and pieces of what she's burning, scatters the ashes like snow. Pictures of my mother, and of my mother and father together, the only photographs we owned. *No no, no,* I say. She shoves me away. I grab her arm; she grabs my neck and shakes me. I topple, taste dirt and ash. Hear her scrape another match down the side of the can and toss it in. All the scraps of pictures are in flames. *I'm your mammy now,* she says.

I heave myself up out of the chair. Suffering a sudden palsy, I am like one of those decrepit patients at the old folks' home. Jittering from head to foot. A side effect of memory, of shaking loose the promise I made to myself long ago, to erase Flanna from my life. And now she's back again, tagging along with Da, hanging on to him for dear life, refusing to ever let him go.

The pendant flies out of my hand, bounces across the floor, and lands on the far side of the coffee table. It sparkles on the carpet. Worthless. No value whatsoever. That's what Cassie's jeweler said. Water and paste. Nobody ought to have to go through this, I decide. I'm going to get rid of the damned thing. Throw it away. Good riddance to bad rubbish. I snatch it off the floor and head out back to the Dumpster.

Twelve:
Are You Lonesome Tonight?

The Dumpster's just outside the back door, in an alcove near the parking lot, the area lit by a motion-sensor floodlight. As I head out to it, my pumper settles down and the palsy eases, and who do I see on the other side of the glass back door but Duffy. He's sweeping up, or trying to sweep up, a mess of Styrofoam peanuts scattered like drifts of snow around the Dumpster. A careless tenant must've thrown in a carton, and the peanuts have blown back out. So here's Duffy, chasing them down, which is like trying to catch air. He holds a broom in one hand, and in the other one of those nifty dustpans janitors use, with the long handle so you don't have to bend over and the flap in front to hold the dirt inside.

But every time Duffy tries to sweep in the peanuts, only a few go in and the rest blow back out, even farther away, and he chases after them, looking awkward, with the bum leg. He tries really hard, but the harder he sweeps, the more the peanuts fly around, like they're doing it on purpose, just to get his goat. The poor guy bends this way and that, trying different sweeping strokes, like he thinks he can outsmart them. I crack up, can't help it. He turns and sees me, and, if it's possible, his face gets even redder. I push open the door.

"Mrs. Malloy, oh Mrs. Malloy, what brings you out here on such a chilly evening?" His question makes me laugh even harder.

"Stalking. I'm stalking you."

"I should be so lucky," he answers without missing a beat, and I laugh harder still.

"Well, I'm glad to be so entertaining. For the second time in recent memory, I'm putting on a show for you." I picture him on his butt on my bedroom floor and laugh some more.

"No way to outsmart those little devils," I say, pointing to the peanuts between snorts and giggles, and at last he's smiling too. Then I get an idea.

"Where's the box they came in?"

Sure enough, it's right there on top of the Dumpster.

"Fold back the flaps," I tell him, getting myself back together. "Then I'll hold it, and

128

you sweep."

Works like a charm. I bend over to hold the box steady on the ground while Duffy sweeps. In minutes, we scoop up every last one. Then we redo the flaps so the peanuts can't escape and Duffy tosses the box back into the Dumpster while I stand over to the side, breathing hard from laughter and exertion.

"Good thing you came along when you did. I'd be out here all night, still chasing them."

"Don't hate me because I'm efficient," I say in a teasing way, and he grins.

"What brings you out here?" he repeats.

"I was only kidding about the stalking thing."

"I wasn't," he answers. My turn to blush.

"Doing a little trashing of my own," I say, to switch the track of our conversation. I take the pendant out of my pocket. In the floodlight by the door, it's so lovely, my heart aches. You can hardly see the scratch. He gasps.

"You mean to tell me, Mrs. Malloy, that you're going to put that beautiful piece in the Dumpster? Have you lost your senses?"

I nod yes, feeling ridiculous, knowing now I could never toss it.

"If you don't want it, hock it. At least get

a few bucks for it."

I nod.

"Good thing I was out here."

"One good turn deserves another, right?" I grin and look up into his nice eyes.

"That's right. But why toss it?" he persists.

I don't have much of an answer. "It brings back bad memories. Every time I look at it. Memories I don't want to have."

He wraps his big old hand around my small one holding the pendant and presses my hand around it.

"Out of sight, out of mind," he says, like he's some kind of expert on bad memories. "Solves the problem, doesn't it?"

I'm turning to go back inside when I hear him call out again. "I don't suppose, Mrs. Malloy, that you'd want to walk up to Clancy's with me in a bit? It's ladies' night. I'll buy you a beer."

For all the complaining my kids do about this apartment, they fail to see one of its best points: location. Just two blocks from the Square, within easy walking distance of just about anything I'd ever want or need. A pharmacy, a deli, a butcher's, a baker's, a package store, a diner, several Irish pubs, and an underwear place called Fanny's Foundations — not to mention my parish,

Our Lady Queen of Peace, an honest-to-God old cathedral. We could be snowed in for weeks and I could still take care of both my corporal and my spiritual needs. You've got to think about such things when you're old and on your own and living in a cold climate.

Duffy and I agree on a time to meet by the front door, leaving plenty of time for the two of us to shower and change, and before you know it, we're sitting at a barside booth at Clancy's, and we're lighting up with a couple of frosty ones in front of us. I'm not crazy about beer — too gassy — but when Duffy said he'd buy me one, it seemed pushy to say I'd prefer a highball.

"It's all your fault," I tell him once the beers are placed before us.

"My fault? What's my fault, Mrs. Malloy?" I've told him at least a million times to call me Mimi, or even Maire, but he insists on Mrs. Malloy. Which I now realize seems to be a little tease, because the way he says it, it has a sexy sound to it. *Mrs. Malloy.*

"When you came to check that leak and the closet shelf fell down. That's when I found the pendant — on the floor, like someone had just dropped it there. It was my mother's, but I have no idea how it ended up in my closet."

He nods like he wants me to go on.

"Well, we lost her when I was six, no seven, my mother. She died when my baby sister was born."

"Not so unusual back then, not like now. Still, forgetting isn't always such a bad thing," he says. "Sometimes you've got to in order to go on." I look at him, grateful that he seems to understand. "Forget too much, though, and you risk forgetting who you are." He takes a swallow of his beer.

"Perish the thought," I say, and we both laugh.

"So you decided to throw it away, the pendant?"

"Well, I was looking at it, and all of a sudden, I saw my stepmother, who was worse than the worst one in a fairy tale. I mean, she was right there with me, in my living room. Like she'd come back to finish the job she started when we were kids. Scared the hell out of me."

"Finish the job?"

"Ruin us all, all over again. That's why I decided to throw the pendant away."

"She doesn't live inside the pendant."

"No, it was an irrational fear. I know that."

"But you survived." He smiles, like he's glad about this fact. Before I can answer, the waitress appears. She's an old gal like me, but with dangly earrings. She's got red hair, with a quarter inch of pure-white new growth like an outline around her skull. Asks if we want another, and Duffy tells her yes, then asks me am I hungry? It's Friday, fish-and-chips night, and everybody knows Clancy's fish and chips are the best on the South Shore. Chunks of boneless haddock, batter-dipped and deep-fried. The chips hand cut and shining with hot oil when they bring them to the table. A nightmare of saturated fat, but truly scrumptious, especially with the tartar sauce and coleslaw. How can I say no? But thinking of the havoc the coleslaw will wreak on my stomach, I decline the second beer.

"What about something else? Whatever you want."

"A highball," I tell the waitress. "A nice rye and ginger, with lots of ice."

When she's gone I tell Duffy, "Thanks so much." He's the kind of man who treats you right. I can't remember the last time I sat across a table from a man who wanted to hear what I have to say. "This is lovely. But I'll spare you the grim details of my childhood."

"I'm interested. I mean, if you want to talk."

I shrug, not sure I believe him. I think

about Cassie and her healing therapies.

"You've seen my oldest, right? Cassandra?" He nods. "Well, she's been in therapy for ages, every time I turn around, a different type of therapy, names I can't even remember, with Twelve Steps this and Twelve Steps that. Behavioral, cognitive, whatever. She's made a career of it." I catch my breath. "All because of the quote-unquote dysfunction in our family."

Duffy grins. It's familiar to him, this aggravation from the kids, so I play it up a bit.

"She goes to seminars 'on the family' and to expensive retreats about codependency. Whatever that means. Codependency. She's never been able to explain it in a way that makes sense."

Now Duffy's chuckling. "Adult children," he says, shaking his head.

"Adult children. Perfect," I repeat, and it tickles me that he gets it. We're on the same page.

"Once, when Cassie was in the middle of one of these therapies, she tells me I must've suffered child abuse when I was growing up. That I'm emotionally absent because of this child abuse. Emotionally absent. Me." We laugh as the waitress shows up with our drinks. We touch glasses, say cheers, and have a swallow.

"I told her that we didn't have child abuse when I was growing up. 'You mean you didn't have a word for it,' she says, correcting me in this high-and-mighty tone she has. 'No,' I tell her, 'I mean we didn't have it. People raised their kids however they saw fit and everybody else minded their own business. Nobody had anything to say about it. The kids were expected to carry on.' Isn't that right?" I ask Duffy.

"You bet," he says. "Not like now. Nowadays you bring your kid into the emergency room after he falls off a bike, and they give you the third degree, suspect you've committed child abuse, or something worse."

"What's worse?"

He shakes his head no. His cheeks turn pinker.

"Well, Cass won't leave it alone. She can't leave anything alone. Tells me maybe my problems — I have problems just because I'm not perfect — my so-called problems stem from post traumatic stress disorder. That I show symptoms of PTSD. That's what she called it. PTSD. 'Alphabet soup,' I answered."

The waitress shows up with our food, a golden display, except for the coleslaw and tartar sauce in little cups on the side. Steam rises from our platters and Duffy says, "Dig in." And that's exactly what we do.

The fish and chips don't disappoint, and while we eat, I think about how we've known each other for the almost fifteen years I've lived in Centennial Square. Knew he was a widower, a disabled World War II vet, but our friendship never went beyond that. Of course, until recently, I worked full-time. Always rushing off to work, and too pooped to pop after I got home. Weekends were taken up with housework, and socializing with my kids and sisters. And me, the walking wounded, I wasn't close to being ready to take a chance on another guy. Jack did me in. But in the past year, since my retirement, we keep running into each other, and when we sit and share a smoke, I feel a warmth — not the hot-flash type — but something softer and deeper.

Now, between bites and swallows, he tells me about his two sons, the married one in Vermont, but not far too from Ruthie in New Hampshire, and the other in Bridge-water. Three grandchildren. Grew up in Southie, married a girl from Dedham, then went off to war, like all the other good Irish boys. Served in the Navy on a destroyer, the *Quincy II,* built right here at the yard. Took part in D-Day. He processed the bodies of the American dead, a job guaranteed to send most people over the edge, but Duffy apparently kept his act together, even after he took a piece of shrapnel in the thigh. Won a Purple Heart; was permanently disabled. His wife, Virginia, a junior high school teacher, died of breast cancer at forty-three, when the boys were in their teens. That's when he moved into Centennial Square, where, between his disability benefits and his free rent and salary as a super, he was able to make ends meet.

"Well, up until a few months ago, I worked at the VA Hospital over in Jamaica Plain. Medical records."

"Then you know it's real, PTSD."

"Sure, but that's for combat vets, not a little girl growing up on the South Shore."

"Maybe you shuffled some of my papers."

I look up at him, and it feels a whole lot more personal than it ought to, this shuffling of his papers. Odd that among the thousands of files I handled every week, some might've belonged to Himself: Mr. Richard J. Duffy, the silver-haired super of my apartment complex. Not a dead ringer for Paul Newman, Paul being Jewish, after all, but close enough to give me those zings and ring-a-ding dings that Frankie sings about, especially when I look deep into his eyes. They're hazel, Duffy's eyes — like the color of the sea, but in a darker shade, instead of Paul's sapphire blue.

"Forgetting's not always such a bad thing," he says again. I nod in agreement but close my eyes, shutting myself off from his sympathy, or maybe it's my shame. Even after all this time, I still feel it.

"Getcha anything else, hon?" I hear the waitress say, and I turn to her, pretending I was only blinking. We order coffee and agree, without saying a word, to leave the dark place of ancient history, and instead talk about the rising cost of gasoline and how much snow we figure we'll get this winter. Duffy pays in cash, and leaves a generous tip in the middle of the table. He helps me with my coat.

Outside the air's still but very cold, cold enough to suck away our breath. The sky is clear and full of stars. About halfway home, he takes my hand, but both of us are wearing gloves, Gore-Tex lined with Thinsulate, the kind you need to protect yourself from frostbite during a Boston winter. I'm still wondering what his hand would feel like when we get to the front entrance of Paul Revere. I punch in my code. Next thing I know, he touches my cheek with his bare hand, kisses the spot he touched, and then disappears into the night.

THIRTEEN:
IN THE WEE SMALL
HOURS OF THE MORNING

My head is spinning after I climb into bed, but not from the beer and the highball. I had a date with Duffy. A date with Duffy. He bought me dinner, walked me home, and kissed me at my door. That part keeps replaying, Duffy touching my cheek with his sandpapery hand, then kissing me on the cheekbone, just below my eye. A sweet kiss, and him gone by the time I realize what he's done. Just as well. I might've grabbed him and kissed him back, assuming I can remember how to kiss a man. But maybe it's like riding a bike: once you've got it, you never lose it.

I toss and turn. Can't quiet my mind. Lots of uninvited guests stopping by, my kids, my sisters, my ex. A regular family reunion, chaotic like always. So many people blabbering at once I can't understand a word. Then Fagan emerges out of the chaos, as if she'd been there all this time — almost sixty years. Fagan. I loved her so, but I forgot what it was like to feel that love after she got sent away. Da called her his squeaky wheel, his fire engine. *Cute as the devil,* Da said. With her red hair, bright and shiny, like a new penny. *A holy terror.* That's what everybody called her. Pale white skin with freckles, cinnamon sprinkles, across her nose and cheeks. Da's bright eyes.

Back when we were little, we girls could never keep our fingers off a scab, and my own daughters, I'm sorry to say, repeated this disgusting habit. Mostly skinned knees and elbows, nothing serious. No matter how often we were warned about infection, told that the scab was a good thing, allowing healing underneath. Did my sisters and I listen? Not on your life. We'd pick away at the brown crust — sneakily, enjoying the pricks of pain — until we saw the shiny pink new skin underneath. Left behind worse scars than if we'd done what we were supposed to and left the scabs alone. Alone now, in the wee small hours, I can't help picking at the scab, the unhealed place where the memories of my first baby sister wait. Why did she get sent away? And why didn't anyone in our family say one word about it?

Thinking hard, hard, hard about her, I get

a dark feeling, then a hot flash. Fagan was a whiner and a pest. After Mam died, she never stopped. Pressed my buttons more times than I could count, and wouldn't stop even when I warned her off. Fagan, the Olympic gold-medal champion of button-pushing. Knew how to get everyone's goat without even trying, causing trouble was her special gift. *She deserves to be sent away.* That's what I thought when it happened, that Fagan was the source of all the trouble in our family. *She deserved to be sent back to Ireland, to Cullyhanna, County Armagh, where she would learn how to be good.*

Well, it worked. What a relief! Because after Fagan Sent Away, everything was peaceful. For a little while, at least.

You're a brat, a baby.

Am not!

You are too. Fusspot! Tattletale!

What could we have been fighting about, Fagan and me? Back then, everything was life and death, a piece of candy, a doll, a soft place in the bed, all the things we wanted in a world of Not Enough. I remember when she scribbled on every single page of my coloring book. I could have killed her. And I might have tried, knocking her to the floor, twisting her arms behind her back.

Another time, she ripped my favorite paper dolls. Not on purpose, by accident, but what difference did that make? She destroyed them. Talk about the pain of loss! My Shirley Temple paper dolls! Still, I loved Fagan, I really did, in spite of all of that. Fussy little Fagan, Da's holy terror. She couldn't help herself.

All of us, except maybe Eden, wore hand-me-downs. That's how it worked, not just for us, but for all the other kids we knew. Anything usable was passed down to the next one. In our family, by the time a dress or sweater got to Fagan, it had already been worn by three or four others.

Once Fagan got passed an old pair of my Mary Janes, blue, with T-straps and pretty perforations on the toe. My favorite shoes. Granted, they'd been Alberta's before they got to me, but they were still in pretty good shape, and Da brought them to the cobbler for new buckles and new heels.

Me, I'd know enough to be grateful. I'd have kissed Da like he'd given me a gift of finest gold. But those shoes weren't good enough for Fagan. She blew a gasket when Da gave them to her. She hollered and threw herself onto the floor, kicking, flailing her arms, turning herself purple. Then she opened the door of the old black stove and tossed them in. Da tried to get them out with an iron poker, but they were already burning, stinking up the house.

I'll put you over my knee and warm your little bottom for you, Da threatened, but all of us, including Fagan, knew he wouldn't. Da never laid a finger on any of us in anger. Next thing we knew, Fagan had new Mary Janes, red ones, that turned me green with envy. She never took them off, never missed a chance to make me jealous, tap-dancing around the house in them. She even tried to sleep with them on her feet. I know because I saw her.

Fagan must have burned the old Mary Janes between the time Mam died and Flanna Flanagan showed up. Because everything changed once Flanna arrived. Well, Fagan didn't change. She was her same old self, a squeaky wheel, and nobody could oil her into silence.

One Sunday morning not too long after Flanna became our new mother, all of us were getting ready to go to church, a big deal in those days. Everybody dressed up in their best, all the girls with a hat or scarf or veil to cover their heads. Fasting from suppertime the night before, and then there were all the preparations, shoe polishing, hair curling, dress ironing. Well, Fagan was supposed to wear a pink ruffled dress that Flanna had starched and pressed for her, a pretty dress that had already made its way from the top of the line on down to her. But the starch and ruffles scratched her delicate skin and, again, she threw a fit, a Fagan fit.

Over my dead body you'll take off that dress, said Flanna, who kept going about her business, getting herself ready for church — wearing, I might add, another of my mother's dresses. Next thing we knew, Fagan had cut the skirt of her dress into ribbons. Somehow, she found Flanna's sewing shears and went to work. While she was still wearing it. Hilarious, so funny, my sisters and I thought, but we knew enough not to laugh.

At Flanna's insistence, Daddy took the rest of us to Mass. Flanna and Fagan stayed home. When we got back, with a box of pastries from Hanrahan's, Daddy's way of smoothing troubled waters, Fagan was nowhere to be found. Flanna refused to let her have a pastry, and the next time we saw her, her beautiful red hair was cut off into spiky little tufts and she was wearing only underpants. She had to stay in just her underpants for a week or more.

That'll teach you, you devil, Flanna kept repeating, her accent so thick we made fun of her behind her back. Alberta, a hot ticket, was the best. She could do a perfect Flanna until the rest of us were paralyzed with laughter. That Sunday, we three oldest saved Fagan pieces of our pastries, crushed and stale by the time we got them to her. Fagan gobbled them down.

Lick your mouth and fingers, I warned her, *so Flanna doesn't know.*

Fagan Sent Away, an ancient injury that hasn't healed at all. My pistol of a sister. A piece of work they'd call her nowadays. Yes, Fagan was a piece of work. Then she was gone. Just like that.

I sit up in bed with the light still on. The pressure of the black spots hurts, places where the stories end before they're over. I pick up the blue pendant, run my fingertip around its edges. I'm glad Duffy made me keep it, yet I'm still afraid of what it holds.

Queer light shines at the edges of my vision. Flanna Flanagan, Da's secret rose, my stepmother. At the sight of her, my heart kicks into overdrive and a lump swells in my throat. Got to get around her, past her, no matter how much it hurts; no matter how afraid I am. Wade into the red tide, even if it poisons me. I have to remember how things were before she came, and everything that happened afterward.

A searing pain flashes behind my eyes. A black spot bursting open. Mam's gone, but Da is with us. He takes us, one by one, my sisters and me, to the neighbor's to wait while the midwife birthed the baby. That's how it was done in those days, not like now, in the hospitals, where parents-to-be, my daughters tell me, take lessons on how to breathe during labor, then get Champagne and filet mignon to celebrate after the baby's born. Learning how to breathe. It's all I can do to keep a straight face when my girls show me how they huff and puff. Oh, and their husbands have to huff and puff along with them because, somehow or other, they tell me, it doesn't hurt so bad that way.

Da walks me down the street to the Callahans'. "Let's Have Another Cup of Coffee," he sings, and he makes me sing too, to mimic him, in his silly voices so I won't cry about leaving Mam. *Just around the corner, there's a rainbow in the sky, so let's have another cup of coffee and another piece of pie.* I laugh and laugh, and Da laughs, too. *There's a rainbow in the sky, let's eat another slice of pie.*

I played hopscotch on the sidewalk with the Callahan kids, but it was February, too cold to play outside for long. Afterward, we colored in the kitchen where Mrs. Callahan was cooking. We ate mayonnaise sandwiches for lunch. Finally I stood by myself, by the storm door down the back stairs. Suppertime, because the Callahan children were squabbling at the table, and I smelled their stew. But I wasn't hungry. Knew, though I could not tell time, that I'd waited long past the time Da ought to have come back for me. Waiting and waiting. Finally, I walked downstairs to the back door and pressed my face against the glass so I could see up the street in the direction Da would come from.

Mrs. Callahan let me go. Didn't say a word. Let me stand in the shadows by the back door while she fed her family. By then she must have known, even without a telephone, that something had gone wrong, that too much time had passed. It felt like forever before I heard Da whistling, saw him stepping out of the shadows. He had a loping walk, scarecrow-skinny Da. That's how I knew him in the dark.

He comes toward me, but I do not run out to him. Still he whistles, such a sad song, no more cup of coffee, no more rainbow in the sky. When he sees me, he breaks into a run. *My sweet little contrary Maire.* He opens the door, gathers me up, tosses me into the air so the dark sky spins around. He catches me, hugs me tight, so that his whiskers scratch my face. *You have another little sister, a real beauty,* he whispers. The sharp smell of whiskey stings my eyes.

I get up out of bed. It's three thirty A.M., too late to call anyone. They'd have me put away for sure. I get up and get Patty's questionnaire and a pen, and bring them back to bed with me. I look at the questions, and the lines where you fill in the answers. All it asks for are facts, no spaces for the blood, sweat, and tears attached to them; my mother, Maire Margaret Ahearn Sheehan, a green-eyed brunette, black Irish, who played piano and loved to sing; who had, despite her family's poverty, graduated from teachers college and worked as an elementary school teacher before becoming a mother. She died at thirty-four, leaving behind a husband and seven daughters, most of us Irish twins, and one set of real ones.

Maybe the grown-ups thought we girls were too young to notice Mam was gone. Looking back, that's the only explanation I can come up with — they thought we wouldn't notice our mother had disappeared. Wanting to make them happy, I suppose, we pretended that we didn't. We girls ranged in age from eleven to three, not counting the new baby we didn't see for a couple of years, but we weren't allowed to cry. I don't remember that we did, except maybe into our pillows, scrunched up in the beds we shared, swallowing the hiccups so no one else would hear.

Irish wakes, I've heard, are the best parties in the world. They last for days, with singing, dancing, and drinking; the old women keening. But you can't prove this by me. When Mammy died, my father, my grandparents, my aunts and uncles acted like it hadn't happened. Mammy, who got to live less than half her life — who didn't get to raise her own kids — didn't get any kind of royal send-off.

If there was a funeral, we girls didn't go to it. We didn't even know our mother had been buried, let alone where. Afterward, it was as if she had never been. No one ever spoke her name. Then one day, who knows how long after that, Da came home with Flanna and said she was our new mother.

I fill in the spaces with these facts, the ones my sisters will repeat on their questionnaires. I lost my mother young. A fact of my life. When I was too young to know what losing a mother meant. I've already lived so much longer, but I've never once thought about it, how Mam got cheated out of living most of her life, and we got cheated out of having her in ours. How nobody I know of, not even her own daughters, ever keened for her.

I wake up with the pen still in my hand, the light still on. It's after nine A.M., but I feel like I haven't slept. I get up, get dressed, drink a cup of coffee. Looking through the blinds, I see it's gloomy outside, the parking lot smeared with ice and dirty snow. I put on a warm coat, hat, and gloves, and go out to warm up my little Shadow because she gets balky in the cold. On the far side of the parking lot, Duffy's sprinkling salt along the walkways. I wave to him as I drive by. He stops to watch me go.

Turns out to be one of the coldest days of the year and the roads are terrible, ice everywhere. Metro Boston during a deep freeze, last week's snow not yet melted. I skid a couple of times. Can't remember if you turn into or away from the skid, if you tap the brakes or take your foot off. I'm scared, but I figure what the hell. Half a century has gone by now, and I am going to visit Da. I have some questions for him; don't know why I haven't thought of them before. At least I know where he's buried.

Gate of Heaven Cemetery. Yes, Da was buried there, way back when, more than half a century ago. I have trouble finding it. I make a couple of wrong turns, and when I finally get there, the whole cemetery is covered under a blanket of snow.

What could I have been thinking? I drive slowly along the cemetery's curved and hilly lanes, through a garden of granite stones, but only the biggest stick out of the snow, and Da, I'm certain, doesn't have one of the biggest. I park near where I think Da might be, get out, and trudge ahead, but I can't remember if Da's buried to the right side or the left. Can't even remember the last time I was here. I step through the snow, colder and deeper than I'd figured. It spills into my Rockports. I get a terrible feeling of being lost.

I stumble across a stone with a familiar name — Jimmy Callahan, our paperboy, the grandson of the neighbor who watched me the day Mam died. Brown-eyed and freckle-faced, full of the Dickens. Jimmy used to babysit my girls, playing and roughhousing with them so every one of them had the biggest crush on him. He was walking home from school late one day when a drunk driver struck him, crushed him against a utility pole, just a few steps from his home.

Later I'll feel sad for Jimmy Callahan, but at the moment I'm too cold. I see the white cottage where the cemetery's caretaker works. Smoke is coming from its chimney. I go over and knock. After a few minutes, a middle-aged man opens the door, gestures for me to enter. Fire spits and crackles in a wood-burning stove. He's listening to an oldies station out of Boston. A *Globe* is folded neatly by his rocking chair.

"I'm looking for my father," I say. "Joe Sheehan. Can you tell me where he's buried?"

"Joe Sheehan?" His voice is high-pitched, whiny. "Which one?"

"Which one?" I'm still shivering, and he gestures for me to warm myself by the fire. I step closer to it, holding out my hands, feeling like a lost child in a fairy tale, Gretel without Hansel.

"We got a half dozen. At least."

"Joseph Daniel," I say. "Died back in '37."

He gives me a look, one that says I'm a nut case, but I'm much too old — and cold — to care. He takes out a big brown ledger, thicker than the Boston phone book, and he turns the pages slowly, sighing and grunting. At last he shakes his head yes, and tells me where to go.

"Any other time, I'd be happy to drive you in the golf cart," he says in a way that does not convince me, "but I can't use it in the snow."

"Not a problem," I tell him, and go back outside, the wind and cold snatching away my breath.

Just a few minutes later, on the far edge of the cemetery, I find Da. His plot abuts a chain link fence that runs along the back-yards of the houses on the street next to the cemetery. On the other side, behind Da's plot, there's an aboveground pool and a deck with a barbecue grill attached, a clothesline with frozen blue jeans hanging on it. Da's stone doesn't quite make it up through the snow. I kneel down to clear it and then I see his name: *Joseph Daniel Sheehan, August 10, 1896–July 4, 1937.* Daddy, dead a month shy of his forty-first birthday. I scrape away more snow, expect-ing to find Flanna's name and her date of death. But all that's there is Da's; the dates of his birth and death, and some silly line from a Yeats poem. No hint whatsoever of what happened in between those dates, or of what happened to her.

"Why did you let her go, Daddy?" I say the words loud and clear because nobody's around to hear. I don't even have to say Fagan's name. Da knows who I mean. "Why didn't you try to get her back?"

I feel better having asked. Kneeling in the snow, knowing I'll pay big when I try to stand back up. I take hold of the stone. "Will you tell me?" Poor Da. He's dust by now. Old bones, no longer capable of answering. I hold the slab of cold stone anyway, and promise I'll come back in spring, to plant daffodils and violets.

Fourteen:
Baubles, Bangles, and Beads

Keeley's birthday, the big six-one, is right around the corner, and as soon as the roads are clear enough for us old girls to get behind the wheel, Cass plans a celebration. We would have celebrated last year, the big six-oh making more sense, but her husband preempted us; took her on a two-week cruise along the Mediterranean, the type I've always dreamed about but have given up on ever experiencing. Big treat, we're going to the new Marriott in Quincy even though we don't have any coupons. We'll have to pay full price. But we figure, what the hey, we'll blow a couple of extra bucks to make things really nice. In one of her morning phone calls, Cassie insists that we go shopping.

"You can't wear those old-lady clothes of yours if we're going to the new Marriott."

"My old-lady clothes?"

"You know, those pull-on pants you get in

the mail. And the baggy over-blouses with the big flowers and the sailboats."

"Thanks a lot." What every mother needs in her golden years, a brat like Cassandra working on her personal style.

"You used to be so stylish, Mimi." She sighs. "Never leave the house without looking your best. You drilled that into us. And now you're letting yourself go. I just can't believe you're letting yourself go like this."

"Letting myself go like this?" Something Jack would say. "I'm not letting myself go. How many times do I have to tell you? I just don't care anymore."

After being forced into retirement, and with the little that I'd settled for from Jack, I had to pick and choose what mattered, and I decided that beautiful clothes didn't. Not at my age, on my budget.

At least Cassandra puts her money where her mouth is. A couple of days before the brunch, she takes me to the Little Lady, a pricey boutique at the mall, and treats me to two outfits, a dressy and a casual, at prices that give me palpitations. "My dime, my dime," she keeps saying.

First she asks the salesgirl to take a guess at my size. A moment of mortification, with those two staring me up and down.

"Twelve, petite," the salesgirl guesses.

"Short and round, I could have told you."

Cassie shakes her head, then roots through all the racks, enlisting the salesgirl's help, hunting for clothes she thinks might look good. Actually, "presentable" is the word she uses. Presentable. That's a notch or two below good. We're there for ages, with me trying stuff on while Cassie sits in a comfy chair in front of the three-way mirror, and the salesgirl stands behind her. At one point I come out in a navy skirt and sweater with red trim on the sailor collar and a big red bow in front. "Well, I've always been small," I say, turning like a runway model. "Am I sophisticated now?"

"Mimi, you're impossible, just impossible." Cassie yammers to the clerk about how difficult I can be, no matter how generous she is. In the end, we choose gray slacks and a matching blazer, a pinstripe shirt, and a little silk scarf and earrings. And I have to admit that these good clothes feel wonderful; I almost feel like my old self again, although that's the last thing I'd tell Cassandra. We also pick out some black dress shoes with low heels that don't hurt my bunions too much, and some navy-blue knit pants and a matching zip-up jacket for working out. "So you'll look decent while you're getting into shape," Cassie says.

"I'll look just like a stewardess," I say when we're at the counter and the salesgirl is wrapping up the slacks. "Fly me."

"Flight attendant," murmurs Cass. Neither of them smiles.

Fifteen:
I Guess I'll Have to
Dream the Rest

Mixed feelings, that's what I've got about this birthday brunch. Been there, done that, I'm thinking when Cassandra drops me off, and I scoot with my shopping bags into Paul Revere. Don't bother to hang up the new clothes. Instead, I grab the pendant and take a load off on the couch, my aching feet up on a pillow.

Our get-togethers always turn out the same, and the fact that we're celebrating Keeley's birthday won't change anything. One drink, and my sisters are off and running, down the beaten track to the old days in Weymouth and Quincy, back before the roads were paved, when everybody grew veggies in their Victory gardens and swam in the Fore River Shipyard basin, and the big excitement of the week was when the ragman came.

If only my sisters would leave it at that, the good times. But no, they've got to keep on going, straight back to our grandparents, parents, sisters, aunts, uncles, and cousins, both dead and living, and who did what to whom way back when. But once we get there, to who did what to whom, we have serious disagreements. I cling to certain truths, which I hold to be self-evident, and my surviving sisters insist I'm nuts, that I've got it wrong. Now Patty's genealogy is giving them an additional excuse to pick and poke at all those painful places best left undisturbed.

In the early winter of our lives, as Patty puts it, my sisters love nothing better than picking at our past like it's the carcass of a rotisserie chicken, oohing and aahing when they find a juicy morsel, a bit of crispy skin. It's a love that came upon them, one by one, after the Change. Maybe it's a side effect, like night sweats and hot flashes. But to me, it's just charred bones. It's always the same, and I, with my rotten memory, have memorized the script. First we'll meet for Mass at Our Lady Queen of Peace, what's left of us: Patty and Josephine, the real twins, fraternal; the baby Keeley; and finally me, the oldest of the survivors.

After Mass, we'll head out in Keeley's brand-new Avalon to one of those all-you-can-eat Sunday brunches cardiologists warn against, with crepes, bacon, sausage, cheese Danish, and at least four kinds of potatoes. Using coupons from the Entertainment Book, especially the buy-one-get-ones, we check out all the good Sunday brunches on the South Shore. They always seat us by the kitchen door, or maybe a table with a window that overlooks the parking lot, guessing, incorrectly, that we're so far over the hill we won't know how to tip. We're used to it by now.

On my first trip to the buffet, I'll grab some eggs Benedict, my favorite — love that Hollandaise — but I'll be hoping for a Belgian waffle before we are through. Enough food for a week, but no doggy bags allowed. You've got to eat it all right there.

I always look around the table a couple of times to get my bearings, to see what's left of the glorious Sheehan girls. Four sixty-somethings in knit pantsuits and me with the Rockport Walkers, only Keeley still in pumps, with little diamond earrings and a snazzy silk scarf tied around her neck. Patty and Keeley with puffy hairdos from their weekly wash 'n' sets, and Jo with the same pixie cut she's worn for thirty years or more. Me, I go for the short perm, extra-curly, so it lasts longer. Wash-and-wear hair. The glorious Sheehan girls.

"Alberta was such a card," Josephine will say, speaking of one of our departed sisters, the second oldest, and the second one to go. As Jo sips her drink, her cheeks will begin to glow. "Three husbands: Buddy, Buster, and Bub."

"But four marriages," Patty will say. "She married Buddy twice."

"No," Jo will argue. "It was Buster, not Buddy, she married twice, wasn't it?" She'll look to Keeley for support.

"But isn't Buster the one who knocked out her front teeth?" Keeley will ask. "And he's the one she loved the most."

"Poor Alberta!" That will be Patty, who still has her red hair and freckles — a worn-out version of the doll she used to be, and on the verge of tears. "She really let herself go those last few years."

Letting oneself go, a recurring theme.

"She couldn't help it." Jo will take Patty's hand. "She was broke."

"And broken," I'll throw in. Because she was, Alberta. Shattered, physically and emotionally. No getting around that fact, no matter how hard they try. Alberta, brunette like me and well-built. She loved nothing better than a good laugh, but never seemed to get them with her Buddys, Busters, and Bubs.

"If Eden had seen her, she would've been heartbroken too." Patty's reply. And every time it's true.

Eden and Alberta, the top of the line, both gone before their time; Eden at forty-three of a female cancer, no health insurance, and Alberta of cirrhosis at forty-six. And all that heartbreak before the two of them moved on.

"Eden kept herself up until the very end," one or the other of them will say, all of them so impressed that she didn't let herself go.

"I can still see her," someone else will say, "with her lipstick and her earrings, right up to the day she died."

Now, relaxing on my sofa, lighting up a True Blue, I see Eden too — darling Eden, baptized Aiden, a boy's name for the son my parents longed to have. She's in the spare room of my house, our house, the house Jack built for me. On her deathbed, weighing less than seventy-five pounds, her famous silky skin the color and texture of a turnip. Shriveling from the inside out. Eden, thin and silent, still lovely. Early on, she changed the spelling of her name, just as Patty later did. The new way, she said, would make everybody think of Eden, the garden of. Spent her whole life drifting from man to man, most of them married, and from job to job, most of them beneath her. Wandered from place to place, Baltimore, Miami, Las Vegas, always coming back to the South Shore, lovelier and more hurt than ever before. I always kept that room for her. I always let her in.

"They're happy together, in heaven, I'm sure of it," one or the other of them will say, the cul-de-sac at the end of every meeting of the Yik Yak Club. They repeat it like a litany. The two of them are happy together in heaven, Eden and Alberta, life eternal, happy, happy, blah, blah, blah.

Sixteen:
Come Rain or Come Shine

Cass picks me up in her Bimmer, me wearing my new outfit, shoes included. Per usual, and against my better judgment, I'm joining my sisters for brunch. I couldn't hurt Keeley's feelings.

"You look great, Mimi," Cass tells me when I climb in, smiling a grateful smile because she doesn't have to be embarrassed to be seen with me. "Like a new woman," she adds, happier with the new one than the old. But maybe I am new. The clothes are a big upgrade, the type Jack used to buy for me. Don't even recognize my feet in the new pumps. I hope God the Father, not to mention His only son, will recognize and remember me.

We drive the few blocks to the church instead of walking them. Sunday Mass at Our Lady Queen of Peace. Wouldn't miss it for the world, and I haven't once for as far back as I can remember. The cathedral's right in downtown Quincy, surrounded now by so many bars, banks, clam shacks, drugstores, and doughnut shops that the Blessed Trinity must have trouble squeezing in. Our Lady Queen of Peace, with its vaulted ceilings so high your prayers can float straight up, and the smell of myrrh and incense so you know for sure you've been to church. Oh, and the stained-glass windows of the Stations of the Cross — Jesus dragging the cross, Jesus falling under the weight of the cross, Jesus hanging from the cross, the weeping women all around him. An act by which he redeemed all of humanity and gave us all eternal life.

When it's sunny, like today, light streams through the stained-glass windows and splashes pretty colors, a benediction over all of us. We take a pew close to Veronica Wipes the Face of Jesus, number six, my favorite station. But today I have trouble getting into the prayers. Lots of unwanted company stopping by, like at night when I can't get to sleep. My dead sisters, Eden and Alberta, up in heaven now, and Fagan Sent Away. We go to the altar for Communion, no point to Mass without the sacrament. We take the Eucharist on the tongue, we Sheehan girls — forget that in-the-palm-of-the-hand malarkey — *Body of Christ, amen,* but I don't get my usual lift from swallowing the Host. Today it's just a dry wafer sticking to the roof of my mouth, leaving a sour aftertaste.

At long last we're at the restaurant of the Marriott, on a big hill overlooking Beantown, to celebrate Keeley's big day one year late. The room is beautiful, two or three stories high, and a guy in a tux sits at a grand piano playing soothing music. "Moon River." "I Enjoy Being a Girl." Here, we're taken to a lovely window table, covered in pink cloth, with a vase of bright pink roses in the middle.

"Tea roses," says Cassandra.

And surprise, surprise, the window doesn't overlook a parking lot but instead a landscaped courtyard with a fountain in the middle. But the fountain isn't flowing and no flowers are in bloom. The trees are crusted with ice, the shrubs wrapped in burlap against winter kill. We order Bloody Marys, and I'm betting we'll go through another round or two before we finish with this celebration.

First thing, we raise our glasses to Keeley. Her fiery tresses have darkened over the years, aided and abetted lately by L'Oréal. She's worth it.

"Cheers, many happy returns of the day," all of us say at once.

"You didn't have to," Keeley answers, embarrassed to be the center of attention but also loving it.

"We did, yes, we did," we cry.

"You're more than just my godmother, Keeley," says Cassandra, smiling at my sister in a way she never smiles at me. "Summer vacations at your house were the best times of my life." That would be at Keeley's second home, her Cape house on the beach in Chatham.

"Hear, hear," the others chime.

Now Keeley holds out her hand, her wrist cuffed with a gold bracelet set with amethysts and diamonds, a gift from her husband, Frank, who's done all right, working his way up from letter carrier to postmaster of Weymouth.

"Beautiful," says Cassie breathlessly, fingering the gems. Keeley takes it off and hands it to Cassandra to try on, which she does. She holds out her arm so the bracelet glitters. Worth a fortune, and I figure that sooner or later, if Cass plays her cards right, she'll inherit it — and I've no doubt she will.

"Life is good," announces Patty, the one in charge of life, or maybe only goodness.

"Oh, yes, very, very good," my baby sister answers, smiling her million-dollar smile. She works in the development office of a hospital in Attleboro, throwing parties for rich people, raking in the big bucks. The bracelet matches the sparklers on her ears. She passes it around the table. I pass it on quickly when my turn comes.

"I'd be afraid to wear it. Afraid I'd lose it or get mugged."

I'm not jealous, not a bit. Keeley deserves whatever she gets. She grew up motherless, after all. I must confess, though, that I don't know Keeley as well as I know the others. We never shared a bed, and, therefore, not too many secrets. Instead of kids, she and Frank bred golden retrievers, and built that nice house on the Cape. Once each summer, we're all invited for a cookout. Except for Cass, who's always managed to stay most of the summer. She's done well, our Keeley, if you count having dogs instead of kids.

"Sixty-one years since our mother passed."

The words fly out of my mouth before I know I've spoken.

"How could you, Mimi?" Josephine and Patty chime like bells. They look at me, eyes wide, their mouths perfect O's.

"Mimi!" Cassandra, who's next to me,

smacks my hand. The sting wakes me up.

"Oh, my God, I'm so sorry, honey." I try to reach across the table to Keeley, but can't quite touch her. The table is round, big enough for six.

"See?" Cassie wails, so loud that some other diners turn around. "See what I'm talking about? She's losing it. I swear to God, she's losing it."

"I'm losing it?" I'm trying not to blow my stack. "I am not losing it, Cassandra. I haven't lost one damned thing I can't live without. And, by the way, I've kept some things I could. . . ." I reach for my purse, take out the little pouch holding the blue pendant. I slide the pendant out, slam it down onto the table. Cass grabs it, she wants to hide it, but Patty, the pint-sized potentate, holds out her own hand.

"Mam's," she whispers.

"It's her fault." I point to my daughter as the pendant makes its way around the table, on the same path as Keeley's bracelet, the scratch visible to all. Cassandra's face turns the color of the tea roses.

"I only wanted to find out how much it's worth." She starts to cry, tear tracks running through her foundation like cracks in a crust, with my real daughter, the one who hardly ever shows herself, sobbing underneath.

"How much it's worth?" Jo's eyes fill up. "Well, then, Cass, tell us. How much is it worth?"

"Worthless," I interject.

"I didn't know he'd ruin it," Cassandra says. "I know it's ruined, and I'm really sorry, but that wasn't my intention."

"Ruination," whispers Keeley, a word the priest used during Mass.

"Ruination," I repeat, a close relative of deterioration.

The server shows up at our table, worried maybe that we'll cause a scene, a worse one than we already have. Cass suggests we order off the menu.

"I'm not sure I could make it to the buffet table," she says.

All of us agree. We take forever choosing our meals, discussing every last detail of the menu, which offers temptations too numerous to count. I go for the eggs Benedict, one of the few items I recognize, but with a layer of baby spinach in place of the Canadian bacon.

"Get the Hollandaise on the side," Cassie says in a stage whisper, then repeats this order to the waiter. "Do you know how many fat grams are in that?" she asks once he's gone. Nobody answers. "Just dip your fork into the sauce. You save hundreds of calories that way."

But miss out on all the flavor, I think.

The restaurant is full. A lighted candelabra, like Liberace's, decorates the top of the grand piano, though the pianist's tuxedo is plain black. All the well-dressed diners are talking softly, and, like them, we try to behave, yammering on about the weather and our kids and grandkids and dogs until the waiter brings our food.

The Hollandaise is to die for. When Cassie isn't looking, I pour the little cup all over my eggs. Strengthened, after a bite or two, I open my big mouth again. "It's all your fault," I say to Patty, "you and your damned genealogy."

"Stop your cursing. You've just taken Holy Communion."

"And we're drinking Bloody Marys," I answer. "Speaking of which . . ."

Cassandra hails the waiter and orders another round.

"What's Aunt Patty's fault?" asks Cassie once he's on his way. "Don't try to blame her for your bad manners."

"I'm not blaming her for that. I mean this trip I've been taking down Memory Lane. Thinking about the old days. It's an obstacle course, worse than the ones they use to train Marines."

"Well, you're new to it," says Patty. "The rest of us have been training for a while."

"I keep thinking about Flanna." They nod and hmm. "Not that I want to. But all of a sudden, after all these years, she's back."

"Flanna," Jo whispers, nodding, but I can't tell if she's pro or con.

"Once," says Patty, "she sewed matching dresses for me and Jo out of one of her hand-me-downs."

"You mean our mother's," I say. "She took all of our mother's clothes."

"She gave me minty candies shaped like flowers." Keeley.

"You always shared." Jo.

"Da's secret rose." Patty laughs. "He loved her so much."

Da's secret rose. But all I got were thorns.

"Once she told us the faeries took our mother off on a horse." Jo.

"A white horse," adds Patty. "Then the faeries brought Da to her."

"Flanna and her nonsense."

"A white horse?" Cassandra.

"Only explanation we ever got for our mother's death," Jo tells Cass. "The faeries took away our mother, on a white horse, in a white gown, with her hair streaming out behind her. Believe me, Flanna could tell a story. We lapped up every word."

Like kittens at the bowl.

"She could cast a spell." Patty.

"Which is what she did to Da." Again, they ignore me.

"I thought Flanna was my mother," says Keeley. "What did I know? But sometimes she called me Fagan."

"Fagan?" A chorus, like in church, at the high part of the liturgy.

"I was so confused. Sometimes I thought I *was* Fagan. Not that I ever knew her."

In my memories, too, Keeley replaced Fagan. The hole Fagan left closed up, so there was no loss to feel. But as soon as I think about that closed-up hole, I get an awful feeling, one that comes on me whenever the Yik Yak Club is in session. As if I'm alone, locked in a small, dark place, choking on smoke, and the air is running out. Eden and Alberta are gone. No one's left with me to loathe and fear Da's woman of shining loveliness.

"Loose lips sink ships," Patty declares, like she's just that moment thought of it.

"Keep mum, chum," echoes Jo. They nod over these words of wisdom from posters at the shipyard forever ago — the shipyard, a vast city with countless top-secret contracts, more than thirty-two thousand workers during the war.

"Keep mum, chum? What the hell's that supposed to mean?" I have trouble keeping my voice under control. "You're the ones who told Cassandra about Fagan. You two let the cat out of the bag." The twins look at me as though I've just run over the cat. "Well, you did. After we promised one another. Best of luck now putting it back in."

"Fagan was our sister," says Patty. "She belongs on the family tree."

"My aunt," adds Cass.

"How can we put her there if we don't know what happened to her?"

"We know what happened to her." Patty, the great historian. "She got sent away and died before we could get her back."

"You and your all-important genealogy." I take another sip of my Bloody Mary, which is what I feel like at this moment — bloody Mimi, mad as hell. "We agreed to let bygones be bygones." I look around the table, hardly recognizing what's left of my own sisters. Now I wonder if we ever actually did agree.

"Remember Alberta's prayer?" I say, not looking at them but at the blue pendant by my plate. "Accept what you can't change,

change what you can, and so forth?" The rest of it escapes me, but Alberta couldn't live by it anyway. Too much she could not accept; so little she could change. "We can't change anything that happened."

Patty's silent, everyone's silent for so long, it's as if we've fallen out of time. Time enough for me to realize I've really done it now, I've ruined Keeley's birthday.

"Oh, Keeley," I say, trying to apologize again, but Patty cuts me off.

"Cassandra is your firstborn," she says at last. "She's got a right to know. Why do we have to keep pretending?"

"Pretending? Who's pretending? I erased her. Ages ago."

"You can't just erase one of your sisters," she says.

"You girls need group therapy," Cass announces, as if over a PA system. "I know somebody who's done a lot of family-of-origin work. Maybe he could fit you in, I mean the bunch of you together. The glorious Sheehan girls."

" 'Family-of-origin work'?" A moment of comic relief. Patty, Jo, and Keeley crack up. Their laughter silences Cassandra. Family-of-origin work. It's the only kind of work Cassie's ever done.

"I'm so sorry, baby, I really am," I say

again to Keeley, but she stops me.

"No, Mimi, you're right," she says. "It's the anniversary of our mother's death, and we've never said it before. Not once in sixty years. I'm glad to have it out there." Her eyes fill with tears. I could kick myself.

"I never knew Mam, not like the rest of you." Keeley twists her cloth napkin. She doesn't look at us. "I never knew anything about her. But from day one, as far back as I can remember, you girls, plus Eden and Alberta, took care of me. You never wanted me to suffer. You were always trying to make it up to me. But our mother died the day I was born. My birth stole her from the rest of you."

Bam! My ticker starts to whine and sputter like my old Mixmaster just before I tossed it out. I'm looking at, listening to my baby sister, but my heart spins and stalls in my chest, a tire stuck in ice and snow. Keeley, Patty, and Jo fill their coffee cups from the silver pot on our table. I watch like it's *Search for Tomorrow* on an ancient black-and-white TV. They yak and yak but the sound's muffled, the volume stuck just above a whisper, the picture snowy. I'm slipping away, pulled under, as if by a wave at Nantasket Beach. Out toward Eden and Alberta, who slipped beyond my reach so long

177

ago. Who struggled so hard out there in the deep water, my old sweethearts. The other dead are out farther, heads like buoys bobbing, warning of the water's depth, its shallows and submerged obstacles.

The lights flicker and dim. A power outage, I think, but no, it's my lights on the verge of going out. Jesus. I'm having a myocardial infraction, or something else I'm not sure how to spell, right here at the table, my arteries clogged from all that Hollandaise.

I push away my plate. Rush, fast as I'm able, to the bathroom. Almost run into the men's. Bump into a slick young fellow coming out.

"Watch it!"

He gives me a dirty look, like I'm polluting his environment. No respect at all. Knocks me back to my senses.

In the ladies', I pee and splash cold water on my face. I lean against the sink until the trembling stops. Not a myocardial whatever, but one of my old episodes. Claustrophobia, like in that MRI machine. My ex used to pick on me about it, my fear of the dark, of enclosed places; the trouble I had with closets and cellars and sometimes, with sitting in the car at night, when I'd be alone waiting to pick up one of our girls someplace. This awful feeling would seize me, hands reaching out of the dark to grab my neck and squeeze it hard. No air, no light.

When our daughters were very young, I took the doors off all their closets. "What the hell?" my husband asked. "So nobody will ever be shut inside," I answered. "Wacky," he said, twirling his index finger by his ear. But that was back when he still loved me, so I won. Once our girls were teenagers and could take care of their own things, Mr. Malloy Himself put those doors back on, cussing up a storm as he lined up the hinges with the drill holes in the frames.

Way back when, when my ex still cared, he would tease me and call me Scaredy Cat. He'd comfort me, and we'd end up doing it wherever we happened to be. But in later years, he lost patience. "Get over it," he told me. "Don't pass your craziness on to our girls." Good point, I figured, but I couldn't help it. That's the part he didn't get.

Mimi's Episodes, a running gag between my husband and my daughters the whole time we were together. Then all of them were gone, my girls into their own lives, my ex into the arms of the new wife. I moved into an apartment without a cellar and just the one big closet all along the bedroom wall. With a sensor light so you couldn't ever get caught there in the dark.

I take a hard look at my face in the mirror. Oh, Mimi, not again, I tell her. No more episodes. No more claustrophobia. Been there, done that. I slap my cheek, good and hard, so it stings, the way I used to keep my daughters in line when they got snippy. A harmless crack on the cheek. It almost always did the trick. What's real is real, I tell that old gal in the mirror.

When I get back to the table, it's clear that none of them even noticed I was gone. "So, Mimi," says Patty, smiling like the cat that just ate the worm, "we've done a little research and it turns out that we Sheehans — yes, us — we really were somebodies back in the day. Not just poor potato farmers, landless peasants who crossed the ocean in desperation."

"What on earth? . . ." I try to ask.

"Not by a long shot." Jo's so excited, her hands are out like the priest's during the Consecration. "It turns out that, a few centuries ago, we had a castle up there on Northern Ireland's coast."

"Ages before the Troubles." Keeley's eyes sparkle like the gems on her ears and wrist. "Before there was a Republic and this other northern country."

"How on earth did you get here?" I missed two hundred years of family history while I was going to the bathroom. "A minute ago you were talking about Fagan."

"The genealogy," says Cass, glowing, smiling like she's just gotten something she's longed for her entire life. "We had a castle. We were somebodies."

Swell, I think, but bite my tongue while the others clap their hands and sigh. The Sheehans really were somebodies. Just wunnerful.

"The Sheehans through two centuries," Patty declares, her cheeks the color of her Bloody Mary. "Growing like clematis along the South Shore, through Quincy, Weymouth, Braintree, Hingham."

Then a ruckus breaks out. Keeley and Jo and Patty and Cassandra argue about who gets to tell which part of the story. Then they start to blabber about a feature film, a television miniseries.

"We could call it *Those Glorious Sheehan Girls from Quincy,*" says Jo.

"You mean the Nobodies from No Place," I say.

The bunch of them fall silent, give me the gimlet eye.

Seventeen:
How Deep Is the Ocean?

Story of my life, the ringing telephone. I take my time getting to it, pick up on the fourth or fifth ring, expect to hear about a cruise to nowhere I've just won, or a request for a donation from the PBA. Instead, it's Duffy.

"Mrs. Malloy," he says, "if you're not too busy, I wonder if you'd like to take a ride with me? I've got to check up on my best girl, see how she's holding up in all this cold weather. I'd like to introduce the two of you."

"Your best girl?" See how she's holding up? Duffy can't see me, but I'm red as boiled beets. I'd rather have a stranger trying to sell me thermal windows or lightbulbs they swear will last forever.

"Can you meet me outside in an hour?"

Can't think fast enough to say no. What to do? Never dreamed it would come to this, me meeting Duffy's best girl. After hanging up, I get out some Lancôme Cassie bought for me at Filene's and try to do my face the way she showed me, outlining my lips, putting mascara on my lashes. Afterward, I check it in the natural light, like Cassie told me, to make sure the blush isn't too bright and that my lips are on straight. I spray on the Trésor that Delilah got for me, the two of them in cahoots — sprucing up the old girl — for my last birthday. Then I put on the casual outfit Cass bought me, at least a cut above the other things I own. If I'm going to meet Duffy's best girl, the least I can do is stand my ground. I'd hate to meet her looking frumpy or not smelling my best.

Another bitter day, with a cutting wind, but the sun shines like it's summer. Duffy does a little double-take when he sees me. Not sure if that's good or bad. He holds the door of the Caprice for me, and as we head out, his face turns a little redder. I begin to wonder if there's something wrong with mine after all. Or maybe it's the perfume. I look at the visor, hoping there's a mirror, but no such luck in the old Caprice. I'm imagining my lipstick smudged, or my mascara streaked, and I can't do a damned thing about it. So I hold my head high. I pretend I'm twenty years younger and twenty pounds lighter, with my face on straight.

I've always believed you can tell a lot about a man by the way he drives a car. My ex, hunched over the wheel in his late-model luxury sedan, expected everything else on the road to get out of his way, and, for whatever reason, they almost always did. I can't tell you how many times the streams of traffic parted when I was with him so that Jack F. X. Malloy could glide through.

It's how I knew Cassandra's future husband, Mike Sr., was a stinker back when they were dating — I could tell by the way he drove. Made Jack Malloy look like a turtle by comparison. Weaving in and out in heavy traffic, cutting people off just for the fun of it, speeding down the breakdown lane if he felt like it, running red lights. No consideration for anyone else. Would Cassie listen? No, she knew best. My oldest daughter knew it all. She was pregnant with their second kid, a girl, when Mike used his rotten judgment at a busy intersection in Weymouth. He escaped without a scratch, but Cassandra's pelvis was broken in three places. She lost the baby, and the doctors told her she'd never have another.

"Don't say a word. Don't say anything,"

she cried when I walked into her hospital room. "I know what you're thinking, but don't say it." Of course I wouldn't. That day, when just the two of us were in the room, she broke down, and I held her for a long time while she cried and cried. "Let it all out, baby," I kept saying, and she did, rivers of tears, until the nurses came to give her an injection. I'm the only person in the world whom Cassandra would cry with like that, wordlessly, the two of us together mourning her lost child. Not too long afterward, she filed the papers.

We have thick crusts, Cassandra and me. Thick crusts with many layers, like an Armenian pastry that's impossible to make without many years of practice. Often, these layers rub, one against the other, generating an awful friction between the two of us. Then, without warning, a layer of crust will crumble, hers or mine, or both of ours at once. That's when we'll find the soft layer beneath the crumbling crust, the real mother and real daughter. That's how it was when Cassandra lost her baby.

Duffy's a different breed of cat, though, nothing at all like Cassandra's ex or my own. Never in a rush, never driving above the speed limit. He's got all the time in the world. Anybody wants to pass, and he'll do what he can to let them. He yields when he's supposed to, always cuts the other guy a break. He keeps the radio tuned to a smooth-jazz station out of Boston, so whenever I get into the car, I know I'll be hearing my boy Frankie, or maybe Sarah Vaughan, or Tony Bennett. If we get stuck in traffic, he'll light up, crack the window, listen to the music — peaceful, like the old Caprice is a refuge, not an unguided missile. Today, as we head away from downtown Quincy, out along Shore Drive, ancient neighborhoods crowded on one side, the Atlantic shining on the other, I'm thinking Duffy knows exactly who he is and what he's doing. He doesn't have to prove anything to anyone. He's comfy in his own skin, no small achievement in times like these.

Once, not long after I got laid off, I tried Senior Bingo over at Our Lady Queen of Peace. Big mistake. A roomful of blue-haired biddies with greedy eyes behind their bifocals. Many from my complex, Centennial Square. A couple of times his name came up, Duffy's, these antediluvian women gossiping about the only man nearby who was still warm and walking. Whispering about how cute he was, and also about his troubles, his burdens. Whispering. I didn't listen. I hold to that old maxim, *Whispering,*

whispering is a sin; when you get to heaven, God won't let you in. I've got better things to do with my time. Like take a ride with Duffy to visit his best girl.

I begin to regret the Trésor. It's too heavy for this enclosed space. Also realize that Duffy's best girl must have a place right on the water, maybe in one of those pricey new condos out at Marina Bay.

"She's got a waterfront place?" He shakes his head yes, staring hard through the windshield, his own cheeks bright red. She must be a rich old broad, I think. Skinny, too, no doubt.

"Must be nice." Again he nods. I'm trying to keep it together, wishing I was anyplace but in Duffy's station wagon heading out to meet his best girl with her place right on the water, and me wearing too much Trésor.

There are some nice new condos out there — high-rises — and, I'll admit, I'd envy anyone who could afford one. Then I see the buildings up ahead, glossy pink granite, their big windows facing out over the water, all shiny in the sunlight. Pink elephants, I say to myself. Totally out of place on the South Shore, way too showy. Not my type of thing at all. Give me Paul Revere any day of the week.

We're driving down Victory Boulevard, almost there, when Duffy makes a sharp right. Next thing, we're at Marina Bay's winter storage facility for boats. On both sides of the road, as far as I can see, pleasure craft are up in dry dock, shrink-wrapped against the elements. Cabin cruisers, luxury sailboats, little yachts. Rich folks' toys, wrapped tight in plastic, like leftover meatloaf or ham. Duffy gets out and punches in a code to open the gates. Once we're inside, he parks, and I let him open the door for me. I wonder what else I can do to put off what's coming next.

"She works here?" I ask him as we walk along the rows of boats, looking for an office or some such thing where a human being might be working. He grins and shakes his head, no this time. "I wouldn't say so, no," he says. He stops to light up, cupping the flame from his Zippo with his hands. We walk farther, down a row of shrink-wrapped boats up on platforms. It's exactly how I feel at this moment, shrink-wrapped, my skin too tight. We stop at the end of a row, right above the water, next to a nice big cabin cruiser. This one isn't shrink-wrapped, but instead is wrapped in a green tarpaulin and protected by a canvas tent instead. The tarp has come loose and is flapping in the wind. When we get closer, I see the name, *Miss Nomer,* printed in big black letters across her backside.

"Here she is," says Duffy, exhaling a puff of smoke into the cold air. "My best girl, *Miss Nomer.* Isn't she a beauty?"

I start to laugh, can't help it. I'm dying of embarrassment. Duffy's smoking, inhaling deeply, staring straight ahead at his best girl, his eyes twinkling, like he can't hear me laugh. Oh, he got me but good, and he knows it, but he'll let me keep whatever little shred of pride I have left.

"She's gorgeous, a knockout." I stifle more laughter. I run my hand along her hull. It's wood, dark and shiny, with white-painted decks and nice chrome fittings here and there.

"She's a Chris-Craft," he says. "A twenty-six-foot Express Cruiser. Semi-enclosed. Built in 1957."

"You do like old things." The minute I say this, I think, Me and my big mouth.

"Not all old things are created equal," he answers. "This is vintage Chris-Craft. Mahogany. They don't make 'em like this anymore. Everything's fiberglass now. Me and my boys rescued her in the '70s. Bought her for almost nothing at an estate sale. Fixing her up was our project. Kept us sane, or me, anyway, during Virginia's illness."

"Nice name. *Miss Nomer.*"

Again Duffy nods. "In junior high, my oldest, Thomas, turned into a real pain in the ass, a know-it-all. Every time I turned around, he was correcting me. Every word out of my mouth was another misnomer. According to Thomas, anyway. So when the boat was finished, that's what I christened her. The *Miss Nomer.*"

"She's elegant, a classic." I take in her gleaming wooden sides, her graceful hull, her windshield and red leather seats. "She must be worth a fortune." Duffy owns a cabin cruiser he docks at Marina Bay. Who'd a thunk it?

Duffy shrugs. "Maybe. I haven't checked, because she's not for sale. But the whole point of Chris-Craft, in its day, was to make quality pleasure boats affordable to working people."

"In its day?"

"Fiberglass killed 'em. Well, it didn't exactly kill 'em. They sold the company for millions. Wood boats were their thing. They didn't want to deal with glass."

Duffy starts to replace the tarp, and I ask him why he doesn't shrink-wrap her, like all the other boats.

"You can't shrink-wrap a wooden boat.

It'd rot right out. Wood's got to breathe."

"You learn something new every day."

"Stick with me, kid," he says. "Let's check her out before I cover her again." He climbs up a ladder on her side, his bum leg dragging just a little. He reaches down to help me, his rough hands warm and strong. Take it easy, Mimi, I warn myself as he pulls me up. I try to climb on board with at least a smidgeon of grace.

We stand side by side, looking through the windshield toward the water, which is icy blue with whitecaps here and there. "Here, take a load off," he says, wiping a spot for me on the red leather seats, which are covered in tiny droplets of ice and water. He sits next to me and offers me a smoke, which I accept. The Atlantic stretches out in front of us, the horizon a blue blur. If I weren't so cold, I could almost believe we were out there, sailing, instead of up in dry dock. Then I see the two of us, Duffy and me, on a hot summer day, in the *Miss Nomer,* speeding out across the harbor.

He puts an arm around me. "It's heaven in the summer," he says.

"I'll bet," I say, exhaling. The smell of our cigarettes mixed with the salt air makes my heart race, but in a good way, not like that myocardial thing.

"The first nice day, I'm going to take you out."

"Threat or promise?"

"Oh, a promise, Mrs. Malloy. You can bet your life on it."

I lean in closer to him, imagining myself out there next to him, sunbathing. The image falls apart when I see myself in a bathing suit. Cellulite. My thighs like candles melting. Got to get serious about getting fit and losing weight.

"Centennial Square's my real life," Duffy's saying, "and the *Miss Nomer* is my dream of life. You know, I don't really fish. I just sit on the deck holding the rod. If something swims onto my hook, so much the better."

"How often does that happen?"

"Often enough to make life interesting," he says, and gives me a little squeeze. I turn to look at him, but he's staring out at the water.

I've lived my entire life surrounded by the water but have never once gone out on it in a pleasure boat. That was something wealthy people did. Far beyond the reach of us Sheehan girls.

"I've never been in a boat like this, Duffy," I say. "Not ever. The closest I got was one of the inner tubes I used to bring to the beach with the girls."

He laughs. "No comparison." I shrug. "Poor Mrs. Malloy, you're deprived," he says. "We'll fix that, the first nice day. We'll take you on your maiden voyage."

"My ex was a marine architect," I tell him, just by way of conversation. "Spent his career designing big ships."

"No kidding?" Duffy's not particularly interested.

"That's how he explained it. He built great ships to ply the waters of the world. But after he came home from the war, the Navy, like you, Jack never again rode the high seas, or the low ones, for that matter. He made his living engineering ships, but he never boarded one again."

"Couldn't live without it, myself," says Duff, nowhere near as interested as I am in this irony. He turns to me. "So, what do you think, Mrs. Malloy? Come spring we'll take a sail?"

"You bet," I say.

Eighteen:
Let it Snow! Let it Snow! Let it Snow!

Dawn. Cold gloom. A naked child, smoldering, her arms outstretched, her face too close to mine, yet blurred. Stinking of smoke, vomit, pee. She nudges me, shaking me awake. Tries to tell me something without using words. Who is she? An alarm sounds, but not one for waking up. Where is the alarm coming from? Even in my terror, I know it's coming from the naked child, but how? Why? I sit up, she disappears, and it's my telephone, my own damn phone that's ringing. My bedside clock says 9:18 A.M. Cassandra.

"Don't even think about driving in this," she wails.

"What, in what?" My voice is thick.

"You're still in bed." She sounds as if the eastern seaboard is about to fall into the Atlantic because her mother overslept.

"It's Saturday."

"Don't even think about driving in this,"

she repeats. "It's a blizzard, a beaut." As if I would. "Stay put. We're supposed to get a foot."

"Don't worry, honey." I use my most soothing Mom voice. "I'm not going anyplace. I've got everything I need right here."

"I'll call you back in a couple of hours to make sure."

Snow. A sudden winter storm. Before the ice and drifts from the last one have even melted. When I hang up from Cassie, I snuggle back under the soft, clean covers of my bed, my Sealy Posturepedic, while the snow whirls around me. I reach out for the blue pendant on my bedside table, squeeze it in my fist, rub my face into my feather pillow. I doze off and another child is there, like a stray cat you made the mistake of feeding once.

I sit up. *Stop haunting me,* I say, or maybe I only think it. The girl's face begins to clarify, like a photo coming into focus. She's a brunette with hazel eyes who looks a lot like me. My sister Alberta, close enough to touch, but I don't touch her. Her face is bruised, her lip swollen, but she's too young for this damage to have been done by Buddy, Buster, or Bub. Her eyes glow like those laser pointers they sell to drive cats crazy. Behind her, a shadow, a black spot.

She came out of it — she's going back, and wants me to go along.

My old sweetheart Alberta, standing in front of me, wanting me to go with her, the way I always used to. Something spins inside me, like I'm in a blender on the puree setting. I love Alberta so much, a humming, spinning love, but I don't want to go. I couldn't follow her in life, and I don't want to now. I'd give anything not to go. But I can't stop what's happening. Can't find the right button on the blender. It spins and spins until a younger me emerges, eight or nine years old.

We're in our bed, Alberta and me. Where's Eden? We cling to each other. Where's Eden? She's gone. We have to find her, bring her back. We wait for ages, listening through the wrought-iron heat register in the floor until we're certain Flanna is asleep. We sneak downstairs. Flanna at the kitchen table, her head on its wooden surface, her mouth open, drool like a teardrop falling from her lips, her hair spilling out across her arm. In a shiny blue dress, black high heels. Waiting for Da, waiting and waiting, just like me and my sisters. All of us, forever waiting for Da to get home.

On the table, an ashtray full of butts, each smeared red from her lipstick. The whiskey bottle, almost empty, not far from her hand. "If it was full, I'd brain her with it," I whisper to Alberta. She picks up the bottle, takes a big swallow, coughs as it goes down. I shake my head no when she offers it to me.

Flanna, enchanting beauty. Sleeping, she's as pretty as a saint on a prayer card, all pink cheeks and shiny curls. Still, she has that power. She makes a shuddering sound, her lips vibrating when she exhales. Ever so carefully, I reach into her pocket, take out her keys. She jerks. I jump back. She's waking up, but no, she settles back into her noisy sleep. I grab a couple of slices of bread and a cup of water. Alberta and I head back upstairs.

That old house was full of closets, eaves, nooks, cupboards. Eden's locked in one of them. Sobs when she hears our footsteps. "Amelia Earhart," I whisper so she knows it's us, not Flanna. "Amelia Earhart loves to fly," Alberta chimes. When we open the cupboard door, Eden reaches for us, her face shiny with snot and tears. She grabs the bread and water. She pees into the cup once it's empty. We try to take her with us, back to our own bed.

"Flanna's drunk, she won't remember."

"No, no, no." Eden scrunches up her eyes and waves her hands. No, no, no. She refuses the pillow we brought for her. She goes back into her little prison. "Lock it. Lock it now before she comes."

Snow blows against my windows. The icy bits make a clattering sound. It's 10:15 A.M. I feel a little crazy, seeing my dead sisters sneaking around in the dark like that. I get up and put on coffee. My heart pumps in a wild rhythm. Maybe it's the A-fib, Jesus, the dreaded A-fib. If it throws off a clot, well, I'll be history, another Sheehan sister down the tubes. Every one of us dropping like flies.

I stand by the counter, watch the coffee bubble up into the glass knob of my electric perk. Nothing like a fresh-brewed cup with a spoonful of real cream, one of my guilty pleasures. When we were kids, the milkman used to leave the glass bottles in a metal crate by the front door, before milk was homogenized and bought at stores. My sisters and I used to sneak spoonfuls of the cream on top whenever we could get away with it. Nothing today tastes as good as that cream. I take my coffee to the table. Now, that's my type of memory, a happy one, of days gone by.

Through the curtains, the sidewalk and parking lots glisten with snow. Duffy's already out there, all bundled up with a ski mask over his face, clearing the sidewalks on a tractor with a plow attached to it. I make a mental note to call him, invite him over for coffee, a bite to eat. I could use some company. Then I remember I've got a brisket in the freezer. I'll stick it into the slow cooker, with carrots and potatoes. Pot roast, the perfect meal on a day like this. When his work is done, we'll share a nice hot meal and watch *Family Feud* together, or maybe a rerun of *Magnum, P.I.*

I'm betting that if I don't call them first, every one of my sisters and my kids will call me, everybody worrying about everybody else, but also glad to have this unexpected snow day, a chance to do absolutely nothing and enjoy it. Sure enough, I've just finished my coffee when Patty calls.

I'm fine, I'm fine, I tell her, and she tells me she's fine too. No hard feelings about what was or was not said at Keeley's birthday brunch. But once we get that squared away, I can't help but bring it all up again. That image of Al and Eden haunts me.

"Patty, our past feels like a curse. I like forgetting better."

"That's what some of the old folks said about us, that we were cursed." She chuckles. "But you," she says, "you exaggerate everything. You older girls were drama queens." My ears ring with the pain of her words. "Everything was life and death with you, plural."

"That's not fair," I cry. "Eden and Alberta aren't even here to defend themselves."

Her remark slices through me, and I slam down the receiver, a blunt instrument silencing her voice. Every time we stroll down Memory Lane, we Sheehan sisters, we end up on opposite sides of the street, shouting back and forth about what happened and what didn't.

I pop an English muffin in the toaster, burn it, and eat it anyway. I'm much too thrifty to throw food away, recalling times when my sisters and I would have killed for a bit of an English muffin, burned or otherwise. In that world, the world of Not Enough, we Sheehan girls held on to one another, gained strength from one another, and that's how we survived. That's why it upsets me so much now that we have this great divide.

My sisters and I shared beds in two little rooms in the back of the house. We three oldest in one big bed, and in the next room the twins and the baby — Fagan or Keeley, whichever one it was — in two small beds pushed together, all of us like honeysuckle, tangled up together; grateful, during the brutal winters, to have each other's bodies to snuggle up to for warmth. After Mam passed, we often climbed into bed with each other at night, all six of us. So close like that, sleeping, breathing softly together, it was like we shared just one body. Lots of arms and legs, but a single heart and soul. Every now and again, this heart would break. The sounds of it breaking — bleats, squeaks, sobs, hiccups — issued from the one body, filling the dark silence of the room.

After all that happened, all things considered, the twins turned out OK. Jo — supposedly the quiet one — was born four minutes after Patty and ended up four inches taller. Grew an inch for every extra minute in the womb, we always joked. Once bossy Patty was born, Jo finally had room to grow. As for her name, I figure they grabbed the closest one at hand, my father's, although Jo insists that being named for him was a special honor, like me with my mother's name.

Both are nurses, Patty a retired pediatric RN and Jo a BSN who supervises a long-term care facility for permanently disabled kids. Not long after the war, they went to nursing school together, paying their own way. Unlike Eden and Alberta, profligate with everything — their money, their bodies, their love — the twins were savers, penny pinchers. Still in their twenties when they bought a house, a sturdy double-decker in Dorchester, worth a fortune now and paid for long ago. "We'll always have a roof over our heads," they said at the time, haunted by our orphan years, when Nana Sheehan would sometimes have to farm us out to other relatives because she didn't always have enough to feed us.

Patty lives on the first floor with her husband, Wesley, and their four kids. Jo, who never married, lives upstairs. No, Jo never married. She could've have had any guy she wanted, but she didn't want. She gave up her glamour-girl ways when she went to nursing school. Keeps her hair cut short and hasn't bought a rouge or lipstick since. "This way," she says, "I'm always driving my own bus." She can take it anywhere she wants, whenever she wants. Not that she's ever been alone. Besides being a second mother to Patty's kids and to a couple of mine, she's always had foster kids, fifteen or twenty over the years, many of them disabled in one way or another, all of them abandoned. "At risk," is the term Jo uses. At risk. She takes them in one or two at a time, lavishing her love upon them, banking their government stipends so they'll have a little nest egg when they move on, and they always keep in touch. She's got more "grandkids" than me. Her refrigerator's covered with their pictures. A saint, that's Jo. When the sun shines just right, you can see her halo.

Pouring another cup of coffee, the snow and wind still howling, I reconsider the silence. Glutton for punishment that I am, I call Jo. She, too, is home safe and sound, doing a jigsaw puzzle with her foster kids. We, too, agree to forget/forgive — take your pick — what happened at Keeley's birthday party, then move on to the subject of our mutual safety. Nobody's going anywhere. Once we get that settled, she launches into what's really on both our minds.

"Patty called and told me you got mad and hung up on her. The truth hurts you too much, she said."

"What's the truth?"

"If we only knew."

"You agree we don't?" No answer, just the sounds of her foster kids squabbling and laughing in the background. "Patty said we older girls were drama queens. That cuts deep."

More silence.

"Jo, we were not drama queens. Not at all. You know that. How could Patty ever think that about Eden and Alberta? Or me? Tell me you don't believe it too."

Jo's too honest and too loyal to answer one way or another. "Sorry, but I can't do this on the phone, Mimi, not now."

I'm about to ask what "this" is, but suddenly I'm exhausted. I drop it. Then Jo tells me one of her kids is doing a fund-raiser for his basketball team, selling gourmet popcorn in a dozen flavors. I promise to buy three packs, six bucks a pop.

"It better be really good."

Jo laughs her sweet laugh. "It will be, I promise."

I hang up, more puzzled now than angry. It's so unlike Patty to cast aspersions upon her sisters, and especially upon the departed ones — "drama queens." Again, I think about how we Sheehan sisters held on to one another, always, all throughout our lives. *Amelia Earhart loves to fly. Amelia Earhart will never die.* A rhyme we made up, to remind us of who we were and how we had to stick together, although, in Fagan's case, we didn't hold on tight enough.

As for Al and Eden, once they passed, I cut them loose. Had to. Their sad lives, their untimely deaths, weighed on me like cement shoes, pulling me down, down, down. If I hadn't let them go, I would have gone under too. Once and for all. So many of those years with Jack, those middle years at home raising our daughters, I struggled just to keep my head above the water. I needed a ballast. I couldn't take on more weight.

Eden never married, but Alberta made up for her, each of her husbands a bigger jerk than the last one, except for whichever one it was she married twice.

At Alberta's funeral, as the gravediggers lowered that cheap box into the ground, I collapsed with grief, ready to climb down there with her. That's when Jack F. X. Malloy whispered, "All Alberta ever did was cry into her whiskey, feeling sorry for herself. Drank herself to death, just like your father," a point he never tired of making. Jack had nothing to say when Eden died from the cancer, not a single word.

"Girls as beautiful as those two had to work really hard to make such messes of their lives," Jack once said.

"What do you mean by that?" I was furious in a way that only Jack could make me.

"Life is easier for good-looking people," he said.

"Oh, you should know." I spoke sarcastically, but Jack took it as a compliment.

"Well, it's a fact." I don't remember where we had this conversation, but I do remember he was breathing on my neck, rubbing my hip in a way that always weakened me. "Also, common sense if you think about it," he went on. "Any number of successful men would've been happy to take care of them. But they always found the losers."

"Speak for yourself," I said, pushing his hand away. I felt shredded like carrots in a coleslaw every time he bad-mouthed Eden and Alberta. "Anyway, you always had a thing for Eden. Maybe you wish you'd married her."

He shrugged, blushed. "She was a knockout, a movie star, but she didn't know how to get out of her own way."

During Eden's last weeks, in a room with lots of sunlight where she could see the water, my daughters kept running in and out to keep her company. She loved it when they climbed into bed with her; she held them like they were her own. Jack, known far and wide as a cheapskate, paid to keep fresh flowers in her room, bouquets of lilies and white roses that covered up her dying smell. He sat with her and held her hand, feeding her orange sherbet with the little spoon we used for baby food. It was the only thing she could keep down.

By then, Eden's worldly goods consisted of a driver's license and two small suitcases stuffed full of cheap clothes with lots of lace and sparkles. After she passed, my daughters found the suitcases and played dress-up in them. They loved pretending to be Eden. They'd take me by surprise, Cassandra, or Celestine, or Ruthie, in Eden's sequins and high heels, like she'd dropped by for a quick chat. My heart stopped every time. More than anything I wanted to throw those clothes away, but the girls hid them so I couldn't.

While the snow blows and the wind howls, I give Duffy a ringy-dingy, leave a message about the pot roast. While I chop the carrots and potatoes, I listen to the TV. The blather about storm tracks and cold fronts and icy moisture in the upper atmosphere calms me down. Pretty soon, my apartment smells of nice rich stew, bay leaf, onions, and thyme. When it's almost done, I'll throw in some dumplings.

After that, I turn off the TV, pick up the pendant, take it to my recliner. Sit there holding it, rubbing my finger on the scratch. I hear the thrum of those deep and dreaded feelings. Fear and longing, flies buzzing around the black spots.

Some things, like sneaking cream from the milk, I remember perfectly, and I hold on to these memories as proof positive that I didn't spring full-grown onto the Earth as a mother in my twenties, hitched to Jack Malloy. Which is what I often felt like as I raised my girls, that I'd just been born that day, without any experience or memory.

No idea at all what I was doing as a mother, but I couldn't tell anyone, not my sisters, and least of all Jack. Boiling glass bottles for the formula — no breastfeeding, Jack's eleventh commandment! My breasts belonged to him alone — mixing big pots of formula on the stove; soaking the soiled diapers in the toilet, wringing them out, flushing; laundering them by the dozens, hanging them outside on the line . . . no dryer, not yet. Not knowing what to do when Cass or Ruthie or Cellie wouldn't stop crying, and Jack was never there. I just muddled through.

Yet I loved that house by the water, where, from the clothesline in the yard, I could see way across the bay to the shipyard, where Jack was working. And I knew that, no matter what, he would come back home to me.

A house not anything at all like Da's in Quincy, with its cupboards, closets, crannies, cellar, hiding places, places to be scared. No wonder we all slept together in one bed. But Flanna put an end to that. She separated us, kept the six of us from sharing a single bed. Turned Da into an enforcer, something he'd never been. She sent him to check on us, and often checked herself, a swooping shadow. "Stay put, you stinkers," she'd hiss after Daddy was asleep. Like if we got back together, we'd plot against her. *Thick as thieves,* she called us.

I had so much trouble sleeping after Flanna came. No more one body. Even with my eyes closed, snug under the covers, I couldn't fall asleep. Couldn't keep my eyes closed for any length of time. The slightest sound — a sigh, a rustle, a whoosh through the registers, a creak on the stairs — would jerk me awake and ages passed before I could close my eyes again. Sometimes a cold gust awakened me, and when it did, I smelled sharp stinging herbs, nothing like those in my pot roast, no; instead herbs that burned my eyes, and I'd believe a ghost, not a holy one, had come into our room, might be there still. Sometimes, after waking up and checking to make sure the coast was clear, I sneaked into my sisters' room just to count the lumps in the bed. Sometimes I counted wrong. An overactive imagination, my father and my sisters said, and then my husband, too.

World War II may have been hell on Earth for everybody except me and my sisters. Those were our glory days, or as close to glory days as we'd ever get, we glorious Sheehan girls. One by one, we finished high school and went to work at the shipyard, where our father, along with various uncles, cousins, and other relatives, had worked back when Joe Kennedy, the father of the future president, ran the place. Girls replaced the boys who'd gone off to war, Jack Malloy among them, although at the time I hadn't met him yet.

As in World War I, the Fore River Shipyard had countless naval contracts, turning out aircraft carriers, destroyers, landing ships, and heavy cruisers at a crazy rate. Triple shifts, the shipyard in full operation 'round the clock. Workers grabbing extra shifts, as many as they could handle, for as long as they could stay upright at their task. As fast as one ship was torpedoed, another would slide off the ways and into the water, chugging off to the European or Pacific theaters.

While under construction, the ships had hull numbers instead of names; from the 1400s up past the 1600s when I was there. Like babies, the ships got their names when they were christened. I remember a group of heavy cruisers with the names of American cities: *Boston, Baltimore, Pittsburgh, St. Paul, Providence,* and, of course, the *Quincy,* torpedoed in 1942. That same year, the battleship *Massachusetts* was christened — the heaviest ship ever launched at the yard — nicknamed Big Mamie by her crew. The types of ships, their names, were my poetry, taught to me first by my father and then my husband. When the *Wasp,* a magnificent aircraft carrier — cutting-edge, a wonder — was torpedoed in '42, we mourned her as though that craft were one of us. The men who built those ships were classified as essential and did not have to serve. But thousands of them, men like Jack, volunteered for combat, and off they went.

I suppose we Sheehan girls really were beautiful back then, with clear eyes, shiny hair, small waists, nice bust lines. Oh, and pretty ankles! Must not forget the ankles, all that I've got left. During school, we wore saddle shoes and bobby socks, pleated skirts and sweaters. But when we started at the shipyard, some of us, depending upon our job, wore sweaters, skirts, and heels like Lana Turner, and others jumpsuits like Rosie the Riveter. For the first time in our lives, we had a buck or two to spend, even after we paid Nana Sheehan for our room and board. We bought lipstick and nail polish and shiny pumps.

We Sheehan girls made quite a splash over there. So many of us, and everybody raving about how alike we looked despite the various colors of our hair, brunettes and redheads, and Eden, the drop-dead gorgeous natural blond. Those days, my sisters and I fought about everything, from the underwear on out. First up, best dressed. We'd claw one another's eyes out to wear the blouse we wanted. We had so few belongings, and we longed for everything! Not that our fights were ever serious. My sisters and I forgave one another everything. *Amelia Earhart loves to fly. Amelia Earhart will never die.*

What we didn't understand is that it didn't matter what we wore, what color we painted our lips. The entire bunch of us could've gone out barefoot in potato sacks and all the doors that opened to us would've opened anyway. Because the war had given us a future, and we had our youth, if not our innocence.

My phone rings again and I grab it. Duffy.

"That's a sweet offer, Mrs. Malloy, one I can't refuse."

"Well, all right then, great. How about six?"

"Can I bring anything?"

"Just yourself. I've got everything else we need."

"Looking forward to it." The line goes dead, but I still feel like we're connected. Duffy, I feel so comfortable with him, in a way I never felt with Jack. Not worried sick about meeting some mysterious standard, one so high it was impossible to reach.

Looking back, it's hard to believe how Jack Malloy swept me off my feet. Our romance was as fast and thrilling as the roller-coaster ride at Nantasket Beach, where we often went that first summer we were dating. Jack, a handsome devil — tall, with slicked-back hair, wire-frame eyeglasses, and shiny cuff-links on the wrists of his starched, pressed shirts. The spitting image of Artie Shaw, his idol.

The first time I saw him, he was walking into the drafting room at the shipyard, where I was a clerk. I fell head over heels for him, a regular Kodak moment: Jack, just back from the war, walks in and everything stops. Bright light shines all around him, and I know without the slightest doubt that he's the One. Oh, yes! A sweet memory I keep on hand for troubled times. And I

wasn't alone in my conviction. Every girl at
the shipyard, and there were dozens of us,
felt the same way. All the girls had the biggest crush on him, but I'm the one he
chose. Jack, a big shot, the one who finally
figured out how to move great ships through
the shallow channels of the Fore River into
Quincy Bay, and beyond that, the great
Atlantic. His words. And he was always
happy to tell anyone who'd listen.

Jack might've been my father's boss if my
father were still alive. Not laboring beside
Da in the dark, hot hull of a ship, but working high above him at a desk in the drafting
room, which was bigger than a football field
and surrounded by sparkling windows with
great views of the water.

Even our wedding was spectacular, with
Jack's parents picking up the tab, a recep-
tion in the church hall of their parish, St.
Jerome's, a three-tiered cake, and Jack's
musician buddies — a real swing band —
playing halfway through the night. All of my
sisters were bridesmaids, each in a pastel
satin gown. We sewed them ourselves on
Nana's treadle machine. Alberta, the maid
of honor, in lavender, and me, a virgin, in
pure white satin with a sweetheart neckline,
a train, a flowing veil, and dozens of white
roses.

Eden and Alberta figured I'd hit the jackpot when I hitched up with Jack. That's what Alberta called him, even to his face, Jackpot. Why, he'd built a brand-new house for us, a little Cape Cod cottage across the street from his parents', above the Fore River. A new house of our own! My sisters couldn't get over how lucky I was. My future was assured, they said, and I wouldn't even have to work. Outside the home, anyway. I was the one who was going to "make it," the two of them kept saying. But those girls didn't have an ounce of good judgment between them. If you asked them what "it" was, neither of them could have said.

No doubt my life looked great compared to theirs. Eden, always searching, never finding. Alberta, finding losers, one after the other. By the time she reached her thirties, her nose had been broken more than once, her eyes blackened, her smile marred by missing teeth, and her bank account, the little she had, emptied out. She had a son and a daughter, half-siblings. Miracle of miracles, the daughter's a high school history teacher, married to another teacher now, and the mother of three. She doesn't keep in touch, much as I'd love to see her. But who could blame her?

Alberta's son, Danny, the cutest kid, the first boy born into the family in ages, died at eighteen. A dead ringer for Da, Alberta always bragged about him, so proud of this fact. *Smart as a whip, and so good with his hands.* Alberta's sun rose and set on him. He died alone, on a sidewalk in Brockton, of a heroin overdose. His druggie friends got scared and took off, leaving him alone, convulsing in an alley. The medical examiner said he was alive for several hours after the convulsions started. If someone had intervened, Narcan, a simple shot of Narcan, would've saved him.

The rest of us chipped in for his funeral, as we would soon after for Alberta's. In spite of everything else Alberta had been through, she kept functioning, but the death of Danny crushed her. *Left to die there like a dog.* She couldn't stop saying it, couldn't get the picture out of her head. After Danny's death I didn't see Alberta much. Couldn't handle her grief — a depth charge, so many bad things exploding to the surface, the sludge and slime of our early lives.

Since the two of them have passed, my sisters, I rarely talk about them, try not to think about them. No point. I get all tangled up in the messes they made out of their lives and while I'm tangled there, I hear Jack

216

Malloy: *A drunk and a slut, that's what you've got for sisters.* I tried so many times to explain to him that it wasn't always like that, but he didn't want to listen. He liked his version better.

I set the pendant down. Go stir the stew even though the point of the slow cooker is to turn it on and leave it be. The potatoes are still hard. I take the Scrubbing Bubbles from under the kitchen sink and head into the bathroom. I spray a nice foam over the tub, the toilet, and the sink in case Duffy has to go, let it set while I Windex the bathroom mirror. Then I give the toilet bowl a good go-round with a brush, working up a lot of suds, getting up under the rim and as deep into the hole as the curved handle will let me. I lift the lid and wipe it, and when the toilet's spotless, I flush, certain that it will pass muster even if God Himself has gotta pee.

I'm in the kitchen peeling off my rubber gloves when the two of them return to me, Al and Eden at seventeen and eighteen. Bobby-socksers. A blonde and a brunette, at the height of their beauty. My heart skips when I see them, my old sweethearts. Nobody who saw them like that, in their pretty skirts and sweaters, with their shiny

217

Breck Girl hair, would ever have had a clue how they'd already suffered in their lives. I try my best to ignore them.

I get out the vac, a nice little Dirt Devil that Ruthie and her boys gave me last Christmas. Lightweight, so I can lug it around without throwing out my back. My kitchen, bath, and entryway are tiled, so I sweep them, but the living room and bedroom are wall-to-wall, a comfy shag my daughters say is hopelessly out of date. But it's in such good shape, I tell them, it would be a shame to replace it. I start in the bedroom, working up a sweat. Aerobic exercise. I'll have to tell Cassandra.

I hope the noise of the Dirt Devil will drown out my sisters' pleas. No such luck. They hang around, and keep telling me without words to look, look, look. No, I say a million times. Look, they demand again, and in a moment of weakness, I obey. I look. I see through their clothes. Marks on their bellies, backs, and thighs, the work of Flanna Flanagan. Flanna with her garden shears, pliers, wire cutters. Her spatulas, paring knives, soup ladles. Her mortar and pestle. Her matches and cigarettes. You learned fast not to rile her.

Flanna, Da's secret rose, in our mother's clothes, mumbling prayers we didn't understand. Right off the boat, they said about her, and we girls, right off the bat, we understood that she was nuts. We also understood that Daddy loved her, more than he loved us. He forgot all about our mammy. Never spoke her name. Put Flanna in our mother's bed — even in her under-wear for all I knew — in all the places where Mam used to be, and thought the rest of us should do the same. That way, none of us would have to feel the pain of loss. He'd found a mother for his daughters, a wife for himself. We tried to stay out of her way, but it hardly ever worked. She found us, always.

I get down on my knees to run the nozzle of the vac all the way under my bed. Can't stand dust bunnies, never could. The Termi-nator is what my daughters call me. I take it as a compliment. But it's my late sisters, not my daughters, who wait under the bed. The Dirt Devil does not suck them up. They stand and watch me with their sad bright eyes. *Go away,* I tell them. *Let me live in peace.* They bow their heads like nuns in prayer. *What did I ever do to you?* I ask, but on second thought, I don't want an answer. Don't want to know how I failed them. *Don't let our suffering be in vain,* they chorus in high voices, like it's a hymn. I think of Duffy by the Dumpster, closing my hand around the pendant. Out of sight, out of mind. Pull shut the pouch of memory. That's what I'll do. But when I try, Alberta cries, *No, Mimi, no. . . . Keep trying to remember.*

"Cut me a break," I whisper above the howling snow. I could howl too. Because Patty didn't go through what we went through. And we did our best to keep it from her, from all of them. Didn't want the younger ones to know what we knew.

I trip on the vacuum cord and fall, end up on my bottom on the bedroom floor. But the floor gives way beneath me. I keep tumbling, down, down, landing in a darker place.

Flanna pushes me down the stairs, into the coal cellar. I bump and bounce and flop, a broken doll, wearing only panties. Flanna stripped me, took my clothes. Left me naked and ashamed. "That'll teach ya!" Flanna hollers. "Ya stinkin' brat!" I land with a thud, a hard landing that shakes loose something inside of me, a mystery as dark as my surroundings. I howl so everyone will hear. Howl loud enough to wake the dead, hoping Mam will come back for me, but the dead do not awaken. Howl until I cannot howl anymore. Lose my voice, lose track of time. It slips away. I'm hungry, and so thirsty, my mouth dry as ashes. "Da, Da," I cry both inside and outside myself. "Da, Da." But Daddy, Da, my father, doesn't answer.

I try to get up from the floor of my bedroom, with its outdated wall-to-wall and the beautiful quilt Ruthie sewed for me. Home. It's a long way up, though, and every joint and muscle's creaking. I don't quite make it, and down I go again, collapsing the way I did in the cellar long ago. Maybe I should start with the glucosamine and chondroitin. Duffy swears by it, though he tells me it's expensive, and Medicare won't cover it. He buys it, two for one, when it's on sale at CVS. Maybe we can share.

The wind's still howling, just like me, and the snow still blows against the windows. I unplug the Dirt Devil. God, I hate to leave my sisters. I hate to leave them again, the way I did before. Hooking up with Jack, going down the path he laid out for us, a path too narrow for Eden and Alberta and their messed-up lives. Not once looking back. I have to get back to my own. Not that it's so great, but at least I know, more or less, what's going to happen next.

NINETEEN:
ZING! WENT THE STRINGS OF MY HEART

Praise the Lord for Duffy, *Family Feud,* and pot roast. He shows up around six P.M., just in time, because I can't turn off the spigots. I cry and hiccup and cry some more. Me. Mimi with her heart of stone. Bawling her eyes out. Her tear ducts, like the bathroom pipe, have sprung a leak. Before he rings the bell, I try to fix my face, but the telltale signs are there. Red nose. Puffy eyes.

"What's up, Mrs. Malloy?" He puts his warm hand on my shoulder. He's wearing gray slacks, a light-blue shirt with a navy-blue cardigan. His silver hair is slicked back nicely and he smells of aftershave.

"Don't give me any sympathy," I say. "I'll fall apart again."

"It's this awful weather. It'd give anyone the blues."

"Maybe that's it," I say, even though I know it isn't. "Had the whole day to walk down Memory Lane. Big mistake."

He nods but doesn't say a thing. I can talk about it, or not, is the feeling I get from him. I decide not. I'm done for the day. I mix each of us a Manhattan, straight-up, which we sip on my couch while we watch the Weather Channel.

"This'll warm the cockles of your heart," he says, lighting up.

"You betcha." I settle into the cushions, let him light my cigarette. Right away my nerves calm down.

"Good thing we got over to the boat," he says as we listen to reports of all the damage up and down the coast. "I must have had an intuition. If I hadn't fixed that tarp . . ."

"She's beautiful, Duff, the *Miss Nomer*. Classy."

"Almost lost her a couple of times," he says, looking at the TV, not at me. "Put her up for collateral, and almost lost her. That's when I put my foot down. I realized I couldn't live without her."

I blush, and hope to hell he doesn't see. Because I'm wishing, all of a sudden and very strongly, that Duffy was talking about me. But no, he's got his eye on the TV, on the maps of storm tracks swirling eastward toward coastal Massachusetts. They look almost like the maps that radiologist made of the inside of my skull, except without the black spots.

"Age hasn't diminished her a bit," I say.

"No," he says, glancing at me, then back at the TV, "she's only gotten more beautiful."

Embarrassment and longing collide inside me and my trusty sharp tongue fails me. I can't think of anything to say.

"You know, Mrs. Malloy, you can only lose so much, and then you have to put your foot down. You just can't lose any more." His sad tone pulls me back from another meltdown. Loss and sadness I can handle. I'm an expert on those.

"I hear ya loud and clear." I sip my Manhattan. He nods, still watching TV, but his eyes are shadowed with that darkness. The subject's closed for now.

When we've finished our drinks, I whip up the dumplings, one of my ex's favorites — a thought I wish I didn't have — and, minutes later, I serve the pot roast on my best white Corelle. We eat at my table with the TV on. But as soon as I dig in, I'm disappointed.

"You should be able to cut this with a fork." I struggle with a steak knife to cut my meat into little bites.

"It's the gravy, and the dumplings, Mrs.

Malloy." He smiles at me with his eyes. "Best I've had in years." He chows down like a trooper.

"You can really put it away." I'm pleased by his appetite. Who wouldn't be?

"Cold weather and hard work. That'll do it every time."

When we finish eating, he helps me with the dishes, washing while I dry and put away. While we clean up, we listen to the news, not talking much. We don't even get in each other's way, which is quite a trick in these small kitchens.

"My ex never helped me with the dishes," I remark when we're almost done, and Duffy turns bright red, then I'm embarrassed too. Me and my big mouth. There's an awkward silence and I put on a pot of coffee.

"You still attached to him, Mrs. Malloy?" he asks. I want to die. Attached. I think of buttons on overcoats. Stamps on envelopes. IV lines in a vein.

"Attached?"

"You still carrying the torch?" Duffy's voice is kind and curious.

"The torch? Uh-uh." I take out the mugs, set them by the percolator, keep my back to him. Don't want him to see the color of my face. "No way. That flame died out long ago.

I still love a good torch song, though. 'Am I Blue?' 'Cry Me a River' . . . 'Here's That Rainy Day.' "

" 'Can't Help Lovin' That Man of Mine'?" Duff adds to the list, but still kind, still curious.

"Nope. I know for sure I don't love him anymore." Even the thought of it appalls me. "Been divorced for fifteen years. He remarried years ago."

"But you never got over him?" His question probes deep as a plumber's snake. I can't help turning around to look at him.

"I was with him thirty years. Married him at nineteen. He was ten years older. We had six kids. I don't love him anymore. That flame died long before we parted, but it's also true that I'm not over him."

"You wish you were."

I shake my head yes. "And you, Duff, you're not over Virginia, are you? You weren't ready for her to go, and you haven't ever let her."

He nods slowly.

"You can't when you've got kids. Even grown-up kids."

"Much as you might want to. Healthy as it might be if you could."

He nods yes, the two of us on the same page, even though we're holding our own ground, on opposite sides of my kitchen.

"I can't bring her back," he says. "And you can't make Jack any better than he was for you."

The coffee's ready, and I pour each of us a cup.

"Remember when we went out to the *Miss Nomer,* and you said you don't really fish?" I ask, my back to him. "You just drop your line into the water to see if anything comes along?"

He's chuckling, the nicest sound. He sees my point before I make it.

"Am I a fish who just happened to swim onto your hook?"

"Oh, I don't know about that, Mrs. Malloy." He picks up our cups and carries them into the living room. "Before we could say for sure, we'd have to know which one of us put the line in the water first."

"Oh, but I've never fished in my life," I tell him, refusing to laugh. "Never even been out on the water. Told you that before. I wouldn't know a hook from a lure if my life depended on it."

"Well, in that case, it couldn't have been you," he says, teasing, as we settle onto the couch for our after-dinner cigarettes and coffee. We're just in time for a rerun of *Magnum, P.I.* We sit close to each other,

Duffy's thigh touching mine. I feel peaceful, such a relief! Next thing I know, I'm waking up during the eleven o'clock news, my head on Duffy's shoulder.

"You missed Tom getting the bad guy," he says, shaking me ever so gently. "You've been sleeping like a baby. But now I've got to go. Work tomorrow."

I sit up, laughing, embarrassed all over again. "Jeepers, aren't I great company? I was out like a light."

Duffy laughs too. "I'm the one who's great company. Bored you to sleep."

"No way," I protest, walking him to the door. We pause there for a moment.

"Mrs. Malloy," he says with his sweetest smile, "could you give an old man a little squeeze to send him on his way?"

"My pleasure," I say, and so I do. Standing in my doorway, I give Duffy a great big hug, and he hugs me back, warm and strong. We stay there for a moment, before we break apart, and I close the door behind him.

Twenty:
A Million Dreams Ago

Cassie shows up on Ash Wednesday and she's got Delilah in tow. Delilah, the head bobber. Pretty as a picture, my Delilah, all smooth and soft and blond, unlike Cassie, who has starved herself into sharp angles, bones sticking out everywhere. Of course, Cassie's ten years older, in her forties, and who knows what Delilah will look like in ten more years. Delilah's been married twice, her first marriage short, anything but sweet, and childless as well. Now she's with a hunky Boston cop named Steve O'Neil. Her second time around seems to be going better. So far, their marriage has resulted in two daughters who look exactly like her — blond beauties, as if Steve, black Irish, got left on the deck of the gene pool.

Cassie, without enough to do, her own son Mikey grown if not exactly gone — he lives off the fat of the land in that big house in Hingham — has taken Delilah under her wing. As if Delilah can't fend for herself. Every time I turn around, Cassie's up there, at Delilah's lovely home in Reading, telling her how to run her house and raise her kids and probably what to do in bed with Steve. Delilah just smiles and nods like it's fine by her. I've already told Jo and Patty, this one's gonna blow up in a year or so. The cop will have had it up to here with Cassie's meddling and Delilah's head-nodding, and I hope I'm living on another planet when it does.

The three of us get ashes at Our Lady Queen of Peace, where the priests make a big deal out of burning last year's palms. We carry in our palms from last year, my daughters' covered with a furry layer of dust, but mine is clean as a whistle. It spent the past year wrapped around the crucifix hanging over my bed, and was dusted on a regular basis. We stand around praying while the priest sets them on fire in this special marble bowl in the front of the church. My daughters watch, but I turn away. I hate the sight, the smell of anything burning. Never been one for candles, or even cookouts. Never wanted a fireplace. *Ashes, ashes, we all fall down.* The fire in the marble bowl burns out, small wisps of smoke rising in the chilly air, wafting away. We stay for

Mass, take communion, then go to lunch at my favorite seafood place over at Marina Bay, McCrann's, my daughters treating.

Driving from the church to McCrann's in Delilah's SUV, an Excretion or Exterminator or some such thing — a vehicle I need help climbing into — I keep thinking about the words the priest whispered as he rubbed ashes onto our foreheads: "Remember man that thou art dust and unto dust thou shalt return." *Remember man that thou art dust.*

The hostess leads us to a leather booth where we can see Quincy Bay out the window, the three of us with smudges of ash on our foreheads. It's a cold gray day with occasional flurries, and I tell my girls we should've done lunch the day before, Mardi Gras, when we could eat, drink, and be merry before the fasting began.

"We're eating fish, aren't we?" Cassie asks and looks at Delilah, who nods her answer, yes. My girls order broiled scrod and salads with the dressing on the side. They also order a bottle of white wine and the waiter, like the priest with the palms, makes the biggest deal out of opening it, giving Cass a taste.

"What the hell," I say, smiling at the waiter. "I'm dust and unto dust I shall return. Bring me the fried clam platter."

My daughters' faces turn bright red.

Turns out, however, that the lovely lunch with my daughters isn't a random act of kindness. I realize this when they're halfway through their scrod, which they supplement by snitching my fried clams, their forks darting out to stab one every few minutes. Not that I blame them. A deep-fried Ipswich clam, belly and all, dipped in tartar sauce, has to be one of the world's great delicacies, especially at McCrann's. I could never finish all of them.

"There's a new apartment complex for senior citizens going up just a few miles from Delilah's," Cassie announces.

"Squantum River Two? Another storage facility for unwanted antiques?" I say, trying to warn them off.

"Oh, no, it's even nicer." Cassandra's oblivious, or she pretends to be in a convincing way. "Federally subsidized, and you pay based on your income." She takes a pen and notebook out of her purse, and, sure enough, she's figured out my monthly income, and what I'd have to pay.

Last summer, just to appease my daughters, we went to a so-called open house. Everywhere we looked, down the long hallways, with numbered metal doors, grown-up children were visiting their parents, but nobody smiled. Irritation radiated off of them like heat off the pavement in July. In one empty hallway with no view, a man old enough to be my own father if he'd lived a normal life span sat and rocked in a wooden chair. His eyes were open but empty. No reaction whatsoever to all the people walking by. That's what the offspring do to you when your useful days have ended. Not mine. No way, no how.

"Remember that last place we visited?" I ask. "I couldn't get out fast enough. I decided then and there that I wasn't going to move. Ever."

"You should see the plans," she says, as if I haven't spoken. "It's gorgeous. Like a Club Med, right in the Boston burbs. Valhalla, I think it's called. It'll have a health club and a screening room right on the premises. They also have an assisted-living wing that you can move into when you're ready."

"Oh, and let me guess, another wing for those lost to Old Timer's disease. Another three-winged creature."

I sip my wine and speak softly, but my blood pressure, Old Faithful, is shooting upward. My daughters never stop.

"You'd be right around the corner from me," Delilah chimes in, proving, after all, that she can speak. "I could bring the girls over anytime you want. And they'll have full-time medical support, to make sure residents take their pills, stuff like that."

"I'm not decrepit. I know when and how to take my medications."

"We know people," Cassie adds. "We could get you moved to the top of the list."

"The developer owes Steve a big one," says Delilah.

"I thought we'd been through this." I feel angrier than I sound. "I thought I'd made myself clear on this point."

They shrug in unison, as if they'd practiced.

"We're worried about you, Mimi," Cassie declares. To my chagrin, several other diners turn around to look at us.

"We want to keep you around for as long as possible," adds Delilah.

"I'm happy where I am."

"You're in denial about your health situation." Cassandra.

"Am not."

"Are too."

"You're not safe where you are." Delilah.

"Not safe? Why not?"

"Even Steve says so. He says those windows are so flimsy, and with those shrubs around them, you're asking for a break-in."

Great, now we've got the cop in on the act.

"Plus it costs too much." Cassie.

"What if something happened?" Delilah.

"What if you slipped in the tub?"

"I put down those sticky butterflies."

"Or fell down in the bedroom?"

"I've got a phone in there."

"What if you couldn't reach it? You could be there for days."

"Without anybody knowing."

My chance to tell them about Duffy, but I won't.

Then Del launches into a story about her ex-husband's sister-in-law. Her elderly mother fell down in her bedroom the day after Christmas, her arm wedged between the headboard and the wall, and she was unable to reach a phone. For three days nobody called her because they'd all just seen her on Christmas. By the time one of her kids figured out the mother was MIA and got the super to let her into the apartment, the mother's more than half dead; semiconscious and dehydrated with the broken arm, which a week later had to be amputated because of all the damage done during the days she lay there helpless on the floor slipping in and out of it.

"I'm not elderly," I say, as if they'll listen.

"I'm pretty good on my feet. I'll study tai chi. They've got senior classes at the Y. And how on earth did her arm get stuck behind the headboard?"

"She was chasing dust bunnies." Cassie. "Behind a couple of Martinis."

"That's what they said." Delilah.

"I'll give up my Manhattans on cleaning day."

"Now she lives with one of her kids. They built a bedroom and a bathroom onto the back of the house, with a separate entrance. Nice place, but a major, major guilt trip."

"She's bitter. Angry and depressed all the time because of the lost arm."

"She lived for golf."

"Can you imagine? No more chipping or putting."

In my mind's eye, I see this gray-haired granny, in a visor and a golf skort, trying a one-armed swing. It just about kills me not to laugh.

"A tragedy that could have been avoided if she'd had appropriate living arrangements." Cassie.

"For a woman her age." Delilah. "In her situation."

"A built-in support system." Cass.

"You mean those alarm thingies you can pull in the bedroom and the bathroom? Or

that thing you wear around your neck?"
They nod together.

"And people to check up on you." Cassie.
"On a daily basis."

"Nosing into my business."

They shrug again, a syncopated move.

"It's only because we love you, Mimi."
Cassie. "That's the part you don't get."

"And we worry about you all the time."
Delilah.

"We've got a great superintendent, a fellow named Dick Duffy," I hear myself say against my own better judgment. "He's there 24/7. Keeps an eye on everything, just to make sure everything's OK. If I forget to pick up my mail, even for a day, he'll come check on me." That's all I'm going to say, and I hope I don't regret it.

By now Cassie's eyes look moist, and a tear is dripping down Delilah's lovely cheek. They're good. They're really, really good, my girls. First-class connivers, just like their old man.

"Put me in a pine box," I tell them now, but in a calmer voice. "That's how you'll move me out of my place. I've told you that before, and I mean it. The only way I'm leaving is in a pine box."

Last summer, on the way back home from that open house, so much fury raged in Cassandra's car, I'm surprised the windows didn't blow out. Me alone in back, the two of them in front, talking about me as if I wasn't there. As if I was just a memory, a bad one. Stubborn. Secretive. Sneaky. Self-centered. Cold.

So today, in the restaurant, looking out at the water, I make a promise.

"Cross my heart that I will never, ever be a burden to you." The two of them look at me with their beautiful blue eyes. "You, my lovely daughters, owe me nothing. I do not expect, nor would I ask for, end-of-life care from you. I want you to move forward, expect you to. Live your own lives. But please, let me make my own choices while I can."

Lunch goes smoother after that. We finish the wine and clean our plates, Cassie and Delilah ruining my plans to take home a doggy bag. Stuffed to the gills, we can't even think about coffee or dessert. We're heading back in Delilah's gas guzzler and again I hear the priest, *Remember man that thou art dust.* We'll be driving practically right by Gate of Heaven, and I think, Hey, why not introduce my daughters to their grandfather?

"Would you like to see where your grandfather is buried?" I ask. They try to catch each other's eyes, but it's tough with me riding shotgun and Cassie in the back. "Gate of Heaven. It's on the way."

Delilah says she knows how to get there, and next thing you know, we're at the gate. Most of the snow has melted, though icy mounds still shine against the stones. I look out across the acres of gray, glinting with old snow and ice.

We park and make our way along the concrete pathways, but this time I know where I'm going. Cassie stops before we've gone very far.

"What a dump," she announces. She's standing, one hand on her hip, a manicured finger on her chin. Turning this way and that, shaking her head, like a movie star from the '40s. Bette Davis or Joan Crawford. "This must be where they buried the poor people."

Delilah is looking all around too, but at least she doesn't bob her head. "It isn't taken care of very well."

"Well, it's an older cemetery. Lots of the people buried here don't have anyone left to tend their plots. That's what happens, sooner or later."

"Still." Cassie's snotty tone tweaks a nerve. Then I realize that's how we raised her, to believe she was privileged, a princess.

To expect the best, to demand it. I helped make her who she is.

"I guess I never showed you." My voice sounds thin and cold. Suddenly I'm flooded with sadness, like a cellar after weeks of rain.

Up ahead, beyond a chain link fence, is the backyard with the barbecue grill and the aboveground pool. In the background, not fifteen feet from where Da lies buried, is the clothesline, one of the round ones that spins on a metal pole. Underwear, frozen stiff, is hanging on it, men's cotton boxers in crazy prints — tigers on one, hearts on another — and women's bras and undies.

"Victoria's Secret knockoffs," says Cassie from behind me.

I kneel down to wipe dirt and snow off Da's stone. Instead I see his face, his shame and sorrow, a face he doesn't want me to see. He covers his face with his hands.

The ground's covered with icy slush. My knit pants soak it up. My girls reach down to help me up, one on each side, pulling me away, as if from something not one of us can bear to see. They stand close, not letting go. The three of us stand for the longest time, looking down at Da's grave and holding hands.

Joseph Daniel Sheehan
August 10, 1896–July 4, 1937

*. . . the world's more full of weeping than
you can understand . . .*

Four decades between the dates, me in his
life for only eleven years.

Del's voice breaks the cold silence. "He
died at forty," she says. "He didn't even
make it to the prime of his own life."

People aged faster then, I'm thinking, but
what I say is, "I want to be buried here. Put
me here when I pass."

"Would you stop?" Cassie screeches.
"You're so fucking morbid."

"Don't use that language around me!"
Can't tolerate the F word, never could, and
Cassie knows it.

Cassie's looking to Delilah, her ally, for
the nod, but Delilah's blubbering. What's
gotten into her? I wonder.

"We never knew him," she gasps, "we
never knew anything about him."

Then I see Da in the parlor, the cornet to
his lips, his music slipping and sliding all
around us. No, they never heard Da's music
nor saw his laughing eyes.

"Time to go." Cassie tugs on my arm.
Delilah's still snuffling. I want to comfort

her but don't know how. By the time we reach the Guzzler, she's going strong again, weeping and repeating, "We never ever knew him. You never told us anything," over and over.

"I'll drive," says Cass.

Delilah hoists me into the backseat, and the whole way to my place she weeps and snuffles. Reaching from the backseat, I pat her shoulder.

"We never had him in our lives, Mimi," she says again when we arrive. "I'll never know who he was. Neither will my girls. None of us ever will."

"I wish I could tell you more about him," I say, and in that instant, as Cass turns off the ignition, I'm overwhelmed with remorse. What would my girls' lives have been like if my father had been in them? "I don't even have his picture."

TWENTY-ONE:
PENNIES FROM HEAVEN

A couple of days later, Patty calls to tell me her grandson's project, the genealogy, is due, wailing like the earth might stop spinning if he doesn't get it in on time.

"We still have unanswered questions!" Including me in that first-person plural, though I do not include myself. "We've gotta call your dreaded Yik Yak Club into session."

"So what if we leave a few things blank?"

"Where can we meet? Not in public. No repeats of Keeley's birthday party."

A bust, the three of us plus Cassie, bawling at the pink table with the tea roses in the middle.

"How about your place?" she asks, like she's just that moment thought of it. But I know better: payback for wrecking Keeley's birthday.

"Sure, why not? I could make lunch." When I make this offer to Patty, I'm thinking only of us, the surviving Sheehan sisters — the Fab Four, Ruthie calls us. But Patty tells Cassandra, who immediately invites herself and then she calls a couple of her sisters to invite them, too. And they all call Patty — not me — to say they'll be there.

In a few hours, after countless phone calls and endless datebook checking, it's settled. Me and my sisters and a few — not all — of my daughters will get together for an official meeting of the Yik Yak Club. At my place, with the stipulation that I don't light up while the meeting's going on. The plan is, we'll bring our rag bags, we Sheehan girls. We'll piece the scraps together, try to stitch up the holes — not just in Aidan's genealogy, but in our lives as well. Not that I care all that much. I'm happy to go on as-is, holes and all.

As the big day approaches, I'm a bundle of nerves, like a pageant contestant facing the final judges. My daughters and my sisters. Well, not my sisters, really. I usually don't have to prove myself to them, except when they call me a drama queen, which makes me see red, and, when that happens, I cannot think, let alone prove, anything at all. But my daughters are another story. A harsh group. Exacting. Not anything like yours truly, who's always willing to cut a guy a break.

As grown-ups, my daughters have become divided into two camps, and each, for different reasons, finds me full of faults. Celestine and Ruth Ann on the one side; Cassandra, Siobhan, and Delilah on the other. I don't count Malvina, who's all by her lonesome in the Bronx.

Two peas in a pod are Celestine and Ruth Ann — a brainy but critical pod, self-certain, and one I prayed they'd break out of at Boston College, Jack Malloy's alma mater, where they graduated from, one year after the other. But no such luck. The pod got thicker. Trust the Jesuits to shape a really fine mind, and they've shaped four out of my six — five if you count Malvina, a Fordham dropout. Cellie, who tends to be a nitpicker, runs a copy desk at a newspaper in Philadelphia. Once she tried explaining what she did to me, and how important it was. Crossing t's and dotting i's and putting in periods and commas where they belong, plus checking facts, like is Nome or Fairbanks the capital of Alaska. All day long. So they can put it in the newspaper. What I got out of it is that my daughter bosses around a bunch of other nitpickers, and that she's paid well for it.

Ruth Ann is, or was, a folklorist, an expert

in American quilts, though I usually think of it as guilts. Now, she's mostly just a mother who sews all the time, stitching together bits of bright fabric in patterns so complex I get a headache just from looking at them. But who knows, maybe it's a skill that will come in handy for the YikYak Club.

Then there's Cass, who married well if income is your measure of success, a CPA with a big corporate practice named Michael Broome. You go girl, I said when she finally dumped him. Sweep him out of your life, Mrs. Broome. Once, at Christmas, all of us — me and Cassie and Mike Sr. and Mikey — went out to a Christmas tree farm to chop down their tree, which we would then drag home and decorate, celebrating the spirit of the season. This splendid tree would fill the big front window of their Georgian colonial, showing all their neighbors and the passersby how joyful they were. During the fall, they'd gone and tagged one, and now the day had come to chop it down. We rode around in a golf cart with a chain saw, and finally found the tree with the tag that said Broome Family. Right next to it was a bigger, nicer tree. Mike checked the tag. It was somebody he knew, a big-shot lawyer he couldn't stand. So he switched the tags and cut down the lawyer's tree and that's what we took home. The three of them thought it was hilarious, but I was mad enough to spit. When I told them so, Mike Sr. called me a killjoy. "What's your problem?" Cassie asked me. "Have you forgotten how to laugh?" Little Mikey, grinning, topped them both. "Get a life, Mimi," he said.

As for my two youngest, Del and Siobhan, the blond betrayers, they're still floundering around in their lives, with Jack Malloy always rushing to the rescue. Del's an efficiency expert at BankBoston who is always short of cash. And Steve buys the groceries and pays the household bills because, despite her MBA, she can't ever quite get her act together. So fragile, Delilah — bursts into tears at the slightest provocation, her lovely face and perfect body a container for unending sorrow, but you'd never guess by looking at her. And finally, the second youngest, Siobhan. A feminist scholar in Irish studies, her education dragging on, year after year, no end in sight. She's ABD, our Siobhan. That means, she explained to me, All But Dissertation, which is like a book she's got to write, but not one that I would like to read. Heading back to the old country every chance she gets, Siobhan is, with me reminding her, "Honey, you're going in the wrong direction. The ancestors couldn't wait to leave. They were lined up at the docks."

I'm a wreck over this all-important pow-wow, and I don't think very well when I get nervous, but Duffy, that prince, he helps. He suggests a deli platter, so I order up a nice big one with turkey, roast beef, baked Virginia ham, and several types of cheese; sides of pickles, potato salad, and coleslaw. We go together to pick it up, along with bags of chips and sodas and wine coolers and all the paper products I'll need to serve them. Everything fits nicely in the back of the Caprice.

We're heading back to Paul Revere, slowed, as usual, by the congestion in downtown Quincy, when I notice a white envelope half wedged in the crack between the seat and the seatback. Without thinking, I tug it out and see it's unsealed, with cash inside and the name Christopher J. Duffy handwritten across the front. Quicker than a wink, Duffy snatches it from my hand and sticks it into his own pocket. I want to melt into my seat.

"Thanks for finding that, Mrs. Malloy." He smiles, but he keeps his eyes on the road in front of him as we pull into the parking lot at Centennial Square. His cheeks are pinker than usual, his eyes a brighter hue.

"No problem," I answer, afraid I've just trespassed against him, finding an envelope full of cash with his son's name on it. I wish he'd meet my eye. He doesn't. *Forgive us our trespasses*, I pray to myself as we unload the Caprice, as if the incident didn't happen. We carry the bags inside and put everything where it goes, me clearing a big space in the fridge for the deli platter. After that, we walk to Hanrahan's Bakery in the Square for rolls, the very same bakery where Da used to buy those pastries. It's run now by the great-grandchildren, and still a first-class place. They've really kept up with the times, selling things I personally wouldn't dream of eating, breads filled with olives and sundried tomatoes and cheeses whose names I can't pronounce. I stick with my old favorites, the snowflake rolls and Parker House rolls, hot out of the oven. The smell of warm bread from that bakery drives me crazy. On the way back home, Duffy smiles with his eyes and says, "I won't tell if you don't," and we dip into the bag and share a warm roll. I've been forgiven, or my trespass has been forgotten. When the roll is gone, I take his hand and squeeze, and we walk home that way.

■ ■ ■ ■

The morning of our meeting, Duffy brings over folding chairs and a card table that he keeps in storage for just such occasions. He puts orange cones on the parking spaces nearest to my place so the girls won't have to walk too far, or drive around looking for a place to park. He attaches little signs to them with duct tape that say "Malloy Party." Just before the girls arrive, he shows up with a bouquet of cut flowers: mums, dahlias, and yellow roses. I open the door and he's standing there, holding this big bouquet from the florist down the street, his face bright red. Suddenly, my heart warms up, like it's wrapped in clover.

"For your table," he says, shoving the flowers at me, then taking off like a shy little schoolboy.

As I arrange the flowers in a vase, Lenox crystal — another gift from you-know-who — I forget about my dread of spending time with these women whom I love but do not always trust. It tickles me, the way Duffy shoved the flowers at me and took off, and it keeps tickling me every time I see them on my table. Before the others arrive, I sniff the flowers, convincing myself that I can get through what's coming next. Of course I won't say one word about him. Duffy and I agree on this point. We're just good friends. No big deal. Why drag the kids into it?

Twenty-Two:
I've Got You
Under My Skin

Keeley is the first to arrive, in one of those shiny jogging suits Cassandra favors. I give her a big hug. "I didn't mean to ruin your birthday," I say.

"You didn't, not at all," she insists with her sweet smile. "That happened a long time ago."

"I love you, Keel. I wouldn't hurt you for the world."

"I love you too, Mimi. You were the wind beneath my wings when I was growing up."

"The wind beneath your wings?" I'm about to make a crack when I realize Keeley's sincere, one hundred percent. I bite my tongue and hug her again. Realize, maybe for the first time, that Keeley is more precious than any of that fancy jewelry Frank buys for her. She helped me raise my girls, though I don't believe I've ever told her. Keeley gave them things I couldn't, like fun and her rapt attention: *Keeley's the best aunt EVER,* a continual refrain I heard throughout their childhood, although it hurt sometimes when my daughters didn't want to come back home to me.

Cassandra shows up with the twins, Jo and Patty, dressed in turtlenecks and sweatshirts and fur-lined boots. Patty's carrying a big box of pastries from Hanrahan's.

"Cream puffs and éclairs. A taste from childhood," Patty says, putting the box on my counter next to the deli platter.

Cassandra, in her pricey Talbots weekend wear, eyeballs me up and down, her lips curling. I'm back in my Rockport Walkers, my black pull-on pants, and a polyester top with purple flowers.

"Just want to be comfy," I say, not meeting her eye. "And besides, I'm not taking it public."

I carry their coats into the bedroom, and when I come back out, Ruth Ann's arrived but without her sidekick Cellie, who lives too far away to come.

"I like the orange cones, Mimi," Ruthie says. She's in jeans and a crewneck sweater, like she's still in college. "You must have good connections here."

"Oh, I do. Friends in high places."

"That Dick Duffy character, right?" says Cass, and my insides realign themselves.

When did she meet him? What does she know?

"Dick Duffy? Who's he?" asks Ruthie.

"The super," Cassandra answers.

Just then Delilah and Siobhan arrive, short-circuiting that line of conversation (yay!) and yapping about the traffic through the city and how the Big Dig is only making matters worse so far — all of the usual Boston laments, plus their gripes about the smell of tobacco in my place.

"I'm allergic, you know," says Del.

"I've opened the windows. You can sit right next to one."

"Daddy sends his best wishes," says Siobhan while I'm taking her coat.

"Yes, he told us to give you his regards," adds Del. Both are wearing full-length leather, butter soft, one caramel, the other forest green.

"Tell him he can stuff it."

"The least you could do is be polite, Mimi," says Delilah, outraged. "He's polite to you. It would make our lives so much easier."

"Less stressful," chimes Siobhan. "I don't know what you've got against him anyway."

"Against him? Shall I write a list? Send you a memo?" They shoot daggers at me. "Oh, I'm sorry, I'm sorry." I don't want to rekindle the old rage, but I can't help it sometimes. Its embers still glow hot beneath the ashes, ready to burst into flame at the slightest provocation. I lay their coats across my bed, take a few slow breaths, get myself together.

"I'll try to control myself."

"Please do," they say together.

Everybody comments on the pretty flowers, Cass happy because I've used her vase. "The crystal does those lovely flowers justice. Where'd you get them?" she asks. Everyone's waiting for the answer.

"A secret admirer," I say, but I know they don't believe me. It doesn't occur to them that anyone might buy me flowers, not even the lowly super.

Pretty soon, everybody's helping themselves and finding a spot to sit down, my daughters at the card table and my sisters at my window table, more people than I've ever fed in my place. They tell me how great the food is, and I tell them, "The only thing I did was drive over to the deli to pick it up. That's me, slaving over a hot takeout window."

When the time comes, when everyone's eaten and dropped their paper plates into the trash, we move the chairs into a circle in front of my couch as best we can, with the coffee table in the middle. Everyone except Delilah, that is, who keeps her folding chair by the open window in order to breathe clean air. I look around at the two generations, my sisters and my daughters, blondes and redheads plus Ruthie, the brunette. The younger generation is well groomed and lovely, done up right, the way I taught them. We older gals, Keeley excepted, are somewhat dowdy — Cassandra's word — having let ourselves go. Approaching our "use-by" date, or maybe past it. I look around my crowded living room, and those old bad feelings start to seep into me again.

If they could, they'd have me put away.

"Let's get back to Aidan's project," says Patty, who's wearing her WORLD'S GREATEST GRANDMA sweatshirt. She pulls a notebook and some files out of her tote, clicks her Bic, and looks at us.

"Yes, let's figure out what happened to Fagan and when it happened," says Cassandra, even louder, like she's the one in charge. She, too, has a notebook — a fancy little moleskin, along with her gold pen.

"Don't think it's any wonder we don't know," Patty says to Cass. "Our lives were in chaos when she was sent back."

"To Cullyhanna, County Armagh." Jo

"Leaving a big hole in our lives." Me. "Filled by Keeley."

All of us turn to Keeley, who looks at least a decade younger than her years, maybe because she raised golden retrievers instead of kids. She flushes, shaking her head no, when Siobhan cries, "Cullyhanna, County Armagh?" The words roll like music off her tongue.

"It's so beautiful there," she raves, her eyes lit up as if the words have flipped a switch. "You should see it."

"You've been there?" I can hardly contain my surprise. That's how much I know about my kid.

Siobhan nods.

"We don't know exactly when she left," says Patty, getting all excited too. "And we don't know when she died, only that it happened before Nana could send for her."

"We were grown-ups when we finally learned the cause of death. Marasmus." Jo looks around the room.

"Who told us?"

"Nana." Patty frowns at me, her pen and notebook at the ready. "On her deathbed."

"You were there, for heaven's sake," says Jo, her halo not on view today. Another black spot.

"Marasmus means starvation," Cassandra interjects. "I looked it up. Failure to grow. Emaciation as the result of protein energy malnutrition. It's fairly common in developing countries among young children."

"Fagan was five when she got sent away," I throw in.

"Fagan starved to death in Ireland?" asks Siobhan, and the pain of it almost knocks me over. Poor Fagan. And me, I let her go without a peep. Now, I swear, her warm breath is on my neck. She's on my lap after one of her tantrums, and I'm rocking her to sleep. Baby Fay.

"When she lived with us, she was anything but wasting," says Jo. "She was a spitfire, full of energy."

"Chubby," adds Patty, scribbling down a few words. "Something happened after she got sent over."

"Fagan, the holy terror," says Jo. "It came down to Fagan or Flanna. The war of the worlds."

"A death match?" asks Delilah, still by the open window, trying to breathe unpolluted air.

"Da had to choose, one or the other," Patty says. "He chose Flanna."

He chose Flanna. These three little words pitch me backward, pull the floor out from under me, make me lose my footing. Fagan: here today, gone tomorrow.

"Da gathered the rest of us together to explain," Patty says. "In the parlor, all of us sitting on the shiny sofa. 'We had to send your sister, Little Fay, away to Ireland to grow up,' he said. His face was wet with tears, and Flanna was crying too — the picture of desolation."

I take over, hearing Da's voice and imitating it: " 'She'll live with family, she'll learn how to behave, and then she'll come back home.' "

" 'Learn how to behave'?" asks Siobhan. "In Cullyhanna, County Armagh?"

"Someone's family was taking her in, Nana's or Flanna's. Nobody remembers."

"Then Da took out a map," Patty interrupts. "He pointed to a spot on it, the point in Europe closest to America, 'Not so bad, huh, my little beauties?' he told us" — Patty imitates his accent perfectly — "and he ran his finger on the map from Boston to Belfast, just a few inches after all. 'She's really not so far away. We'll send her letters and packages, OK?' "

Hearing Patty, my skin feels burned, the way it would after one of Flanna's punishments. She'd draw scalding water in the bathtub, force us to bathe in it, we three oldest girls together. She'd dare us to make the slightest sound: *You do, and I'll warm your little bottoms for you.* A joke, maybe, since our bottoms were already burning, and would for hours afterward.

"There must be someone left who'd know," says Cass. My sisters shake their heads.

"Flanna took all of our birth and baptismal certificates, whatever was left in Da's house, after Da died." Patty. "The house and all inside it, that's what Nana used to say. Da's uniform, his cornet, our mother's things, whatever few belongings we girls had."

"Then the house got torn down, for an exit ramp on Route 3A," I add.

"Our mother's things?" says Jo. "Flanna took them over the minute she arrived."

"Back then, you didn't throw good things away," says Patty.

"She didn't get the blue pendant," I say, "though who knows how it ended up with me, on my closet floor of all places."

"She smelled funny," says Jo.

"Like the herbs she was forever boiling." Patty. "She grew them in the yard, in a garden where we weren't allowed to go."

"Not anything like Mam's." Jo. "Her smell."

"What did Mam smell like?" asks Keeley.

"Like a Hanrahan's pastry," says Patty. "Sweet."

"You never knew when that hand of hers would fly out, smack you on the cheek," says Jo. "Or whatever body part was reachable."

"Flanna, not our mother," Patty clarifies.

"She'd hit you with whatever she was holding." Jo. "A hairbrush, a spatula."

"A soup ladle, a spade." Patty.

"Her cigarette." Me.

My daughters hum and chirp, their lovely feathers ruffled. Mine are ruffling too, a peculiar sensation deep under my skin. "Patty, how can you call us drama queens when you know all of us were hurt?"

Hurt. This hard little word ricochets around the room, repeated by the older and then the younger generation.

"Hurt," my daughters echo.

"Beaten or burned." The twins shake their heads no, but I hold my ground. "Or both."

Now my girls are whispering to one another, like I'm making it all up. I look at them, beautiful birds perched on the shaky limb of our family tree. Suddenly I'm furious at them, with the safe lives Jack and I worked so hard to give them, keeping everything from them so they'd never have to know. Made sure they'd never have bad dreams, never be afraid. Not once did I ever ask them for sympathy — and certainly not for pity — but a little bit of respect would go a long way. I roll up the sleeve of my big shirt with its pretty purple flowers. I hold my arm out so they can see a spray of scars.

"That was fat splatter from the stove!" wails Patty.

"Fat splatter," repeats Jo, looking like a bobble-head doll, nodding so hard just to agree.

"Daddy was cooking bacon," the twins recite together. "You were standing too close to the stove when he dropped the spatula and the fat splattered and burned your arm. That's what Daddy said."

Nope. I find the correct black spot inside my head: Flanna grabbed me and held me close to the stove. Slammed the spatula into the bubbling oil on purpose. She screeched when it hit my arm, not my face. I tried to run, but she grabbed my arm again. Looked at the blisters bubbling. Did this without anger, without any feeling I recognized. Her brown eyes were so beautiful — a place for getting lost in, the way Da did. But when I looked into her brown eyes, I refused to get lost. Refused to cry. Put on my plaster of Paris mask, the one I used so often growing up. A plaster mask that pushed Flanna closer to the edge. She reached for the pan of hot oil, ready to throw it at me. I broke away just in the nick of time. Whatever that means, the nick of time.

"It wasn't Da. It was Flanna. She burned me on purpose."

"When?" asks Patty. "When did she do that?"

"I don't know when. Can't remember."

"Traumatic amnesia," babbles Cassandra, scribbling into her notebook.

"Stop it, Mimi, just stop it," Patty begs.

"Things were bad enough." Jo. "Don't make them worse by making things up."

The twins glare at me, their faces white and hard.

My daughters steal glances at one another. Mad Mimi, telling another whopper, like the one about the secret admirer who gave her flowers.

"I'm not making things up. Eden and Alberta had scars too. Worse ones, and you know it. Flanna was jealous of their youth, their beauty. She didn't want to share Da with us, with anyone. She refused to let him love us." At least that's my theory, all I could come up with.

I roll down my sleeve, hiding the scars, closing off that memory, at least for now. To hell with my sisters' version of our lives.

Other memories roll toward me now like waves on the shores of the Fore River, after a big ship had been launched. I'm stepping right into that swirling cold water. I'm going to tell it like it was.

Twenty-Three:
Last Call for Love

Ruthie gets up and grabs a wine cooler, one of those fruity kinds that looks and tastes like soda. "Alcohol content, three point two percent," she reads. "I don't think that's strong enough to get me through this."

"I've got a box of something stronger in the fridge," I say. Next thing you know, my Franzia Chardonnay is out there on the counter, and they're all lined up, holding paper cups up to the spigot, even Cassie. I'm way too hurt to join them.

I watch while they fill up, my sisters and my daughters. I wish they'd all leave. I'd like nothing better than to light up, mix myself a Manhattan, call up Duffy, and turn on Sinatra's "If You Go Away." The last place in the world I want to go is back to Flanna hurting us, or to Fagan Sent Away.

But while I'm thinking this, Eden and Alberta show up and press against me, one on either side. They've got my arms, the three of us together, the way we were so often growing up. I remember Flanna chasing after Eden and Alberta with her Lucky Strikes. *Reach for a Lucky instead of a sweet.* Flanna's words to live by. I try to break free of these memories, to push them away again like I did before, but Eden and Alberta won't let me go.

"Flanna wasn't always vicious," Patty says, her face no longer icy white but flushed. The room is heating up now, even with the open window.

"That was the crazy part." Jo. "She could be sweet and caring, curling our hair, ironing our dresses, parading us in front of Da, showing off how well she took care of us."

"You never knew which Flanna you'd get." Patty.

The memory of the other Flanna cuts through me. I might've keeled over from the pain, but Al and Eden hold me up. *They take me into a terrible dark place, but it's familiar, with fearful sounds and smells. I gag. Switch off my ears and nose. Alberta holds my wrist, her little hand a clamp. Eden, on the other side, holds me too, but gently. She leans her head on my shoulder. Her silky hair feathers my cheek. "Amelia Earhart loves to fly," they whisper, and I join them. "Amelia Earhart will never die."*

I stumble between them, leg bones melting, until I recognize the place where they are taking me, the coal cellar of our house. The stink is worse. My throat closes up. I cannot breathe, no air. I struggle to break free, but Eden and Alberta hold me until Flanna steps out of the shadows. She holds aloft some type of pole, the poker, its tip glowing in the dark, red hot. "I'm your mother now," she says.

"We loved the good Flanna," says Patty, jolting me back in to my living room. "We wanted her to be that way all the time."

"That's why we never told on her." Jo.

"Fagan got the worst from her," I say.

"Worse than being burned with hot oil?" Ruthie asks.

"Fagan couldn't go with the flow," says Patty. "She was always fighting."

"Defiant." Jo. "It was her nature."

"Oppositional defiant disorder?" asks Cassie, the expert, using the new lingo.

"A brat," I answer. "Don't you remember when Fagan burned the shoes? The blue Mary Janes? Back before Flanna came?"

My living sisters chuckle, then I have to tell the story so my daughters get it. Fagan throwing the hand-me-downs into the fire, Da trying to pull them out, then buying her new red ones. My daughters love it, so I haul out another.

"Remember how Fagan was always taking off her diaper because she said she was a big girl, not a baby? Then she'd pee the bed again."

"Hey, that's my story, not yours," Patty cries.

"You didn't have to share a bed with her," Jo adds, like the two of them hold a copyright.

"No, but you two tried to climb in with us whenever she wet yours."

"We learned our lesson after Flanna came, though," says Jo. "The first night we told on her, she poured the chamber pot over Fagan's head."

"Showered her with pee," adds Patty. "Wouldn't let Fagan wash. Fagan had to sit in the corner all night, covered with pee."

"Chamber pot?" says Delilah, turning to look at us, risking an intake of foul air.

"That's right," I say. "That's how ancient we are. When we were growing up, people still kept chamber pots in the bedrooms at night. Houses didn't have fifteen bathrooms, not like now." Delilah's house had four at last count. She and Steve are planning major renovations.

"She poured it over Fagan's head?" Siobhan asks.

"Yes, she poured pee over Fagan's head

when she wet the bed at night."

Fagan, wet and smelly, whimpers in the corner of the bedroom. I sneak over to her so she won't be alone. Fagan, wet and whimpering, and me, a few feet away, whispering nonsense. "Wee Willie Winkie runs through the town." I can't hug her or even touch her because if I do I'll get her pee stink on me, and Flanna will find out.

"Flanna couldn't control her. Sometimes I could, and so could Da, if he was home. But not Flanna."

"Fagan never missed a chance to get Flanna's goat," says Jo. " 'You're not my Mammy, not Mammy.' She said it half a dozen times a day."

"Not Mammy."

The words ignite a fuse. It sparks and hisses in my skull.

"Flanna couldn't have children of her own." Patty. "Nothing made her madder than to be reminded of it."

"If only Da had known enough to stay single." Jo.

"That wasn't an option," says Patty. "And besides, he really did love Flanna."

"He was always spouting Irish poetry." Jo looks at my daughters, who watch us like we're actors in a foreign film and they're having trouble with the subtitles.

269

"Yeats," adds Keeley.

"Yeats shmates," I say, snapped out of my trance by their nonsense.

"He thought Flanna was an angel, or a creature from a poem." Patty. "His secret rose. That's what he called her. He worshiped the ground she walked on."

"Da and his poetry," cries Jo. *"A man that had six mortal wounds, a man violent and famous, strode among the dead . . ."*

"And that other one he used to read us, something about *No better than a beast, upon all fours?"* says Patty. "It was Da's favorite."

"That's when he was worshiping the ground Flanna walked on." Unbidden, Da appears to me like that; on his hands and knees, clutching at the ground. But where? Maybe in some sort of garden? But not Flanna's. Flanna isn't anywhere around.

"What was Da thinking, reading us that stuff?" Jo asks.

"Other kids got Mother Goose and we got 'Cuchulain Comforted.' " Patty.

My daughters watch, flushed and alert. Then Siobhan, almost always silent, speaks again. "Yeats? Your father read you Yeats?"

"Your grandfather," I say. "Even if you never knew him."

"The Rose, The Wind Among the Reeds,

The Tower, his favorite books," says Jo. "He always had one with him."

Da's poetry. I put it in the same category as Flanna's mumbo-jumbo.

"Awhile back, just for the heck of it, I picked up Yeats's collected poems," Jo says. "Flipping through the pages, I saw all these poems Da used to read to us, so I bought the book." She shrugs. "It isn't airplane reading, but it sure did bring back memories."

I shake my head. "Sinatra's all the poetry I need."

"Sinatra has never written a word," argues Ruthie. "Not one word."

"He only sings them," says Cassandra.

"Not even 'Nancy with the Smiling Face.' " Ruthie.

"Who cares? He sings my own feelings," I say. "*How far would I travel to be where you are? How far is the distance between here and a star?* I don't get that other stuff. Makes my brain hurt."

And again, I see Da, right there in front of me, just like my sisters, but unshaven, his blue eyes rimmed red and a crusted cut across one cheek. He's on his hands and knees, on the ground, a place that seems familiar even though I can't place it.

"The Ahearns never stopped blaming him

271

for our mother's death," says Keeley. She gets up with the box of Chardonnay, and walks around the room, slim and shapely, holding it up so the others can help themselves to refills. "Knocking her up so many times, I guess. Seven kids in eleven years. And then not having enough money to bury her. They paid for her funeral, the Ahearns did, and never forgave Da for it."

"When Da remarried, forget about it." Jo. "They were outraged. He didn't even wait a year."

"A year?" Patty laughs. "How long did he wait? No more than two or three months."

"After that," says Jo, "they didn't give a rat's ass about us." It's the strongest language I've ever heard her use.

"Flanna expected us to fall all over her with love from day one." Patty. "Alberta and Eden did. At least at first."

"Look where it got them."

Again, Siobhan speaks. "You said Flanna was right off the boat."

My sisters and I nod.

"We don't know where she came from." Patty.

"She was supposed to be some type of healer," I say, thinking about her garden, her awful concoctions. "The old folks were always coming by the house for remedies.

Healing potions."

"And also for help with their bad luck." Jo. "Can you imagine?" She and Patty laugh. "Flanna, making their lives better."

"She gave them herbs, elixirs, prayers to say." Patty.

"Flanna might have been a *cailleach,*" says Siobhan, who, after all, is ABD in Irish Studies.

"A what?" we chorus.

"Kyle-yuck?" I try to copy Siobhan's pronunciation, but the word won't go deep enough into my throat.

"Cailleach," Siobhan repeats, the strange word tumbling all through my childhood, like when Flanna pushed me down the cellar stairs. "A faerie healer."

"Faeries? Jesus," chime her sisters.

"What was that word?" I want to hear it again, this word I can either pronounce nor spell.

"Cailleach," Siobhan repeats, yet again, and looks at her sisters. "Laugh if you want, but faeries weren't always funny leprechauns, wee folks on cereal boxes. Back in the last century, in rural Ireland, an entire preliterate cosmology —"

" 'Preliterate cosmology'?" Cassandra and Ruthie echo, a sharp edge to their voices, a warning. If Siobhan gets too big for her breeches, they'll cut her down with her own words, a life skill the Sheehans and the Malloys have both perfected.

"An entire world view was built around this belief in faeries, the so-called good people, who weren't always good but could also be sneaky, spiteful, and treacherous. Kind of like the Irish themselves."

Speak for yourself, I want to say, but stop.

"I thought it might relate, you know, faerie belief," Siobhan adds. "You said Flanna poured the chamber pot over Fagan's head."

"What's that got to do with it?" I ask.

"Maybe nothing. But it is something a *cailleach* might do if she thought the faeries had taken over a human child."

"The revenge of the faeries," says Ruth Ann.

Del and Cassandra giggle. "Taken over a human child?" Delilah asks.

"Laugh if you want," says Siobhan in a snippy voice, like she's arguing that Tom Cruise is better-looking than George Clooney and nobody agrees. "But I'm telling you, it was powerful stuff. It kept the peasants in line long after the Catholics converted them."

"Flanna used to tell us the faeries took our mother off on a white horse." Patty looks at Jo, then Keeley. "She died from toxemia, but Flanna said the faeries took her."

"She said the faeries wore shining white robes and had beautiful long hair." Jo. "I thought faeries were like angels. I thought it was a good thing."

"Some faeries are like angels," says Siobhan. "According to the myths, they were angels before they got kicked out of heaven. They kept their wings."

"Kicked out of heaven? Kept their wings?" Cass, Del, and Ruthie think that's hilarious. Their cackles cut right through me.

"Thanks for the lesson, Professor Smarty-Pants," says Cass. "Very edifying!"

Again, Del and Ruthie chuckle.

"She said we had a *piseog* on us," says Jo. "Flanna did."

"A *piseog*?" Siobhan perks up again. A *piseog*. That's news to me. More language I don't understand.

"Faerie nonsense," Patty says. "That's what Nana called it."

"No, no," says Siobhan, her eyes bright, her fingers fidgeting. "It's a spell, a curse. Like voodoo. Somebody puts an object in or near your house. Rotten meat, say, wrapped up in something belonging to your family. Maybe a towel or a diaper stolen from the clothesline. A lock of hair from a dead child. They'd put it in the cellar, or under the front steps, make an evil wish. Its spell would keep working unless someone found it and burned it to ash."

"A faerie healer," several of them murmur, turning the words over like precious objects they desire, even though they can't quite appreciate their worth.

"Yes," I say, "a faerie healer who brought every last one of us to heel."

"Healer, my tush," says Jo. "She was a drunk, like Da."

Now you could hear a pin drop. Dead silence. Poor Da. I never told my girls. Not a word about Flanna or my scars; not a word about Da's drinking. Not to mention Fagan. No point. I couldn't stain their lives with so much shame and sorrow.

"Well, it's true, isn't it?" Jo says. The Chardonnay has gone straight to her head. "Much as we all hate to admit it. We're all ashamed."

"Shame is toxic," says Cassandra, our own resident healer. "Always toxic."

"I was wondering when we were going to get to him," Ruth Ann interrupts in that tone she used on me at Dunk's. "Where was he in all of this? Didn't he take any responsibility?" Her cheeks too are flushed, and her eyes shine the color of the sky outside.

"He was the kindest, the most loving man I've ever known," I say, and I glimpse him on the steps of our old house, passing out our cookies, teasing us with magic, his spiky hair, his dimpled smile.

"But weak, obviously, and irresponsible," answers Ruthie. She looks to Cass. They nod in agreement. I'd like to smack them both.

"I wouldn't say that at all," interrupts Patty, the potentate. My daughters wouldn't dream of talking back to her. "He did the best he could under terrible circumstances, most of which he couldn't control. Don't forget the Depression. Everyone was out of work."

"When our mother was alive, he was always working," says Jo. "He was a riveter, a hellish job, hot and dangerous, all through the Depression. That's how he bought the house, and kept it, even in the worst of times. He had a second job, part-time, as a chauffeur for a wealthy family, the Mortons. Not to mention playing his horn whenever he had the chance. He provided. He treated us like queens, or maybe princesses. At least until Mam died, and *she* came along."

No need to specify who "she" is.

"Called us his bouquet of beauties. Remember, Mimi?" says Patty. And I nod, because I do. Words I'll never forget, nor the sound of Da's voice when he said them. *My little bouquet of beauties.*

"Then everything fell apart."

"The shipyard just about shut down in the '30s," Patty says. "The workforce reduced to a few hundred. The Mortons lost everything in the Crash; our mother died. He married Flanna, who couldn't handle Fagan. Fagan got sent away. The rest is history."

"He turned into a drunk?" asks Ruth Ann.

"That's what some people said about him," I say. "But the way I think of it, Da just couldn't chew and swallow all the bitter pills life dished out to him. He got a handful, all at once."

"Bitter pills," Jo repeats.

"What about everybody else? Your aunts and uncles? Your neighbors?" asks Ruth Ann.

"The other grown-ups?" Patty shrugs. "All of them had troubles of their own. Hard times. We grew up during hard times, honey, not like now."

She looks at my daughters who are all, I see, quite beautiful, the way my sisters and I used to be. The difference is, they've never once gone hungry, or worried about how to make ends meet. They've never had the rug pulled out from under them just when they thought they'd finally found their footing.

"No, we didn't talk about it." Jo. "And nobody, not our aunts or uncles or grand-parents or neighbors, asked us anything. Nobody wanted to know. Da had married a beautiful young woman to give his girls a mother. We had a mother. It was official. That's all that seemed to matter."

By now the sun is setting. My apartment, sterile with its beige walls, the sheer white curtains at the windows, is full of shadows, plus the spirits of Eden and Alberta. Then there's Da, on his knees, in that strange place of earth and stones. Behind them, in a darker place, is Flanna — enchanting Flanna, our stepmother.

But where could Fagan be?

"How about some coffee?"

I get up to put on a pot, hi-test, just what everybody needs. I end up making a second pot to have enough to go around. I swear my black spots throb.

When everybody's got coffee and are settled back in their seats — me in my throne, the La-Z-Boy — Cass grabs the box from Hanrahan's and picks out an éclair.

"Hog," says Ruthie before she takes the box and grabs one too.

The box makes its way around our circle,

nobody worried about plates or napkins, or about carbs or fat grams or calories. We've got bigger fish to fry. Soon all of us are drinking coffee and pigging out on those scrumptious treats.

"The world's more full of weeping," says Delilah, out of nowhere. She turns toward us, forcing herself to breathe the air in my apartment. She chews thoughtfully on a cream puff. *"The world's more full of weeping . . ."*

"Than you can understand," adds Cass.

"That's a Yeats poem, 'The Stolen Child,' " says Siobhan.

"The stolen child," Jo and Patty chime.

"That's written on his gravestone," says Delilah. "Your father's."

"Your grandfather's," corrects Patty.

"Mimi brought us to the cemetery on Ash Wednesday," Del explains to Ruthie and Siobhan, like they missed out on something big.

"Mimi brought you to the cemetery?" Ruthie points to me as though I'd committed a sin.

"Da always used to read that poem," says Keeley. "I remember the weeping part."

"It's so depressing. Why would he pick that for his headstone?" says Cassandra.

"He didn't pick it." Patty is outraged.

280

"How could he pick it? He keeled over at forty. Right in front of us. He wasn't planning to die."

"Come away, O human child!" Siobhan recites. *"To the waters and the wild, with a faery hand in hand, for the world's more full of weeping than you can understand."*

Come away, O human child! I've heard those words before, but the sight of Da keeling over, right in front of us, collides with them. My late sisters, Eden and Alberta, give me a good hard shake. Flanna. She's the one who said them.

Twenty-Four:
Looking for Yesterday

Next thing I know, Ruthie's gathering her purse and parka. "Gotta go be a soccer mom," she says, blowing air kisses to her aunts and heading toward the door. "I'm not all that into Yeats."

She pauses and looks back, gesturing to Delilah and Siobhan, expecting them to join her. I do too. Thanks for the memories, Mimi. We're outta here. Then they'll stand outside in the parking lot gabbing about all my shortcomings. But the blond betrayers stay. The truth about Da's death has got them riveted to Duffy's folding chairs. They don't even wave good-bye to Ruthie.

The minute she's gone, Cassandra pulls a folding chair next to my recliner. She drops her pen and notebook; holds one of my hands in two of hers. "Your father keeled over right in front of you?"

The twins and Keeley nod.

"He died on the Fourth of July," says Del.

"In 1937. It's on his gravestone."

"Two days after Amelia Earhart disappeared." Patty.

"Amelia Earhart?" Del.

"It was all over the news." Jo gestures to show the big headlines. "Amelia Earhart and her copilot, Fred Something, disappear over the Pacific."

"Without a trace. Until a year or so ago, right?"

Jo nods. "An explorer found a rubber heel and an empty whiskey bottle on that island in the South Pacific where they supposedly went down."

"The copilot having been, supposedly, a drunk." Patty. "More booze on board than fuel."

"That whole first week of July, it was all anybody talked about." Jo. "Biggest news ever."

"Amelia Earhart, the beautiful, high-flying aviatrix, disappears without a trace." Keeley. "Not that I remember. Too young, but I've read a lot about it."

"Remember Nana in the kitchen?" Jo asks. "With the RCA Victor radio turned up loud so she could hear it while she worked? She wanted every detail."

"We lived with Nana then." Patty. "We girls got up and got dressed to go to the

Independence Day parade. Nana had ironed our best dresses, and we got to wear our shoes."

"We couldn't wait to go, but Nana wasn't in the mood to celebrate anything." Jo.

"She'd seen enough parades."

"She made us toast and eggs, and sent us off." Patty.

"While we ate, the radio was on, Amelia Earhart gone." Jo. "We kept looking at each other."

"We three oldest were thinking about our silly rhyme. *Amelia Earhart loves to fly. Amelia Earhart will never die.*"

"But she did," my daughters chorus as I slip back to that hot bright Fourth, humid with a pounding sun.

"We heard the drums before we even got there." Keeley.

A pulse that ran through my body as we squeezed our way out to the front, the six of us together, holding hands. Eden, Alberta, Maire, Josephine, Patty, and Keeley, the glorious Sheehan girls, in our pretty summer dresses, our faces shiny bright, our hair curled and tied with ribbons, our patent leather shoes buffed to a high shine.

"There were floats, marching bands, baton twirlers, and old soldiers with pins and ribbons on their chests. They marched right by

284

us," says Patty, the great historian. "The parade went on and on. Sousa marches. And finally, a military band, like the one our father used to play in."

"That's when we saw Da." I see him again, emerging slowly, as if from one of those Polaroid cameras, the picture blurred at first, then turning crystal clear. "He ran out behind the military band, trying to catch up." Wire-thin Da, running, running, running, trying to catch up to the parade. The jacket of his uniform! I know it from the cedar chest upstairs, but its shiny buttons are unbuttoned. The sides flap out like broken wings.

"He ran and ran, holding on to his cornet." Keeley.

"I couldn't wait to hear him play." Patty. "I felt so proud, Da joining the parade."

"But the minute people noticed him, they started to laugh." Jo.

"I wanted to run out to march with him," Keeley says. "But you, Mimi, you pulled me back."

"I called out to him, right?" I ask my sisters. "Didn't I call out, 'Daddy, stop, it doesn't matter,' but he didn't hear me." The people around us just laughed harder.

" 'We don't care about a stinky old parade!' Jo and I yelled," says Patty, all excited, this shared memory keeping us together, Da keeling over right in front of us, his life over and ours hardly yet begun. "We kept yelling, but he didn't hear us, never saw us."

My late sisters nudge me, longing to be included.

"Eden and Alberta were paralyzed, weren't they?" They press against me once again, just like they did that day. "Even Alberta, who loved a good laugh better than anything." They clung to me and to each other, watching Da run.

"All around us, everyone laughed. 'Joe Sheehan, drunk again.' " Patty. " 'Look at Joe, that fool.' "

" 'A shame, with that beautiful girl he married,' " adds Keeley. " 'If I'd been lucky enough to get her, I'd behave myself.' "

" 'Oh, yes, the second Mrs. Sheehan is a beauty.' " Jo imitates those awful accents, those brogues we Sheehan sisters refused to speak. " 'And him with all those lovely girls to raise.' "

Slow down, slow down, it doesn't matter, I screamed, or wanted to; the way he was running made me afraid.

"He ran right past us," says Patty. "A short way down the street, he fell." He fell flat, like a tree that's lost its roots, all at once.

Slam, onto the ground, facedown. "Like in a cartoon. Splat!"

"Laughter, a great roar of laughter," says Jo. " 'Joe Sheehan, that drunk.' "

Nobody moved to help him, not even us. The others talked and pointed and snickered as if we weren't there.

"Their words cut deep," says Jo, hugging herself, protecting herself from those still-sharp blades.

Cassandra squeezes my hands. Across the room, Delilah and Siobhan huddle against the window, clinging to each other. They stare at us as if they are looking at a wreck on the highway. Rubbernecking. Curiosity factor, clogging traffic everywhere.

"Everything stopped when Da fell." I realize this as I say it. "My life ground to a halt and I had trouble starting it up again."

"The parade kept going." Jo. "Another damned Sousa march."

"Down a street lined with red maples." Keeley.

"Nothing I hate more than a Sousa march," says Patty. "Makes my blood boil."

Not a single Sheehan sister disagrees.

"Da-didda-da-da-da," Jo stutters, a Sousa tune, "Da-didda-da-da-da!"

"Shut up!" commands Patty.

"You'd think we'd be wailing like banshees," says Keeley, looking at my daughters, "but not one of us made a sound."

"It took forever for the parade to pass," says Patty. "Then we ran across the street to him."

I remember somebody rolling him over, but I looked away. Da lying on the ground, peaceful, like he was sleeping, but I knew it was something worse.

"I couldn't look at him. I looked at the grass around him, soft and green, like the grass he raved about in Ireland. The grass where Fagan lived."

All of us are stuck there, in the sunlight, on the roadside long ago.

"Faerie struck!" Siobhan's voice rings out like a bell, calling all of us to attention. "Your Da was faerie struck."

"Faerie struck?" Delilah elbows Siobhan, a good hard jab.

"Zapped by faeries. Having a stroke."

We stare at Siobhan. Her silky pale skin turns pink, her eyes a deep, deep blue.

"That's the etymology of the word 'stroke.' "

"Etymology?" Cassandra grimaces.

"Sounds like a disease." Delilah. "Contagious."

"Its source," Siobhan explains. "Isn't that what he died of? A stroke?"

"Of drink," I say. "Drank himself to death. Pure and simple."

"You don't keel over like that from drink."

"Since when did you get a cause of death?" Cassandra reaches for her sparkly pen and notebook.

"I could hardly think about it, ever," I tell Siobhan. "Thinking of my father dead drunk on the roadside. No. It made me so ashamed."

"We were only kids." Jo. "What did we know?"

"Then Aunty Alberta followed in his footsteps," says Cassandra, like she understands everything. "She carried on the family tradition, substance abuse, and after her, her son, my cousin Danny."

"I'll bet it was a stroke, not alcohol," says Siobhan. "It goes back to the faeries."

All eyes turn to her. I'm relieved, can't help it. We've got another lunatic in our midst.

"Is it any wonder I needed therapy?" says Cass, scribbling into her notebook. "Or that I keep recommending it?"

"Before anybody understood a thing about brain hemorrhages," Siobhan continues, ignoring her, "or any other type of cardiovascular issue, if someone suddenly became paralyzed, experienced aphasia, or maybe even dropped dead in their tracks, they were called faerie struck."

"You were orphans, you and your sisters." Delilah, on the brink of a breakdown.

"We never thought of ourselves like that," says Jo. "We had Nana. She took us in without a second thought. Lace curtain, not shanty, that's what we Sheehan sisters were. Plus we had each other. That made us as good as anybody else. At least, we thought so."

"Nana refused to give us any pity, and we didn't pity ourselves." Keeley.

"Wasn't your father born in Ireland?"

"Your grandfather," somebody corrects.

"In the north, County Antrim. The family worked in shipbuilding. For a while, his family went back and forth. But his mother, Nana, once she settled here, she wouldn't allow any talk about the old country or the old ways. 'We're here, now. Look ahead.' Nana meant it, believe me."

"Half our roots are missing." Siobhan looks pained. Maybe that's what she's searching for every time she goes back to Ireland. "When we were growing up, you never said a word about our grandparents. Never once mentioned your own father."

It's true, I didn't, but I didn't plan the silence. I didn't do it on purpose; it just happened.

"He was a lovely man, but life just didn't go his way," I say. "That's all you need to know."

"But we're just now finding out about him." Delilah.

"We've got holes in our family history." Cassandra.

I shrug, afraid she'll start to cry again. All of them on the verge of a meltdown, the room a bubbling pot of anger and sorrow.

"What did you do?" Delilah, face scrunched, holding back the tears. "I mean, with your father, on the roadside, dead. What happened next?"

"We just stood there," says Patty. "We didn't know what else to do."

"We didn't do anything, only looked," says Jo.

"Everyone forgot us. We were standing in plain sight, but it was as if we'd been erased." Keeley.

"Finally a couple of our uncles, Leo and Teddy, got to him." Patty.

"I saw his cornet in the grass. I picked it up." Keeley.

"Our uncles hoisted him up and rushed with him back to Nana's." They lifted him from the ground carefully, lovingly, and without a sound, cradling Da the way he'd carried me that time he took me to the doctor's.

"We followed them back to Nana's house, running down Commercial Street, away from the parade."

When we walk through Nana's front door, it's like entering an ice cloud, a place where I can't see or feel. The only sense I have is sound, and what I hear, through hushed voices of frantic grown-ups, is Nana's aching cry. "No, God, no. Please don't take my Joe. No, God, not my Joey, no."

"Our uncles sent Jo and me upstairs to find a clean white sheet in the hallway closet," says Patty. "We stood there for the longest time, maybe hoping that if we froze, right there, we could stop what was coming next."

"We looked through stacks and stacks of crisp and neatly folded linens, ironed by Nana on the mangle in her kitchen." Jo. "One of our uncles hollered from downstairs. 'Whatcha waitin' for? Hell to freeze over?'"

"We chose a sheet with yellow flowers along the edge, flowers Nana embroidered for her dowry," says Patty.

"Years before Da was born." Me, because Nana told me, showed me all her beautiful linens in that closet. Tried to teach me to embroider, with silky threads and a flashing needle, but I was all thumbs; couldn't ever learn. "That's what they used to cover Da before the undertakers came and carried him away." Everyone's so quiet we hear the hum of my Frigidaire, the slamming of car doors in the parking lot. I toss in two more cents' worth. "The whole world wept for Amelia Earhart, but we were the only ones who cried for Da."

"The rest is history," says Keeley.

"History? What history?" Cassandra holds her pen, her fancy little notebook, ready to take it all down.

Slowly, Jo and Patty start to unwind the rest of it, a film with hazy pictures, but I'm stuck in Nana's house, my da covered in the sheet, even his face, especially his face; his handsome, handsome face, the one I'd built my world around. Sun and moon. Stars and planets. The entire solar system. No matter what he'd ever done or failed to do, Da remained the center of everything. He was the known world.

Within hours, Flanna Flanagan claimed him. She barred all of us, even Nana, from the wake and funeral. There was no way for us to say good-bye. Flanna buried him according to her own wishes, and ages passed before Nana found his plot in the Gate of

Heaven Cemetery.

"When Da died, we weren't allowed to cry, so I used to think about how he put his beloved horn away."

"His ritual," Jo says, smiling.

"Everything had to be done just so." Patty.

"At night, to keep myself from crying, I'd imagine the hands of angels getting him ready to be put away, with the same care he used to put away his horn. They would bathe him and shave him and comb his hair and change his clothes. They would turn him back into handsome Da, the man who always made me laugh and always made me proud."

"The riveter, the chauffeur." Jo.

"The musician, the poet." Keeley.

"The good father who ran with me to the doctor's when I broke my arm."

"Who walked us home, up the hill." Patty.

"Who brought us treats on payday." Jo.

We're all silent until Delilah demands, "That's it? The end? The angels cleaned him up?"

"Oh, these angels were so beautiful," I say. "Like on the cards Cassie sells. They took their time, working with great care. They laid Da out in a beautiful box lined with red velvet." I give my girls a chance to pick on me for being such a nut. They don't.

"The angels stretched him out in this box, and I could see him snug and safe. Nothing could hurt him anymore. Like his cornet in its case. Then the angels closed the lid and snapped shut the brass clasps, just the way Da did with his horn."

"Before last week, you never even took us to the cemetery." Cass.

"You never said a word about him." Del.

"And all this time, Mimi," says Siobhan, her face lit by the late sun and her own strong feelings. "I could have been looking for Fagan. I was right there, in the place she got sent to. I might have been able to find the place where she's buried."

TWENTY-FIVE:
BEGIN THE BEGUINE

It's after dark by the time my sisters and my daughters have sobered up and gone. The box of Franzia is empty. So's the box from Hanrahan's. I throw them into a giant trash bag, along with all the paper cups and plates. The bag of trash is full, but I get that old empty feeling. The Yik Yak Club accomplished nothing except stirring up more sorrow. Eden, Alberta and Fagan, Mam and Da, Nana — all gone. Which is exactly why I prefer to look ahead instead of back. And the Yik Yak Club never even figured out the date of Fagan's departure, the main purpose of our meeting. I head out to the Dumpster with the bag and toss it in. I'd like to do the same with my childhood. Back inside, I go to close the windows and the blinds and see Duffy outside, picking up the cones. He's had his share of losses, but he always seems to know exactly what he's doing, and what he has to do next. That bum leg doesn't stop him or even slow him down. It must be badly scarred, with all that shrapnel in his thigh. Scars everywhere. . . . Nobody escapes.

I go back to cleaning up. A few minutes later, he's knocking on my door. I know the sound by now.

"Mrs. Malloy," he says as I open it. "I hope I'm not disturbing you."

"That happened awhile back," I say, flushing while he grins. "You'll be picking up those chairs and the table?"

In a sec, we've got them folded, ready to go. I carry the table behind him as he takes the chairs to a storage closet at the end of the hallway.

"How about a cup of coffee?" I ask him when we're done. "I just brewed a fresh pot."

"Can't turn down a cup of your coffee, Mrs. Malloy," he says, but I know what he really wants is company, my company. As I want his. Next thing you know, we're back at my place, and I turn on Sinatra. Nothing like good, soothing music. No torch songs tonight.

"You've got some hungry women in your family," Duffy says when he sees the little bit of cold cuts left. Two pickles. A tablespoon of potato salad. Not a chip or a crumb of pastry in sight.

"You know it. Just enough left to make you a sandwich."

"Twist my arm."

When we're settled on the couch, and he's digging into the nice, thick triple-decker I've built for him, he asks how the get-together went. I shrug.

"They yak and yak, but we never get to the heart of what happened. At least, I don't think we do."

"You could just let it alone, Mrs. Malloy," he says, taking a long swallow of hot coffee. "Happened so long ago. Let sleeping dogs lie."

"My philosophy precisely," I tell him. "That's what I've done all my life, but the dogs aren't sleeping anymore. They're awake and howling."

"The silver pendant with the blue stone," he says. It's almost, but not quite, a question. I nod again.

"Not to mention Patty's damned genealogy."

I curl up next to Duffy on my couch, smoking and drinking coffee, while he finishes his sandwich. With my remotes, he switches off Sinatra, and switches on the television news to catch the weather report. I tell him how Fagan was sent away and died before we could get her back; sent to Cullyhanna, County Armagh, but nobody knows when she passed, or even where she's buried.

"You've got to keep track of where your dead are buried," Duff says, and I think about his chore during the war. How he kept track of the bodies of those boys, no matter what condition they were in, every bit and piece, to make sure they got back home. Their families got to keep whatever was left of them, and to know where they'd been laid to rest. I'm lost in thought when Duffy grabs the remote and turns up the volume on the TV.

I watch him watch TV for several moments before I tune in, something about the high-tech prison complex, on thirty acres of rural land in Bridgewater. A state-of-the-art place, the Bridgewater Correctional Complex, aka the Old Colony Correctional Center.

The reporter, a young Asian woman, stands in front of a high fence and a sprawling brick building. "Even the name 'Old Colony,' " she says, "signals what's going on here, a new type of corrections. In deference to our early settlers, its name fosters a sense of hope and renewal."

"Good lord," I say, but Duffy's mute.

"In keeping with the theme of hope and renewal," the reporter continues, "each of the housing units within the institution is named after a Revolutionary War hero." Among them, Paul Revere, naturally, plus Patrick Henry, William Dawes, and Crispus Attucks.

"Can you believe it? Just like Centennial Square," I say, but Duffy just stares at the screen. The most innovative part of the complex, the reporter informs us, is the Treatment Center, capital letters, the place for sexually dangerous persons. Rapists, pedophiles, predators, sex traffickers.

"Here, men committed both civilly and criminally are mixed together, treated together, in the most humane but rigorous way possible."

" 'Sexually dangerous persons,' " I murmur, just to try it out.

"The only problem so far," the reporter says, "is overcrowding. There are now more inmates than the most generous projections allowed for, and almost more than the facility can handle. Most of the men are double-bunked in single rooms."

Microphone in hand, the reporter strolls up to the fourteen-foot-high chain link fence, which is topped with razor wire. She pats it with her pretty hand. "Behind this fence is another identical fence," she says, and the camera zooms in close so we can see the second row of fencing. "In between the fences are motion sensors, connected to a microwave system that alerts the towers the moment an intruder is perceived." She smiles and steps closer to the camera, which zooms in on her face.

"It's impossible to get out of here until they decide to let you go," she says. Then the program segues to an ad for tartar-control toothpaste. Duffy clicks off the TV and clicks back on Sinatra.

"Maybe your daughter wasn't so far off," he says, as if the past few minutes hadn't happened. He puts his arm around me, pulls me closer. "I mean, when she said you have some kind of post traumatic stress disorder."

"Maybe I do," I answer, not exactly willing to concede the point, yet feeling myself softening in the sadness of all these recollections.

"Not a flaw, just a fact," he murmurs, hugging me tighter. I lean against him, a thrill to press my cheek to. Sinatra croons and we smoke and drink our coffee, not talking for a while.

Twenty-Six:
I'll Never Smile Again

The next morning, the phone starts ringing before I even get a chance to pour my first cup. I've got no desire to chat with Cass or my sisters. Not interested. But I give in on the seventh or eighth ring.

"I'm so glad I caught you, Mimi," cries Ruthie, panting, her voice edged with a siren's squall.

"Is everything OK?" I ask. "The boys? They're OK?"

"Do you know who your super is?"

"My super?" I feel the air whoosh out of me, her question like a puncture wound. I grab hold of the kitchen counter.

"Dick Duffy. I met him outside yesterday. We introduced ourselves. Well, I introduced myself to him and we talked for a while. I wanted to make sure he keeps an eye on you."

Oh, Duffy, don't, I'm thinking. Don't betray us. Don't break our promise to each other.

"The name, his name, rang a bell, a distant bell, but still I had to check it out."

"There's millions of Duffys. It's like Smith or Jones. Common as common could be."

Not a black spot, but a black hole, opening up this time. *Last night when you came over, you didn't even tell me you'd met my Ruth Ann.*

Ruthie has always been our doyenne of disaster, our catastrophe collector, forever calling with some horror story or another. She's addicted to true crime books and reads at least three newspapers every day, and always the most gruesome stories. She'll retell them to anyone who'll listen: The mother who left her kids in the car on a hot day while she shopped and came back to find them roasted like capons; the boys in her town who sledded down a steep hill right into an oncoming SUV; a kid who committed suicide by hanging himself from the mouth of the soccer goal at the school where his mother was the principal. Her latest, pedophile priests, one of them from Fall River who admitted to molesting more than a hundred boys and girls, an equal-opportunity offender. She goes on and on about them, half the time quivering with fear and the other half marching into battle.

This time, it's battle.

"No, Mimi, I did my research before I called. I saw the news story about the new prison. I put two and two together. Your Dick Duffy there is the father of a pedophile."

My Dick Duffy.

Ruthie pauses to let her words sink in, and I sink down the side of my counter. I crumple into myself, like those accordion cups they used to sell so you could take your pills even if you weren't at home. They had a little cover and collapsed to fit right into your purse or pocket. I'm small enough to do that now.

"His name's Christopher. Convicted on multiple counts of sexual assault on minor children. You remember. Don't you? He was a martial-arts instructor, and you know how pedophiles always find ways to be with kids. That's a fact. Now he's doing, like, twelve years at Bridgewater. Not half enough in my opinion. Do you know how freaking hard it is to get a sex-abuse conviction?"

I don't. "Not a clue," I whisper.

"So damned hard," she goes on, suddenly an expert on the criminal justice system. "From what I've read, the evidence against him is overwhelming. So many victims. He —"

"No. No, I don't want to hear."

"Most child abusers have themselves been abused as kids —"

"Stop, baby, please stop."

"Mimi, are you OK? You're not in some kind of relationship with this guy, are you?"

"No. No I'm not," I'm able to declare with a bit more strength.

"Be careful, Mimi. Just be careful. You're so vulnerable."

"I'm ancient, honey, not a child. Who'd want me? Anyway, the sins of a son, should they be visited upon the father?"

"It goes the other way," my daughter contends, as if I didn't know. "The apple doesn't fall far from the tree. We've always agreed about that. I thought you'd want to know."

No, I didn't. I didn't want to know. But she hangs up before I get to tell her. I sit there, on my kitchen floor, my little hopes and dreams in pieces all around me. Nobody to help me put them back together, or to even get back up.

I have no idea at all of what to do with Ruthie's news — which I'm sure she's already shared with all her sisters — when the phone rings again. It's Duffy. "Feel like taking a ride?" he asks.

I hesitate, not sure I do. "Mmm, no

thanks," I say.

"I'd really appreciate it," he urges in a voice that sounds as sincere to me as a man's voice can sound. "I just . . . well, there's something I want to show you."

"You've got another best girl?" I hate the brittle sound of my own voice.

"No, I don't."

"How far?" I ask. I'm swallowing, can't help myself, even though I'm leery, and longing for some downtime.

"We'll be gone a couple of hours. No more. I promise. I need to do this."

"Need?"

He doesn't speak, but in my mind's eye I see him nodding yes, and I feel his hope that I won't let him down echo through my receiver.

We set a time, and I clean myself up, but forgo the Trésor, the makeup, the fashionable upgraded clothes. All the while, doubt and fear, hope and longing brawl inside me, fighting for control. Should I go or should I stay? OK. OK. I'll go. I decide to go because Duffy's earned that much from me, but it will have to be a "come as you are" party. Plain old Mimi is the one he's going to get.

I meet him outside. He opens the passenger-side door of the Caprice for me, then slides behind the wheel. We don't speak. I can't think of anything to say. Once we're under way, he stays focused on the road as we navigate through the complicated arithmetic of local and state roads until we reach I-495.

"We're heading south," he says, a redundancy, because I've read the big green highway sign we've just followed. I expect him to tell me more, but he doesn't. Mum's the word. Then he turns on a soft jazz station out of Boston, Nat King Cole, the smoothest of smooth crooners, but I don't feel the least bit relaxed.

"Smoked three packs a day," Duffy says out of the blue, like I'm supposed to understand what he's talking about. I frown at him, a first. "He believed it made his voice sound better."

Got it: Nat King Cole. *I found a dream that I could speak to . . . A thrill to press my cheek to . . .*

"Before every recording session, he smoked one after the other — Kool menthols."

"It killed him," I say, recalling my sadness over Nat's untimely death. I realize both of us are smoking, our windows cracked. "Lung cancer in his forties."

Duffy turns off the radio.

In the quiet, our journey feels more

urgent, Duffy driving faster than usual. Thinking of Nat's demise, the silencing of his inimitable voice, I smush out my cigarette in the little ashtray but leave the window cracked. Shopping strips, industrial parks, and housing developments blur past. In this rare silence, it only takes a few minutes for me to figure out where we're headed: Bridgewater.

At last we get off the highway, follow a bunch of twisting roads. Duffy drives more slowly, squinting straight ahead. I get the feeling that he could drive this route blindfolded, that he's done it so many times, and over and over again in his dreams. But I don't say a thing. Loose lips sink ships. Then, in the distance, huge and shadowy, is a place I've never seen in person but recognize right away. Concrete buildings surrounded by miles of chain link and razor wire, its guard towers glowing in the light of the setting sun. The infamous prison and loony bin, the Old Colony Correctional Center — historical, like so much else around here. It's where his son must be incarcerated — a word I've never used before or even thought about. "Incarcerated." Your body, your soul confined in a place it does not choose to be. The unlighted place in Duffy's eyes.

I wait for him to tell me about his son. He doesn't know I know. He stops in the parking lot but leaves the motor running. His hands grip the wheel. We're as close as we can get, but still quite far away. The prison's gloomy; no interior lights are visible. Armed guards pace its towers, their weapons silhouetted against the sky.

"Medium security." Duffy's voice is weak and scratchy, like it might, at any moment, break. Medium security, like it's some kind of triumph.

"Before this thing goes any further," he starts to say, then stops. "Before this thing goes any further . . ."

Now his face is red, not pink. His nose and ears look scalded, like Flanna got to him with one of her potions. For the first time since I've known him, he's having trouble spitting out what he's got to say.

"What thing?"

"This thing." He nods to me, taps himself on the chest. "Our thing."

"OK, our thing. What are you trying to say?"

He hands me a folded piece of paper, an official notice of some type, stamped with the seal of the Suffolk County Superior Court. What on earth, I wonder until I open it and read the words: "Level three sex offender," and below them, a mug shot of a younger Duffy. Christopher Joseph Duffy. Now forty-two years old. Convicted of indecent assault and battery on a child under fourteen years of age. Three kids. Nine counts. Like Ruthie told me on the phone, he's the father of a convicted pedophile.

Then, in a voice from far away, a voice shaky with sorrow, Duffy tells me how his son had been arrested, tried, and convicted on trumped-up charges of child molestation. How the past decade of Duff's life has been bound up by the tribulations of his son, a Vietnam veteran, a hapless but good-hearted guy, a black belt who'd owned a karate studio in a shopping center in Rockland. He names it and I have the vaguest memory of having passed the place.

"If he has a weakness," Duff insists, "it's women, not little boys." I look at the handsome fellow in the photo wondering, can't help it, if what Duffy says is true, or if he's in denial. His son was convicted, after all.

"He messed with some of the young mothers of the kids at his karate school, true, one of them the wife of a cop. No big deal, in his opinion. They're all consenting grown-ups. That's how he looked at it. The cop caught them, right in the act, in an office at the school. Next thing you know, he's arrested, charged with umpteen counts of sex abuse. For touching his students inappropriately during classes. When he'd actually been touching the cop's wife. But they've got the kids, including two of hers, lined up to tell their horror stories."

"Teaching karate, you'd have to touch the kids," I say. "How could you teach them without touching them?" He nods, exhales a long stream of cigarette smoke.

"Three trials, three sets of charges," Duffy says. "Over three years. He could've taken a plea. Could've done a sexual-predator rehabilitation program, eighteen months in and out, instead of hard time in prison. But he tells me, 'Dad, I can't plead guilty to something I didn't do. I can't admit I'm a child molester if I'm not.' He took his chances at the trial, and he lost. Had a public defender, all we could afford."

Anyone who lives in Massachusetts, especially in Suffolk County, is familiar with our attorney general. He got his start as an ambitious DA a few years back, the same one who prosecuted Duffy's son. Sexual predators were his thing, and he found them everywhere. Routed them from all their hiding places, determined to make the Commonwealth of Massachusetts safe for children. That was his slogan, and by everyone's account, he succeeded. On TV they brag about how the Commonwealth of Massachusetts has more sexual-predator convictions than any other state, and that Suffolk County has the most in Massachusetts. Now it's only grown-ups who need to worry.

"Here's the thing," says Duff, flicking his butt out the window, then opening the door to stomp on it, make sure it's out. "Christopher's new lawyer knows for a fact that during the first set of interviews the three boys who testified insisted that nothing inappropriate had happened, ever. But the recordings disappeared. Don't forget, the husband of the woman he had an affair with was a cop. In later interviews, the boys changed their stories, and their stories were identical, down to the last detail."

"Why three trials? Why didn't they do them all together?"

"The DA figured he'd get more mileage from three trials than from one. Which he did. He was right. More media coverage, more outrage. Dragged it out as long as possible. Now the new lawyer says the DA did it that way because the kids' stories were identical in all three trials. He's got the transcripts. And that's a sure sign of false memory. Even the wording was the same. If the same jury had heard them all, they'd have realized something was up."

"False memory? How can a memory be false?"

"Kids remembering things that didn't happen. The precise details of things that didn't happen because they were fed to them by adults. It's a common phenomenon, even in families. It doesn't just apply to crimes.

"I read the transcripts from the pretrial interviews, which lasted hours, with a parent always present. They asked questions they could not ask in the courtroom. Like, for instance, 'Is that when Christopher Duffy, the karate instructor, put his hand on your right buttock and squeezed?' That sort of thing."

Chris had been appealing on the grounds of prosecutorial misconduct, arguing that the prosecutors themselves, aided and abetted by the boys' parents, had planted the false memories. Recently, a young defense attorney with some connection to an advocacy group for the wrongfully convicted — a lawyer as ambitious as Mr. District Attorney but fighting for the other side — was only too happy to take his case pro bono.

"And, already, through these advanced therapies they do, showing, if you can

313

believe it, different types of pornography to the offenders, to figure out what . . . what rings their bell and they've demonstrated conclusively . . ."

Duffy looks away, at a loss for words. I doubt his face could get any redder. I understand his shame.

"Don't explain," I say, pained by his pain. A sad old Billie Holiday song. "Don't Explain."

"I need to tell someone," he says, turning to me, looking at me eye to eye, in a way that somehow thrills me, in spite of everything he's just said, and even in the dimming light. He trusts me. And I decide to trust him back. Despite my panicked moments earlier today, my fear of betrayal.

"They cover these guys with electrodes, like in an EKG, and then show them pornography." Duffy pauses, gathering strength. "They do brain imagery, measure a million bodily reactions . . . Costs a fortune. The state wouldn't pay, but the lawyer got a grant from some foundation for the wrongfully convicted. And the tests demonstrate that Chris has no sexual interest whatsoever in children. He had the opposite reactions — anger, disgust, nausea. No matter how many times they tested him, the results were always the same. His lawyer will use this as new exculpatory evidence."

"Exculpatory," another new word. I roll it around in my mind. Exculpatory. Duff sits silent for a minute, exhausted, I think, but the silence is OK. I put my arm around him and rub his shoulder, for whatever that might be worth.

"By the time they hear the case, Chris will be released," he says. "He'll have served his time. Good behavior."

"Then what's the point?"

"His name. No 'level three sex offender' next to it for the rest of his life. He had a new girlfriend, and they'd been going steady for a while. He was ready to settle down when all this started. She tried hard to stand by him, but she had to move on. If his name is cleared, Chris, too, might be able to move on." That notion hangs there, Duffy's son being able to move on, a small bright spot in the darkening parking lot, the prison a forbidding edifice, way too close for comfort.

"That envelope, in the Caprice that day," I start to ask.

"Chump change." Duffy laughs a bitter laugh. "Money for Chris to use at the prison commissary."

Chris, his son Chris, a grown-up; incarcerated, but with a chance, however slim, to clear his name. Redemption. What all of us are hoping for. I look at Duffy, and he's still looking straight ahead at the place where his son is doing time, hard time, the only kind a man can do at Bridgewater.

Duffy holds up the flyer. "Every police station and post office in the state has one of these. And, when he gets out, unless he's cleared, they'll inform everyone in the neighborhood, wherever he decides to live, that a pedophile is living close by. I wanted you to know." He's looking at the flyer, not at me. "Before we go any farther with this thing."

"This thing?"

He shakes his head, repeats himself.

"This thing. I didn't want you to hear it from anybody else."

"Like my daughters?"

"One of them buttonholed me yesterday."

"I know. She called." Duffy doesn't answer. He looks at me, and I see an old guy, the lines on his face a map of all he's been through. But he still has a child's eyes, full of wonder and longing, and I can tell, even in the shadows here, that he's gotten to a place where he really wants to be. With me. And in a quiet place inside myself, I make a decision: I believe him. I'm on his side, no matter what his son has done or not done.

Duffy. I trust him.

"Well, now you'll have somebody to keep you company on court dates and visits. If you want her to. Only if you want her to."

"Too late to visit today. They're very strict. And when I do, they've got this Plexiglas wall between us."

I take his hand. "We'll come back another day. Just say the word."

TWENTY-SEVEN: AIN'T SHE SWEET

Another morning, another ringing telephone. I've no sooner put my coffee on and plugged the phone back in when it starts. Last night when I got home, I'd unplugged the damned thing in case my daughters or my sisters were in the mood to gab. I wasn't. I was all gabbed out. I had some new vocabulary — "incarcerated," "false memory," "exculpatory" — and these words hung in my mind, blotting out anything else I might want to say. We went our separate ways when we got back, Duffy and I. Didn't even talk on the way home, just listened to the music. A warm and necessary silence, as if we were still communicating, not like that colder silence on our trip south. At last I pick it up.

"Hi, Mimi, it's me," says the voice. "I've been trying and trying to reach you."

"Oh, Cassandra, I'm fine. I just needed a little time off. I mean, from the phone."

"Cassandra?" the voice wails. Whoops. Which one is it?

"It's Siobhan, your fifth child," she says, all huffy.

"Who gave you my number?"

"Very funny."

"Well, when's the last time you used it?" Silence. She can't remember, but I can, me with all the black spots. Not once in all the years I've lived here has Siobhan called to say hello or for any other reason.

"When do you call me?" she asks.

"Once in a while."

"A great, great while, Mimi. To remind me to send a birthday card to Aunt Keeley or some such thing. You never ever call to ask me how I am. Never."

"Well, how are you?"

"Very funny."

We could waste the whole morning, pointing out what I've done to her and she's done to me, or what we've failed to do.

"OK, what's up?" I pour my coffee, the phone cradled by my ear. "What's so important you had to call?" Her breathing still sounds funny, but, hey, the truth's the truth.

"Can I come over?"

"Sure, why not?"

"I've been thinking . . ."

"About what?" I stifle the mean retorts

my lips unload so easily.

"I'll be there ASAP."

Siobhan lives on the other side of Beantown, in Andover, not far from Delilah in Reading. It'll take her an hour or so to get here. While I wait, I drink coffee at my table by the window and think about her, something I've hardly ever done over the past fifteen years or so. Siobhan, a feminist scholar in Irish studies. Of course, I also wonder what she's been thinking about, why she has this sudden urgent need to visit me. Maybe it's about what a rotten mother I have been.

Siobhan and I, we never spend time together. I mean, time alone together. When I left Jack, I left the way you leave a burning house — in a mad rush, knowing some things will be lost to you forever. Siobhan was one of those things, but I couldn't let myself feel anything about it. I had too many other things to feel.

Siobhan, the only one of my girls without a nickname. When she was little, she pronounced her name Shibbon. We tried out Shibby on her, but she wouldn't have it, wouldn't answer to it. Siobhan or nothing. Siobhan is what she insisted upon and it's what she got. This name, I think, is what got her into Irish Studies in the first place, though the truth is, I haven't paid close enough attention to know for sure.

She's soon to be Dr. Siobhan Sheehan Malloy, because, being a feminist, she's keeping my name too. Which makes me proud, though I've never told her. She swears that if she ever marries, she'll keep this name. Though she's already told her sisters, she doesn't plan on having children, a tidbit they've passed on to me. She's doesn't want to do what was done to her to an innocent and helpless child. Whatever that might be.

Siobhan's the biggest of my girls, taller and wider than the rest of them. Not that she has a weight problem, not by any means. She's just bigger boned, like the women in Jack's family, instead of mine. Plus, she's perfectly proportioned, and carries her size well, but she's always been jealous of the others, especially Del and Cass, because they're so fit and thin. Size 4, where she's probably a 10. No biggie, in my book, but it practically kills her. That's what her sisters tell me, anyway. She does spinning and peelatays and a million other things to stay in shape. And she's always on one weird diet or another. She's also into fang shway, and everything in her apartment is placed perfectly so she gets the best vibrations. Siobhan does it by the book. Or so her sisters say. I wouldn't know because I've never been there. Never been invited.

Siobhan's a control freak, I'm pretty sure, though she tries to keep this part of her personality under wraps. Or maybe she doesn't even recognize it. No doubt about it, she's a brain, our Siobhan, quiet and studious all her life — hiding in her room, reading, trying to stay out of the line of fire. Smart, but without a clue about herself. It's funny because she's older, bigger, and better educated, but Del leads her around by the nose, telling her what to think and how to feel. Then, when Cassie gets in on the act, forget about it. The three of them together. Whoa. Or maybe woe.

Siobhan shows up in jeans and a beautiful Irish sweater she picked up on her last trip. She's already thirtysomething, although she looks much younger. It's that gorgeous skin. Where did the time go? I wonder when I look at her. She was in high school when I left Jack, and now she's all grown up, a woman I hardly know.

We don't hug. Never do. I invite her in, and right away she starts coughing and waving her hands around because of the cigarette smoke.

"How can you stand it?" she asks.

"I don't notice." I open a window, trying to keep my cool.

I pour her a cup of coffee, and we sit at my table. Neither of us speaks. The old hurts and betrayals push us apart.

"You've never forgiven me for leaving you." This sentence is out before I even think it. It thrashes in the air between us, a snake about to strike.

Siobhan bursts out crying. She stands and spins around, her hands over her face, howling like one of those car alarms that go right through you and seem to never stop. I stand up too. I want to go to her but can't. She might push me away. I watch her have this fit, spinning like Rumpelstiltskin after the princess guessed his name. Not the shy, chubby teenager I left behind, but a grown woman, sad and smart and so confused. Wailing like a broken car alarm. Did she really come out of me?

"Come on, sit down," I say, enfolding her as best I can given the difference in our sizes. I lead her to my couch and sit beside her. I keep my arm around her, and make soothing sounds. *Now, now, sweetheart, now, now.* She's still crying, but it turns into a more normal type of sobbing, tears running down her cheeks, hiccupping — the type of sad that I can handle.

"After you left, you never cared a thing about me," she says between the hiccups. "You never paid attention. You wouldn't even go to my high school graduation party because it was at Daddy's house, and I was the valedictorian. I had a scholarship to Georgetown. And my own mother was MIA."

"That was fifteen years ago, for heaven's sake," I say, staggered by her first blow. "It's ancient history. Water under the dam. Or the bridge. Wherever water goes."

But it's also true. I went to the graduation ceremony, but hung out in back, refusing to sit up front with Jack and Miss Piggy, though Siobhan had reserved a seat for me there. And I refused to go to the party at Jack's house because, of course, Miss Piggy would be there, playing hostess in my former home, with my former husband, and my good china and silverware.

"You were too busy hating Daddy to think about me. You still are, Mimi. You're eaten up with bitterness."

"Am not!" Leave it to your offspring to tally up your failings and remind you of your every weakness. "And leave your father out of this."

"We can't leave him out," she says. "He's

324

here whether we want him or not. And you don't have any idea who I am." We're sitting close together, and I've got my arm around her, but we're not looking at each other.

"Do you know me?" I ask.

"You don't want me to."

"I don't want you to?" I take her chin and force her, gently, to turn toward me. We look at each other, Siobhan and I, her eyes that same lovely blue as her father's, her head crammed full of learning.

"You're full of secrets." She shrugs. "Always hiding."

I drop my hand. I can't even answer that. I've said it all before, so many times, to one or another of her sisters. All of my daughters. I've got no secrets, not a one. For a time, we're quiet, except for the occasional sob or hiccup.

"Siobhan, I know I got off track with you, and I don't know how to get back on. I don't know if it's possible. All these years, I thought you didn't care. I thought you hated me so much you didn't want to get to know me."

"I never hated you, Mimi. Never, ever. You ripped my heart out a few times but I was smart enough to know that's not what you meant to do. I just happened to be there. Wrong place, wrong time."

"Would it help for me to say I'm sorry? Truly sorry for leaving you behind?"

She nods yes, but corrects me.

"You didn't leave me behind. You abandoned me."

"I'm sorry for that, too. But maybe we can, I don't know, try to get to know each other now," I say. "Take it slow."

She nods but doesn't speak, her nose red, her cheeks tearstained, like when she was a little girl and came to me with her upsets and her hurts. I pull her toward me and hold her the way I used to, way back when, patting her soft hair. She sobs some more. We sit that way for a while.

"But this isn't what you came here for, is it?" I say at last, unable to deal with Siobhan's hurt any longer.

"No." For once, she agrees with me. "It's not."

We get up and take turns in the bathroom, washing our faces and putting on fresh makeup. When she's finished, Siobhan shoves a big plastic bag at me.

"Got it for you on my last trip," she says. "I forgot to bring it last time I was here."

Inside's an Irish sweater, a light-green cardigan with a pretty design around the neckline and the hem.

"You're trying to upgrade my image too,"

I say, then want to kick myself.

"No," she says. "I just thought it would look good on you. The color matches your eyes."

I go into my bedroom, slip it on over my turtleneck. Siobhan watches in the doorway.

"It does, Mimi," she says. "I was right. It looks really good on you."

"Wow, it does," I say, smiling at her, seeing how pleased she is. I'm afraid the sweater might be itchy or too hot, but I'll keep my big mouth shut. I'll wear it no matter what.

"Let's get out of here," she says, suddenly taking deep breaths. "I'm having trouble breathing."

TWENTY-EIGHT:
WITCHCRAFT

We drive over to Marina Bay, where we can walk on the promenade by the water and window shop. After I park and we climb out of my Shadow and into the fresh salty air, I take Siobhan by the arm. " 'Come away, O human child,' " I say, and she smiles. As we walk around the shops and piers, the two of us in our Irish sweaters, the weight of what she's said presses down on me. Even still, I can't help but notice the way my daughter draws attention, clueless though she may be. Men like to look at her, the way they used to like to look at me.

We pass a Vietnam War memorial, a miniature version of the one in Washington — black marble, shiny as a mirror, engraved with the names of the local dead. Siobhan points to a name, tells me it was the younger brother of Del's ex-husband.

"Would've been my brother-in-law if he'd lived. Or if Del had stayed married to him."

"The dead are all around us."

"Just like the faeries," says Siobhan, and she squeezes my arm tighter.

"Is that what you wanted to talk about? Faeries?"

"It might relate," she says, her cheeks going pink.

"To what?"

"To what happened in your family."

Then, scholar that she is, she launches into a lecture, about how, back in the day, in the old country — the one that she's obsessed with, just like the grandfather she never knew — the ancient beliefs of the peasantry got mixed up with stories from the Bible.

"The preliterate . . ." I can't remember the next word.

"Cosmology, world view."

"Right."

"Like when God expelled Lucifer from heaven with all the other rebel angels. The rebel angels were already falling through the sky when Jesus told his Father that heaven might end up empty, with so much rebellion going on."

"Everybody getting into the act."

She nods.

"When God the Father stopped to think," she says, stopping in her tracks so we can stare into the window of a sweet shop where they're dipping big red strawberries into a vat of melted chocolate, "the falling angels stopped wherever they happened to be." She touches the window with her fingertip. The strawberry dippers smile at us. "Yummy," she says, then goes on with the lesson. "That's why you've got faeries in the air, in the water, under the earth, and on top of it."

I look at those luscious berries being dipped into the even more luscious chocolate. I try to imagine God the Father thinking, and the falling angels stopping wherever they happened to be. I can't quite see it. I look at Siobhan.

"So this is that preliterate cosmosomething?"

"Cosmology," she repeats, nodding patiently, like I'm slow but catching on. "Most of the time, they're invisible, the faeries, at least to most people, but if you could see them, they'd look human."

"I'll treat you to a strawberry," I interrupt. My daughter doesn't even pretend to protest. We buy four, two each, picking out the biggest ones on the tray.

It's warm enough to sit on one of the benches by the water, especially in these heavy sweaters. We find an empty one and take a seat. "Most were male," she says, and it takes me a second to catch up. "The faeries. That's why, when they kidnapped, they chose girls and women. Most of the time."

"When they kidnapped?"

"Stole a human child. Replaced a human child with a changeling."

"Folks in Ireland believed this stuff?" I ask my daughter, but I already know the answer. I've always known, somewhere deep inside, though I've kept it there — a dark secret I did not want to figure out. The old folks in Ireland believed some crazy things and built their lives around this craziness, their preliterate cosmology. Some, like Nana, dumped those beliefs into the Atlantic as they crossed over to North America, but others, like Da, held on to them — held on for dear life — into their new lives in the new country, a place where those beliefs would mark them as ignorant and backward, something Nana understood.

"Any disturbance in the predictable order of things could be blamed on faeries. Madness, illness, a deformity. A death in childbirth, like your mother's. Misfortune was interpreted as a form of revenge, a failure to appease the little people."

Siobhan has forgotten her strawberries,

though I'm nibbling one of mine. It's a disappointment beneath the chocolate coating, dry and mealy. A lesson in deceiving looks.

"They understood the world through the stories they told each other, sitting around peat fires at night. There was no electricity well into the twentieth century. And remember, the Irish Free State wasn't formed until 1922, and even afterward, most people didn't know how to read or write."

Siobhan glows as if she's sitting by one of those fires instead of on a bench with me, Quincy Bay heaving just beyond us, the sky overhead a clear and gorgeous blue. 1922, just a few years before I was born. Suddenly, I feel ancient; a crone, with this cold breeze stirring up the ashes at the bottom of my soul.

Flanna wasn't an ordinary madwoman. She was a *cailleach,* a woman with special power. *Cailleach,* a word that makes you gag if you pronounce it right. She understood the wee folk, could talk to them, could hear them. Which is why Da chose her. Da himself believed in spirits, faeries, wee people. He believed in Flanna.

"When I was a kid, I imagined Flanna getting off a big sailboat right out there," I point, "right in Quincy Harbor, walking on the water, making her way toward us, with her big black satchel."

"What was in the satchel?"

"Herbs. Whiskey."

"Nice combo."

"She boiled up plants she grew in the yard, and made us drink them. If we didn't, there'd be hell to pay."

"Hell to pay," Siobhan repeats. "Probably purple foxglove, and St. John's wort, both used in faerie medicine. *Come away, O human child.* It all goes back to the line you just mentioned, from the Yeats poem. The same one that's on Da's headstone." Da. She's calling her grandfather Da, and in that way, she's claiming him.

I nod. Without wanting to, I see Flanna rushing through the house, muttering mumbo-jumbo. Hiding things. Finding things. Boiling things. Burning things. Whispering. Listening.

As I think about Flanna parceling out her concoctions to the old folks at the back door, Siobhan tells me about how, back in the day, poor rural families — and almost all families were rural poor — couldn't afford kids who didn't obey. Kids had to do their part for families to survive. Life was just too hard. If a defiant child couldn't be gotten under control, parents and priests and healers might gather to exorcise the evil thing from the child who was causing all the trouble. They'd break the kids' spirits, along with a few bones, if that's what was necessary to get them to behave, to stop wreaking havoc in the family.

" 'The Stolen Child,' " I say, and the words work like a wire whisk whipping up my dread. "But I don't see the connection."

What I see is Flanna in the coal cellar, next to the furnace, holding the shovel she used to dump in the coal. The furnace door is open, filled with flames. That's when Fagan shows up beside me, her bright, furious self. Clutches me, as Flanna shovels in the coal. I can't see her, only feel her. Fagan. Hot as embers, even out here in the cold.

"Mimi." Siobhan hugs me. She smells scrumptious, like cinnamon and lilies. A scent that overwhelms the stench of Fagan, filthy Fagan, furious Fagan, hanging on for dear life. I lean closer to Siobhan, inhale deeply.

"Flanna believed Fagan was a changeling," Siobhan says. "That's the connection. I'll bet anything."

"For heaven's sake, Siobhan, a changeling?"

"That the faeries stole the real Fagan and left behind the disobedient monster who looked just like her." I look at my daughter, so smart, and so grown-up and serious, telling me one of the nuttiest things I've ever heard. Fagan, a changeling. She blushes again, her cheeks the color of the bits of yarn in the design around her neckline.

"And if she did?"

She doesn't answer, stares out at the water.

"Siobhan!" I shout, as if she were still an adolescent and I was struggling to control her. "Siobhan," I say again, my voice softer, gentler; I'm calling her back to me.

"Well," she starts to say, "if that's what she believed, she'd do what she had to do to get the real Fagan back."

" 'What she had to do'?"

"You said Flanna poured the pee pot over Fagan. That was one way to make the faeries let a changeling go. One of the first things they'd do, drench the changeling with piss. If that didn't work, they'd try emetics. By inducing vomiting, they believed they could force the faeries to release the child."

Flanna in the kitchen, forcing Fagan to drink one of her disgusting concoctions. Fagan pukes into the sink, and Flanna smacks her back to make her throw up more. I see, if only dimly and in flashes, induced nausea, enemas, terrible hot baths — the purifying of our systems, Flanna trying to force the evil out.

"Fire was the last resort."

"The last resort?" No place to vacation, this last resort.

"After the dousing and the emetics. If everything else failed, Flanna could have threatened Fagan with fire as a warning to the faeries."

"A warning?"

"To the faeries. To let her go."

In my mind's eye, where everything now seems to be 20/20, I see the burn can in the backyard, the black stove in the kitchen, the coal-burning furnace in the cellar. Beside it, the shovel for scooping up the coal, the bucket with the slanted lip for pouring coal into the furnace, the poker for stoking up the coals. Like a house, the furnace had a front door. *When Flanna opens it, the flames inside shoot up, red and ravenous, warning us how close we are to hell. Flanna commands all of us to stand behind her, to see how, in just a few minutes, she turns that poker redhot from the flames.*

"Fire was the last resort," Siobhan repeats. I look into her earnest eyes, her lovely face, the sunlight on it. "Sometimes the warnings worked. Little kids could be and often were terrified into docility."

Eden, unbidden, comes back to mind. Early on, she lost her spirit if not her soul. Turned passive in all things, wouldn't or couldn't stick up for herself. A doormat, we'd often wisecrack. Eden, the beautiful doormat. Alberta and I kept her going, then finally just Alberta.

"Children could have the spirit beaten out of them," says Siobhan. "It was common practice, handed down through the generations. If they were ill, they could get well. Believers interpreted these things as successful faerie interventions."

"Faerie interventions?" The last time I heard that word, "intervention," was from Alberta's daughter, a year or two before my sister's death. She wanted us to help with one, but we said no. We loved Alberta, understood her and accepted her as she was. We could not turn on her. And that was the last we heard from her, our niece.

"Faerie literature is full of stories about so-called wise women bringing mortal children back. About changelings flying up out of their beds and disappearing into the night, leaving the normal child behind." Siobhan squeezes my hand. But instead I feel Fagan's fingers dig deep, deep into me. "Stories about how, when a *cailleach* builds up the fire and threatens to put the child on top, what looks like an ordinary child flies up and out the window."

"I'm so glad she got sent away," I tell Siobhan. "That was the right thing for Da to do. Imagine what might have happened if she stayed."

"Cullyhanna," murmurs Siobhan.

"Why don't we go back?" I ask, stunning myself because the trip never seemed possible to me before. "You could help me look for Fagan. I mean, her grave." Me, Mimi, thinking of going back when I've never ever desired to set a foot there. Ireland, land of mystery and sorrow.

"We could do that," says Siobhan, but when I look at her, she's staring out at the water.

"It's funny. After Fagan was sent away, Flanna would call Keeley Fagan all the time."

"Fagan?" She turns to look at me, and this time the knowledge in her gaze frightens me. "Back then, when a child died, families often blamed the death on faeries. Then, when the next child came along, they'd name it after the dead one."

"The dead one? Fagan didn't die til later, after she got sent away."

Shrieking, hollering, though not one of us actually saw Fagan go.

Not Mammy, my sister's everlasting lamentation. Flanna chases Fagan through the house. They holler loud enough to wake up the neighborhood, but the only ones who wake up are Eden, Alberta, and me. *Not Mammy.* Over and over again, Flanna grabbed Fagan, but Fagan escaped. The two of them ran and ran, cartoon characters racing around the kitchen table, so fast they were a blur. Comical if you didn't know what was going on.

"The new baby was seen as a gift from the faeries who'd stolen the first one," Siobhan says. "That's what they believed."

Now my own mind might be on fire, the same fuse that got lit the other day. Because I see Flanna caressing Keeley, only she calls her Fagan. *Fagan, my wee love.* Which drove Keeley nuts, because she never once thought Flanna was confused. No, not for a minute. *She's thinks I'm Fagan, but I'm not. I'm me, Keeley.* All that conflict always, over who was who and what was what.

"That's why," says Siobhan, "when you walk through the cemeteries in the countryside, you'll see families with two Bridgets or Annies or Padraics born within a couple of years of each other. The second child replaced the first."

No loss to feel.

But I've never walked through cemeteries in the Irish countryside, and I've never planned to do so. Unless, that is, Siobhan and I go to search for Fagan.

I look around, see how normal we look sitting here, a mother and daughter, enjoying the fresh air in our lovely Irish sweaters. Perfectly normal, that's us. The water's churning, with little whitecaps here and there. Siobhan's squinting out at it. I look at her face with Da's clear blue eyes. My heart swells, a feeling as good as that myocardial thing is bad. I love her, this Siobhan, and for the first time, I realize how much I'd hurt her. Me, Mimi Malloy, who swore deep down in her own soul, and with all her might, that she would never, ever hurt her children.

Now both of us are shivering. We lean closer to each other. An icy gust blows up off the water, and trash flies around our feet. It's so cold, it feels like winter's coming back.

Twenty-Nine:
Something's Gotta Give

When I walk into my apartment, my brain is so full of sparks I'm afraid it might explode. I get the blue pendant from my bedroom, sit with it in my recliner. I don't turn on any lights. The dark feels good right now, and maybe necessary. I've got this dull ache deep inside, like just before my miscarriage, the one I had between Malvina and Siobhan. Those ashes at the bottom of my soul send up clouds, making my eyes water. Everything I see blurs and shines through a veil of tears.

Instead of thinking about my second-youngest daughter, or my first baby sister, I think about the baby I lost, though it wasn't, either in my mind or in my body, yet a baby, not really. I was just far enough along to feel the baby move, the quickening, a word I've never understood.

I wasn't thrilled about the pregnancy, my fifth in seven years. I was twenty-seven and hadn't been out of maternity clothes since my teens. No, I wasn't thrilled, to say the least. I didn't want another baby, I was already in way over my head with the four I already had, and I knew it, but I told Jack the opposite. I insisted I was happy: God was giving us another one. He agreed that we were blessed. We were propagating the faith, and our faith was everything.

Then, one morning I woke up, sat up, but did not throw up. Yippee, I thought, I'm past the worst part. But over the next couple of days, I realized something wasn't right. No throwing up, but also no more of those feathery tickles down inside. Then, in the middle of the night, I woke up, drenched with sweat and with a dull ache down where the baby was supposed to be growing. "Something's wrong," I told Jack, shaking him awake. "Go back to sleep," he said. In the morning I called my doctor. "You're fine, it's all in your head," he told me. He'd see me the next month. After that, I called my sisters. "Keep us posted," Jo and Patty said. "Whatever you need, whenever you need it. We'll be there." It was the twins who came to help, that afternoon, when I started bleeding. I went into labor, sharp, intense contractions, but no baby would be born.

By the time the twins arrived, I was

hemorrhaging, gushing blood. No more pain, just this river of blood, with Cassandra and Celestine and Ruthie hollering and sobbing at the sight of me. Jo called the hospital. She told them to get ready for an emergency D&C. She was bringing me in. Patty packed Malvie's diapers between my legs, cloth ones, from the stack folded neatly in the bathroom. She grabbed an armload for us to take along in the car. One after the other, they got drenched. Blood was flowing out of me, and I couldn't do anything to stop it. Patty stayed with the girls and tried to comfort them while Jo drove me to the hospital. That's all I remember. Nothing about the surgery, waking up, the rest of it, though it's one of the twins' favorite stories when the Yik Yak Club's in session. How they saved my life. Talk about drama queens.

My sisters were furious with Jack and they've always held it against him. Because he never showed, never thanked them, never expressed regret about the baby, or concern about me. But me, I didn't expect any of those things. I wasn't angry, not surprised, either. Jack F. X. Malloy abhors the sight of blood. He doesn't do hospitals, that's just how it is. Yes, I lost the baby; no telling, back then, if it was a boy or girl. The next few months were hard. I went into the deepest mourning, a grief out of all proportion. Strange, because part of me had wished that baby dead, though I never told a soul. I wept for days on end, the last time I'd cry for many years. "Get over it, we'll make another one," Jack kept saying, especially in bed at night when he wanted some. Soon enough, a couple of years later, we did, we made another one, Siobhan, and I forgot about the lost one, the one I didn't want. I tucked it away, neatly, into a black spot, like a sandwich into a Ziploc bag.

Siobhan, the one who came next. Still sitting in my recliner, I put down the blue pendant to check my hands, wondering if they're stained with the blood of her broken heart. Eaten up with bitterness, that's me. That's what my daughter thinks. Oh, and that I abandoned her. My own child. Of course, poor thing, she was my fifth in a decade, with the miscarriage in between. I was worn out by the time Siobhan showed up, that much I'll admit. She didn't get the best of me. But abandoned?

My mind churns around the idea that I've known her all her life without knowing her at all. How does that happen? How can you give birth to a kid and raise her, and end up not knowing her? She's got her father's brains but nothing of me — nothing visible, anyway, unless you count what she considers her weight problem, the one nobody else can see.

When we said goodbye today, we promised to call each other once a week or so, just to say hello. We agreed we wouldn't let Cassandra be our go-between, running our relationship for us. We agreed to let bygones be bygones. To try to trust each other.

Which reminds me.

I grab my personal directory, pick up the phone, and punch in Malvina's number in the Bronx. Cassandra wrote it in my book the last time she was here and now, after all this time, I want to talk to her, make it up to her. I can't help imagining her surprise when she hears my voice, "Hello, darling." We'll make a plan to get together. I'll take the train to New York to meet my grandsons, spend a few days there with them — Mimi in the City. But Malvina's phone rings and rings. Nobody picks up, not even the answering machine. I promise myself to try again later. I hope I remember.

I decide to call Cassandra — press that speed-dial number and ta-da, she picks up after the first ring. "What's up, Mimi? Everything OK?" Worried, always worried, like I'm so flimsy that I'll collapse at any moment.

"I'm fine, baby, just fine. Siobhan visited today."

"Siobhan? That's a first."

"A first, but not a last." Then I'm quiet, unable to figure out how to say what I want to say next.

"Great, but what's —"

"That got to do with you? I want to go on a field trip. I want to go back to Da's house, or where our house used to be."

"Ooookaayy. . . ." She's says it like I'm the real nut she's always suspected me to be. The house, after all, was demolished ages ago. I imagine her rolling her gorgeous eyes, shadowed and mascaraed, wondering what craziness is coming next.

"We ran away and never went back. I want to retrace our steps. I want to see what we can see."

"You ran away? To your grandmother's house?"

"Yes, that's all I remember, showing up at Nana's house." Nana's lovely house in Weymouth, just over the bridge from Quincy. Nana in the kitchen, working, forever making soups and jams and breads, Nana playing the radio, tuning in to the Boston stations, and practicing her American accent by mimicking the announcers: *"Coca-Cola,*

346

ice-cold sunshine! Wonder Bread! It's Slo-baked."

"I don't remember anything that happened right before."

"Like traumatic amnesia?"

"Something like that."

"Tomorrow morning?"

"Great."

THIRTY:
MAKIN' WHOOPEE

I'm no sooner settled back in my chair than Duffy's knocking on the door, calling in that funny way he has, "Mrs. Malloy, oh, Mrs. Malloy."

When I open the door, Duff's smiling like a little boy, embarrassed, maybe because he's showed up unexpected, and he's brought me a treat. He holds a big brown bag, and a rich steamy smell escapes from it.

"Moo Goo Gai Pan," he says. "Chow Mei Fun."

"My favorites." I smile, too, though I haven't got a clue what either dish tastes like. I'd hug him if he wasn't so loaded down. I drag him inside.

"Lovely sweater," he says, putting the bag down on my counter, taking out the little white cartons. "Looks great on you, Mrs. Malloy." He makes a throaty sound, like I'm so delicious he could eat me up.

348

My face burns.

"My daughter Siobhan brought it to me from Ireland." I hold out my arm for him to feel. He rubs his hand along the sleeve and then puts his arms around me, pulls me close. He kisses the top of my head. I almost start to cry, but stop. Stay in the moment, I tell myself, some of Cassie's psychobabble. But this time I get it. I'll stay in the moment.

"You must've read my mind, coming by with Chinese. I'm starving. Went out with my kid, but all we ate was strawberries. They're always on my case about my weight."

"You're looking fine to me, Mrs. Malloy."

I smile up into his twinkling eyes. The feeling's mutual, but I can't bring myself to say so. He's wearing a pale blue sweater and jeans with a thin white stripe down the front from being pressed so many times. Probably brings them to the Chinese laundry on the corner, next to the takeout place. Kills two birds with one stone.

But now Duff pulls away and hands me a package he must have brought in with the Chinese food. A thin rectangle, too big for my mailbox in the foyer.

"Figured I'd make a personal delivery," Duff says, but in a way that makes my heart go pitter-pat. Of course, he keeps packages for all the tenants, saving us a trip to the PO, but usually he'll just leave a note, and we'll pick it up in his office.

"Thanks so much, Duff." I see the return address: Keeley. I shake my head. Can't escape the Yik Yak Club, no matter what. I set it aside, but then curiosity gets the best of me. While Duff divvies up the food and puts on a pot of coffee, I open the package. Inside is a posed portrait of a family. A black-and-white photograph, unframed, and crudely colorized. A mother, father, and six daughters. Just like us, I'm thinking, when I realize it *is* us, the Sheehans, way back when. I'd know Da and Eden and Alberta anywhere, Mam not so much.

"Oh, Duff, it's us." I look again. A note in the package has fallen to the floor. Duffy stoops to pick it up before reaching for me. He walks me into the living room, helps me onto the couch.

"Let me get the coffee," he says, and while he does, I read.

Dear Mimi,
   Katie Bain, that cousin I went to high school with, called last week to say she'd found some things we might want when she was cleaning out her mother's place.

This was one of them. Our family minus me.

Katie's the one who came to see me when her mother (our aunt!!!) was a patient. The old lady, our mother's sister Maeve, died before I got to meet her. Not that she wanted to meet me. She was in her nineties, still holding a grudge.

Love,
Keeley

On the back of the photo is a note, handwritten in pencil:

Joseph Sheehan and family
Sea Street, Quincy
August 1932

Joe and Mary, so young, so good-looking. Got the world on a string, that's what you'd think, looking at the picture. Da's got his arm around my mother and we three oldest are standing next to him, crammed together, peas in a pod. The twins, Patty and Josephine, stand, one each in front of each of them, and Fagan is in my mother's arms. Her head's resting on my mother's shoulder and her index finger is knuckle-deep up her nose. Darling Fagan, picking her nose for posterity.

The black-and-white picture has been colorized the old-fashioned way, the colors painted over the print, but bleeding just outside the lines. Each of us girls, brunettes, redheads, and Eden, the only blonde, appear to be wearing a pastel-colored dress, yellow, pink, baby blue, mint green, lavender. Alberta and Eden, at ten and eleven, are just as beautiful as I remember. My mother's lips are red, her cheeks bright pink, and Da's eyes are too, too blue. I wish I could peel back this layer of color to see what they really looked like. Still, I'm grateful for this shot of all of us together.

I don't realize Duffy's next to me until I smell the coffee.

"My family," I say. "My first one."

"Sweet."

"Right before disaster struck."

"You mean the Depression?"

Again I check the date on the back, shake my head no. "My mother was pregnant with Keeley. Her birth was the beginning of the end."

"What a burden for her to bear, your sister."

"I like to think we've helped lighten her load. We tried. She's done well. She's got the love of a good man. They've made a nice life together."

The love of a good man. This part of the sentence echoes louder than the rest. Duff puts his arm around me. His fingers press the soft part of my upper arm. My body burns — embarrassment, not lust, but the one, I'm finding, doesn't necessarily rule out the other.

"Hey, I'm starved," I say. "How 'bout that Moo Goo Gai Pan?" I jump up and turn to look at him. Duffy smiles. I've blown him off, but he can take it. He'll try again.

While we eat, I prop the photo on the window ledge over the table.

"Six daughters," he says once we've dug in, using chopsticks and laughing every time the Chow Mei Fun falls back onto the plate. We've agreed, without using words, that tonight we won't talk about his son; about incarceration, false memory, exculpation. "How'd you manage to duplicate that?" His question hangs there while the two of us turn redder than the peppers in the sweet and sour.

"The propagation of the faith," I say, innocent as could be.

" 'The propagation of the faith'?" He takes a sip of coffee and shakes his head.

"Isn't that the duty of every Catholic couple? Increasing the ranks of the faithful?

My ex was really big on that."

"We stopped at two, Virginia and me," he says. "It's all we could handle, to hell with the propagation of the faith. Turns out, they pushed us to the edge. Over it a couple of times."

He shrugs, looks at me. I nod, I get it. No more needs to be said.

"Hey, it's good to know your limits," I say. "Neither Jack nor I ever did."

Again, Duff looks at the picture. He can't get over how beautiful Eden and Alberta were. "You look just like them," he adds.

"Time to get your eyes checked."

"My eyes are great, except for the fine print. That's when I need glasses." He takes out his glasses. He puts them on and gives me a hard stare. I swear Duff's look goes right through me, like a shot of whiskey, burning all the way.

"You're lookin' good either way, Mrs. Malloy. Mighty good."

I don't know where to look or what to say. Me, who lost my looks years ago. I pretend I haven't heard him, try but fail to pincer a bit of chicken in the Moo Goo Gai Pan. "I keep wondering about my parents. Who, in the end, had seven daughters in eleven years."

"Only doing their Catholic duty?" Duffy's

eyes twinkle.

"Even the propagation of the faith can't account for that level of reproduction, I don't think. And Da wasn't devout. He just went through the motions. What I keep wondering is, did my father and mother have a true passion for each other? Did they risk it all and lose it all because they wanted a son? Or because they couldn't get enough of one another?"

He reaches across the table for my hand.

"Does it make a difference now?" His eyes blaze a trail deep inside me.

"All the difference," I say, although I'm not clear why.

"A true passion," he repeats.

It's a statement, not a question, and next thing I know, we're standing and holding each other. We head toward my bedroom, moving slowly, like children going to some-place we've never been, instead of old folks traveling backward down a familiar but neglected path.

Thirty-One:
The Lady Is a Tramp

Duffy's up and gone at the crack of dawn. I can tell the time by the way the light comes in around my curtains. I pretend to be asleep, roll over onto his side of the bed, enjoying the last warmth from his body, and the nice smell he left behind. When I roll, the hinges of my body creak, a door that hasn't opened for ages, but I'm oh so glad it did. Aren't I just the lucky duck? I think, finding this at last. Whatever "this" is, "this" will do.

But when I sit up, figuring I'll let the coffee brew while I hop into the shower, my sciatica howls. Sharp, hot pain starts deep inside my butt cheek and shoots all down my leg. Great, I think, I finally get laid and now I can't even hobble out of bed.

If only Alberta were around to tell. The sight of me in agony after rolling in the hay with Duffy would send her into orbit. *Mimi screws an old guy and ends up needing trac-*

tion. God, Alberta. She kept her sense of humor through it all, right up til Danny died. We shared more laughs than you could count. If she were alive, I'd call her, just to crack her up. *You made my day, honey,* she'd say.

Once, when we were kids, we were at the kitchen table, all of us together, eating elbow macaroni — one of our favorites — and were laughing our heads off about something, when a piece of macaroni shot out of Alberta's nose and landed in the middle of the table. A complete accident, because she'd been laughing with her mouth full. We — the twins, Eden, me, and Alberta — doubled over at the sight of that piece of macaroni in the middle of the table. Then all of us had to try it, snorting and sucking up the macaroni, but not one of us succeeded. We were in hysterics when another elbow macaroni flew out of Alberta's nose, and she wasn't even trying. By then, we were crying we were laughing so hard, and Alberta laughed the loudest of all. After that, she used it as a party trick, blowing macaroni out her nose. It always got a giggle. God, if she could see me now, with love in the air, and my sciatica screaming in a way it hasn't since I carried all those babies on my hip all day. She'd be tickled pink.

A nice hot bath and some Advil ought to do the trick, if only I can get myself to the bathroom. I haul myself up, make my painful way into the kitchen to put on the coffee, swallow a couple of pills. The coffee hasn't even started to bubble up into the glass knob when the buzzer sounds. Cassandra, I think, remembering our date this morning. But, no, it can't be Cass because she's got a key and always lets herself in. And besides, she's not due for at least half an hour. Slowly, ever so slowly, I go to the intercom in the front hallway.

"It's me, Patty, with Jo." My sister's voice sounds muffled. "You gonna let us in? Or make us stand out here in the cold?"

"I ought to let you freeze, the two of you," I joke, but I'm still miffed at the pair of them for calling me a liar in front of my daughters. No memory lapse in that regard.

"Open the damned door," Patty orders.

I buzz them in, crack my apartment door, then go, fast as I'm able, into my room and throw on some sweats. Getting my legs into the pants is a new form of torture. But I'm glad they're here, those two. I'm going to give them a piece of my mind — a small one, at least, considering what's left of it.

But when I walk out of the bedroom, they're shivering in my foyer like the pair of hungry orphans they used to be, all bundled up in down jackets and fur-trimmed hats. Patty shoves an envelope into my hand.

"Greeks bearing gifts," I say.

"Shut up," she answers. "Sit before you open it."

We plunk down onto my couch. Ouch. Inside the envelope are an embroidered hankie and a lock of bright red hair. Fagan's hair. I'd know it anywhere.

"Nana gave it to us," says Patty. "On her deathbed."

"She didn't give it to us," Jo corrects. "She told us where to look for it. In her bureau, under the lining of a drawer."

"A *piseog*," I say, one step ahead of them. "The *piseog*." I fold the hankie back around Fagan's silky hair, just as soft and vibrant as it used to be.

"I forgot we had it," says Jo.

"Until Siobhan started talking about the faeries." Patty.

"The wee people." Jo tries to laugh, but it sounds like something's stuck in her throat.

"Well now, Patty," I tell her, still holding the *piseog*, "your prince of a grandson can include this with his genealogy. Maybe he can laminate it or something." Can't help it. I'm still miffed.

"Too late," says Patty. "He already turned it in. Got a C+ because of all the missing info." She looks crushed because he didn't get an A, but I feel a small surge of vindication: the Sheehan genealogy, an ill-fated project from the start.

"Flanna brought it over to Nana, after Da was buried," Patty says, grabbing back the *piseog*. "She showed up at Nana's, banging on the front door, calling in her sweetie-sweet voice."

"In our mother's black silk dress, and wearing a black hat with a pink feather." I see it plain as day: Flanna on the porch, pink feather on her hat, *piseog* in her black-gloved hand. She held it out to Nana. We hid in the parlor, all six of us crammed behind the curtains and the couch. Scared. But still, still we wanted to look at her, wanted to see her again, Da's woman of shining loveliness. *You put it there, you,* Flanna wailed while Nana stood there, her white hair in its neat bun, her old face gathered like a fist, her squinted eyes sharp as blades. The *piseog*. Our real mother's hankie, and a lock of Fagan's hair.

"Nana wouldn't let Flanna in, remember, Mimi?" Patty asks, and I do. Made Flanna stand outside, on the porch. " 'You'll burn in hell for what you did to Fagan and my Joey,' she said."

The twins slip off their parkas, stand in front of me.

"Its evil spell is broken," snarls Patty, taking on the role of Flanna as the twins act out the ancient drama. Her accent isn't perfect, not like when she does Da, but it's good enough to scare me. She jabs her finger right in front of Josephine's face.

"I've broken it myself, without even burning it to ash, and now I want my Fagan back."

"That's right," I interrupt. "She didn't say Keeley. She called her Fagan. *'Fagan belongs to me.'* That's what she said." A chill wind gusts around me, even colder than out at Marina Bay.

"Fagan's my daughter. They brought her back to me. You've no right to keep her. I don't care about the rest of them. Brats and trouble-makers. But Fagan, she's mine."

"Fagan's gone," spits Jo, playing Nana's part. *"You know that better than anyone, Miss Flanna Flanagan. And she won't be coming back. It's Keeley we've got here. And she's staying put."*

Not for a split second would I confuse my sisters for my stepmother and grandmother. Patty hasn't got a speck of Flanna's glamour and Jo lacks Nana's ferocity. But in spite of their bad acting, they've got their lines down to a T.

Patty: *"She's Fagan and she's mine."*

"Ha-ha-ha-ha," hacks Jo, imitating Nana laughing in Flanna's face. *"Get out and take your faerie business with you. Take yourself and your faeries and your silly curses back to Ireland. On the next boat, and good riddance to ya."*

"Then Flanna started mumbling, using words we didn't understand." I see her and hear her, on the front steps of Nana's house.

"She'll be haunting you all your days, will Fagan," hollers Jo as Nana. She raises her arms, shakes them, as if to ward off Flanna.

"That's when Flanna took off," says Patty, back to herself, her eyes bright, her face aglow.

"The last time any of us saw her," I say. They nod. "Let's have coffee, huh? The smell of the fresh brew is driving me nuts." I get up and make my slow way to the kitchen.

"Why are you limping?" they ask at the same time.

"Me? Limping?"

"You're walking funny," says Patty. "What happened?"

"I was throwing the trash from the party into the Dumpster," I lie, fast and slick. "I must've thrown my back out."

"Gosh, nothing works the way it used to, does it?" says Jo.

If only she knew, I think, but my lips are sealed.

Once we're settled back in my living room with coffee, I try to give them that small piece of my mind.

"Last week, you two acted like I'm a liar or a lunatic when you know how Flanna hurt us. 'Fat splatter.' Right in front of my girls."

The twins cling to each other. Sixtysomething years evaporate.

"We came to apologize." Little Patty, with her faded red hair, her mind still sharp and shiny, like those multipurpose tools they sell on TV late at night.

"When we were driving home last week, the car was full of angry ghosts." Jo.

"We felt them flying around inside the car." Patty.

"Eden and Alberta and Da," I say. The twins eyeball me. "They were with us at lunch. Maybe they followed you out." Jo looks around.

"The soul has everlasting life." We learned that in our Baltimore Catechism way, way, way back when, the immortality of the soul.

It's one of the few points of Catholic teaching that we all agree about. Couldn't keep going if I did not have that faith.

"Flanna hurt all of us." Jo.

"We pretended to the outside world it wasn't happening." Patty.

"Nobody would've believed us."

"You're shaking," my sisters say together. They move onto the couch beside me, wrap their arms around me, the way Eden and Alberta used to do.

"We knew you were scarred." Patty's hug keeps me from falling apart.

"We knew it couldn't have been an accident." Jo.

"Which means Da lied."

"Or he was lied to." Patty.

"May he rest in peace." Jo.

"He's not in peace," I say, as convinced of this as I am of my own existence. "You two know he isn't either."

Patty nods. "Da knew about your scars. But he went along with Flanna's story, about the accident."

The pain of Da's betrayal still sends convulsions through me, even after all this time.

"Da wanted to believe it, all of us did. We preferred the made-up story." This time, the twins recite their lines together. We were all so good at pretending. Blah-blah-blah.

"But you accused me of making things up, right in front of my own daughters. And you know how hard it's been for my daughters and me . . . Jack always undermining. Giving them permission, right from the start, to put me down. 'Don't make things worse than they were,' that's what you said. You two, who chew over the past like it's an Omaha steak."

"We look for the sweet and tender parts," says Patty.

"You try to make it better than it was," I say.

"Well, Mrs. Mimi Malloy, all these years you've acted as if none of it ever happened." Patty, in her snippy voice.

"You're in denial." Jo.

"Denial? No way," I wail. "Never pretended. I didn't remember. I didn't want to. And now my brain is full of black spots."

"It's those little strokes you've been having." Patty. "With the name I can't pronounce."

"You're waiting for the Big One." Jo.

Their words smack me as hard as Flanna's hand. I can't stand having my health status a topic of chitchat. I'm furious.

"Cassie and her big mouth."

"She's only looking out for you."

"Nothing's sacred in this family."

"She looking out for your best interests." Jo and Patty.

Just then there's a light knock at my door, and then the sound of it opening.

"Mimi?" Cassandra calls.

"Speak of the devil."

Cassandra rushes in, stops short at the sight of her aunts. Huffing and puffing, like she's just run the Boston Marathon, except she's carrying a box of Dunkin' Donuts and looks like she won the lottery.

"I've found a guy, a great guy in Scituate." She drops the box of doughnuts on the coffee table, still panting, then hugs Jo and Patty. "He does repressed-memory therapy."

Repressed-memory therapy, the twins echo. My sisters and I look at one another and crack up.

"He cures psychogenic amnesia. We might solve this mystery once and for all, the mystery of Fagan Sent Away."

"With doughnuts?"

"Not doughnuts, Mimi, hypnosis. He's great, that's the buzz. Hypnosis, but no hard-core drugs."

Cass opens the doughnut box, puts it in the center of the coffee table. My favorite, vanilla crème with powdered sugar, sits right there on top, calling out to me. It'd be rude not to eat it after Cass went to all that trouble.

"Are they coming too?" Cass asks, pointing to her aunts.

"Where we going?" Patty, up for anything, assuming she's included.

"We're following the route you took when you ran away." Cass.

"I can't remember any of it, just showing up on Nana Sheehan's doorstep. The summer of '37."

"Wasn't that a movie?" asks Cassandra.

"No, that was *Summer of '42.*" Patty. "An entirely different thing."

"Just after school got out," says Jo. "A hot summer day. All six of us setting out. Sad and scared, but excited, too."

Another of those memories that binds us together, we Sheehan girls, forever. That's when Eden and Alberta press against me, like they've got to certify the memory. In my living room, the twins sit facing Cass and me, all of us with traces of sugar sprinkles, flecks of jelly, on our chins and chests.

"You remember Flanna and her tea?" asks Patty.

"No." When I try, and I try hard as I can,

my mind goes dark. Lights out, nobody home.

"It had to be just so, just sweet enough and hot enough, or there'd be hell to pay." Jo and Patty nod together, like it's a story they've told a million times. Al and Eden embrace me now, like they want to hold me up.

"Hot afternoon, nothing to do," I say, the black spot slowly dissolving. All of us in the kitchen, with its big black coal-burning stove. Flanna, the queen of her domain, holding Keeley on her lap — two pink-cheeked beauties, mother and daughter.

"Flanna demands to be served her tea." Patty. "She doesn't care how hot it is outside. She wants her hot tea and she wants it now."

"Alberta makes her tea," I say. "Right?" Slowly, encouraged by my dearly departeds, it's all coming back to me. "She puts the loose leaves in Flanna's tea steeper and we knew, all of us, that if she could have, Alberta would have poisoned it."

"Instead she makes it scalding hot," continues Patty, the historian. "We're watching because we know Alberta's up to something. Alberta sets the teacup in its saucer next to Flanna, as nice as could be, but before she's cooled it down."

"Flanna took one sip and threw it, cup and all." I feel triumphant as the scene unfolds before me, like a drama on *Hallmark Hall of Fame*. "Alberta screamed."

"Flanna dropped Keeley and charged after Al." Patty pauses. "Poor Alberta. She always bore that scar on her chest."

"Like a stain." It never went away, a shadow always over her breast. " 'Just as well,' she used to say. She used to joke that, without it, she could've made her living as a stripper, but who'd pay to look at that?"

"She said that?" Cass. "Auntie Alberta?"

"She was only kidding," says Jo.

"Alberta was a card, a hot ticket. That's what the fellas used to call her over at the shipyard."

"She howled like a trapped beast when Flanna threw the tea at her, though." Jo. "Then Flanna chased her down and smacked her."

"Da came home." I remember now. "Al tried to show him, but he wouldn't look. He shook his head, like a little boy, and took off again." A recovered memory. Da refusing to help. Running away.

"He left you with her?" asks Cassandra. We nod yes, me feeling again the pain of Da's betrayal, as fresh as the crocuses pushing up through the snow outside and sharper than a spade.

"He left us with her."

"After that, Flanna gave Alberta a royal beating." Patty.

I couldn't see the beating, only hear it. Those sounds convinced me of what I had to do.

"But the story didn't end there." Jo smiles, her halo glowing.

"That's where you came in, Mimi," says Patty. "After Flanna beat Alberta, she went upstairs for a nap, still wailing about her burned tongue. She took Keeley with her, but the minute Flanna was asleep, Keeley ran downstairs to us. Then you got us organized."

" 'Gather a few things,' you told each of us." Jo. " 'Shoes, a change of underpants. We put everything in pillowcases.' "

"We waited to be sure she was sound asleep," I say. "Then the six of us took off." Sitting in my living room, stuffed with vanilla crème and honey-glazed doughnuts, I see us, in pairs, creeping out the back door. And for the first time, I also see or understand that I was making a choice that day, a choice to stay with Da and Flanna or to go. It was a choice that rippled through our lives, all of them. If Da was going to run away, then we could too.

As Alberta sat there trembling from her burn and beating, I grew certain she'd be next. The next Sheehan sister to be sent away to Cullyhanna, to learn how to be good. I could not let that happen. We had to run away. We'd be leaving Da, I knew that, knew that we'd be leaving him, the center of our universe — my universe — but he'd just turned his back on Alberta when she was in pain, hurt yet again by Flanna Flanagan. So we left, Eden holding on to Alberta, carrying her things.

"You two were bawling your eyes out." I see the twins as frightened children, jabbering and weeping. "I told you to cut it out so you wouldn't wake her up."

"You said we weren't allowed to cry til we got to Nana Sheehan's." Jo. "Then we could cry all we wanted to."

"You carried Keeley, piggyback."

"We were leaving Da that day," I say. "We were leaving him for good."

"The father you loved was already gone," Cass cuts in.

"No, he wasn't," corrects Patty. "The father we loved was the same one who left us with Flanna. Let her hurt us."

Everything is quiet for a while, all of us thinking about that hot afternoon in Quincy when our family fell apart once and for all.

371

"How blessed we were to have Nana in our lives," I say. To know that she would take us in, no questions asked. That we'd be welcome in her home.

Now Patty tosses Cassandra the *piseog*.

"Check it out," she says. "The *piseog*."

"That hair, that wonderful hair," Cass whispers, fingering Fagan's locks, the color of flame.

While Cass is examining Fagan's hair, I finally see my chance to escape and grab it. "Let me hop into the shower."

I use the word "hop" very loosely.

THIRTY-TWO:
THE BEST IS YET TO COME

After my shower, I put on the nice workout clothes Cass bought for me, though I've got no plans to exercise — not on the treadmill, anyway. When I'm done, the three of them are still sitting around my coffee table, eating doughnuts, drinking coffee, and jabbering about memories — repressed and otherwise — hypnosis, and *piseogs.* Everything is moving just a bit too fast.

"Where'd you get this?" Jo and Patty ask together, holding up the photo Keeley sent. I'd left it on the coffee table.

"From Keeley." Cass answers for me when she sees I've stuffed another honey glazed into my mouth. "See the return address? But where did Keeley get it?"

I take Keeley's note from the envelope. They take turns reading it. " 'Our family minus me,' " reads Patty, then she goes back to the picture.

"Your parents were so young, so good-looking," says Cass.

"Your grandparents." She nods. "And every one of us in the picture clueless about what the future held." Fagan picking her nose. Our mother, as if her entire life's ahead of her instead of just a few more months. Da so proud of his girls.

I pick up the phone, speed-dial Keeley's work number. She picks up, sounding elegant and efficient. "Thanks for that photograph, Keeley. It's beautiful." I tell her the twins and Cass are with me, looking at it. They holler their hellos.

"It's hard, so hard for me," Keeley says, and I turn away from the others.

"Why, Keel?"

"Because I'm not in the picture and never knew our mother. Because my birth caused it all."

"No, it didn't. Get that thought out of your head."

"Aidan's genealogy has really done a number on me."

"I hear you. That's why I've always hated ancient history, the blighted family tree."

"Honestly, I'd never thought much about our real mother dying a few hours after I was born. Flanna was my mother. And then, of course, she, too, was gone."

"Your mother? Perish the thought."

"No, I never knew our mother. Or Fagan. She was gone by the time I showed up. And when I think about Da, I only remember him bringing us treats, and spoiling me. You girls spoiled me too."

"Spoiled?" I hate that word. "We never ever spoiled you, Keeley. Spoiled means rotten and self-centered. You've never been either of those things."

"No, spoiled," she insists, "because I never understood anything. I don't remember anything bad. Everybody loved me. I lived in a fog."

"You weren't spoiled, baby, you were protected. What's wrong with that? You've turned out kind and thoughtful, Keeley. You've got a great husband, a successful career, two homes, and those beautiful dogs. My daughters love you." Probably more than me, I'm thinking, but I don't add this part. Cassandra grabs the phone.

"When were you born?" she asks, knowing darn well the answer. February 11, 1933.

"Well, then you are in the picture," says Cass. "It was taken in August 1932. You were there, right where you were supposed to be, in your mother's belly, gestating away." Leave it to Cassandra to do the math.

I grab the phone back. Keeley's making a

funny sound, laughing or crying, I can't tell.

"Cassie's right, Keeley. You're in the picture. Our mother would have been three months pregnant. So all of us are there, together." The funny noises get louder.

"Thank God I've got a private office," she says.

"Oh, Keeley," I say, "I'll get some copies made."

The twins take the phone from me. I catch my breath, but then Cass pulls me down beside her on the couch.

"The memories you've recovered so far explain so much."

"Recovered memories? Explain so much?" I'm thinking, More of Cassandra's blah-blah, but then I realize with a pang she might be right: the recovered memories seem to be pushing out the false ones, me remembering things the way they didn't happen.

"You've finally found the courage to let them come up into the light," she says.

"Courage?" I say loud it enough that the others turn around. I didn't hear them hang up. "Courage has nothing to do with it."

"Does too," says Patty the potentate. "You had more than Daddy did."

"What do you mean?"

"Some men rise to the occasion, whatever

376

the occasion is, and some men fall below it."

Jo nods. "Our father, who art in heaven, did not rise to the occasion."

"What occasion?" Cassandra interrupts.

"His life, our lives," I say, seeing the sad truth of it. "Our father fell below the occasion of his own life."

"Which doesn't mean we loved him any less." Jo.

"No, we didn't love him any less."

All four of us look at the photo, Cass running her French-manicured fingertip over the ancient image of Da's face. Next to him, untouched, our mother, a woman we never got a chance to know and not one of us remembers. Our mother, lost to us forever. Our father, Da, despite his best efforts, unable to be the father I'm sure he longed to be. Pulled too hard, in too many directions, as if on a rack of his own making, and right there in the village square for everyone to see.

Again it comes to me, that image of my da, unshaven, his eyes bloodshot, the crusted cut across one cheek. Fallen, *a beast upon all fours,* in that familiar place I can't quite recognize, one of earth and stones. When did I see him like that?

"Keeley says you saved her life." Jo.

"That's what she just said." Patty.

"When we ran away." Jo. "You saved her life."

That hot summer day, the six of us setting out barefoot, pillowcases holding our few belongings, then showing up at Nana Sheehan's, not far from the Fore River Bridge. Nana's house, with its smells of baking bread and flowers. It wasn't Keeley's but Alberta's life I was trying to save.

The four of us, plus the ghosts of Eden and Alberta, head out in Cassie's Bimmer, back through Quincy, onto Route 3A, to see where the old house used to be on 27 Sea Street. Taken by the Commonwealth of Massachusetts and demolished in the late 1950s or early '60s. No trace of the old neighborhood, just a big loop of asphalt three lanes across, marked with guardrails, reflectors, and tall steel poles for the mercury vapor lights. Even though bits and pieces of our journey have come back to me, I still want to see it, the tiny patch of earth on which our home had stood, and my departed sisters urge me on.

"Pull over," I order Cass when we reach the spot where I think our house might have been. There's a breakdown lane just wide enough for a car if she pulls up against the guardrail.

"It's dangerous."

"Pull over anyway." She does, putting on her emergency lights. I get out. My sisters, both dead and living, join me. Soon Cassandra does too, the four of us, or the six — depending upon how you count — staring over the guardrail into the valley of dead grass. Styrofoam cups, shreds of the *Globe* and the *Ledger,* beer cans, broken bottles, a sneaker, a Filene's bag, a CVS sales flyer, a golden crown from Burger King. Not one damned thing of us. History wiped out. I can't tell where anything would have been, not the house itself, not Flanna's gardens, the foundation, or even a trace of that old coal cellar. I'd hoped to get a glimpse of Fagan dancing in the kitchen, or Flanna by the burn can, but all I see is this bowl of grass, filled with litter, a million motor vehicles speeding past it night and day.

"Seen enough?" Cass asks, not meanly, just wondering. I nod. Not one of my other sisters speaks. For all we know, Flanna made out like a bandit, getting paid the house's full market value just to leave so they could bring in the wrecker's ball. Maybe Flanna went back to the old country with her satchel full of money, back to Cullyhanna, County Armagh. But I wouldn't know.

Because even though 27 Sea Street was just one town over, only a few miles from Nana's, it might as well have been on the far side of the moon.

Nana herself never brought it up, except to mutter that Flanna took the house and all inside it. We never heard the other grown-ups talking. Not a word about our father, our stepmother, our little sister. After we ran away to Nana's house we started our lives over, just the way Nana had when she came to America. That's what she taught us, how to leave things behind, how to start again — how to look ahead, not back. A lesson that made life possible for me.

We get back into Cassandra's Bimmer, the traffic pushing us forward, everything outside the car a blur. Now Cassandra, directed by Patty, exits the highway near Quincy Point and drives along the narrow streets of double-deckers and small cottages, just a few blocks from the water, and when the wind is right, the residents get that fresh salty smell. But when the tide is out, the air is filled with another type of smell, nowhere near as invigorating.

Our old neighborhood is gone, but the adjacent neighborhood remains, crammed up against the highway. The streets twist and turn. Started out as cow paths, never intended for use by SUVs. The houses still huddle close together, the way they always have. All that's changed in the years since we grew up are the cars — lots more cars — and of course more power lines and satellite dishes on the rooftops. Many of the houses have added upper floors and roof decks to give them views of the water.

"The whole neighborhood used to be full of shipyard workers." Jo. "Riveters, lofts men, welders."

"I couldn't stand living like this, the houses so close together," Cass complains. "Everybody in your business."

"These houses were built back when people still needed one another," says Jo. "They didn't mind if your kids and pets ran through their yards. They didn't have cars, so they didn't need driveways or garages."

In Cassie's luxury sedan, comfy as could be, we make our way through the old streets, then turn back onto Route 3A. We see the same ugly stretch of road connecting Quincy to Weymouth, a mess of bars, boatyards, banks, dollar stores, nail salons, and fast-food joints. When we were growing up, there was hardly any traffic, and just a grocery and the bakery.

Now, just ahead, is the Fore River Bridge, a steel truss drawbridge. Almost brand-new the summer we ran away, one of the wonders of the world when we were growing up. Every ship built at the Quincy yard had to pass beneath it to make its way out to sea.

"Eden was terrified of the bridge," says Jo. "Afraid every step of the way that it was going to open." I feel her fluttering, jostling Alberta, glad that her fear is being remembered.

"I've always had dreams, no, nightmares, about that. Still do," says Patty. "The bridge opening, while we're walking across it. We're just about in the center when it swings open like a book, and the six of us go flying."

I see us hurrying on foot across the bridge, then plunging toward the water after the bridge opens to let a big ship through.

"I never see where we land."

THIRTY-THREE:
SWINGIN' ON A STAR

Minutes later, less than four miles from where our old house used to be, we pull up in front of Nana's, or what once was Nana's, a bungalow a couple of blocks from the water. Part of a row, all with front porches and postage-stamp lawns. We park across the street.

"Craftsman cottages," says Cass. "Worth maybe four hundred thousand today if they've got the original woodwork."

"When Nana lived here, she had the most beautiful gardens," Jo says. "Her kitchen garden was right here on this busy street."

"Of course, it wasn't all that busy back then." Patty.

"A young family must be living there now." Jo points to a swing set and a little yellow playhouse.

We get out. It's just after noon and the street is quiet. Down the block, a mailman with a big leather sack walks from house to house. A mother pushes her baby in a stroller.

"I can't say that Nana was glad to see us," says Patty

"No, she didn't smile or hug us, but she opened her door and let us in." Jo.

"Maybe she expected us." Me.

That day we showed up on her doorstep, she brought us in and fed us soup and toast and butter, which we were glad to have despite the heat. She looked at Alberta's burn, swollen and bubbled, then sent me and Eden around the corner to the doctor's — the same doctor who'd set my broken wrist a lifetime before. Later that evening, he came to tend to Alberta, and to give her something for the pain. Afterward, Nana made each of us scrub our feet in a tub of water on the kitchen floor. She gave us ointment to put on our blisters, and a clean pair of socks for each of us to wear so our blisters wouldn't get infected. Then she sent us up to bed.

Nana, Annie Sheehan, widowed for as long as any of us could remember, was a tiny woman, with pure-white hair rolled into a knot. She had sharp blue eyes, cold and lovely, and thin lips that were almost always pressed tightly together. She had a clean, pressed housedress, flower-printed, for each day of the week, and a work apron hanging on a hook by the soapstone kitchen sink. Nana, with hardly any accent, because she'd struggled so hard to become American.

Nana couldn't waste time talking when she could be working. Hard work was how her family had survived the Hunger and made it to the USA, although they lost too many along the way. Hard work, along with expecting and accepting loss. That's how Nana lived. She never explained the world to us. She figured we'd get it on our own.

We shared two bedrooms, one in front and one in back, with chenille bedspreads in pretty designs, and green pull shades at the windows. These rooms seemed to be ready for us. Nana slept in a small room downstairs, and on the front porch during the summer. That night, for the first time in ages, I slept through the night, knowing nothing bad would happen.

Suddenly Patty rushes across the street, like she's being dragged or chased. Doesn't even bother to look both ways.

"What's gotten into you?" shouts Jo, chasing after her. Cass and I follow, running too.

We run straight down the driveway to the edge of the garage, where Nana's compost pile used to be. Scraggly grass. Dead leaves left over from the fall. A crocus or two pushing through, all that might be left from Nana's garden. We're trespassing, and I'm really hoping no one's home. I'd be so embarrassed.

"The night before Da died, I saw a banshee in the yard," announces Patty. "In this yard. Right here."

"A banshee?"

"A banshee with streaming white hair. She wailed in the most awful way. Jo woke up too."

Patty herself has gone white.

"Recovered memory," says Cass, taking out a notebook and a pen so she can get it down in writing.

"I heard the wailing," says Jo, "but I didn't see the banshee. By the time I got to the window, she was gone." The twins look at each other, identical expressions on their faces.

"We were so scared." Patty.

"What exactly is a banshee?" Cassandra asks.

"A female spirit." Patty.

"Whose wailing foretells a death in the family." Jo.

"We jumped back into bed and pulled the covers up." Patty.

"The wailing only lasted for a few minutes." Jo. "Then we both went back to sleep."

"And sure enough, the next day, Da was dead." Patty.

As we look around Nana's yard, Eden and Alberta press close, and I swear Fagan shows up too — fierce, feisty Fagan. The story of the banshee washes over me, and I see Da prostrate, his clothes filthy. In agony or maybe just drunk, in that place of earth and stones. Something hard ricochets in my chest. Da. *A beast upon all fours.*

"Take me home, please." Suddenly I'm out of gas, right there at the end of the driveway of what used to be Nana's house, a house that's hardly recognizable anymore.

"Take me home now." Cass gives me a look, like she's about to argue, but changes her mind. She puts away her pen and notebook, takes my arm, and walks me back across the street to the Bimmer. The others follow.

"Call me Greta Garbo," I say once we're all belted in. "I vant to be alone."

I feel full and empty at the same time, everything I'm learning, everything I'm remembering and thinking — memories, either false or recovered — are spinning, like a load of laundry on its final cycle.

Thirty-Four:
We Just Couldn't
Say Goodbye

What I want more than anything right now is to sit by myself and think. Too much is happening, and too fast, after nothing at all for so many years. It's like that feeling I got when I went to Ruthie's, looking out the window, the train moving forward as it pulled out of the station, but everything around me seemed to be sliding in reverse. I pick up the phone, call Siobhan, leave a message, tell her that I want to see her soon. Oh, and that I love her, which is still easier to say into the machine than to her face. Then I call Ruth Ann, Celestine, and Delilah, just to say hello, trying not to feel my grudges, duct tape wound tightly around my heart. We exchange pleasantries, which we've never done before. What's doing, how's work, how are the kids, etc., and "I love you," before hanging up.

I'm still jittery from the phone calls, my sciatica in excruciating mode, when Duffy tap, tap, taps on my door. Who else would it be? So much for my downtime. So much for my chance to think.

"Mrs. Malloy, oh, Mrs. Malloy!" His voice is edgier than usual, some shard of pain in it.

"Mrs. Malloy?" he calls again, sharper, a question.

Suddenly I'm full of dread. We finally make whoopee and now he wants to dump me. Just my luck. I put out and get put in the trash. On my coffee table, within reach, is the photo of my family, my mother's hankie, the lock of Fagan's hair. I'd like to trash them, too.

"Mrs. Malloy," he says one more time, and then I hear the key turning in the lock. Himself is letting himself in. The nerve. Of course, or maybe curse, he's got the master key.

"I'm here, I'm here," I call, but I can't crank up the volume. My voice stuck on low. And furthermore, I'm stuck in the recliner, and I'll be damned if I'll let him see me hobbling around.

But once he starts walking toward me, I see the look on that old face — weathered like the masthead of an old ship, but looking better with age — and I read the worry and sorrow in his eyes, the fear that I wouldn't answer, or maybe that something bad had happened to me.

"I saw you come in," he says. "I knew you were here. When you didn't answer, I . . . I . . . I . . ."

He's at a loss for words. An old Irishman at a loss for words. That's got to be a first.

I move the recliner to its upright position. If only I had that kind where you pull the lever and it ejects you from the seat. Ed Mc-Mahon advertises them on TV.

"Duff. Oh, Duff."

"Mimi," he answers, and I'm stunned. Mimi. Such a beautiful little word. "You OK?"

I can tell by his dazzling eyes, focused so steadily on me, how much he wants me to be OK. So I tell him, sure, sure, I'm fine, even though I'm feeling like a nut case, strange feelings storming around inside my skull, my sciatica riled up, plus me loving him way too much.

He sits down at the edge of the couch without me asking him to. He's got something to say, but now I'm pretty sure he isn't going to dump me.

"I'll mix us a Manhattan," I say. Without thinking, I stand up and let out a yelp, cringing from the pain. If only the floor would open up to swallow me. Instead,

Duffy grabs my arm.

"Poor Mimi," he murmurs, reseating me gently onto the couch beside him, like I'm a combat vet, enfeebled by an old war wound. "Tell me where the whiskey is."

Duff gets up and goes into the kitchen. He's not exactly limping, just that list from his old wound, but he's moving slowly; stooped, maybe, from the weight of what he's said, or possibly from our roll in the hay. I watch him, thinking of the two of us together, of his son in that awful other place. I remember, vaguely, Cass and Delilah gabbing about the case when he went to trial, how terrible it was; this karate instructor, an Army veteran with a girlfriend, you couldn't trust anyone anymore. But I didn't pay much attention, and never made the connections. Minutes later, Duffy's back with our drinks, straight-up, in those glasses that are so hard to hold if your hand is shaking, even a little bit. I don't think mine is until I see the amber liquid slosh.

After a few swallows, my sciatica settles down. I sip my Manhattan, my hand less shaky now.

Duffy lights up, but I pass. No desire for a smoke. Instead, I make us breakfast for dinner, one of my favorites. Eggs, bacon, toast, and home fries.

"Do you like 'em straight-up or over-easy?" I ask from the kitchen, where I'm cracking eggs and stretching the strips of bacon neatly into the pan. Just enough to satisfy, but not enough to clog our arteries.

"Over-easy, Mrs. Malloy," Duffy says from the living room, his voice sweet and warm as syrup. "Over-easy every time." I'm glad he can't see me blush. He'd think I have a dirty mind.

The next day, Duffy and I run errands — the bank, post office, Stop & Shop. Each of us picks up a few things, coffee, English muffins, the usual. We don't talk much. No need. He's the type of guy who doesn't mind a little silence, which is exactly what I need right now, plus some Advil for the pain. Peace and quiet. He's what we used to call the strong, silent type. But whenever he looks at me now, ever since our trip to Bridgewater, plus our trip to, well, anyway . . . Since then, his eyes, the color of deep salt water — the color of the Atlantic — are fully lighted in a way that makes me glad. Gladness, a new feeling at my age.

When we're done with our errands, Duffy suggests the Squantum Diner for a quick bite. All morning I've felt Duffy's sorrow, plus the presence of his incarcerated son,

Christopher, who's with us now, like all of my dearly departeds. A regular entourage. While I down a turkey club and he polishes off the Hungry Man Special — eggs and pancakes and hash browns and three types of grilled meat — Duffy gives me a lesson on wrongful convictions.

"Wrongful conviction?" It's still hard to believe everything that's happened to his son.

"Happens more often than you'd think," he tells me, "the main reasons being inadequate defense, prosecutorial misconduct, eyewitness misidentification, and false confessions."

"What about false memories?" I ask. "Isn't that a big reason?"

"Well, the false memories come under prosecutorial misconduct. In cases of alleged child abuse. Mostly because kids are easy to manipulate, easy to convince that something happened when it didn't."

I order coffee and sip it while he tells me that this advocacy organization, Justice for the Wrongfully Convicted, is convinced of Chris's innocence. With its help, and the help of law students from Boston University, his lawyer has been developing his appeal on the basis of prosecutorial misconduct, and he thinks they've got a better than even shot of winning.

"Wow," I say, considering that the original prosecutor is now our attorney general. *Good luck to them and the Red Sox,* I'm about to add, when I remember my commitment to believe in him. Still, I struggle to understand.

"From the start it was a bad case," he says. "No DNA. Nothing except the testimony of these kids, two of them sons of the cop whose wife Chris messed around with. They actually started off with six kids, but the others insisted Chris had never done anything inappropriate, and the prosecutors dropped them from the case."

"Dirty business," I say. Can't help it, but Duffy doesn't disagree.

"Chris was thirty at the time, still immature, still sowing his wild oats."

"Bad judgment."

"Terrible, the worst," says Duffy, nodding, agreeing, not angry at all. "But he doesn't deserve incarceration, or to have his name in the state's official registry of sex offenders for the rest of his life."

"An appeal based on prosecutorial misconduct," I say, just to try it out.

Then Duffy lists all the things that the prosecution had done wrong. He's memorized them: the missing first recordings of the so-called victim interviews; the trial transcripts demonstrating the children's identical testimony; the lack of any physical evidence — no injuries to the children, no signs that sexual abuse occurred — plus the results of the brain tests showing Chris's reaction to the pornography.

"Lastly," he says, "they'll subpoena the cop's wife. She'll have to testify under oath."

"A hot mess," I say.

"Doesn't get much hotter or much messier," he answers, "but I'm in it for the long haul. What else can I do?"

"We have to follow them, don't we, go to the places our children take us, even if we don't want to go there."

He nods and takes my hand, his eyes brighter, his cheeks pinker than before. And I realize looking at him that Duffy is a father who has risen to the occasion. He's stepped up for his son. What else can you ask for in a man?

We finish up in silence. Duffy lights up and offers one to me. I shake my head no. He raises his eyebrows.

"You quitting?"

"Trying. Doctor's orders."

"I quit for more than twenty years," says Duffy, taking a last deep drag, then stubbing out his half-smoked cigarette. "Then

Chris got into this mess. Within a few days I was lighting up like I'd never stopped."

"Want to try again?"

He shrugs, like it's a no-brainer, no answer necessary.

"We'll try together."

"You bet."

Duffy pays the bill. As we get up to leave he asks, "Anything else you'd like to do, Mrs. Malloy? Your wish is my command." His eyes twinkle and a sweet smile tugs at his lips. He feels better now. He needed to talk and I needed to listen. "The rest of my day is yours."

"Bowling," I tell him. "Let's go bowling. I haven't been in ages."

So we head over to the Colonial Lanes, where the Angel Babies used to play. Waste the afternoon laughing at each other, a regular laugh riot. Turns out we get a senior discount for playing on a Tuesday afternoon. He ties my shoes, and I tie his, and we make the biggest deal picking out our balls. I have trouble finding one light enough for me to handle. Not that it matters. Most of my balls end up rolling into the gutter, and every time he's up, Duffy has to do a funny little hop to make up for his bad leg. I laugh, and he exaggerates a bit, just to entertain me. Duffy, with his bum leg and big heart.

"I've really lost my touch," I say whenever my ball rolls into the gutter. "I really held my own back when I was with the Angel Babies," I tell him, and he insists he never had one to begin with.

"Nope, bowling's never been my game," he says. "I prefer other indoor sports. I'm a little better at them."

I'm probably supposed to ask which indoor sports, but I don't. "I should hope so," I say instead, and he throws his head back, laughing. I don't bother to look at him. Instead I take another turn, and again, halfway down the lane, my ball slides into the gutter. Duffy applauds and I take a little bow. Pretty soon, we give up keeping score. No point. Instead, we keep slamming the big balls down that gleaming alley, clapping when we knock down a pin or two, laughing our heads off when we don't. Lucky for us, the place is almost empty. Otherwise we'd have gotten dirty looks.

THIRTY-FIVE:
CALL ME IRRESPONSIBLE

Nobody has ever accused me of being deep — quite the opposite, in fact — and that's always been fine by me. Never claimed to be a deep thinker. I leave the profundities to Jack and my daughters. If it looks good, it probably is good, that's my philosophy, always has been. Celestine, my third, the copyeditor who lives in Philadelphia, once said I'm as deep as Formica. Me, Mimi, deep as Formica. I happen to love Formica, how durable it is, how easy it is to keep clean, plus all the pretty colors. I took it as a compliment until Ruthie clued me in. "A laminate. No depth, get it?"

This story always gets a big laugh from my daughters, and no doubt from their father, too. But Celestine was right: Mimi Malloy, with her strong and sturdy surface, is tough and made for wear. What you see is what you get. Who cares what's underneath?

But now, with all that's happened, I can't

stay on the surface. A laminate won't do. Got to go deeper.

False memory. Recovered memory. The two of them colliding.

As a result of the first, an innocent man is punished. Years in jail, his reputation ruined, for a crime he did not commit. Without a whiff of mercy from his accusers, whose lives have now been ruined too, having been tricked into believing that a horrific thing had happened to them when it hadn't. As a result of the second, we now know who the guilty party is, the witch at the heart of all the trouble in my family, but it's way too late for punishment. That's been meted out to the survivors.

False memory, remembering things that didn't happen. Recovered memory, at last remembering things that did. A banshee in the yard the night before Da died. Cozy in my own bed, alone, holding the blue pendant, I poke around the edges of Patty's recollection, called back to it by the banshee's wail.

It had to have been July 3, 1937. Amelia Earhart, the beautiful, high-flying aviatrix, disappeared over the Pacific on July 2, but we didn't hear about it until the next day, News moved slower then.

AMELIA'S PLANE VANISHES!!!
LADY LINDY LOST!

Amelia with her copilot, Fred Something, gone, just like that.

A mistake. We thought it was a terrible mistake. *Amelia Earhart loves to fly. Amelia Earhart will never die.* Keeley and the twins were too young to understand, but Eden, Alberta, and I stumbled around in shock, whispering our rhyme, looking at one another, trying to figure out how to feel.

PACIFIC CLAIMS AMELIA'S PLANE!!!
LADY LINDY LOST!

That day was so hot and bright, and all of us had chores to do, no sloth in Nana's house. We made beds, swept floors, hand-washed laundry in Nana's black soapstone sink, then hung it outside on the line. Nana, in the kitchen, peeled potatoes and rolled out pie dough, the RCA Victor radio turned up loud so everyone could hear. And we did, we heard the news all through the house, over and over again while we worked, the harsh twang of the broadcaster's voice: *Amelia Earhart, beautiful and fearless, has disappeared over the Pacific.*

Nana kept two gardens, one for flowers,

and one for vegetables. To the side of the flower garden was Nana's shrine to Mary, a statue of the Virgin, tall enough that I saw eye to eye with her when I was four or five years old. The Virgin, chipped and weather-beaten, yes, but still with her shiny marble eyes, her gold crown and blue robe, the serpent arched beneath her sandaled foot. In Nana's garden, flowers bloomed near Mary from March until November. Cro-cuses, tulips, hyacinths, and daffodils in the early spring; then peonies, my favorites, and irises, roses, dahlias, gladioli, hydrangeas, and hollyhocks through summer, and at last, in fall, chrysanthemums and marigolds.

In a plot next to the flowers, in careful rows, grew Nana's peas, squash, potatoes, carrots, tomatoes, peppers, corn, and on-ions. Here I inhaled the smell of the earth, and of the root crops, which I loved pulling out of the ground. Nana counted on her vegetables to survive, but the flowers, the flowers gave her something else: peace, or maybe joy — something she did not, in her silence, get any other way.

Ages before, when he was still in school, Da had built his mother a wooden bench next to the shrine. Most afternoons, during good weather, Nana said her rosary there, her face porcelain, as unchanging as the

Virgin's, her lips shaping the words of the Our Fathers, the Hail Marys, but no sound coming out. We knew enough not to interrupt her when she prayed.

When Nana said her daily rosary, we girls had our free time. We played canasta, did jigsaw puzzles, tried out new hairstyles, or sewed ourselves skirts and blouses. Now and then, I slipped outside to watch Nana pray. Her rosary beads were black wood — no frills — shiny as licorice lozenges. Nana kept them in the pocket of her housedress, where she'd finger them throughout the day. Whenever she moved, they clattered. That's how you could tell when Nana was nearby, the soft rattle of her rosary beads.

The day we heard about Amelia Earhart, Nana said her rosary, as usual. She sat on Da's bench, in front of the Virgin, amid the flowers — cosmos, daisies, and gladioli — her head bent, her hands pressed together, the shiny beads twined around her fingers. *Hail Mary, full of grace, the lord is with thee.*

Nana knew all the holy mysteries, the five each for the Joyful, the Glorious, and the Sorrowful, and she knew which set of holy mysteries was correct for each day of the year. Who knows which set was the right one for July 3, 1937, but in my mind, it had to be the Sorrowful, hands-down, and in particular the Agony in the Garden, which Nana prayed over and over again. I watched her for a long time, hanging close to the back door. From time to time, Nana stared up at the bright sky as if she hoped to see Amelia in her plane. But the sky was empty, not even any clouds. Nana prayed and prayed. It was like I was witnessing a transfiguration of some kind, something I couldn't, and didn't, try to explain to my sisters. The Agony in the Garden. But why was Nana crying for Amelia? That's what my nine-year-old mind couldn't figure out.

That night, the six of us went to bed exhausted. No trouble whatsoever falling asleep, despite the awful heat. The next morning we were going to the Independence Day parade, one of the greatest events of the year back then in Weymouth. We couldn't wait.

I fell into a deep, deep sleep. Dreamed Da was calling out to me, calling and calling, *Maire, Maire, Quite Contrary. How does your garden grow?* Deep into my dream. But at some point, loud angry voices, urgent cries, cut through it. I sat up shaking. Da was really there. Yes, he was there calling out to me, and my dreams had spun themselves around his voice. I tiptoed to the top of the stairs to see what was going on. Knew enough to hide.

On the front porch stood Da and Nana. My heart thumped when I saw him. Da, Daddy, he'd come for us. He'd come to take us home. It took everything I had not to run down to him and hug him. But their voices, tones I'd never heard before, held me back. Da and Nana fighting. I crept partway down the stairs to see them better. Crouched against the railing on the landing, out of sight.

I could see Da clearly under the front porch light. My handsome, handsome Da. Cheeks red, eyes bloodshot, an open cut beneath one eye. Hair matted like a bum's. Daddy, who'd always groomed himself to perfection. I wanted to run down the stairs and kiss his cut and tell him I'd make his hurt go away, the way he'd done for me when I was small. But I didn't. I hid on the stairs, my arms around the railings.

I've told you so many times, Joseph Daniel Sheehan, Nana cried, *you want to see those girls, you show up sober. I'm not going to let you see them when you're drunk.*

Not drunk, Da answered, but his slurred words told the truth. *Just had a couple to settle my nerves.*

Settle your nerves? You think you're the only one with nerves?

Please, Ma. Please.

You stink, said Nana. *You need a bath and a shave. I won't let your daughters see you like this. You should be ashamed. Now, get out of here.*

Maire, at least let me see Maire. I have to tell her something.

Where's your self-respect? Your pride? You, Joey, you, the smartest and best-looking of them all, and you've turned into a drunk.

Da tried to push past his mother, but all four feet eleven inches of Annie Sheehan stood firm in the doorway. Then she shoved him. He lost his balance, stumbled backward down the steps, sprawled into the grass. I couldn't tell if he was laughing or crying.

Come back when you're sober, Nana cried. *Then you can talk to her all you want.* Nana slammed shut the door.

Shaking so hard I thought my joints might snap, I tiptoed through the still heat of the upstairs, to the room where the younger ones were sleeping. I looked out their window, hoping I'd see Da stumbling off down the street. If I had, I might have jumped out the window and run after him. But Da had disappeared. I got back into bed, hearing their voices all over again, swirling and shrieking, Da and Nana fighting on the porch.

Maybe I'd gone back to sleep by the time I heard something against the window screen. I sat up, hearing it again, and realized it was a stone.

I hurried to the window in the dark. There was Da, outside in the yard, a finger by his lips, making a shushing sound.

Oh, Da, Da, I cried.

You did the right thing, Maire. I'm betting you were the instigator, and I want you to know you did the right thing, running away. His hoarse half-whisper cut through the still air. I started laughing. Couldn't help it. Da whispering loud enough to wake the dead. Or at least his own mother.

Sorry isn't good enough, but I'm sorry anyway, he said.

Now I wonder what he meant, what he was sorry for. At the time it didn't matter. Because he seemed to be so close to me, close enough that I could feel the warmth of his breath and smell the whiskey on it. Close enough for me to look into his eyes and see the kind of pain no man should ever have to feel.

Listen to me good, Maire, his whisper echoed through the night. *I'll come back for you and the other girls. OK? You wait. And be good. Not so contrary, huh? I'll be back. Soon*

*as I can figure out how to take care of the
bunch of you by myself. No more Flanna, OK?
We're done with her.*

I love you, Da, so much. I was about to
yell my love down to him, how I would
always love him, no matter what, when
Nana flew into the yard in her white night-
gown, her white hair flowing down her back.
Get out of here, Joe Sheehan! she shrieked,
her words chased by a strange and awful
sound, a banshee's wail. *You've already
broken my heart. Don't break your daughters',
too. Come back when you're clean and sober.*

I left the window, crawled back into bed.
Couldn't bear to see them out there fighting in the yard, Da and Nana, near her
shrine to the Virgin and the bench he'd built
for her to pray on. But I only stayed in bed
a minute. Nana's cry, a needle in the marrow, yanked me back to the window. When
I looked out I saw Nana running around
the yard, her arms outstretched like she'd
gone mad. She wailed, reaching for the sky,
her white hair streaming. Danced a wild
dance, then fell to her knees before the
statue of the Virgin. She prayed, her palms
pressed hard together, then reaching up,
up, up. Da, our father, was no more than a
shape, a shadow prostrate by the compost
heap, near the garden shed and Nana's

plow. *A beast upon all fours.*

I got back into the bed with my sleeping sisters, Eden and Alberta. Didn't wake them. Didn't tell them what I'd seen. Put the pillow over my head, but still I heard the banshee's wail, Nana's cry.

Thirty-Six:
Dig Down Deep

Yesterday, I woke up thinking about Geraldo Rivera. That fool Geraldo, of all people, and all that hoopla a few years back, about the mystery of Al Capone's vault. There was all kinds of hype about this vault discovered under Al Capone's house in Chicago, locked up since Prohibition, and all the skeletons he must have hidden there. And Geraldo was going to open it, live on national TV.

We couldn't wait to see what was inside, my sisters and me. Of course, the bones of Al Capone's victims, those he'd had whacked, plus bags of cash and documents confirming ancient crimes. We gathered at Patty's place to watch, with her kids, and Jo's, and a couple of mine. She made popcorn, buckets of it to have enough to go around. But when Geraldo finally got the damned thing open, the only thing inside was an empty Four Roses bottle. Oh, and some dust bunnies. It doesn't get much funnier than that. We Sheehan sisters loved it. Laughed for days over that big-shot Geraldo, and Al Capone's empty vault.

So I woke up thinking about Geraldo, but saw, superimposed over Al Capone's vault, the furnace of our old house in Quincy. The image is black-and-white, blurred at the edges, exactly as the cellar used to be, unlighted, shadowy, cobwebs hanging everywhere; the coal bin and the big black furnace taking up most of the space; smells of soot and ash. Again, I see the bucket, the shovel, the poker, propped against the wall by the coal bin. Flanna opening the furnace door, flames exploding outward, enough to silence all of us. All of us except Fagan.

These images came to me after I dreamed of falling a great distance — falling precipitously, unexpectedly — the way my grandfather fell off the scaffolding on a ship oh so long ago, leaving Nana widowed and alone. A terrible fall, a fall of many stories, because some fool had left a coiled rope on the pathway to the riveters. A great fall that, for my grandfather, ended in his death.

After my grandfather's fall came my father's, right there in the street, at the July Fourth parade. Me, witnessing those falls, experiencing those falls, a sensation of falling and falling with no place to land.

I thought about Amelia falling from the sky, *Amelia Earhart loves to fly.* Lady Lindy Lost. A fall that captured the world's attention the way Flanna captured Da's and changed all of our lives.

Eden and Alberta, falling through their lives, forever stumbling and falling, picking themselves back up, but only for a while, never quite getting their footing. Then, too, Alberta's son, falling, dying alone on the sidewalk in Brockton, an event that brought Alberta down for good. That time when she fell she couldn't get back up.

Finally, those rebel angels, falling out of heaven, falling and falling from a place even higher than Amelia, falling and falling, stopping wherever they happened to be because God the Father stopped to think. Landing in Flanna's world where she could see them, hear them, believed she could outsmart them.

Our fear of falling, falling through the open drawbridge when we ran away. At last, my own falls, first down the stairs when I broke my wrist and Da helped me get it fixed; again when Flanna pushed me down into the cellar; and, last, a fall from grace, fast and straight down — *ashes, ashes, we all fall down.* A real memory pasted over with the false ones of Fagan Sent Away.

411

I woke up in my own sweet bed, in Duffy's arms, with all that falling on my mind and in my heart. But I also woke up with a feeling of elation, the hope that I, Mimi Malloy, might get another shot. The minute Duff went on his way, I called Siobhan, and I told her to do what she does best, brain that she is, and she told me that she would. ASAP. No questions asked. After that, I only had to wait.

Today, we're heading back to Weymouth in a little caravan, and this time I'm going to keep my act together. Maybe I'll come up empty, like Geraldo, looking like a fool, the way he did, not on national TV but in front of my sisters and my daughters. But I'm pretty sure I've solved the ancient mystery in the middle of our lives, what really happened before Fagan Sent Away, before Keeley showed up on our doorstep walking and talking like a Chatty Cathy doll. I won't know for sure until we get there. And it's worth the risk of looking like a fool.

I'm in the lead, me in my trusty Shadow with Siobhan beside me, the two of us in our pretty sweaters. Keeley follows in her Avalon, with the twins, Jo and Patty. I invited Ruthie, but she said no — too busy, too much to do to make the trip. But Cass and Del will join us in a few — in the Bimmer, natch. They'll meet us at the beach around the corner from Nana's house, what we used to call Nana's Beach. After that, we'll go back to the house, and I'll say everything I've got to say. Whatever that is. I'll know when we get there.

Over the bridge to Nana's house, like when we ran away, except everything is different now. The bridge is short and narrow, steep in the middle. The middle stretch is steel mesh, the water visible below. When you drive over it, this surface makes a high-pitched hum, a keening sound, like women wailing for the dead. The only time I ever walked it was the day we ran away. Once was enough. Today I put the pedal to the metal. Less time for those wailing women.

These days, the bridge hardly ever opens. No more big ships gliding out from the yard, only an occasional tanker down from Canada or other points north. Still, there's a bridge tender who gives plenty of warning, whistles and blinking red lights and such when the bridge is about to open. When it does, you're stuck there swaying on the open bridge for however long it takes for the ship to pass. To avoid that situation, you can check for scheduled openings in the newspaper or on the radio. I always do.

None are scheduled for this morning.

Yes, today's gorgeous, a reminder that winter's over, spring is here, and summer's just around the corner. Like Nana's Beach is just around the corner from her house. Not much of a beach, really, compared to others nearby, developed beaches like Wessagusset, Wollaston, and Nantasket. It's small, well off the beaten path — down a winding gravel road, with no facilities, and used only by the few neighbors who live nearby. They're the only folks who know the beach is there. When we lived at Nana's, we would walk to it, and swim in old clothes because we didn't own bathing suits. Back then, during the war, it didn't matter because nobody else did either.

After I married Jack and we moved into our new house on the bluff just above it, we swam there again, but in bathing suits this time, Jack always wanting us to look our best, to show off our prosperity to the world. I took the girls down every day when the tide was in. We still called it Nana's Beach.

I park at the end of the little lane, careful not to go too far and get stuck in the sand or mud flats. Keeley pulls in next to us, and all of us get out. Nobody asks me what we're up to. For once, the Sheehan sisters

414

and their nieces are silent. Mum's the word. We walk the few steps toward the water. It's blue and calm, the tide low, the water's edge clumped with debris, the high tide line a snake of seaweed, driftwood, Styrofoam packaging, tampon casings, beer cans. I have an urge to grab a bucket and start cleaning it up. If I had one, I would. From here, we can see, way across the water, the backside of the shipyard — a rusted hulk that ought to be torn down, all traces of it carted off.

Every spring, way back when, Jack organized the other men in the neighborhood and they spent a weekend or two cleaning up the beach, raking up the driftwood and sea glass and clumps of tar from the shipyard. Jack always got the town to carry the trash away and bring in a few truckloads of white sand for the water's edge. Our own, mostly private, white-sand beach. My girls loved playing in the sand, the water, the smelly mud flats when the tide was out. That's when we'd dig for clams and I'd make Jack a nice rich chowder for his dinner.

Now Jo and Patty point upward, toward the bluff. A wooden staircase, recently constructed, zigzags up the side of it not far from where we stand. Our old house sits on top, all those windows still shining out toward the water, just the way they used to.

"Your first house," they chime together. The house Jack built for me, I think, and me the maiden all forlorn. We laid the hardwood floors ourselves, Jack and I. We painted all the rooms. So happy then, building our own world.

Its cedar shingles have weathered to a lovely brownish gray. The windows are trimmed white, and the shutters are bright blue. A sweet New England cottage with a deck out back for looking at the water, and now the new staircase leading down to it. When we lived there, we had to walk around by way of an unpaved lane to reach the beach. Back then, we couldn't afford to build a staircase. We had to count every penny. Once we could, Jack decided to move.

"It's stood the test of time," I say, feeling a sharp pinprick, but no longer a stabbing pain, looking at this home no longer mine.

"Worth a fortune now," says Patty. "Waterfront and all."

"A small fortune!" yells Cassandra, walking toward us, Delilah following, the pair of them in tight jeans and high heels. Cassandra and Delilah, my oldest and my youngest, wobble toward us through the sand. I focus on Delilah, once my precious baby. She and Siobhan, the blond betrayers. Got to forgive her. Watching her walk toward us, I know that I got stuck on her flaws behind her pretty face, had trouble getting past them. But she's got her own strength and goodness, a sharp mind and a soft heart, even though I haven't always seen it. What I see now is her heart and it's in the right place, beating there inside her chest despite the damage I've done to it, and my promises to myself that I would never, ever hurt my children. We've forgiven each other, Siobhan and I, and now I must forgive Delilah, too, and hope that the forgiveness will be mutual.

Cassandra and Delilah join hands to give each other balance, laughing at themselves as they walk in their ridiculous shoes. I laugh too, can't help it. I laugh and that abiding anger lifts and floats away. Delilah, my baby. Codependent, I think, looking at the two of them holding each other up. Codependent, another of Cassandra's psychobabble words, but so what? What else are sisters for?

"You're the expert," Patty says to Cassandra once they reach us. Back to real estate. Patty's being sarcastic, but Cass nods, accepting it as a compliment. Because she does consider herself the expert on fortunes, both large and small, and, in a way, she is.

"In the mid–six figures," she says.

"We built it for next to nothing." But my words float away.

The two of them, Cass and Del, look around, as if they've never been here before when, in fact, they spent endless happy hours here as babies and toddlers. Cass curls her lip, shaking her head at the sight of the bedraggled beach, just like she did at Gate of Heaven. I recall the comments she made after I left Jack and moved into my apartment. "You've really come down in the world," she said, my firstborn, who knew darned well what Jack had done with all our assets. "I can't believe how far you've fallen."

"Everything looks so small now," says Siobhan. "Seemed huge when we were growing up."

"I can't believe we actually went into this water," says Delilah, emphasis on "this." "Must be full of toxins."

"We never worried about any of that." Patty. "We loved it. Every high tide, we dove right in. Had a blast. Never hurt a one of us."

"I remember catching minnows," says Siobhan. "Beautiful little iridescent minnows. I trapped them in a jelly jar."

"When the tide was in on hot nights, Daddy took us down after he got home from work," says Cass. "He took us into the water and tossed us high up into the air. We took turns diving off his hands. We wouldn't stop until we wore him out." My daughters, adoring their father, just as I'd done mine.

"When you got back, we washed you girls down outside with the garden hose and Ivory soap." Me, seeing my little girls, all six of them, naked, slick with suds, giggling and twirling under the spraying water in the last light of the day.

"Mimi, remember how much Daddy loved you with a tan?" asks Cass. My face is scorched by a sudden sunburn.

"All those babies born in April and May," my sisters say.

"No, Jack couldn't keep his hands off you when you had a tan, could he?" adds Patty, and the three of them chuckle while my daughters look away. Cass just stands there, embarrassed into silence, though she's the one who started it.

"Ruined my skin." I hold out my hands so they can see the wrinkles and age spots on the back of them. "It was my skin, not my brain, that aged prematurely. I went to a dermatologist a few years back. She was horrified. Wanted me to have some kind of abrasion, a chemical peel I couldn't afford. It sounded like torture. I said the hell with it. Love the skin you're in."

THIRTY-SEVEN:
ALL OR NOTHING AT ALL

Soon, without any discussion, we begin the easy walk back around to Nana's house — seven of us: me, plus three of my sisters and three of my daughters. Eden and Alberta will catch up soon enough. I keep Siobhan close by me because she helps me feel calm. Siobhan, of all people, the daughter I ignored for many years. Looking at her lovely face, strange and familiar at the same time, I feel substantial. She's my kid, after all. I gave birth to her. She's got a strength and wisdom neither Jack nor I ever had. All those shy years of hers when she was growing up, she must have been thinking, paying attention, taking it all in. Her knowledge changed everything, a halogen light shined into in the blackest black spot in my brain, a light so bright it hurts. Yes, Siobhan was the first among us to imagine that our family's dark history might make some kind of sense. She didn't accept the conventional wisdom, that her mother was just a nut job, someone to put down or ignore. Someone to stash for the duration of her existence in an overpriced storage facility like Squantum River Living.

The bunch of us walk close together, the way we used to do when we were small, when we ran away, and again, when my girls were growing up.

Nana's house is painted yellow now with blue trim. No sign that anyone's home. We cross the street to the end of the driveway, tar macadam where Nana's garden used to be. The front porch where Nana slept on hot nights, and the steps where Da and Nana fought. Glassed-in now, and a big central air-conditioning unit in the ground next to it. At the end of the driveway, the new two-car garage is there in place of her garden shed and compost heap. *Da on his knees in a place of earth and stone.* I feel the ghosts of my dead sisters fluttering around me. Eden and Alberta, they've gotten here just in time.

We're close, ever so close now, standing at the end of the driveway, looking at the scraggly grass, the plastic playhouse, the swing set. My sisters and my daughters reach for me; Eden and Alberta, too. I'm aware, if only dimly, that we're no longer

422

inconspicuous, the bunch of us — the glorious Sheehan girls, plus my daughters, standing in a driveway where we have no right to be.

I look down the driveway toward the new garage, but instead I see Fagan, ages ago, tap-dancing in her new Mary Janes with the shiny buckles. Shuffle, hop, step; shuffle, hop, step. Then again in her little panties, hand-me-downs sagging in the bottom — droopy drawers, we teased — her flame-red hair cut off into spikes, tears spilling down her cheeks. Fagan, part of the one body in the one bed after our mother died, the sister who has haunted me, stepping out of my dreams, my nightmares. For most of my life, I didn't just confuse Keeley with Fagan. I hid Fagan behind Keeley, because I could not bear to see her. No loss to feel.

Eden, Alberta, and me. Just the three of us, the twins still sleeping in their own bed, but Fagan's place in it is empty. She's not in the closet; not under the bed, places she sometimes hides and where we sometimes find her. We stand, we three, in the dark upstairs hallway holding hands, so alike it's hard to tell where one of us stops and the other one begins. Brave together, nothing when we are apart. *Amelia Earhart loves to fly; Amelia Earhart will never die.*

Not Mammy. We hear Fagan's cry, from a distant planet. *Not Mammy.* We squeeze one another's hands. We've heard this cry so many times before. *Not Mammy.* It echoes and repeats. *Not Mammy.* We hear other things, not with our ears but with our bodies — unnamable things, painful even now. Why couldn't Fagan just go along with the program? I wonder for the umpteenth time. Still don't have an answer.

Ashes, ashes, we all fall down.

"What woke us up that night? Fagan crying? Or Flanna muttering her nonsense? . . ."

"What night?" somebody asks.

"The night before Fagan got sent away. Eden, Alberta, and I got up to look into the other bedroom, but Fagan wasn't there. You two were sound asleep." I point to Jo and Patty. "Da nowhere to be found."

"We hesitated in the upstairs hallway, then, through the registers, heard Flanna mumbling her incantations. And, beneath that, Fagan crying, *'Not Mammy.'* "

"You three went downstairs?" Cassandra prods.

"Only so far. We stopped. We stopped halfway down the cellar stairs. Eden whispered 'Amelia Earhart.' Our rhyme. *Amelia*

Earhart loves to fly. Amelia Earhart will never die.*"*

"But she did, she disappeared without a trace," says Cassandra.

"Like Fagan." Delilah.

I prefer to leave the story there, on the cellar steps, but Eden and Alberta are with me now, the way it used to be; the three of us as one, feeling one another's feelings, knowing one another's thoughts. Plus Fagan, clutching at me with her death grip. She has finally reached me, our stolen child.

"I told Eden and Alberta that we had to save her. We thought we could overcome Flanna. Rescue Fagan. We tiptoed down, a few stairs at a time, holding hands." Siobhan reaches for me and hugs me close. "The smell was awful, something burning but not for heat. So many voices. We thought four or five people must have been down there."

"Faeries," says Siobhan. "The faeries in a pitched battle for Fagan's soul."

Fagan drags me with her. Eden and Alberta, too. This time, there's no way out. I'm triple-teamed, right up to the furnace.

"Flanna was there, in the shadows. The furnace door was open. She held Fagan close to its flaming mouth. Fagan kicked and screamed. *Not Mammy. Not Mammy.*

Flanna laughed and cried at the same time. Speaking in those tongues, or whatever it was she did at times like that."

Ashes, ashes, we all fall down.

Everything stops. Everyone is quiet, as if we've fallen out of time.

"Flanna killed her?" Cassandra breaks the silence.

"In the cellar. With fire," says Delilah. "Fagan was never sent away."

"What did you do, Mimi?" Cassandra, just a whisper.

"We ran back upstairs. Hid in our bed. Left Fagan there with Flanna." My own great fall, running back upstairs. Maire Sheehan Malloy's fall from grace.

A great uproar — that's what I expected after this revelation, my confession. Instead, moments of agonizing silence pass. Don't they believe me? That's what I begin to wonder. Then, all at once, they rush me, gasping and sobbing, and clasping me and one another. As for me, looking back, I didn't feel anything. I was empty. At eight or nine years old, what could I have felt? Short circuits everywhere. Only ages afterward did I realize that I, Maire Sheehan Malloy, better known as Mimi, was irredeemable, though I was no longer sure why.

"The next day or the day after, Da told us Fagan had been sent away. To Cullyhanna, County Armagh. What a relief!" I shake my head, laughing at the memory of it. "He'd rescued Fagan and sent her to where she would be safe. We didn't have to worry anymore."

"But why are we here?" Delilah points at Nana's house. "Why did you bring us here?"

"Fagan's buried here," Siobhan answers.

"How do you know?" Cass, annoyed that Siobhan knows more than she does.

Siobhan shrugs. "An educated guess."

"Very educated," Delilah digs.

"But she's right." I'm as sure as I've ever been of anything in my life. "Fagan's buried here." Da's place of earth and stone.

Then Siobhan tells us that, at my request, she called several U.S. government agencies and checked all their available archives. She also made some calls to her colleagues and professors at Trinity College, Dublin, to check any records that might relate to Fagan's situation.

"No passport was ever issued for Fagan Marie Sheehan to leave the USA, nor any visa issued for her to stay in Ireland," she says. "No records exist of her ever having lived or died in Cullyhanna."

Important facts, yes, but irrelevant by now.

"We couldn't overpower Flanna."

"How old were you?" asks Delilah.

"Nine," answers Patty, the great historian. "She would have been nine, and Eden and Alberta, twelve and eleven."

The twins hold each other, weeping about what they did or didn't suspect or know, and why and how it happened. But I cannot imagine ever having been so young, or having known what I knew then, at an age when my own daughters worried only about pretty dresses, Brownies, learning to write cursive, and how to read and dance.

"How could she have gotten away with it?" Delilah, full of doubt. Like her sisters, she grew up in a world where more or less everything made sense.

"These days, giving your kid a well-earned smack on the bottom can get you into trouble," adds Cass, speaking from experience, I assume, given the proclivities of her ex.

"Away with it?" says Siobhan. "They weren't seen as doing anything wrong. They were fighting a mortal battle."

"Da must have carried Fagan to his mother's, maybe hoping Nana could save her." I say this, my theory, but I wonder how he did it, how he found her, and if he carried her — or whatever was left of her, Fagan having been silenced now at last — the way he'd carried me when I broke my arm, his chest heaving against her like a bellows.

"Too late," says Siobhan.

"Nana would have called a doctor," says Patty. "She did things by the book. She played by the rules."

"Not exactly," Jo argues. "She'd never have called the police." Nana, like most of the other immigrants, was terrified of the authorities. "But a doctor . . ."

"An Irish doctor," interrupts Siobhan, "one who understood the old ways."

"The one who treated Alberta's burn." Me. "Who set my wrist." Yes, a healer who understood the old ways, who kneeled in his own garden, near a statue of the Virgin and the vanquished serpent.

"Somebody who understood that such an accident, under certain circumstances, was possible, maybe even inevitable." Siobhan. "That Flanna was only trying to make the faeries let her go."

"So now we know where Fagan is." Cassandra.

"We know where Fagan is at last." Me, though I'd known, without knowing that I knew, this entire time. Almost sixty years.

Keeley and the twins bless themselves and start to pray. *Our Father who art in heaven . . .*

Hallowed be thy name . . . and the rest of us join them, on the street in front of the house where we used to live together. Yes, Fagan's little bones, whatever was left of her, are buried under the detached garage, in Da's place of earth and stone. The rest, whatever else happened, is smoky wisps, but I'm pretty sure I've avoided Geralo's fate, ridicule and laughter. My vault of memory, in spite of areas of atrophy, holds more than dust bunnies and an empty whiskey bottle.

Thirty-Eight: Summer Wind

When we get back to the beach, the tide is coming in. We see it, creeping up across the sand toward the last line of debris. Cassandra takes off her heels and strides across the sand, looking out toward the shipyard, heading toward the staircase to our first house. Delilah, barefoot too, follows. I'm afraid they'll climb it, bang on the back door, introduce themselves to the current owners. Instead, they sit together on the next-to-bottom step, and the twins join them there.

Keeley, Siobhan, and I walk over and sit below them, on the bottom step, our feet in the sand. All seven of us are scrunched here, where we have no right to be, looking at the water, like we're waiting for high tide in summer, so we can jump in and splash around.

We sit there, enjoying the sunlight, the promising spring breeze layered over our sorrow. I feel twenty years younger and at least twenty pounds lighter. Yes, me, Maire Sheehan Malloy, known to all — even to God Himself — as Mimi, has solved an ancient mystery. She stumbled around for ages before she discovered the correct path, stunned to realize it had been right in front of her the entire time. Along the way, she fell down, but got back up again. Scorched, scarred, damaged in a million different ways, but still with her warm heart intact. Her hungry heart, A-fib and all, now satisfied.

"Da lied," somebody says, and the rest of us murmur agreement. We lived a lie. We had to live a lie, but didn't understand it. An ancient betrayal, but one that's easier to forgive here in the bright light, looking out over the water toward the shipyard where he toiled year after year for us.

"May he rest in peace," says Jo. "And Fagan, too."

"May perpetual light shine upon them." Patty.

"And on Eden and Alberta." My old sweethearts, who bore witness to Fagan's death with me. I see their weaknesses and their failures in a new light, a perpetual light, the same one in which I see myself; the three of us running back upstairs, hiding in our bed, burying what we'd seen.

"Their lives never went anywhere but down," says Patty.

"No matter how hard we held on to them." Jo.

"I didn't hold on tight enough." Me.

"You held on as tight as you could, Mimi," says Cassandra of all people, defending me. "What else could you have done?"

Cassandra reaches for me, massages my shoulders, a technique she learned in one of her therapies. She reaches below several layers of crust, maybe to the real place, where the two of us, my firstborn and me, will forever be connected. I glance down, see that her bright acrylic talons are gone. In their place, the small pink, white-tipped nails she was born with. I touch her fingernails, my firstborn, the everlasting thorn in my side. Always there. Loyal as a puppy. Day after day she looks out for me. I squeeze her hand, realize I'm a lucky woman. Even though I've yet to say it out loud.

"Flanna . . . Flanna with her herbs and whiskey," says Jo.

"Her prayers and incantations." Patty.

"Her two faces, and her eyes for getting lost in." Me.

"A healer," says Keeley, her voice soft. "A

cailleach. A wise woman with special powers from the countryside where the faeries lived."

"A *cailleach,*" I repeat, the word sticking in my gullet.

"I thought she was my mother." Keeley, paler than I've ever seen her, and trembling like a leaf. "You saved me, Mimi. You saved us, all of us. You got us out of there."

But I never once thought of it that way. Ever. Couldn't see anything but shadows. Couldn't feel anything, not even pain.

"Your episodes," says Delilah. "Now I get it, Mimi. You weren't kidding. They were real."

"The source of them, all those repressed memories." Cassandra massages me some more, getting even closer.

"Well, next time you see your father, you might pass this info on to him. That he wasn't married to your ordinary nut job." Everybody laughs, because Jack will never be convinced.

Now my sisters, both living and dead, surround us, murmuring that there was nothing else we could have done, any of us, to save Fagan from Flanna's madness; her conviction that Fagan was a changeling, left behind by the faeries who kidnapped the real one. *Come away, O human child . . .* We had to save ourselves. A small breeze blows up off the water, then turns and gusts away. Forgiveness. Yes, we forgive our father, Joey Sheehan, forgive him his trespasses, his failures; forgive him for falling so hard and so far below the occasion of his own life. Da loved us, oh, he loved us all — he loved too much, but this love of his could not save us. Daddy. Da. Who knew how to work hard, and did work hard, but didn't know how to manage his feelings or his family. Poor old Da. No, a correction: just poor Da, who never got to be old like me. He did the best he could.

Forgive me, for I have sinned. Me, myself, and I, Mimi Malloy. *Yes, I, too, have sinned.* Fagan, in agony or joy, flies away. An ember in the wind, the soul's eternal life. Beside her are my sidekicks, Eden and Alberta, the top of the line. They're content, I feel it, all three of them together, at peace, at last.

THIRTY-NINE:
ALL THIS AND HEAVEN TOO

Siobhan drives me home, back over the Fore River Bridge, the water below clear and sparkling, the banks and bars and boatyards just as ugly as before, gray and brown, grimed by the elements. We've traded places, my kid and I. She drives the Shadow while I settle down, thinking about all that's happened, the ancient lies and secrets, the tragedy of Fagan's death. Deep inside me, I feel a sense of resolution if not an absolution. Closure. Another word I hate, but I'll take it anyway. And at the last possible minute. Who'd a thunk it?

Instead of black spots, my mind is full of light and laughter, balloons and cotton candy, like Nantasket Beach at night, everybody having the time of their life. I make a mental note to call that snotty brain guy. Order more maps. And I'll bet my life that they'll be brighter this time, full of swirls of color, those areas of atrophy transformed.

I reach into my pocket for the blue pendant, take it out, look at it. As we drive back to Paul Revere, another memory spills out from its sparkle, one I'd buried along with the rest of the shame and sorrow surrounding my da's death and Fagan's disappearance. While Siobhan drives, I tell her about those awful empty days after Da died, the summer of 1937.

"Nana seemed hollowed out and shrunken, and she never did recover. Not unlike Alberta in the next generation, after losing Danny. Couldn't get over the loss of her begotten son.

"One afternoon Nana brought me outside and she sat me beside her on the wooden bench Da built for her. We sat there for a long time, looking at the flowers, the statue of the Virgin, and behind them, the potting shed, the compost heap. She would have known, though I did not, that that's where Fagan was buried. She pressed something into my hand.

" 'Your father wanted you to have this,' she said. I looked down and saw the bright-blue pendant, the color of Da's eyes. 'He brought this over, the night before he died, but he was in his cups, and I wouldn't let him see you.' I nodded, not letting on what I'd seen.

" 'You know, Maire, he started out the best of them, but life didn't go his way.' She wasn't looking at me, instead dropping the blue pendant into its little velvet pouch. She held my hand when she passed it to me. She held it for a long time, the closest she would ever get. She warned me not to tell my sisters, because Da didn't leave anything for them. 'He didn't have anything else to give.' "

When we get to Paul Revere, Siobhan parks in my space up front, and we get out to say good-bye so she can go to her own car. I take Siobhan's hand, the way Nana had taken mine. I press the blue pendant into it. She tries to give it back, but I won't take it.

"Get that scratch fixed, will you please?"

I see the pouch in my daughter's hand and feel it's found its home. She will be its guardian.

Siobhan doesn't speak. She kisses my cheek, then turns and hurries to her own car. I glimpse her heart before she turns. Hers, too, is right where it's supposed to be. Scarred perhaps, but beating strong, glowing, full of life. I watch her go, my brainy kid. She'll be the protector of our heirloom — singular, not plural — Da's wedding gift to Mam, water and paste, the best he could afford. Siobhan will be the keeper of our stories.

FORTY:
GOT THE WORLD ON A STRING

I cannot wait to see Paul Newman, aka Dick Duffy. Of course I love my sisters and my daughters, but we're too much sometimes. Girls, girls, and more girls. *I enjoy being a girl . . .*

No, I can't wait to see Paul Newman, because I have so much to tell him, so much I want to share. Plus, I really do feel twenty pounds lighter and twenty years younger, and I wonder if he'll notice. Don't have long to wait. He shows up just after dusk, knocking, and calling through the door, Oh, Mrs. Malloy. We're back to Mrs. Malloy, which strikes me as funny. I laugh as I open the door.

"What happened?" he asks as soon as he lays eyes on me. "Something's different." His comment tickles me. I pull him inside, and as we heat up the leftovers, mostly Chow Mei Fun, I give the details of all that happened in Weymouth, how great it feels to at last have some closure. I even use that awful word. "Closure."

"Like this huge weight has been lifted, even though my sister's buried under the garage at my grandmother's old house. Even though our stepmother killed her."

We take our plates to my table by the window, turn on the TV: *Family Feud,* with Richard Dawson doing the Big Bucks Challenge.

"Isn't it great he's back?" I ask, nodding toward the TV. Richard Dawson, I mean.

"You bet. I couldn't stand that other one."

I continue with the saga of all that happened, not just in the past, but today. News to Duffy, all that faerie business, and he's engrossed by my story, just the way I want him to be. Now I know, or at least feel, that I won't be an awful burden to him if we keep our relationship together, dragging around my ancient baggage.

"Let's go over to Quincy City Hall tomorrow," says Duffy. "As long as everything's quiet here. And there aren't any emergencies."

"Why? For what?" Good Lord, I'm thinking, I hope not a marriage license. I'm not close to being ready. He chuckles in that way he has, as though he's able to read my thoughts. So embarrassing.

441

"Oh, Mrs. Malloy, the records room, what else?" He grins, the tease. "We'll go to the records room and find your sister's documents, her birth and death certificates, for that all-important genealogy."

"Too late. It's done, handed in for a C+," I say, but then look at him again, like he's some kind of genius. Of course we ought to gather all those records. "Why didn't I think of that? Documented family history, in archives just down the street."

"We can get them for your whole family, at least for anyone who was born or died in Quincy."

"No job is finished until the paperwork is done." That's what I taught my girls way back when, during toilet training.

"Nope, no job is finished until the paperwork is done." Duff laughs. "It will be nice to have those."

Duffy himself is an expert in documents, practically a lawyer after all the legal work he's done for Chris. Duffy, a widower, a combat vet with an old war wound, a man who rose to the occasion of his own life, even the terrible part about his son. And now he's fighting for his son's redemption, or at least the slim hope of redemption, having already earned his own. At least in my book, anyway. Duffy's earned his own.

"So we'll go look for the birth and death certificates?"

" 'Primary documents,' my brainy kid Siobhan would call them." Then I tell him there's another loose end I want to tie up. He raises an eyebrow while munching on the noodles.

"I want to talk to Malvina in the Bronx. I don't even know her sons."

He pauses, shrugs. "Go for it, Mimi, call her," he says. "Right now."

And so I do; I find her number in my book, and punch in the numbers, area code 718. It rings five times. This time the answering machine clicks on. A boy's voice — Rafael or Judah? I can't tell, wouldn't know who was who even if I saw them, because I've never seen or spoken to them, not since Rafael was a newborn.

"You've reached the Malloy-Sosa household," says a happy little voice. I swear to God, a trumpet and a clarinet are playing in the background. "You know what to do. We promise to get back to you."

You know what to do. . . .

"This is Mimi," I say, "Mimi Malloy, your grandmother. I just wanted to say hello." I leave my number, and hang up, trembling. Duffy hugs me, a nice strong hug. Doesn't say a thing.

443

"I hope they keep their promise," I say.

"Promise?"

"You know, to get back to me."

"They'll do what they'll do," he says. We reach for the fortune cookies we didn't eat the other night. I read mine, " 'A well-aimed sword is worth three.' "

" 'It takes more than good memory to have good memories,' " reads Duffy.

"For real?" I grab his paper strip. Sure enough — *It takes more than good memory to have good memories.* Our eyes meet and we laugh. *A well-aimed sword.* We laugh some more.

This is when, in the past — our supper finished, our bellies full — we'd light up. No more. I'm wearing a transdermal smoking cessation patch, and Duffy has one too. Per instructions, we've applied them to the "clean, dry, hairless skin" on the inside of our forearms.

"Hangin' in?" He nods toward my patch, which I'm rubbing, as if trying to squeeze out more nicotine.

"Hangin' in," I answer. He takes my hand, sending me some strength. "I keep thinking how happy my girls and my sisters will be when I tell them."

Then Duffy turns on the TV, to the Weather Channel. On the screen, a map of the USA, colors swirl with storm systems and high-pressure areas moving this way and that. North, east, south, and west. The map looks the way the inside of my head feels right now, the black spots shrunken up, beautiful colors swirling over them, a vast and gorgeous landscape ripe with possibility.

"Whoa, looky-looky." Duff gestures to the screen with the remote.

" 'Looky-looky'?" I echo. "One bowl of Chow Mei Fun and you start to talk Chinese?" He laughs.

"No, check out the weather map. Tomorrow is going to be perfect for a boat ride."

Both of us watch the screen.

"Hey, Mrs. Malloy, what say we save City Hall for another day? Instead, tomorrow, we'll go over to the *Miss Nomer*. We'll get her ready for the water. Get you ready for your maiden voyage."

"An offer I can't refuse." I lean in close to him so I can feel his warmth.

"Have you thought about where you want to go? I mean, on your first boat ride? Wherever you'd like. Your wish is my command."

One of Duffy's favorite phrases, my wish being his command.

"Under the bridge. The Fore River. I want

to ride on all that water under the bridge."

He cracks up. He gets me. As I get him. Then I see the two of us, on Duffy's gleaming Chris-Craft — his cabin cruiser, the *Miss Nomer*, gliding out across the sparkling water. We'll speed around the shipyard, to the basin, where we might glimpse Nana's house and, on the bluff, the sweet cottage Jack built for me a lifetime ago. We'll turn back around on that water under the bridge. After that, we'll head out to the open Atlantic. Who knows where we'll go from there.

ACKNOWLEDGMENTS

I gratefully acknowledge my editor, Elizabeth Bruce, such a gifted one, endowed with all the qualities writers long for in their editors: intelligence, warmth, perspicacity, generosity, and mad skills with the line edit. Thank you.

Also, my agent, Janet Rosen of Sheree Bykofsky Associates, Inc., a woman of wit and passion, a lover of great sentences and stories, a tireless advocate for those whose work she believes in. (A very special thank-you, too, to Sheree for finding me at that writers' conference!)

Last, *mil gracias* to the Geraldine R. Dodge Foundation for funding a residency at the Virginia Center for the Creative Arts, where a first draft of *Mimi* was completed.

ABOUT THE AUTHOR

Julia MacDonnell's fiction has appeared in many literary magazines, and her story "Soy Paco" was nominated for a Pushcart Prize. Her journalism has been featured in *The Boston Globe,* the New York *Daily News,* and *The Philadelphia Inquirer,* among other publications. A tenured professor at Rowan University, she is the nonfiction editor of *Philadelphia Stories.* This is her first novel in twenty years.

AHARON APPELFELD

Illustrations by **VALI MINTZI**
Translated from the Hebrew by
JEFFREY M. GREEN

long summer nights

SEVEN STORIES PRESS
New York • Oakland • London

A TRIANGLE SQUARE BOOK FOR YOUNG READERS
PUBLISHED BY SEVEN STORIES PRESS

SEVEN STORIES PRESS
140 Watts Street
New York, NY 10013
www.sevenstories.com

College professors and high school and middle school teachers may order
free examination copies of Seven Stories Press titles.
To order, visit www.sevenstories.com.

LIBRARY OF CONGRESS CATALOGING IN PUBLICATION DATA
NAMES: Apelfeld, Aharon, author. | Green, Yaacov Jeffrey, translator. |
Mintzi, Vali, illustrator.
TITLES: Long summer nights / Aharon Appelfeld; translated from the Hebrew by
Jeffrey M. Green ; illustrated by Vali Mintzi.
Other titles: Lelot kayits arukim. English.
DESCRIPTION: First edition. | New York: Seven Stories Press, [2019] |
SUMMARY: Eleven-year-old Yanek wanders the countryside with Grandpa
Sergei—the blind former Ukranian army commander to whom the boy has been
entrusted by his Jewish father—avoiding the horrors of war and learning
how to fend for himself and how to care for others.
IDENTIFIERS: LCCN 2019011266| ISBN 9781609808983 (hardback) | ISBN
9781609808990 (ebook)
SUBJECTS: | CYAC: Nomads—Fiction. | Survival—Fiction. | Jews—Europe,
Eastern—Fiction. | Holocaust, Jewish (1939-1945)—Fiction. | BISAC:
JUVENILE FICTION / Historical / Holocaust. | JUVENILE FICTION
/ Religious / Jewish. | JUVENILE FICTION / Boys & Men.
CLASSIFICATION: LCC PZ7.1.A64 Lo 2019 | DDC [Fic]—dc23
LC record available at https://lccn.loc.gov/2019011266

Book design by Dror Cohen and Abigail Miller

Printed in the USA

2 4 6 8 9 7 5 3 1

"And to every people after their language"
BOOK OF ESTHER 1:22

BOOK OF ESTHER 1:22
וְאֶל־עַם
וְעַם כִּלְשׁוֹנ

Published with the support of The Institute for the Translation of Hebrew
Literature, Israel and Consulate–General of Israel in New York.

To my mother, with love, always

long
summer
nights

They walk from field to field, from woods to woods. After walking for an hour, they stop next to a tree, sit in its shade, and then continue.

When their path takes them to a stream or a well, Yanek draws a pail of water, and they rinse their faces and drink until their thirst is quenched.

"Are you tired?" Grandpa Sergei asks.

"No," Yanek answers.

"We'll rest a little and move on."

Thus they wander, always the same sights. In spring and summer they rest under a tree, in fall and winter they sleep in roadside inns or the alcove of a church.

With the small amounts of money people give them, they buy food, but there are days when they're hungry.

They're called wanderers. In some villages people attack them. Grandpa Sergei says: "That's our fate in this world. We mustn't complain. Complainers are miserable."

On the way, they speak little. If Grandpa Sergei asks a question, Yanek answers with a word or two. Grandpa Sergei doesn't like talk and chatter. Sometimes a day passes without his uttering a word.

Usually they reach villages toward evening, when the flocks return from pasture. Yanek loves that hour: the moist smells of mowed clover and the fragrances of milk and bread.

They don't go into the village. They lay their bundles next to a tree, near a grove of trees and a stream.

Yanek tells Grandpa Sergei what his eyes see. The changes aren't many, but when he discovers a change, he's glad to tell them about it. Grandpa Sergei is blind, and he inclines his head attentively. Sometimes he asks about a building or a barn that once impressed him. His memory is vast.

In the summer they sit under a tree during the day, lighting a fire and roasting potatoes. Grandpa is lost in thought, and Yanek looks at all the wonders that surround him.

They eat without speaking. Toward the end of the meal, Grandpa says: "Everything was delicious. We must thank God."

To end the meal, Yanek makes a cup of tea for Grandpa Sergei and lights his pipe for him. For a long time Grandpa sips from the cup and puffs on the pipe.

The summer evenings continue deep into the night. Yanek loves these hours of light. If they have a watermelon, Yanek cuts it, and they both eat the red slices.

Even after midnight the remains of the light still glow. Grandpa asks: "How does the sky look?"
Yanek answers: "There's still a lot of light."

"But still, it's late, and we have to sleep," says Grandpa, laying his head on a folded sack and falling asleep.

Yanek keeps looking at the lights of the night, and while doing so, he sees the path they have taken since morning. Now they will rest here until Sunday.

On Sunday they go to church. They don't allow wanderers, lepers, or insane people to enter. Yanek removes his hat and places it at his feet: a sign that he and the man at his side are asking for charity.

Hearts don't open easily. Mostly the people hurry into the service and ignore the needy, but it sometimes happens that someone removes a banknote from his pocket and lays it in Yanek's hat. Yanek promptly thanks them.

A month ago a man removed a banknote from his pocket and placed it in Yanek's hat. To their surprise, it was for two hundred marks. Grandpa Sergei blessed God and called out loud: "May God preserve your health."

Sometimes they stay where they are after the church service. Usually no one approaches them, but it may happen that a woman brings them hot food and stays with them until they finish eating. In the end she asks: "Where are you headed?" Grandpa Sergei lists the nearby villages and says: "I assume that tonight we'll sleep at Yadovetse."

"Is anyone expecting you?" she asks for some reason.

"No," answers Grandpa curtly.

"And what will you do there?" she keeps asking.

"We'll stay for a few days in the shade of a tree and then move on."

"And where do you want to get to?"

"Wherever our feet take us."

Upon hearing Grandpa Sergei's answer, the woman chuckles out loud. In the end she gathers up the dishes and asks, "Won't you ever get home?"

Grandpa Sergei tells her the truth: "We have no home. The sky is our roof."

The woman looks at him and says: "A person should look for a home."

"Once we looked, but now we've stopped," says Grandpa Sergei, surprising the woman again.

"Anyway, take care of yourselves," she says, and disappears.

2

One night, a year and a half ago, Yanek's father brought him to Grandpa Sergei and said, "I'm leaving my son with you. Take care of him, my friend."

"I'll watch over him," said Grandpa Sergei with his astounding brevity.

"Take this little bundle. There's a little money in it, my wedding ring and my wife's, and my wristwatch. Tomorrow they're driving us out of the city." The money was in the form of bills issued by the German occupation government.

"Don't give anything to me. You'll surely need these valuables more than I do. You're going far, who knows where? I'm staying here."

"Please take it. I don't have a lot to give you. When I get back, I'll pay you many times over."

"Have a cup of tea," Grandpa Sergei urged him.

"I can't, my friend. I have to go back."

He hugged Yanek and whispered in his ear, "Do what Grandpa Sergei tells you to do. The time will pass, and we'll come back home." He went over to Grandpa Sergei, hugged him, and said, "My son's a good boy," and he blocked the tears in his eyes.

Without further delay, he went on his way.

Grandpa Sergei knows Yanek's father very well. For

many years he worked in his lumberyard. After he went blind, he used to come to the lumberyard to advise customers. The customers liked him and his advice. At their ten o'clock break they would eat a sandwich together and drink a cup of coffee. Their friendship lasted for years. Yanek's father kept paying him his salary, even after he went blind, until he got into financial trouble, went bankrupt, and the lumberyard was seized. Already completely blind, with no one to help him, Grandpa Sergei began to wander among the fields from village to village.

After his father disappeared into the darkness, Grandpa Sergei asked Yanek, "Are you hungry?"

"No," Yanek answered.

"Still, you should eat something. How many hours did you walk?"

"Three, maybe four."

"You've got to eat. You'll be wandering together with me. Wanderers have no home. They have to be strong."

After a pause, Grandpa Sergei went on, "We sleep in our clothes, and we don't take off our boots until everything around us is quiet. But don't worry. You'll get used to this life real quick. Wanderers are like soldiers, always on the alert. But there are little pleasures that will make you happy."

Yanek was floored. He didn't know what to say or what to ask. Only that morning he was still at home, next to his mother. Before going out his father had tried to reassure his mother, who was standing next to the stove, trembling.

That night Grandpa Sergei said, "You have to change your name. From now on you'll be Yanek and not Michael. You're smart, and you know why you have to do that. After the war you can go back to your name."

Yanek was tired and foggy. The last days in the cellar, the fear that soldiers might come down and grab him, and finally the confusing walk to Grandpa Sergei had exhausted him. He laid his head on the ground and fell asleep.

When Yanek woke up, he didn't know where he was. Grandpa Sergei was awake, drinking tea and puffing on his pipe.

"How did you sleep?" asked Grandpa Sergei.

"I slept at home," Yanek answered in confusion.

"So it seems to you. But you slept here, in your winter coat."

"They didn't kill me?"

"Don't be afraid. Nothing bad will happen to you. True, I'm blind, but I know this region very well. During my military service I was around here. I did months of training here, and later on I trained other soldiers."

Yanek remembered his father's instructions: "Don't ask a lot of questions, do what Grandpa Sergei tells you to do, and if it's hard for you, don't complain. The war will be over, and I'll come and get you."

Grandpa Sergei sensed that Yanek wasn't at ease. He spoke to him softly, saying, "You have nothing to be afraid of. Rest. After you've rested and gotten used to the place, we'll make lunch."

That very day the unpleasant side of the place was

revealed to him. A boy walked by and hissed at him: "Dirty Jew."

Grandpa Sergei heard and said, "Don't pay attention to that little snake. You'll beat the daylights out of him one day."

In the evening Grandpa Sergei said to him, "You have to change clothes. City clothes will give you away. I have a linen shirt and trousers in my pack. I figure they'll be a bit big on you, but don't worry, you can roll up the pants and take in the waist with a couple of big safety pins that I still have from the army."

Yanek put on the new clothes and felt as if he was in disguise.

Grandpa Sergei went on to say, "Excuse me. To make the camouflage complete I'm going to put a little wooden cross around your neck, so you won't arouse any suspicion."

"Will I wear these clothes all the time?" Yanek asked.

"In a little while you'll get used to them."

The clothes smelled like animals, and Yanek couldn't stop sneezing.

"You'll also get used to the smell, I promise you."

Yanek didn't know what to say or what to ask. He felt as if something of his own had been taken from him. It was hard for him to explain that feeling to Grandpa Sergei. Grandpa Sergei made it easier for him and said, "It's just a temporary camouflage. The day will come, and it's not far off, and you'll take off this camouflage and go back to being what you were."

Grandpa's words calmed him, but at night in a dream he felt heavy and handcuffed. His shouts could be heard all around. With all his strength he tried in vain to flee. In the end he fell from a great height and woke up.

Grandpa Sergei asked, "Don't you feel comfortable in the new clothes? We'll see. Maybe in a few days we'll buy you a shirt and trousers that fit you. Meanwhile you have to get used to this situation. Don't forget, soldiers at the front get used to every situation."

"Are we soldiers?"

"We're like soldiers."

Yanek wanted to ask what it meant to be like soldiers, but he held his tongue. He remembered that his father told him several times, "Don't ask too many questions."

After they'd been wandering for several weeks, it sometimes seemed to Yanek that they'd been on the road forever.

"Are wanderers different from the people who live in houses?" Yanek asked.

After a pause Grandpa Sergei answered, "They don't talk much, and they like to observe and listen."

"Don't they work in the fields?"

"They don't have fields of their own."

"So how do they make a living?"

"You saw, from the gifts of flesh and blood," Grandpa Sergei answered quickly.

Grandpa Sergei handed him a slice of dry bread and said, "Wanderers aren't fussy. They eat what they have."

"Last night a little fox came close to me," Yanek told him.

"Don't be afraid. He won't harm you. You're wearing a strong, thick military coat, and at night I button it up over your head. I even cover your feet with the coat. Are you warm?"

"Very."

"That coat preserved me in the army, and it will preserve you now."

When Yanek curls up in the coat, he sees his father

and mother, and his heart is stirred with longing. That only lasts a moment. The weeks he's spent with Grandpa Sergei have erased the near and beloved sights from his mind. He no longer dreams about the handyman or the housekeeper. He sees the fields before his eyes and the groves of trees that surround them.

Grandpa Sergei doesn't allow him to wander off on his own. You have to study these dangerous areas before you go out into them. He spends most of the day curled up in the military coat, sitting next to Grandpa Sergei and observing him.

"What should I do, Grandpa Sergei, to be a wanderer?"

"Observe and think."

Sometimes it seems to Yanek that his father didn't bring him here to hide from the war, but to learn the ways of the wanderers.

Grandpa Sergei doesn't speak with people much. If they ask him something, he answers briefly, but there are some insolent boys who call him a dirty beggar. Grandpa Sergei doesn't flinch. He gets up and curses them.

Early on he said, "Come, friend, I'll teach you how to brew tea. Tea's a beverage the body thirsts for. We drink it two or three times a day. It nourishes body and soul. Tea, even simple herbal tea, livens the heart."

"At night I get homesick," Yanek told him.

"Homesickness is a noble feeling. It takes us far away from ourselves, to the people we love. Hold on to your homesickness, but don't overdo it. Now pull your legs and head into the coat and close your eyes. Good night."

Sometimes it seems to Yanek that dogs approach them with the intention of biting him. He holds his breath and clings to the edges of the coat.

One morning a girl came up to him and asked, "Where are you from?"

"From here," Yanek answered.

"Do you live in the village?"

"No, we're on our way to another village."

"Are you wanderers?"

"Naturally," Yanek said, because he could find no further words.

"Are you wanderers or beggars?"

Yanek didn't know the difference, and to get out of the tangle he said, "What difference does it make?" But he added right away, "And what do you do?"

"I go to school."

"How old are you?"

"Eleven."

"I'm also eleven, and I'm in sixth grade."

"Where's your school?"

"Grandpa Sergei is my teacher."

"Is he a strict teacher?"

"No."

"That's strange," said the girl.

"Are you a good student?" Yanek asked.

"My report card is okay. Just one grade, in arithmetic, is a D."

"Don't worry. Next year you'll improve it."

"When are you leaving?"

"On Sunday, after church."

"Too bad. Maybe we'll see each other again sometime," she said, and went away.

After the girl went away, Yanek saw his school before his eyes, the children racing down the corridors, Olga, the teacher, standing at the entrance to the playground, smoking a cigarette. That familiar sight, which he'd never paid attention to, moved him, and he wondered, Why am I the only one they expelled from school?

4

One day Grandpa Sergei said, "Today, after breakfast, we'll start training. Without training you'll be weak. The boys in the village will pick on you and insult you. Running is the basis of all physical training. Running at a steady pace with the correct breathing will make you taller, the muscles of your arms and legs will fill out. After a month you'll feel your body and be surprised. Your gloomy thoughts will also disappear as if they never were."

Yanek set out to run around the fields. "Don't rush, just keep a steady pace," Grandpa Sergei instructed him.

When he returned from the run, his leg muscles hurt, and he collapsed on the ground, short of breath and exhausted. Grandpa Sergei told him to massage his legs with some oil. "This is the first step of the way, Yanek. A sound body will protect you and your soul. The soul is soft and delicate, and only a strong body can wrap it up and protect it."

"Can you see the soul?" Yanek asked.

"No, just as it's impossible to see God."

Yanek went out on a morning run every day. At first the runs exhausted him, but gradually he learned to overcome the muscle cramps.

The next task Grandpa Sergei imposed on him was to climb trees. This task also wasn't easy at the beginning. For days he learned to use his arms and legs well, to grasp the branches properly and move from branch to branch. Sometimes he hung from one branch in order to swing himself over to a nearby tree. Grandpa Sergei stood at the foot of the trees and asked, "Where are you? Now what are you doing?" Yanek tried to tell him exactly.

That month Grandpa Sergei also told him to look for logs and train in picking them up.

After two months of tough training, Yanek felt the muscles of his body, and when boys threw stones at him, he went toward them angrily. The first confrontations were hesitant, but as time passed, fear abandoned him.

Grandpa Sergei often repeated his instruction: "You have to keep training. Every workout adds to your strength. Most people are cowards. Daring and firmness scare them. Too bad they're not afraid of God."

One night, two boys tried to steal their bundles. Yanek woke up and leaped at them. In a few minutes he overcame both of the robbers. Grandpa Sergei was pleased by Yanek's quickness and the way he had acted.

When he was young, Grandpa Sergei had been in a special army unit. He was a daring soldier, a champion long-distance runner and weight lifter, a model soldier. Because of that they promoted him to the rank of master sergeant. If he'd finished high school, they would have sent him to the officers training course.

His long military service had made him a nocturnal creature whose hearing was sharp and who caught scents before other people did. His sense of taste was also fine, and he could always tell what was fresh and what was spoiled and thus inedible.

After he went blind, his other senses grew more acute. Sometimes he would stop in the middle of a field and say, "Rain is on the way. We have to find a tree with thick leaves." There might be no signs of rain around them. The sun could be in the middle of the sky, without wind or clouds. But Grandpa Sergei's forecast was always right. The sky would quickly be covered with clouds, and rain would fall.

Blindness spoiled his life, but it didn't affect his faith in God and in good people. When Grandpa gropes with his cane, he looks hesitant, but his voice is clear, and even his silence has great strength. All his conduct shows he was a commander. When they met one of Grandpa Sergei's former trainees, he couldn't get a word out of his mouth because he was so moved. Finally he asked, "How are you, sir?"

"Fine," Grandpa Sergei replied.

"I miss my time in the army," said the man, almost bursting into tears.

"Everything in its own time. When a man is young, he climbs mountains and ties ropes over chasms and welcomes every danger eagerly. When you're older, you have time to think."

"Thinking drives me crazy, sir."

"Say to yourself: For my part I did the best I could, and the rest is in the hands of heaven."

"I haven't attained that high level, sir."

"You have to accept life quietly, Gregor," Grandpa Sergei spoke softly to him.

"How can I accept it quietly? My wife drives me crazy, and my daughters have strayed from the right path."

"As I said: quietly. If not, you'll go crazy. You evaluate the situation, weigh the possibilities, and in the end you decide to act."

"Once, sir, I knew that way. The army and dangers taught me patience."

"Even today you can say: I'm doing what's right in God's eyes, and the rest is in the hands of heaven."

Gregor sighed and said, "I'm so glad I met you, sir. You restored me to the fine days of my youth. I was proud to be under your command. We were all proud of you. Together we were sent to godforsaken places to save people from avalanches and flash floods. Our togetherness was amazing. We would get to dangerous places by foot and try to do everything possible—and even the impossible. Life meant something."

"Gregor, my friend, don't be angry at me if I tell you that life means something today, too."

Gregor bowed his head and didn't answer.

For a long time Gregor sat next to his former commander and didn't utter a syllable. Finally he turned to Grandpa Sergei and said, "Sir, not a day passes when I don't see you before my eyes. May God help you. Who deserves His attention more than you?" Without adding another word, he went on his way.

Summer days are long. Yanek sits for hours and observes the colors of the sky. Grandpa Sergei puffs on his pipe, and he asks, "How's the sky?" Yanek answers, "There's still a lot of light."

Mostly, they're quiet, but from time to time Grandpa Sergei is roused from his silence and tells about his army days, his fellow soldiers, the training, raids, and rescues. Not every soldier is accepted in the rescue unit. The tests are hard. You need stamina and resourcefulness and determination. Anyone who doesn't meet those standards is rejected. Grandpa Sergei reminded his soldiers that service in the special unit was a great privilege. Frequently he would praise a soldier with these words, "You're a soldier in every cell of your body, and at the same time you're moral, and you're not arrogant."

When Grandpa Sergei tells about the time of his military service, his eyelids tremble, and his forehead gleams, and it's clear that his memory is showing him clear pictures.

"Was it hard in the special unit, Grandpa Sergei?" Yanek asks cautiously.

"Hard, but good," answers Grandpa Sergei. "I was young and strong, and I leaped like a panther. All my life was ahead of me, and I had no worries. Those were the most beautiful days of my life. I would come home, and the whole village cheered for me. In time my uniform got full of medals. The village children would look at me with admiration and list my medals according to their importance. On Sundays, in church, the village notables would approach me and shake my hand. To tell you the truth, my heart was proud."

"Grandpa Sergei, will I be in the army, too?"

"I assume so, but you have many years before you're drafted. How old are you?"

"Eleven."

"You have a lot of years before you."

Grandpa Sergei tells his stories briefly, without many details. Yanek listens and doesn't bother him with unnecessary questions. He stores up every story that Grandpa tells in his memory. Yanek loves his voice and the tobacco smell that wafts up from his pipe. When Grandpa Sergei gets excited, he swallows some of his words, and Yanek doesn't catch the whole story, just a few images, but they're retained.

Meanwhile, it's time to get fresh supplies. Yanek goes to a peasant woman from whom he bought before. On the Sunday before, the churchgoers had been kind, and they had received generous contributions. Now Yanek had enough money to buy things. The peasant woman recognizes Yanek and calls him by name. She brings cucumbers, tomatoes, little onions, and potatoes from her garden, and she adds a loaf of brown bread, a jug of milk, and a slice of cheese. The peasant woman names a price, and Yanek immediately answers, "Too expensive. I don't

have that much money."

"How much can you give?" asks the peasant woman.

"I have a fifty-mark bill."

"I won't give you the labor of my hands for fifty marks."

"That's all I have," Yanek answers.

"For fifty marks I can't give you the loaf of bread or the jug of milk."

"I'll go to another farm," says Yanek.

"At another farm you'll get rotten vegetables and sour milk."

"You're an honest woman. Last time you gave me fresh produce," Yanek flatters her.

"Everything I have is fresh, but not for free," says the peasant woman.

"I'll go," says Yanek. "Last time you sold for fifty marks, and you were satisfied."

"Go. We'll see whether anyone will give you fresh produce like mine."

"I'll go," says Yanek.

"Fine," says the peasant woman.

"Take away whatever you want, except for the bread and cheese," Yanek suggests.

"I'll also take away the jug of milk."

"Please leave the jug of milk."

"Go away. I don't want to see you again," says the peasant woman with feigned anger.

In the end Yanek hands her the bill and adds two smaller bills, puts the supplies in his sack, and, with the jug of milk in his hand, he heads for the gate.

"May God bless you," he says.

The peasant woman doesn't respond to his blessing, a sign that she's still annoyed.

Grandpa Sergei hears Yanek's steps as he approaches and calls out, "Yanek."

Yanek removes the sack from his shoulder and tells him what he has brought.

Grandpa Sergei's blind eyes smile. He had also taught Yanek how to bargain, what to say and what not to say, and the main thing, to be calm and avoid eagerness.

"How did the negotiations go?" Grandpa Sergei asks.

"They were long," Yanek answers.

"What did you tell her?"

"I told her I'd go to another peasant woman."

"Brave guy," says Grandpa Sergei, and pats him on the shoulder.

Yanek places a few potatoes in the campfire and hands Grandpa Sergei a piece of bread, cheese, and tomatoes. They sit and eat. The bread is fresh and tasty, and the tomatoes are juicy and sweet.

The supplies will last for two or three days, and then they'll pack up their things and set out on their way.

In the summer wandering is easier: they go from village to village. Some villages are quiet and pleasant, but other villages are hostile to wanderers and beggars and kick them out with threats.

"Don't worry, Yanek, God will make an accounting with them."

6

They thought they would stay here until Sunday, sit at the church door, and wait for charity. But Grandpa Sergei decided they'd better leave the place and move on. A few young men had passed by them and mocked them, and a woman, not a young one, had even shouted at them, "Get out of here."

The next day, after breakfast, after Yanek made his daily run, climbed a tree, and did gymnastic exercises, they went on their way. On the road they saw blossoming trees, white rabbits, and even a cherry tree with ripe fruit. Grandpa Sergei didn't allow Yanek to pick the fruit, even if the trees were on public land, so people wouldn't say, "The wanderers steal."

Before arriving in a village, they wash in the river. The water is warm in the afternoon. They remove their clothes and go in. Grandpa Sergei, despite his age, has a hairy, sturdy body. But he doesn't swim. "Blind people mustn't swim," he says with a slight laugh.

They reach the village in the evening. The tree they had stayed under on an earlier visit has already sprouted thick foliage. The renewed encounter makes them happy. They remove their packs and bundles, and Yanek tells Grandpa Sergei what his eyes see. Meanwhile he builds the fire. They still have a bundle of potatoes, which

Yanek quickly places in the campfire.

A half hour later the meal is ready. Yanek serves a potato to Grandpa Sergei, with a wedge of cheese and some cucumber, and along with that, a cup of warm, brown tea. Grandpa Sergei eats slowly, and after he's finished his meal, Yanek lights his pipe for him. He sits next to him and observes his movements, which are quiet and given over to his reflections.

"Should I go to the tobacco store and buy some more?" Yanek asks.

"No need. I have more than enough," answers Grandpa Sergei.

For a long time they sit without saying anything. Regarding speech, Grandpa Sergei has principles: there's no need to talk; act, don't speak. Speech only causes a fuss. Better to listen. Listening will teach you something.

Since joining Grandpa Sergei he's obeyed these instructions carefully, but now he can't restrain himself, and he asks: "Grandpa Sergei, where have they sent the Jews to?"

"Who knows? But don't worry, your father is smart and resourceful."

After a pause he adds, "They've always driven the Jews out. In the last war they also drove them away, but they came back and fixed up their houses."

"What harm have the Jews done to make people hate them?"

"It's better not to ask questions we can't answer."

At night sleep takes him to his house, and there everything is as it was. In the afternoon Yanek comes home from school, and Father returns from the lumber-yard. Mother has cooked lunch: borscht with sour cream and cheese blintzes. After lunch Father lights a cigarette and sips tea.

"How was the test?" Father asks, and Yanek answers, "I got 'excellent.'"

Upon hearing Yanek's answer, his father's face glows, and Yanek, full of pleasure and dread, wakes up from the dream.

Grandpa Sergei is already awake, with a cup of tea in his hand, spreading pleasant-smelling smoke.

"How did you sleep?"

"Well. I was at home. The house was as it always was."

"Were you pleased?"

"Something didn't seem right to me."

"You were dreaming. Dreams aren't reality."

"What are they?" Yanek asks.

"In a dream, among other things, God shows us what we must do."

Yanek doesn't understand all of Grandpa Sergei's explanations. When Grandpa Sergei talks about God and about His actions in this world, most of what he says is incomprehensible to him. But not to worry—Yanek has decided within himself—he'll make an effort to listen. Maybe he'll also disobey his father's instructions and ask for some details so that the obscure things will be clear to him.

7

This is how a new day begins: Yanek goes out for a run around the fields. Now he is light on his feet and within an hour he returns to Grandpa Sergei.

Grandpa Sergei greets him and asks, "How did the run go?"

"Everything was fine," Yanek answers with a grown-up voice. Without realizing it, Yanek has adopted Grandpa Sergei's words and gestures. He answers briefly, like a soldier executing an order.

Here they'll stay for two or three days. Soon he'll return to the peasant woman, Mary, and he'll buy vegetables, milk, and bread again. Grandpa takes two twenty-mark bills out of his pocket and says, "Bargain with her like a brave soldier."

Yanek remembers the short, sturdy peasant woman, Mary. She hardly utters a word, but she's as stubborn as a mule and won't reduce the price she's stated by even a penny.

Yanek makes his way to her at a run, opens the gate, and here's Mary standing at the door of her house.

"Good morning, Mary," he calls out loud.

"What do you want?"

"Vegetables, dairy products, and bread, like last time."

"I'll show you what I have in the garden."

After some delay, she returns holding a basket: two red tomatoes, a bundle of radishes, green onion, a few cucumbers, and potatoes. She enters the house and brings half a loaf of bread, a jug of milk, and a piece of cheese. She lays it all down on the bench at the entrance.

"What's the price?" asks Yanek.

"No less than forty marks," she surprises Yanek pleasantly.

"Could you add some salt?"

"I'll give it to you."

Yanek pays, places the groceries in the sack, blesses her, and is about to go.

In the end she says, "Don't forget to return the jug."

"I won't forget," says Yanek, and sets his legs in motion.

Grandpa Sergei is pleased with the price and asks, "What happened?"

"I guess she got confused," says Yanek.

Upon hearing his answer, Grandpa Sergei chuckles. They eat breakfast without speaking. After the meal and after drinking their first cup of tea, Yanek lights Grandpa Sergei's pipe, and Grandpa Sergei sinks within himself.

That night Yanek dreams he is at home: everything is in its place. Only his mother's movements are slow, as after an illness, but her face is unchanged. His father's movements are also unusual.

"What's the matter?" Yanek managed to get those few words out of his mouth. His father and mother looked at him and his father said, "We have returned from a very long journey. We suffered a lot. If only we could understand why we suffered. It's hard to speak about it. Maybe it's better not to talk."

"Father, but you haven't changed."

"Inside, my dear. We changed a lot."

Yanek wants to tell the dream to Grandpa Sergei, but he can't find the words to tell it. Since he's been with Grandpa Sergei, the words have grown fewer in his mouth, and it's hard for him to compose a sentence. In his heart Yanek knows that the dream was trying to tell him something.

Grandpa Sergei, drinking his fill of tea and puffing on his pipe, lays his head on the sack and fall asleep. Yanek likes to look at him while he's asleep. It's not the sleep of an old man, but of a soldier after a day of training and a trek. His years of military service are impressed in every one of his movements, in every non-speech of his. Once he said something surprising, "The army prepared me to be a soldier in the army of God."

"How, Grandpa Sergei?"

"I stick to the Ten Commandments as to the Order of the Day. Once I liked going to church, but since I took to wandering on the roads, they don't allow me to enter the church. But there's nothing bad without something good in it: I learned to live without splendid prayer, but to pray within myself."

Once when they were sitting at the entrance to a church, a blind beggar covered with sores stood not far from them. After the service, and after they received generous gifts, Grandpa Sergei said, "Take these two bills and give them to the blind man."

"I'll do it right away," said Yanek.

"The blind man covered with sores was astonished by the gift and asked, "Who gave me this valuable gift?"

"Grandpa Sergei," answered Yanek.

"May God bless him. And who are you?"

"My name is Yanek, and I'm his grandson."

"May God preserve you."

8

Tomorrow is Saturday. Yanek remembers the Sabbath in his home. His father didn't go to synagogue, but there was a calm atmosphere in the home. His father sat in an armchair and looked at the garden. His movements were few. He read or listened to music. Sometimes they went out on a walk in the woods near their house. His mother spread a cloth on the earth, and they sat and ate.

On the Sabbath their talk was also different. His father didn't talk about his business. His mother joined him in not speaking, but still it was pleasant. It all lasted until Saturday night. On Saturday night the house would fill with people. The owner of the sawmill came to ask about a few beams and boards that had to be prepared. He was a tall, sturdy man, silencing everyone with his firm speech. The thin web of moderation and quiet that had enveloped the house was torn to shreds, and you couldn't tell it had been there.

Yanek removes his mind from the sights of home that had surrounded it and returns to reality: tomorrow is Sunday. They will pack their bundles and make their way to the church, they'll sit at some distance from the entrance and wait for people to give them alms.

This humiliating hour is hard for Grandpa Sergei. The soldiers in the special unit Grandpa Sergei had commanded were honorable men who spoke to everyone with respect. They helped weak people to cross a stream over a narrow bridge, and they brought truly helpless people—people who fell and were wounded—to the nearest infirmary. Grandpa Sergei does sit by the church door, but he doesn't ask for gifts from flesh and blood.

"I'm sitting here," says Grandpa Sergei, "because God apparently wants to teach me humility. I won't violate His will. I'm a soldier and I carry out His orders."

Though he went blind, he is never without the Bible. He knows the Book of Psalms by heart. He whispers his prayers. He only raises his voice on rare occasions. Sometimes he'll recite a verse out loud and repeat it several times. He forbade Yanek to extend his hand and beg. "If they give, they'll give. If not, we'll ask God to give us something from His open, broad hand."

Once, when the congregation came out of the church and ignored the wanderers, Grandpa Sergei raised his voice and shouted at them, "God sees you and won't forgive you."

Some time ago, after Grandpa Sergei shouted that way, two bullies attacked him. Grandpa Sergei didn't hold back. He wrestled with them and knocked them down. The bystanders didn't mix in. They saw Grandpa Sergei's courage, and their hearts melted.

That's how their wandering goes. In every corner someone indifferent or evil awaits them. Yanek learned to be cautious and behave with cunning. "We have to know our limitations and prepare ourselves accordingly," Grandpa Sergei speaks to Yanek as if to a military man.

Yanek is proud that Grandpa Sergei is his commander and obeys his orders precisely. Secretly he hopes that Grandpa Sergei's sight will be restored, and he will once again command a unit, and he, Yanek, will be among his outstanding soldiers.

They parted from the tree that had been their home for several days. Yanek checked and checked again to see whether anything had been forgotten, he returned the jug to Mary, and they set out.

The path from the tree to the church isn't a straight line. They walk around the village, to avoid running into people who hate wanderers, and they get to the rear of the church, lay down their belongings, and at some distance from the church they sit down. Grandpa Sergei repeats, "Not by the gift of flesh and blood will we be saved."

Grandpa Sergei's faith in God was strong and unshakable. He constantly repeats, "God has given, and God has taken away." Yanek doesn't understand this sentence.

One of the people going to church not only refused to give them anything, but he also shouted, "Go to work, and don't be parasites." Grandpa Sergei rose to his feet and shouted back, "Shame on you! You're a big hero over invalids and weak people. God won't forget that about you."

After that service, an old woman approached them, bent over, and placed a few banknotes in Yanek's hat. Grandpa Sergei said, "In the name of God I thank you." Grandpa Sergei spoke very loudly. He surprises Yanek anew, time after time. The old woman heard Grandpa Sergei's bellowing voice, was alarmed, and fled for her life.

9

Without delay they set out. The way to the next village was long. It isn't good to arrive at night. It's better to be early.

Grandpa Sergei places his hand on Yanek's shoulder, and they set out at a vigorous pace. Despite his blindness, Grandpa Sergei marches like a soldier. At first Yanek got tired from walking by his side, but now he keeps up with his pace.

Signs of Grandpa Sergei's military service remain in all of his actions: the way he wraps his leggings, sits, listens, raises his voice when iniquity cries out to heaven, his willingness to take risks, and his great power to accept his rigorous life without complaint.

A few days earlier he explained to Yanek, "There's no point in complaining. If you decided not to do something, don't do it. But if you've decided to do something, do it with all your strength. Complaining is just ugly."

He calls unworthy actions "ugly." A criminal act is "base." He calls an evil act "disgusting." Grandpa Sergei tries to be precise in his speech.

For now, there's nothing to worry about. For supper they have bread, cheese, vegetables, and potatoes. If there are mishaps along the way, they'll sit under a tree, eat, and rest.

As they moved forward, a pack of dogs fell upon them.

The dogs were apparently hungry. First Yanek tried to chase them away with sticks, but the dogs didn't give up. In the end Grandpa Sergei pulled his pistol out from his belt, shot, and scattered them.

They reached the village of Yanovka toward evening, together with the flock returning from the pasture. They immediately headed for a plane tree, to sleep at its foot.

Without delay Yanek went to collect twigs from the woods. Fortunately he found plenty of dry branches. In a few minutes the campfire burned with a blue flame. Yanek filled the kettle with water, placed it on the coals, and put some potatoes in the fire.

"Is the sky light?" asked Grandpa Sergei.

"Yes, Grandpa."

"What color is it?"

"Reddish blue."

"It's good that God blessed me and showed me everything that He showed me before I was blind: the colors of the sunset, the flowering trees, the animals, and the faces of the people I loved. Yanek, you should say a blessing every day for everything that God shows you and preserve the sights in your heart. Our life may be short, but it's full of wonders. Observe them. Don't miss even a single sunrise. God deprived me of vision, and it's a good thing He brought you to me, and you can tell me what your eyes see. Without you my blindness would be even greater.

"Once I had a dog that guided me, who guarded my sleep at night, a smart, noble dog. I called him Prince. Suddenly, without any warning signs, he got sick and departed from the world. You should know that animals also have souls. To this day I can feel his rounded body and his fur. I liked to talk with him. Too bad you never knew him."

Yanek prepared the meal, and they sat down to eat. The bread and cheese were still fresh. After the meal he poured a cup of tea for Grandpa Sergei and for himself, and he lit Grandpa Sergei's pipe. Grandpa Sergei immersed himself in sipping the tea and puffing on his pipe.

After an hour's silence, Grandpa Sergei said, "Bring me the sack, please, and I'll lay my head on it. I'm tired from the road." He immediately laid his head on the sack.

Yanek sat where he was and thought: One day is like another. The same steps, the same breaks, the same meals, and the same bad people who hate wanderers.

Grandpa Sergei apparently read his thoughts and said, "Every day is a miracle, and every day shows us new things. But because of minor preoccupations, our eyes don't see them."

From time to time Grandpa Sergei tells Yanek about his childhood in his parents' house in the village. The harvest, sowing, and the rains they awaited. In spring and summer, everything is done outdoors. In the winter people don't leave the house or the storerooms and barns.

"When I was a boy, I would sit by the windows and look at the snow flowing down from the sky. The stove was hot, and we drank milk. Even then I knew there was a God in the world, though I couldn't feel Him. During the winter people repair their tools, change the handles, sharpen the knives and scythes, but the main business was with the wagons: changing wheels, greasing the axles with pitch, and strengthening the shafts."

When Grandpa Sergei talks about his native village, his voice is soft. It's clear that he's connected to it with all the fibers of his soul, and Yanek has the feeling that in that first piece of earth, even if there were wicked people and criminals there, heaven was close to earth, and on Sundays the choir boys in the church raised up the people's souls.

In moments of grace, Grandpa Sergei tells Yanek about his father's lumberyard and about his grandfather. He started to work in the lumberyard after his military service, when Yanek's grandfather was still managing it "and your father was very young."

The lumberyard sprawled over a large area. There were all kinds of boards and beams. "Your grandfather and your father were decent men. They never sold defective merchandise." People from distant villages and towns used to come to buy from them.

"You knew my grandfather well?"

"Yes. He observed the tradition. He was strict with himself. When he passed away, my life was narrowed. I remember every one of his movements and words. He never insulted anyone. He spoke quietly and tried to understand everyone, Jew or gentile."

"Grandpa died before I was born, and I bear his name," Yanek told him.

"That's a great privilege, believe me."

"I'll try to be worthy."

"May God bless you," said Grandpa Sergei. He closed his eyes and fell asleep.

Yanek continued to look at the twilight, which grew redder.

In the morning two peasants showed up, raised their voices, and shouted, "Get out of here, filthy parasites. Clear out, or we'll make you wish you had."

"We've done no harm to anyone." Grandpa Sergei rose from his bedding.

"Beggars aren't wanted here. They steal."

"I'm blind and my grandson Yanek helps me. He who places a stumbling block before a blind man or harms him, God will not forgive him."

"You're not God's spokesman."

"You should be ashamed of yourselves."

"Clear out, or we'll make you wish you had."

"Wicked men. He who dwells on high sees everything. The world isn't lawless."

Grandpa Sergei is in no hurry to clear out. Threats don't deter him. They just strengthen his trust in God. More than once he struggled bravely against tall, sturdy peasants. His old age brings no shame upon his youth. "If we aren't brave, we'll lose the image of God," repeats Grandpa Sergei.

Nevertheless, the night was not peaceful. First it rained, and Yanek quickly removed the tarpaulins from the pack. With a small tarpaulin he covered the packs and bundles, and with the large tarpaulin he covered them.

"The rain smells good," said Grandpa Sergei. "Too bad it put out the fire and wet our clothes."

Grandpa Sergei is sensitive to smells and tastes. When

Yanek serves him fruit or a vegetable, he smells it. According to the smell, he decides whether the fruit or vegetable is good enough to eat.

At the tail end of the night, the rain stopped. Yanek lit the campfire and placed the kettle on it to boil water. There's nothing like a cup of tea in the morning.

"We didn't sleep last night," said Yanek.

"No matter, we'll make up what we lost."

Yanek asked whether there was a difference between wanderers and beggars.

"There is," said Grandpa Sergei with a strong voice. "Beggars are concerned with their lives and nothing more. True wanderers want to purify themselves, to draw near to God, and thereby to help those in need. A wanderer isn't a beggar in his soul. He's a free man. True, from time to time he's forced to sit at the entrance of a church and ask for gifts from flesh and blood. But he doesn't do it as a beggar."

Yanek likes these nighttime conversations with Grandpa Sergei. He doesn't always understand the words, but

When it was fully morning, Yanek asked, "Grandpa
Sergei, should I go to Sonia's to buy supplies?"

"Wait. Let's listen to the mood of the village first."

"Sonia's a good woman. She's friendly to me."

"Wait a bit. We'll eat something and then decide."

As we've said, threats don't unnerve Grandpa Sergei.
On the contrary, in times of danger his movements become quieter. At such a time Yanek doesn't move his eyes
away from Grandpa Sergei.

After Grandpa Sergei sipped some tea and puffed on
his pipe, listening to the noises from the village for a long
time, he said, "Now you can go to Sonia's."

Grandpa Sergei knows the village ways of life, his
hearing is keen, and his nostrils are alert. He knows
when danger is approaching them and when it's moving
away.

After Grandpa Sergei let him go, Yanek lifted his feet
and ran.

Sonia greeted him and asked, "How has it been?"

"Good."

"Are your wanderings difficult?"

"Thank God, reasonable."

"What can I give you?"

"What you gave me last time."

"I'll do that."

She went to the garden right away and brought two red tomatoes, cucumbers, radishes, and a few potatoes. She added a loaf of bread from her kitchen, a hunk of cheese, and a jug of milk.

Yanek handed her a fifty-mark bill, and Sonia didn't bargain with him.

"Thanks," said Yanek. "Tonight I'll return the jug."

"May God preserve you."

In a few minutes he returned to the tree. Grandpa Sergei asked, "How did it go?"

"Everything was fine."

Yanek added some branches to the fire, spread a cloth on the ground, and prepared the meal. While doing that, he thought: Some people are angry at you and throw stones at you, and some people are like Sonia, and God's light hasn't gone out in them. Her question, "Are your wanderings difficult?" touched his heart. She apparently knew from her own body that a person without a roof, exposed to the winds of the skies and the whims of people, deserves a little consideration.

After the meal Yanek asks, "Why do people hate wanderers?"

"In their eyes, every wanderer is a thief, or strange, or a person you can't depend on. True, some of the wanderers are thieves, but not all of them."

"Do they hate wanderers the way they hate Jews?" Yanek wondered.

"They hate the Jews even more."

"Do I look Jewish, Grandpa Sergei?"

"Since we started wandering together, you've changed. I assume your face is tan. But one thing I can tell you: the language you speak is completely Ukrainian now, even though you spoke German at home."

"I don't feel like I've changed."

"That's how life is. You change, and only after a long time do you feel that you've changed."

"Will my parents recognize me?"

"I'm sure they will."

Later Yanek told Grandpa Sergei, "Last night I dreamed that hooligans attacked us. I tried to get up and hit them, but my arms and legs were tied. All my efforts to free myself from the bonds were of no use to me. In the end I fell from a great height and woke up."

Grandpa Sergei listened and said, "Your dream has told us what we must do. It's an ordinary dream. In the army I used to dream that I was falling from a high place, plunging down, and waking up. Sometimes I would dream that a giant was holding me, hoisting me up to a great height and throwing me down."

Grandpa Sergei often said, "Don't let the giant men in your dreams panic you. They're imaginary. When the dream goes away, they evaporate."

"On Sunday will we go to the church?" Yanek asked.

"We'll see," answered Grandpa Sergei. "If the village is quiet, busy with its own affairs and not thinking about wanderers, we'll go. But if the people decide to expel the wanderers, we'd better keep our distance."

On Saturday they didn't move away. Yanek rose early for his daily run, climbed some trees, and did a few new calisthenics that Grandpa Sergei taught him. But aside from that activity, he didn't do anything. Grandpa Sergei sat and listened. From time to time he asked whether people could be seen in the street and whether there was a wagon at the door of the tavern. Grandpa Sergei says that in the tavern not only the beer is in a ferment, but also people's instincts. On Saturday night, men get drunk, and if a wanderer or a leper or a deranged person crosses their path, they have no mercy on him and beat him, and if the wanderer gets up and resists, they slug him till he bleeds.

Grandpa Sergei is attentive to all the little commotions in the village.

At night he came to a decision: "We won't go to the church on Sunday. We'll be on our way at midnight. Before we go, return the jug to Sonia."

Grandpa Sergei makes sure to keep every promise he makes. If you promised to return the jug that night, you have to return it in time, so people won't say: You can't trust wanderers. Only when they're in the woods, which everyone agrees are public property, does Grandpa Sergei allow him to pick cherries or currants.

Yanek loves the forest and the fruit that grows in it. He also loves the animals: the squirrels, the deer, the rabbits. They all have a cautious gait, with tense alertness. Sometimes he sits for a long time without moving in order to catch the silhouette of a deer. Sometimes a bluish green gaze peeks through a thicket: a wolf.

"Grandpa, why don't we sleep in the woods? Is the forest dangerous because of the wolves?"

"The people who live in the forest are more dangerous

than the wolves: robbers, murderers, people who hate mankind and God—their power is great in the forest. They kidnap people and demand a ransom. If they don't get the ransom, they kill the hostages."

Grandpa Sergei is a soldierly man. Before they set out, he thinks through every detail: where they'll cross a stream and where the huts and shelters are located and where people who are liable to attack you are living. Once a tall and wild peasant emerged from a hut. Grandpa Sergei wrestled with him and subdued him. In the end the man pleaded, "Let me go," and Grandpa let him go.

11

At midnight Grandpa Sergei woke up and roused Yanek. Yanek got up quickly, gathered up their belongings, and put them in their packs and in two bundles. Grandpa Sergei asked, "Is everything packed?"

"Packed," answered Yanek with a single word. They left. The night was dark, but Yanek knew the way. After an hour and a half of walking, Grandpa Sergei asked, "Can you already see the first light?"

"You can see it, Grandpa."

Grandpa Sergei pronounced the words "first light" in a special way, as if they didn't refer to something inanimate but to a living creature he was seeing again.

After they put their packs and bundles down at the foot of a tree, Yanek went out to gather firewood. The darkness was still great, but Yanek knew how to walk in the darkness and find branches that were right for the fire.

Grandpa Sergei, as we've said, doesn't talk a lot, especially not at night. But after Yanek poured tea for him and lit his pipe, Grandpa did speak, but not in his ordinary voice. He spoke to God and said, "Thank you, God, for guiding us until now. You have saved us from evil people, and I ask you to keep helping us. Many villages await us before autumn. Both men and women attack wanderers, and even children are happy to see them suffer. We do what we can, but we need your help. Without you, we have no one to guide us in these hostile expanses. Please, extend your kind hand to us."

After that prayer, Grandpa Sergei sank into himself. Yanek remained seated where he was. The words that had left Grandpa Sergei's mouth kept reverberating and slowly sank into the silence of the night.

Grandpa Sergei was a commander in all his limbs. Even when he addressed God, his highest commander, he didn't grovel. Yanek had already heard Grandpa Sergei pray several times, and every time he was amazed by his direct stance, as though he were not speaking to the God of the whole world, but to the God whom Grandpa Sergei knew very well, at whose side he had fought battles.

More than once he had told Yanek, "God sent us here to learn people's ways and so that we can distinguish between good and evil, between servants of God and those hypocrites who just pretend. All our wanderings are study. God has us meet with devoted people and with the hard-hearted. We have to cling to the beautiful and the good and condemn the ugly and the evil."

Meanwhile Yanek sliced the bread and cheese, added a few vegetables, and placed them on the cloth, saying, "Grandpa Sergei, I invite you to supper."

"Thank you, Yanek, there's no one like you!"

Grandpa Sergei tasted the food and said, "The bread is baked well, so it's tasty. Your grandfather, Yanek, said a blessing for all his food, and that's the right thing to do. To eat and drink without a blessing isn't proper."

"Grandpa, are you a religious Christian?" Yanek dared to ask.

"Once I was. Since they stopped allowing me to enter the church, I've been praying in my own way."

"Grandpa, do you know the Jewish way of life?"

"I lived among Jews for many years. Your grandfather and grandmother obeyed the commandments. Your grandfather rose early for prayers, and when he returned from the synagogue your grandmother would serve him two slices of bread spread with butter and a cup of coffee. They were modest people and helped others in secret. Your father and mother don't obey the laws of the religion, but they inherited your grandparents' modesty, and they also help people."

"Why don't my father and mother keep the laws of the religion?" Yanek wondered.

"They serve God in their way. You can serve God in many ways. Helping needy people is an important commandment. It might seem that greeting people pleasantly is not such an important commandment, but that's not true. A man or woman who greets you warmly not only lights up the moment for you, but the whole day."

The night went on. The campfire gave off pleasant warmth. Yanek gave Grandpa another cup of tea and lit another pipe for him. Now Grandpa Sergei will squeeze his eyelids closed and begin his worship of God.

Once Yanek was expecting his father to come and save him from this life in nature. Now he no longer hopes for miracles. Now he loves traveling with Grandpa Sergei and camping under the familiar trees, the cold water he draws from wells or streams, and the silent sitting with Grandpa Sergei toward evening.

During the first months he was shy and didn't know what to say, what to ask. Grandpa Sergei's silences frightened him. Now there was a reason for everything he did. He was glad to follow Grandpa Sergei's instructions. But what he liked best was the training. He enjoyed training. Sometimes it seemed to him that his soul was growing within his body.

They reach the village called Nikolaiev in the morning. Right away they settle in a little grove near the village. Yanek remembers the village very well from their earlier visit. It's different from the others. The houses are small and well maintained and decorated with lilac bushes. Not only that: the villagers don't mistreat wanderers.

A soldier who served in Grandpa Sergei's unit lives in the village. His name is Kiril. They visited him the last time, and he had greeted them warmly, invited them into his house, and called Grandpa Sergei "my commander." After months of wandering, a ceiling covered their heads, and they sat at a table, on chairs.

"How's life," their host asked.

Grandpa responded without delay, "Thank God, God nourishes His creatures, and He has not forgotten us either."

"Were people generous with you?"

"We won't speak ill of His creatures," Grandpa Sergei answered.

Their host hadn't expected that answer.

After he recovered his wits, he said, "Excuse me, my commander, there are good people who deserve to be honored and bad people who should be condemned. Not everyone is worthy of God's grace."

"Leave that be," answered Grandpa Sergei, trying not to argue.

Kiril's wife lay in the bedroom. For years she'd been sick. She didn't speak or open her eyes. She slept most of the time.

Grandpa Sergei hadn't asked about her illness or what the doctors said. If their host wanted to tell him, he would listen to his words. And Kiril did tell: "I feed her three times a day, wash her, and pray to God to restore her to life."

After eating, Grandpa Sergei and Kiril reminisced about their time in the army, and Kiril made a bundle of supplies for them and wished them a successful journey and blessings from God.

This time they didn't go straight to Kiril's house. They settled under a tree. Yanek rushed to gather firewood and make a fire. Before long the kettle on the coals was boiling. He immediately made a cup of strong tea for Grandpa Sergei and placed it in his hands.

"My friend," Grandpa Sergei addressed Yanek, "could you light my pipe for me?"

"Right away."

"Tea without a pipe is like a woman without a husband."

Yanek understood the comparison and laughed.

The morning was fine, and people had risen early to go to the fields. Yanek tried to find the right words to tell Grandpa Sergei about what was happening in the village, but he had no words in his mouth.

"Did they all come out, the women and children, too?" Grandpa Sergei asks.

"The women and children, too."

"That's a sign that the harvest day has come, when everyone goes out together."

Without delay Yanek went to Olga's house, which was on the edge of the village, near the river. Luckily for him, she hadn't gone out to the harvest with the rest of her family.

"My name is Yanek," he introduced himself.

"I remember you. I'll give you what I gave last time."

"I only have forty marks," said Yanek.

"No matter. I'll give you a little less."

In a short time she brought a basket full of vegetables and potatoes, a hunk of cheese, a jug of milk, and a loaf of bread.

"You gave me more than last time," said Yanek.

"I'm allowed to be generous sometimes," Olga said, and they both laughed.

Grandpa heard about Olga's pleasant welcome and said, "God is merciful to us."

Yanek spread the cloth on the ground and prepared the meal.

After praising the bread, the cheese, and the vegetables, Grandpa added that this meal reminded him of other meals in the field. In the army, after a day of training, or after climbing mountains, the bread and cheese were especially tasty. The army prepares a young man for the proper way of life. Physical training is always good, but aside from that, the friendships that are formed in the army are friendships forever.

When Grandpa Sergei speaks about his military service, his eyelids tremble, and he is completely given over to those years.

After the meal, Grandpa Sergei sank into his thoughts and in puffing on his pipe. Yanek sat in his place and saw his home, coming from school, his mother standing on the threshold and waiting for him to come, so she could hug him.

Yanek has happy news. He got "excellent" on his mathematics test. His father comes home from the lumberyard and the happy news widens his eyes. The table is set for lunch. They sit in their regular places. His father says, "Enjoy the meal," and they start to eat.

Now Yanek clearly sees his mother's hands serving soup with a ladle.

Many months have passed since Yank began wandering with Grandpa Sergei. The apprehensions and fears that paralyzed him at first have long since disappeared. Now he runs as if gliding.

Suddenly Grandpa Sergei was roused from his thoughts and asked, "Yanek, what are you thinking about?"

"About my home, about Mother and Father."

"It's good that you're thinking about them. Thoughts attach us to the people we love."

"Can they tell we're thinking about them?" Yanek asked.

"I'm sure they can," said Grandpa Sergei.

The words "I'm sure" were so full that they brought tears to Yanek's eyes.

13

The next morning they slept later than usual. When Grandpa Sergei woke up, Yanek handed him a pitcher of water, so he could wash his hands and face.

Saturdays in the village are different from the other days. Housewives cook and bake for Sunday. The men clean and organize their tools in the storehouse, curry the horses, talk with the neighbors about the harvest and other seasonal matters.

After they ate breakfast and Grandpa silently recited blessings, they went to visit Kiril, Grandpa's soldier. Even in this quiet, decent village of Nikolaiev, where people don't attack homeless people, they aren't pleased to have wanderers drag their bundles along the main street.

When they get close to Kiril's house, Yanek sees immediately: the house is not as it was. Grandpa Sergei stops and listens, asking, "Are the shutters closed?"

"Closed," Yanek answers.

They approach the door, and Grandpa Sergei knocks.

"Come in," says a voice from inside. Kiril is sitting on a wicker chair. His face is gray, and his beard is white. His wife, whom he cared for for many years, has passed away.

Kiril, seeing his commander, says softly, "My wife Magda has departed. She didn't speak in the last years. Her eyes were closed, but I believed she heard me and understood. We were together for many years. We had no children, but I loved her, and she loved me. We did everything together, in the field and at home. In her last days I promised her that we would be together in the next world, too, just as we were here. She suddenly opened her eyes wide, looked at me, and, without saying anything, she returned her soul to her Maker."

Grandpa Sergei stood there, stunned. His friend's sorrow made him mute.

At last he recovered and said, "Kiril, my friend, God is with you even in this hard time. You mustn't despair. I, too, when I went blind, I was sure that God had parted from me. I was wrong. True, He took the light of my eyes from me. God tests us. The way he tested the Patriarchs, but we have learned that it is forbidden to despair. Despair is darkness. It keeps us away from God."

"What can I do?" Kiril murmured, and burst into tears.

Grandpa Sergei didn't restrain himself either, and he cried, but he managed to overcome his sobbing and said to his soldier, "You loved Magda, and Magda loved you. That's a precious treasure to console you."

"Now I have no one to love. I have no children. My parents passed away years ago. My sister, whom I also loved, has also departed. Everyone has passed away. I've been left alone."

"Kiril," Grandpa raised his voice, "you're not alone. God dwells within you."

Upon hearing Grandpa Sergei's voice, Kiril stopped crying. He covered his eyes with both hands and said nothing more.

They were silent for a long while.

Then Kiril recovered and said, "Forgive me, sir. I would like to give you something for the road, but I have nothing. Since Magda's death, I haven't been working in the field or the courtyard. I sit in the wicker chair most of the day. It's the chair Magda liked to sit in."

"Thank God for guiding me to you. I, too, am unable to help you. I'll pray to God to bring a cure to your sorrow," said Grandpa Sergei.

"Who's the boy?" Kiril woke up and asked, forgetting the time before.

"A boy I adopted. He guides me from place to place and buys food for us."

"A handsome boy."

"He's not only handsome, he's also disciplined and helps me cross fields and streams. Without Yanek, I'd be like a stone."

"May God preserve you," said Kiril.

"And you, too."

Before they parted, Kiril gave him a quarter of a sack of cornmeal and said, "So you can cook a warm meal at night."

Grandpa Sergei promised to come and visit him in another four or five months.

They returned to their camp under the tree.

That evening Grandpa Sergei didn't utter a word. Kiril's face didn't leave Yanek's eyes. It seemed to him that most of Kiril's body had departed for the next world with his wife Magda, and the little that was left of him could hardly move.

Meanwhile Yanek prepared bread, cheese, and vegetables, and they sat and ate. Yanek expected Grandpa Sergei to tell him something about Kiril, but Grandpa didn't say a word. In the end he said, "God ordered us to live the lives He allotted to us. Not everything goes smoothly in a person's life. But you mustn't sink into sadness. Sadness lowers us to the underworld. We have to obey God's command: to keep living even if we're harmed. You don't second-guess a commander's order. You obey it. A commander's order is always an order."

When they first began to wander, Yanek didn't understand most of what Grandpa Sergei said. His words sounded like secrets to him, which only his soldiers, whom he had trained, and with whom he eventually went out on missions, could understand. But gradually he learned to share in his thinking: it was thinking that never forgets for a moment that God is a God of justice, and that everyone who seeks justice—God is with them. Injustice darkens the world.

At first Yanek pictured injustice to himself like an overcast day that darkens the world and shortens the breath. Now Yanek knows: injustice is God's enemy. Grandpa Sergei fights it openly and in secret.

14

That night Grandpa Sergei went to sleep early. Yanek stayed awake and watched the sunset, and at the same time he saw his classmates. He didn't try to stand out, but nevertheless he did stand out, in his height and in his knowledge. Some schoolmates admired and liked him, but others mistreated him.

His great love in the last year was Christina. She was not only pretty but also full of little charming things. She sat in the first row, and Yanek sat in the second, behind her. He could see every movement of her face. Christina also liked him. But she was apparently shyer than he was. Every time they met, they would run away from each other.

On his last day of school he took courage and approached Christina, saying to her, "Today's my last day in school. I want to say goodbye to you and to wish you success in your studies."

"Why are you leaving us?"

"Jewish children aren't allowed to go to school."

"Why?" she asked, and her lips were pursed.

"Because they're Jews."

"That's grossly unfair," she said, and suddenly the determination of a girl who stands her ground appeared on her pretty face.

A few pupils approached him, shook his hand, and wished him success in his new life. Christina didn't move away. She kept crying out, "It's terribly unfair. We have to go out into the playground, hold up signs, and proclaim that there will be no such injustice in our school."

The boys who gathered around him weren't willing to go so far. They stood where they were. The bell rang and interrupted that commotion, but Christina didn't stop raising her voice. She said that their class was cowardly. "You can't expel a good friend and a good student just because he's not a Christian. We're commanded to value people not according to their origin, but according to their character and virtues." For a moment she didn't seem like a girl, but like a fighting woman.

Before long the teachers entered the classrooms, the doors were closed, and the silence of discipline was felt in the corridor.

Yanek left quickly, and he arrived home short of breath.

All that night Christina's face never left his eyes. Though they exchanged no words, it seemed to him that he had conveyed a lot of himself to her. For her part, she also conveyed a lot to him. That night he heard her voice clearly, and it was addressed to him. "I'm sorry," she said.

"What are you sorry for?"

"Because I didn't talk to you."

"You did speak, and I also spoke, but it was speech without sound, so that no one would hear."

"Don't feel sad. We will get to speak a lot."

Suddenly she extended her two hands to him and said, "Since they expelled you from school, you've been with me. No hour passes when you're not with me. I pray in my heart that your exile won't be long."

Around noon Yanek asked, "Grandpa, should I make cornmeal porridge?"

"An excellent idea. Thank God we've been provided with that good food. Kiril knew what we needed. Do you know how to make cornmeal porridge?"

"I know. I liked to watch my mother cook cornmeal porridge. I watched her hands."

"You're blessed!"

That way of talking brought tears to Yanek's eyes. He stepped aside so that Grandpa Sergei wouldn't hear him crying.

Within half an hour the porridge was ready. Yanek served Grandpa a full plate and sprinkled bits of cheese on it. He also took some for himself.

Grandpa tasted it and said, "Excellent porridge. It's been many days since we ate hot and tasty food like this. Even simple food is a gift from on high. People tend to undervalue the food they're used to."

After the meal, Yanek thought of going to the store to buy tobacco leaves, but he didn't go, because they had run out of money.

Yanek doesn't say, "There's nothing to be done." Once Grandpa rebuked him for saying, "Nothing can be done," because there was a note of despair in saying that.

Grandpa Sergei is tall and solid, and before he went blind he was probably even taller. People tend to be moody, but moods don't influence Grandpa Sergei. Before folding the sack and laying his head on it, he said, "Let us pray that God will favor Kiril and free him from his melancholy. He was a brave soldier and stormed the enemy fearlessly. Let's pray that his courage won't fail him this time either."

While he was talking, a peasant approached them and asked, "Are you wanderers?"

"True," Grandpa Sergei stood up and answered.

"Isn't it hard to wander?"

"Hard," Grandpa Sergei answered with a single word.

"Don't you have a house?"

"No."

"I don't understand how people can live that way."

"We live," answered Grandpa Sergei, "we've learned not to complain."

"But still, who helps you?"

"God."

The peasant was dumbstruck by the word that had just been flung at him. He stood where he was for a moment, then, without asking anything else, he went on his way.

Grandpa Sergei asked for a cup of tea, and after sipping it and puffing on his pipe he said, "Our life isn't splendid, but it has a purpose."

"Grandpa Sergei, when did you start wandering?" Yanek asked cautiously.

"When your father went bankrupt and lost all his money, and I had nobody in the town, I didn't want to stand in the street and beg, so I decided to go out to the villages and sit in church doorways on Sundays."

"At first was it hard to wander, Grandpa Sergei?"

"Absolutely. But the solitude brought me close to God. I learned to trust him and to love him."

15

Yanek prepared vegetables, bread, and cheese for supper. Grandpa Sergei was content, but gathered into himself. Tomorrow was Sunday. In the morning they would fill their bundles and packs and go to the church. This was a very difficult time for Grandpa Sergei, to sit and wait for gifts from flesh and blood was shameful.

Yanek got up early and took his morning run. He prepared a cup of tea for Grandpa Sergei and lit his pipe for him.

Grandpa Sergei was in a good mood, and he jokingly said, "Let's go to church, and we'll do it like soldiers obeying an order. More than once my unit was sent to clean the garbage that had piled up along the roads. It's a nothing job, just to keep the soldiers busy, so they won't get lazy. We'll do that, too. But in our hearts we'll know that it's a contemptible task and not done by free will."

After a short pause, Grandpa Sergei added, "God sent you to me. What would I do without you?"

"You don't have to thank me. I have to thank you."

They reached the church, stopped, and sat next to the path that led to the entrance. Yanek took off his cap and placed it on the ground.

The first worshippers passed by without noticing them. Yanek got to his feet with his cap in his hand and was about to call out, "Don't ignore the helpless," the way beggars and cripples do, but he restrained himself. Grandpa Sergei forbade him to ask out loud. There was only One whom one addressed and asked for mercy.

One of the worshippers bent over and placed a small bill in Yanek's cap. That little donation pleased him. He hoped that other contributions would follow.

The prayers in the church lasted for a long time. When it was over, the worshippers came out and distributed a few more small bills. Some of them also came to Yanek.

Yanek was disappointed. Grandpa Sergei noticed his disappointment and said, "Thank God, we have plenty of cornmeal and it will nourish us. You mustn't be ungrateful."

Without delay they set out. On the way they met a peasant who was resting in the shade of a tree. Grandpa Sergei asked, "How's the war going?" At first the peasant didn't understand his question, and, once he understood it, he said, "People say the Germans are going from victory to victory, and some people say that the Russians have recovered and launched a counterattack."

"Didn't they take the Jews away from here?" Grandpa Sergei asked.

"They took them to big pits and shot them." The peasant spoke in an objective manner.

"How do you know?"

"I saw it with my own eyes."

"They killed them for no reason?"

"They killed them because they were Jews."

Grandpa Sergei didn't ask any more questions. Without

saying goodbye to the peasant, they went on their way.

At first Yanek hadn't understood the peasant's words, but once he did, his leg muscles froze, and he could barely drag them. In the end he couldn't restrain himself and asked Grandpa Sergei, "Are the peasant's words correct?"

"Peasants tend to exaggerate. Their imagination soars." Grandpa rushed to put out the fire.

"Do the peasants hate the Jews?"

"Yes," he said.

From then on he didn't ask. They stopped beneath a tree. Grandpa Sergei sensed that Yanek was tired, and he lit his pipe by himself and sank into his thoughts.

Yanek wanted to ask Grandpa Sergei about the Jews, but he didn't. The peasant, the way he looked, the way he sat, horrified him, and only now did he feel the dread it sowed in him.

In the end Yanek overcame his reluctance and said, "Grandpa Sergei, I'm afraid."

"Of what? Of whom?"

"Of the peasant we talked with."

"What about him frightened you?"

"What he told us about the Jews."

"You mustn't be afraid, my friend. Fear diminishes you."

Yanek understood that his spirits had flagged, and he had to be strong so he could help his parents and grandparents when they returned from exile.

He was tired and fell right asleep.

In his sleep he was in school. The two class bullies were teasing him, calling him "Jew" and shouting at him: "What are you doing here? Go to the Jews." Yanek stared at them, and with a sharp movement that Grandpa had taught him, he knocked them both to the ground. They lay there and it was apparently hard for them to get up. They were amazed.

Many months had passed since he'd been in school.

Suddenly Christina rose from the bench, stood, and said, "Yanek, where have you been? You've changed a lot. I almost didn't recognize you. Your new height suits you."

"I've been exercising," he answered.

"Wonderful," Christina said. "Will you be with us now?"

"Not yet. I have to finish training."

Christina was wearing a blue sweater that Yanek was particularly fond of. Her pretty face had gotten much prettier since he saw her last.

When he woke from his sleep, the sun was still on the horizon.

16

They reached the village of Karilovka toward evening, when the flocks were returning from pasture.

Grandpa asked as usual, "What do you see?" Yanek quickly answered, "No change."

"And what color is the sky?" asked Grandpa Sergei.

"Reddish green."

"Do you think it's beautiful?"

"Very," Yanek quickly answered.

"Still, there is a change. The sky isn't colored reddish green every day. Every minute something in nature changes. It's too bad we ignore these marvelous changes. A man like me, who can no longer see the wonders, knows what is denied to him. But thank God his imagination shows him what he once saw."

This time they had collected very little, and they wouldn't be able to buy fresh food. But one mustn't be discouraged. There was cornmeal and there was still a piece of cheese, and there was tea.

Yanek made cornmeal porridge and served a full bowl to Grandpa Sergei. Grandpa tasted it and said, "Excellent," and Yanek filled a plate for himself and sat down.

They were tired from the road and got ready to go to sleep. Suddenly a tall, thin man appeared out of the darkness. His hair was long, and he immediately started to blame the wanderers, because all the troubles came from them: disease, the poor harvests, strange deaths, rain at the wrong time. Everything was because of them. Wanderers not only stole, they also frightened children at night. They should be put in prison.

Grandpa Sergei listened and he immediately realized whom he was dealing with. He rose to his feet and said, "Where did you got those falsehoods from?"

"What do you mean? Everybody says it."

"And I tell you that they're falsehoods."

"They are true," said the man, beginning to jump up and down like a boy.

"The Bible says, love thy neighbor as thyself. You're supposed to love every man, whether he lives at home or wanders, or is a cripple. You have to love everyone."

"Why didn't I remember that?" he said, and grabbed his head.

"Now you'll remember."

"It's forbidden to forget the commandments that are written in the Bible," he said, and childish amazement covered his face.

"You won't forget now," said Grandpa Sergei.

"What should I do?" he asked.

"Do good," Grandpa Sergei spoke to him softly.

"True."

"Now go to sleep, it's late already."

"I'll go," he said, and started running toward the village.

They had run into all kinds of people on their way, but they hadn't met such a strange man before.

Yanek served a cup of tea to Grandpa, lit his pipe for him, and for a long time they sat without speaking.

Now Yanek saw the long, bright summer evenings in the garden of his house, the colorful suppers. He and his parents spent most summer nights together, sleeping in the cellar.

The separation had come swiftly, so swiftly that Yanek had barely felt it. Father came down to the cellar at midnight and woke him. He said they had to go immediately and look for Grandpa Sergei.

"Grandpa Sergei will watch over you until we come back."

Yanek remembered seeing Grandpa Sergei standing at the door of the storeroom in the lumberyard, listening with his blind eyes.

They searched for him all night long, and there were moments when they were about to go back home, but suddenly his father saw a man sitting under a tree and smoking a pipe. He recognized him and called out, "Sergei."

That had been more than a year earlier. Since then Yanek had changed. He was taller, his shoulders were broader, his walk was steady. He had outgrown his shoes twice. He leaped easily. Grandpa Sergei insisted on daily training. Recently he had been teaching Yanek how to box. Grandpa Sergei, despite his disability, had often knocked down peasants who were taller than him.

Grandpa Sergei fell asleep. Yanek folded a sack and lay his head on it. He immediately saw Christina before his eyes, not as he had seen her all those years in school—

pretty and quiet—but as he had seen her on the day he was expelled, a girl with great strength in her. Now he also heard her voice: "Injustice is disfiguring the world, and at this moment it's making us ugly," she raged. Her strength of character added to her beauty. Everyone was surprised, but no one said anything. A few children giggled. Yanek was embarrassed and frightened, and all the way home Christina's words trembled in his ears.

When he climbed up the stairs to the house, his mother came out and asked, "What's the matter?"

"They expelled me from school."

"For how long?"

"Forever."

"Did they say why?"

"No."

His mother almost burst into tears, but she restrained herself. In the end she recovered and said, "Don't worry, my boy. You were always an outstanding student, and you still will be. Soon they'll be sorry they expelled you. Soon they'll ask your forgiveness."

That was only the beginning. In just a day their pretty little town turned into a trap. The Jews weren't allowed to leave their houses at night. Gendarmes and soldiers burst into the houses, plundered everything of value, and after the robbery, they took the old people and children away.

17

The next morning Yanek woke up early and went out for a run around the fields. When he returned, Grandpa Sergei was still sleeping. Yanek climbed a tall tree, quickly reached the top, came down easily, and immediately started to get the campfire ready.

Had it not been for Kiril, who had supplied them with a quarter of a sack of cornmeal, their situation would have been desperate.

At noon he would go to the peasant woman, whose name he had forgotten, and buy some dairy products from her with the money they had collected.

"Most of beggars' time is given over to the needs of food and clothing, and they don't make time to contemplate their souls or the purpose of life. We have to be careful not to sink into that muck," Grandpa Sergei warns.

When Grandpa Sergei speaks about matters of faith, he grows taller, his forehead shines, and it's evident that he's connected to another world. Once he had said with enthusiasm, "Yanek, open your eyes and look at all the wonders that surround us. A flowering tree is no trivial matter. It speaks to us the way a calf in a field is pleased to see us from a distance."

When Grandpa Sergei woke up, the water was already boiling, and Yanek started to prepare a cup of tea for him.

"How did you sleep, Yanek?" he asked.

"Well."

"Did you have dreams?"

"I had some, but I forgot them."

"I believe I've already told you that God also talks to us in dreams."

Yanek poured a cup of tea for Grandpa and lit his pipe for him.

"Good tea," said Grandpa Sergei.

Then Yanek went to buy dairy products. Most of the peasants—men, women, the youth—had gone out to harvest the grain. Only old men and women stayed back to watch over their houses. It was quiet. From the stables and cowsheds the whinnying of horses and the mooing of cows could be heard.

Suddenly Yanek stood still and said to himself, "I will always remember this quiet sight."

No sooner had the words left his mouth when, aston-ished at himself, he moved his feet and set out for the house where he had bought bread, dairy products, and vegetables a few months ago.

The members of the family were in the fields, and an old woman stood at the gate and asked, "What do you want?"

"I wish to buy dairy products."

"How much do you have?"

"Twenty marks."

"I'll bring you a slice of cheese and a jug of yogurt."

"Be generous, please, and add some bread and vegeta-bles, Grandma."

"For a twenty-mark bill you want fresh and tasty

produce, and, as if that weren't enough, you have more demands?"

"Grandma, give with the generosity of your heart."

"It's a good thing you can accept what I'm willing to give."

Yanek didn't rush back to the tree. The silence and the blossoming trees captivated his eyes and reminded him of vacations with his parents in pleasant little guesthouses in the mountains, the long walks, the tasty meals in the shade of tall trees.

What had they spoken about during those long, quiet days? He didn't remember. He was reading adventure books by Jules Verne and westerns by Karl May then, and they were his world.

Since leaving the house he had changed. He had forgotten his name from home. When Grandpa Sergei says, "Yanek, would you please . . ." It seems to him that he has always been called Yanek.

The women who sell him groceries also call him Yanek, and often with fondness.

Is Grandpa Michael angry at me for abandoning his name? Yanek wonders, and he doesn't know the answer. He doesn't dare ask Grandpa Sergei.

When the war is over, I'll go back home, and my parents will call me by the name I loved—Michael.

When he got back to the tree, to his dismay he saw that Grandpa Sergei's face was bleeding.

"Grandpa Sergei," he said, sinking to his knees.

"It's nothing. Don't be upset. One of the village bullies stood next to me, cursed me, threatened that if I didn't clear out, he'd hit me. I got to my feet and slugged him.

He tried to knock me down and scratched me. I kept on pounding him."

"Do your wounds hurt, Grandpa Sergei?"

"No, they sting a little."

"I'll wash your face. Mother supplied me with iodine and bandages."

"May God bless your mother."

Grandpa Sergei's face was scratched deeply. Yanek washed it carefully and put iodine on the wounds.

"You could have been a medic in my unit," said Grandpa Sergei.

Yanek didn't know what to answer, but in the end he said, "I hope the iodine will help to cure your scratches."

"We'll eat lunch and in the afternoon we'll leave this place, with what we called an orderly retreat in the army."

Yanek cooked cornmeal porridge for lunch, placing some pieces of cheese and a few spoonfuls of yogurt on the side of the plate. The fresh dairy products gave the meal a fuller taste.

"Does it hurt, Grandpa Sergei?"

"No. A man who's been in the army is used to getting wounded. A soldier without scars isn't a combat soldier."

They ate at their leisure, finished the porridge and the yogurt, and Yanek made a cup of strong tea for Grandpa Sergei, and he lit his pipe for him. Grandpa Sergei gradually sank into himself.

Yanek cleaned the pot and the plates, the spoons and the cups, dried them, and put them in the pack.

During the months with Grandpa he learned to honor

the vessels they used. Vessels for cooking and eating are part of you, and you must treat them like your hands.

It occurred to Yanek to ask Grandpa Sergei, "Where do we want to get to?"

"I assume, to Zhadowa. Not everything is in our hands."

"In the end, where will we get to?" Yanek asked.

"We'll get to the place God wants us to get to."

Yanek didn't ask anymore. Now he would think about the things Grandpa Sergei said to him. Sometimes Grandpa's words trickle into him, and they come back to him in a dream.

They started off again. The backpack and bundle were heavy, but in time Yanek had learned to bear the weight. From time to time he said to himself: It's certainly harder for my parents and grandparents.

Roaming in Grandpa Sergei's company is like being in the army: you train during the day, you're awake and alert and prepared for any attack, but still you're free.

After walking hard for an hour, they stopped and rested under a tall pine tree in the heart of a field.

Grandpa Sergei started to talk, "When you wander, you learn what's essential and what's unimportant, what's temporary and what's permanent and abiding, what's truth and what's a lie. When a person sits comfortably in his home, he forgets the main thing. He's busy with everyday concerns, fights about trivial matters, and he only thinks about himself and his property. But when you're outside, without a house, only the sky above you and the earth beneath you, only then do you know that wandering, as hard as it may be, purifies you."

Yanek listens to every word that comes from Grandpa Sergei's lips. He doesn't understand some of the things. But the melody of his speech is pleasant to his ears. Sometimes it seems to him that Grandpa Sergei's words are only melody.

I have to learn that melody, and maybe then I'll understand his words, he sometimes says to himself.

After that they got up and went on. Now he remembers that the first days with Grandpa Sergei were full of dread, unrest, yearning for his parents, and every night before sleeping he would say to himself: Tomorrow Father will come and take me home.

Grandpa Sergei, for his part, never tried to make things easy for him. He told him that a person who is wandering is exposed to dangers, and he has to learn to defend himself. "You can do it. If you want, you can. God helps those who make an effort."

Once he asked Grandpa Sergei whether soldiers are also afraid.

"Certainly they're afraid. Every living creature is

afraid. But they learn to overcome fear. That's the secret in a nutshell."

They got to the next village in the evening. Thin smoke drifted up from the chimneys of the houses, and it was a quiet time. Housewives were making meals, and in some houses the family was already sitting and eating supper. Yanek remembered his own home at this hour. His father would return from the lumberyard, and his mother would be pleased at his arrival. Yanek liked his mother's blintzes, the wild berry preserves she would pour onto the blintzes. Supper was always light and tasty.

"What are you thinking about?" asked Grandpa Sergei.

"About my home."

"Your home is a good one. Your grandfather is a noble person, and your father inherited quite a bit of his nobility. They always helped people, whether they had the wherewithal or they were in a bad situation. There are no quarrels in your house. Your grandfather observed the tradition, and he often told me: Sergei, you mustn't sink into sorrow, sorrow brings us down to the underworld, a man has to be happy with his lot. At first I didn't understand his words, how can a poor, handicapped man like I am now be happy with his lot? Gradually I understood, that if a man has faith in God, he is happy. I learned a lot of things about God and man from him. He was a man filled with many generations of faith and wisdom."

"Are all Jews like him?" Yanek asked, alarmed by his own question.

"Regrettably, no."

"What happened?"

"They lost their faith."

"All of them?"

"Not all of them, but many."

"Why did that happen to them?"

"It's like a great love. Sometimes the flame goes out. The Jews were devoted to God, heart and soul, for many generations. Suddenly, in the last generation, their faith left them."

"Will faith return to them?"

"I'm sure it will."

"Why does everyone hate the Jews, and only you have compassion for them?"

"I know their life, their faith, and their suffering. It isn't easy to be a Jew, whether you're religious or not. Suddenly they uproot them from their houses and send them to someplace unknown."

Grandpa Sergei stopped talking, as sometimes happened with him, and Yanek didn't ask any more questions.

Yanek went out to gather firewood and brought back a dry branch, immediately sawing it into pieces. Not until he had given Grandpa Sergei a cup of tea and lit his pipe for him did Grandpa Sergei return from the world he had sunk into and ask, "How are things?"

"Everything is fine. I'm about to cook cornmeal porridge."

"God bless you."

They sat and ate for a long time, and Yanek felt that Grandpa Sergei's blessing lay upon his head. He was tired from the events of the day. Without spreading a blanket on the earth or folding a sack to lay his head on, he fell asleep where he was. "Yanek," Grandpa Sergei called, but, since Yanek didn't answer, he understood that he'd fallen asleep.

In his sleep Yanek went to his school, and he felt light, dressed in the peasant clothes Grandpa Sergei had lent him.

It was the eleven o'clock recess. The children ran around in the schoolyard and the corridors. Yanek recognized quite a few of them, but they didn't recognize him. He moved forward, climbed the stairs, and entered his classroom.

Most of his classmates were standing, a few were talking, but most of them were watching the class clown, Edmond, who was imitating the mathematics teacher. They didn't recognize Yanek.

In the end, one of the pupils approached him and asked, "What are you doing here?"

"I came to see my class."

"Did you go to this school?"

"I was even in this class."

"When?"

"More than a year ago."

"What's your name?"

"You have to figure that out."

With a clumsy gesture, the boy turned to his friends and called out: "We have a new student in our class. Do you recognize him?"

"He's a peasant. He comes from a village. He got here by mistake," said a guttural voice.

"Not by mistake," Yanek said softly.

"Who are you?" one of the pupils asked.

"Last year in this class you were studying equations with two unknowns."

"Were you studying with us?"

"Correct."

"Hans," Yanek spoke to one of them, "you were learning to box. Do you still box?"

"Yes."

"Do you want to try me? Let's have a friendly bout," Yanek suggested.

"I'm out of shape."

"It's interesting that you don't remember me. Where's Christina? I'm sure she'll remember me. Where is she?"

"She's sick," answered one of the children.

"Has she been absent from school for a long time?"

"A few months."

"How is she? Did you visit her?"

"She's in a sanatorium far from here."

"And you never thought of going to her?"

"It's far away, one or two hundred miles."

"Why didn't you go to visit Christina?" Yanek raised his voice and at the same time he raised a desk to the ceiling. The desk fell and broke apart. Yanek woke up from the force of the crash.

19

It was the middle of the night. He fell into a deep sleep again.

He was in an unfamiliar place and tried to identify all the objects that surrounded him, but everything he saw was strange to him.

While he was perplexed and wondering where he had ended up, what had brought him there, he heard a voice speaking to him.

"Yanek, you have successfully passed the first, important stage in physical training. Soon the practical actions will begin. Grandpa Sergei gave you what he'd gathered over his life and made you into a warrior. There are many injustices, and you'll have to withstand severe trials. Don't be afraid. Your strength will be with you, and you'll emerge stronger from the struggle."

Yanek woke up. The voices echoed in his ears, clear and emphatic. The first light of dawn glowed on the horizon. Grandpa Sergei was asleep, and Yanek sat up where he was, stunned.

When Grandpa Sergei woke up, Yanek promptly told him about the dream.

Grandpa Sergei wasn't surprised when Yanek repeated the words he had heard and asked, "What am I to do, Grandpa?"

"Store those things up in your heart."

"Still, Grandpa, what am I to do?"

"Don't reveal that secret to anyone."

"Not even to Mother and Father?"

"You may tell it to them."

"But it was just a dream."

"A dream is sometimes truer than reality."

"Grandpa Sergei, may I go out for my daily run now?"

"Go, my friend. It's too bad I'm disabled. I would join you."

As soon as he began to run he felt that his body wasn't as it was. He was light and floated. When he returned, he gave Grandpa Sergei a cup of tea and lit his pipe for him. For a moment he was surprised by Grandpa Sergei's tranquil soul, the way he accepted misfortune without complaint.

The voices he had heard at night remained with him, and he felt a rustling in his ears and a little pain.

"Grandpa Sergei, I feel a slight pain in my ears."

"No wonder. Wouldn't ears that heard voices from somewhere hurt a little?"

"What should I do?"

"Nothing. I assume the pain will pass."

Everything he did and saw that day was different from other days. There were moments when he felt elated and it seemed to him that he could fight against a few bad men and overcome them. But there were moments when he felt weakness and a lack of faith in himself and his strength. Grandpa Sergei knew even without asking that Yanek's spirit wasn't the same as before. Finally he said, "What are you thinking about, Yanek?"

"I'm not thinking. The voices I heard at night are still scurrying around in my head."

"I told you. Hold on to those voices, and you'll be content that they spoke to you in a dream. Agitation and mood swings aren't fitting for a warrior."

"Sorry, Grandpa Sergei."

"It's not a question of being sorry now, but of the correct stance. We have hard days before us, and we have to be calm, to think about the dangers with open eyes and to prepare for them."

Grandpa Sergei, after sipping another cup of tea, turned to Yanek and said, "I want your advice, Yanek."

"What about?" Yanek was alarmed.

"We've run out of food. Except for cornmeal, we have nothing to eat. Your father, among other things, also left us some cash. I didn't think I'd touch the money or the valuables until he came back. But since we have nothing to eat, I want to borrow fifty marks from the money he left us, and with God's help, when I have it, I'll return it to him. What do you think?"

"My opinion is the same as yours, Grandpa," said Yanek, and he was surprised by the words that left his lips.

For a moment Yanek sat without moving. All of Grandpa Sergei's being, his large body, his huge blindness, suddenly seemed to him like a great secret you shouldn't get too close to.

While they were listening to the tranquility of the evening, they heard steps approaching.

"Sergei," called a woman.

"Tanya," Grandpa Sergei recognized her voice. "How did you know I was here?"

"Yesterday I dreamed you were approaching the village, and I went out to meet you."

"Strange. I also saw you in my sleep, but I didn't know whether you'd want to see me."

Tanya and Grandpa Sergei were cousins, and they had been very close friends when they were young. After Grandpa Sergei finished his military service and remained in the city, the connection was broken. Tanya married and had children, and Grandpa Sergei married a woman named Dorka.

"How many years has it been since I've seen you, Sergei?" Tanya asked.

"Many years," answered Grandpa Sergei.

"Have you gone back to visit our village?"

"No. Since my parents died, I haven't been there."

"I haven't gone back either," said Tanya, "but the village stands before my eyes every day. I loved all the seasons there: the blossoming of spring, the summer sun, and the falling leaves in the autumn. But I especially loved the winter. Do you still remember me?"

"How could I forget?"

"We were friends, heart and soul. We used to swim in the river. We jumped off the bridge right into the stream. We used to go into the forest to pick berries. We'd sit and gobble them up, and we kissed each other a lot. We were always happy. Why didn't you come back to the village after your army service, the way you'd promised me you would?"

"The city seduced me: the lights, the coffeehouses, the taverns, the movie theaters. In the end I met Dorka and married her. I didn't live with her long. After three years of life together, she died. She was sick for two weeks, and she passed away without complaining. Four years after her death, I went blind."

"Did you think of me all those years?"

"I did."

"And what did you think?"

"I thought about going back to the village and finding you."

"And why didn't you come back?"

"I already told you. The city seduced me. If it hadn't been for the city, I would have returned to our village, and my life would have been different."

"Do you regret it?"

"Of course I regret it."

"That's what I wanted to hear."

"And now, do you forgive me?"

"No," she said, laughing.

"Not even now, after all the years?" Grandpa Sergei wondered.

"Some sins are hard to forgive. I believed you'd return to me. I prayed and wept for nights on end, and you didn't even send me a postcard."

"I was a prisoner."

"You were a prisoner? The brave soldier, decorated with medals, that I was so proud of, was captured by the city lights? Where was your will, where was your resourcefulness, and where were your promises?"

For a short time they sat together in silence. "Now I'll go home," she said, rising to her feet, and she added, "I'm glad I met you."

"Tanya, you did me a great favor by coming to visit me."

"It was nothing. A few childhood memories. Who's the boy?" she asked.

"His father lent him to me. He helps me and guides me from place to place. He's a sweet boy. Can he buy some supplies from you?"

"If he'll come with me, I'll give some to him."

"Tanya, you've done me a great favor."

Yanek went with her to her house, a big house, with a courtyard, a stable, a dairy, and chicken coops.

"What can I give you?"

"Whatever you want to give us. I have a fifty-mark bill."

She went into the garden and came back with vegetables, and she took cheese and butter from the pantry, and she took a loaf of bread and more cheese down from the shelves, and when Yanek handed her the bill, she said, "No need."

When Yanek returned to the tree and told Grandpa Sergei what had happened, he didn't respond. Even when he spread a cloth on the earth and prepared the meal, Grandpa Sergei didn't ask anything or say a word.

After an hour of silence, Grandpa Sergei asked for the bottle of brandy. Usually Grandpa Sergei doesn't need to drink from that bottle, just in times of great pain, but that evening he was moved and took a few long swigs. He sat, withdrawn into himself, and didn't ask anything or make any remarks.

He didn't get up from his bedding until the end of the evening. "You mustn't drink brandy. Brandy dulls thought, and a person forgets who he is and what's required of him. Next time, if I ask you to give me the brandy bottle, don't give it to me."

"I won't be able to refuse you, Grandpa Sergei."

"I command you."

Yanek didn't respond. This time Grandpa Sergei's voice was determined and not directed at Yanek, but at himself.

The next day Grandpa Sergei spoke about the need to equip themselves for the struggle against the wicked.

"The wicked know that true wanderers wish to purify themselves, but this doesn't stop them from hating them with clenched teeth. We are few, but we are faithful to the Ten Commandments that God gave us," Grandpa Sergei spoke with a strong voice.

"Is it possible to recognize the wicked?" Yanek dared to ask.

"Their deeds testify to them. They seek only to do harm, especially to strangers and the crippled and lepers."

"What must we do?" Yanek asked.

"I cannot prepare myself better than life has prepared me. But you can do exercise after exercise. In a little while I'll pass the pistol on to you and teach you how to use it properly."

"Just the two of us will fight against the wicked?" asked Yanek.

"No, we'll train the weak and the miserable to be stronger and resourceful. We'll take them up from their low place, raise their stature, restore the image of God in them. Without the image of God, there's no way of facing life correctly."

Yanek remembered the tramps who lived in shelters for the poor during the winter: unpleasant people, shouting and cursing, and they had reproaches against the whole world. Last autumn they had lived in a hostel. Grandpa Sergei tried to persuade them that it wasn't proper to use coarse language, that we must preserve the image of God in us. The reaction was swift: "Preach morality to yourself, not to us. We have no interest in God. God takes care of the healthy and rich, not of the needy and those with nothing."

"I was a master sergeant in a special unit. I can teach you things that will be useful to you."

"Don't worry about us. Take care of yourself."

Grandpa didn't give in. "And what about your souls?"

"What you can't see doesn't exist," said one of the poorest of the poor, and he said nothing more.

If Grandpa Sergei's arms hadn't been strong, they would have stolen their bundles.

Would those people fight against the wicked? They themselves were wicked, Yanek almost said, but he stopped himself.

Yanek made supper and Grandpa Sergei's mood became relaxed again.

After the meal and after Yanek poured Grandpa a cup of tea and lit his pipe, Grandpa Sergei remembered his village, his parents, and his elder sister Irena.

"Those were lovely days. We would go out to plow the fields, then sow with broad sweeps of our arms, and after a few weeks we'd see the seedlings again and the growth, and our hearts would overflow. Every few days we would come to see the growth in the fields, and we'd be happy when the rain fell at the right time, and the fields were full of sprouting wheat. Those were the fullest days of my life. Later Tanya became part of my life. She was beautiful, and together we knew love. Then I joined the army and I was sure that after my military service I'd come home to my parents, to the soil, and to Tanya. But for some reason I didn't go back to her. Only God knows why. Suddenly I was captivated by the city lights, bars, cafés, movie houses, and girls who came my way. I would go back to my room dizzy from brandy and sleep restlessly. I knew that my life was polluted, and that I had to recover myself and go back to my parents, to the fields and the gardens and all the good things that the village bestowed on us. I knew, but my feet didn't take me there. God saved me. I don't know why. I wasn't worthy of His mercy.

"One night, I had just left a bar. It was already autumn and a cold wind blew. Suddenly a rather short girl stepped out of an alley. Her hair was gathered in the back, her neck was long. After some hesitation I approached her and introduced myself: 'My name is Sergei. You please me.' I expected a movement of rejection, or a reproach. But, amazingly, she said, 'My name is Dorka.'

"I didn't invite her for a drink or to sit in a café. I walked beside her, embarrassed, and I didn't know what to say. I escorted her to her house, and at the gate, I said, 'Dorka, I'm sure we'll meet again. Meanwhile, good night.'

"That very week I saw her and walked up to her. She smiled and said, 'How are you, Sergei?' Once again, I didn't know what to say, and I stood there like a dummy.

In the end I said, 'I'm very glad to see you.'

"Since that evening, we were together for all the years that God granted us. I didn't move from her side. We were only together for three years. Dorka got sick, with a rare disease, and she went up to heaven like an angel.

"That year I arrived at your grandfather's lumberyard and asked for work. I apparently pleased him, and he hired me. He taught me all about wood, the various beams and planks, what makes some wood expensive, other wood cheap, what's for construction and what's for furniture. In that way my soul and his came to be joined. I liked his way of standing, of speaking, his relation to people. Your father is different from him. He doesn't keep the tradition, but some of your grandfather's nobility is stamped in him. Your father, like your grandfather, also doesn't speak a lot. He likes to listen and treats people with compassion. I worked in their lumberyard until I went blind. Even after I was blind, I kept coming to advise customers. Until the lumber business collapsed. Your father went bankrupt, and I had no choice but to go out and wander.

"Sorry I tired you out with talking. I wanted you to know who your ancestors are. I've trained you a lot, so your body will do its duty. But there wasn't always time to deal with matters of the soul."

That night a gang of three fell upon them. Grandpa Sergei, with the agility of a young man, grabbed the legs of two of them powerfully, knocked them down, and hit them. Yanek did the same to the youngest one. The attackers ran for their lives.

Grandpa Sergei was pleased with Yanek's courage and called him a hero. "We mustn't be complacent. Even on a quiet, bright night, wicked men steal the little that wanderers possess."

Now they didn't go back to sleep. Fortunately there were still branches that had been cut, and Yanek quickly brought the campfire back to life. Grandpa Sergei was upset and didn't cease denouncing the criminals. When Grandpa Sergei vilifies someone, his face turns red, and for a moment it seems to Yanek that soon he'll shed the blindness from his eyes, and the company commander will lead his soldiers again. Meanwhile the sky brightened, and the night withdrew into its lair.

While Grandpa was sunk into himself, a girl dressed in a long smock approached Yanek and asked in wonderment, "Who are you?"

"We're wanderers," Yanek answered quietly.

"So where's your house?"

"We don't have a house. The earth is our floor, and the sky is our roof."

Upon hearing Yanek's words, her eyes opened even wider, and she said, "You wander like this all the time?"

"True."

"Aren't you cold at night?"

"We sleep in our clothes."

"And what do you eat?"

"What everyone eats: bread, cheese, and potatoes."

"So you're like everyone else?"

"True."

"But why do you scare me?"

"There's nothing to be afraid of. We're like everyone."

Hardly had Yanek said that when she picked up her feet and ran away.

It was a fine morning. Thin smoke curled up out of the chimneys of the houses—a sign that the housewives were making semolina porridge, and soon they would serve full plates to all the members of the household.

Yanek also started to prepare breakfast. He asked Grandpa whether to make cornmeal porridge or set out bread and cheese. Grandpa Sergei, after thinking for a while, said, "It's good to heat up the belly with porridge in the morning. Cornmeal porridge reminds me of home, of my father's and mother's faces, and the light in the windows."

Then Grandpa Sergei said, "I'm sorry I didn't appreciate the beauty and the taste of my childhood. Yanek, every day you must choose a sight and say to yourself: I will treasure this sight forever. If you meet an old man, or someone young, and you speak with them, and they say something fine to you, or a meaningful proverb—keep them in your memory."

Yanek loves this clear morning hour. He's with himself and with his thoughts, and suddenly a cool breeze from the woods touches his neck, and he sees his mother sitting in the garden, dressed in summer clothes, and she's pretty. Even then, when he was barely nine years old, he used to say to himself: My mother and father won't die. They'll always be with me. He immediately ran to his mother, and she hugged him and asked, "What were you thinking about?"

"That we won't always be together."

"Why did you think of that?"

"Hermann, my classmate—his mother died last week."

"Don't worry," his mother quickly said. "Your father and I will live for a long time, and we won't go and rest in heaven until we're very old."

His mother's words, and even more her arms when she hugged him, calmed him down. But tears burst from his eyes and wouldn't stop. His mother quickly pressed him to her heart and murmured, "You'll always be with me."

That morning Grandpa Sergei sat with his legs crossed and sang military marches, alternating with nostalgic songs. He sang slowly and emphasized the words. Yanek felt that the melodies were dear to Grandpa Sergei, and he did repeat them several times. In the end he took a deep breath and said, "A person has to have melodies. Without melodies there's no vitality. Do you understand, Yanek?"

"I like to hear my mother sing. I don't sing myself," Yanek told him.

That morning Grandpa Sergei was wrapped in nostalgia. Yanek heard him singing song after song. Suddenly he saw his mother singing and for a moment he wanted to join in with her, but his voice didn't obey him. It made him sad to be blocked, and he laid his head on the sack.

In the afternoon Yanek went to a tobacco and liquor store and bought Grandpa Sergei some tobacco.

In the tobacco store the customers are mainly tall, bulky men, and quite a few drunks. Yanek overcame his fear, approached the counter, and asked for tobacco.

"Leaves or cut?" asked the woman who owned the store.

"Cut."

She immediately brought him a tin box, opened it, and showed him what was inside.

"Fresh tobacco?" asked Yanek.

"Fresh, we just cut it yesterday."

While he was paying her, a peasant approached him and asked, "Who are you?"

Yanek was alarmed, but he recovered his wits and answered, "My name is Yanek, and I'm buying tobacco for Grandpa Sergei."

"And what are you doing here?"

"Grandpa and I are resting in the grove here. We're on our way to the village of Nikolaiev."

"Are you wanderers?"

"We're going to visit Grandpa's sister."

"If I see you again, you'll catch some blows."

Yanek overcame his fear, returned to Grandpa Sergei, and told him what had happened.

Grandpa Sergei listened and said, "Wicked man. He'll go to hell."

Yanek wasn't at ease. He had met a man with a wicked heart. Grandpa Sergei sensed Yanek's fear and said, "I'll also teach you how to deal with people like that. A man, even if he's a giant, is still only a man. He has weak points. You have to be brave, and everything will go right."

Suddenly Yanek saw someone he hadn't seen for many days: Elena, a very pretty Ukrainian girl who had worked in their home until she found a husband. When she stopped working, his mother bought her a lot of clothes, blankets, and sheets, and she gave a going-away party for her.

Yanek was four or five then. He parted from Elena with many tears. The assurances that soon she would come and visit were of no use. He refused to be consoled and kept crying.

Yanek saw Elena before his eyes, her plump, red fingers. They used to play in the house or the garden, always laughing, and when his mother went shopping, they would sit on the bed, and Elena would tell him stories about her village or scary stories that had been told to her in her childhood.

Yanek looked forward to her arrival in the morning, and in the evening, when she put on her coat to go home, he would hold on to her and refuse to let go. His mother used to say, "Elena has to go back to her parents in the evening. She'll come back to us in the morning. You're a big boy, and you're smart, so let go of her."

"I won't let go." Then his mother would approach him

and say, "You mustn't stop Elena. You're hurting her."

He stopped crying. But at the goodbye party the sobbing came back and wouldn't stop.

Meanwhile Grandpa Sergei made a "review of the situation" and decided they would leave that night and start on their way. Everything that had happened during the day, the attack at night, the peasant's threats in the tobacco shop, and other talk that had reached his ears, indicated that it was best to clear out. But not in haste. There was still time to sit and drink a cup of tea and light the pipe.

Meanwhile Grandpa Sergei opened his belt and showed Yanek the pistol. "I got this pistol from the commander of the regiment when I finished my service. Please read what's engraved on the stock."

Yanek read: "To Master Sergeant Sergei Ivanovich for exemplary service, for courage and determination. Signed: Commander of the Seventy-First Regiment."

"It's a good pistol. At the first opportunity, after you've learned to take it apart and put it together, you'll start to train with it."

Yanek was moved and said, "Thank you, Grandpa."

After a silence, Grandpa Sergei said, "Training in a special unit prepares you to live right. First, not to go easy on yourself. Not to say, I can't. Everything is possible if you're ready to dare. We would climb steep mountains, equipped with climbing boots. The abyss lay below, but that didn't stop us from going up.

"After I was released from the army, civilian life

seemed weak to me, without real content, and meaningless. When the time comes, I hope you'll be in a special unit. You'll be outstanding, and they'll send you to officers training. When you return from officers training, you'll rise higher and higher until you're a general. I, to my regret, never studied in high school, and that prevented me from being accepted in officers training. But you, the sky's the limit for you. You have traits and abilities to stand out in every field."

Before they set out, Grandpa Sergei added, "Service in a special unit prepares you to be honest in your ways, to love the truth, and to serve God without reservation. In my wanderings I met a priest who had served in a special unit in his youth. He immediately discovered, without my saying a word, that I was a commander in the special unit, and he saluted me. He invited me to his home and served me a hot meal, and because it was autumn and it was raining without letup outside, he let me live in an alcove of the church until the flood passed.

"On Sunday I wanted to stand at the church door and ask for contributions. The priest's response was: 'It's not right for a commander who served in a special unit to stand at the church door and beg for alms. I'll tell the congregation who you are and what you did in the special unit, and they'll give you a significant contribution in a dignified way.' And that's what happened.

"That fall we talked a lot, the priest and I, about wandering and about what it does for the soul. Wandering is only valuable if it raises up the soul for true service to God."

24

Yanek quickly learned how right Grandpa Sergei had been. After an hour of walking, a volley of stones fell on them. Grandpa Sergei stopped and ordered: Lie down and cover your head with your hands. They were in the middle of a cornfield. It was hard to know where the stones were coming from. In any event, they didn't move.

After lying there for an hour, they heard the voices of boys who were on their way to the village. Grandpa got up and immediately decided: they wouldn't enter the village. They'd go to the forest. Grandpa Sergei knew the area like the palm of his hand. For a long time he had trained his soldiers here. Even now, in his blindness, he pointed out features of the landscape.

"Do you see the telegraph pole?"

"I see it," answered Yanek.

"Is the dirt path still passable?"

"Passable."

"We'll turn to the right, into the forest."

Everybody called the forest the White Forest, because of the many birch trees that grew in it. Within an hour of walking, they were at its edge.

Meanwhile, morning approached. Yanek went to gather dry branches to light the campfire. There were plenty of branches, and it was easy to light the fire.

Every time they escape danger, Grandpa Sergei whispers a few words and immediately sinks into his thoughts. Yanek prepared cornmeal porridge, and Grandpa Sergei fondly remembered Kiril, who had supplied them with that food. "Kiril was a model soldier."

"Yanek, my dear, please read me a psalm. Psalms help us connect with purity."

"Which psalm should I read, Grandpa Sergei?"

"It doesn't matter. All the psalms are precious."

Yanek read slowly, emphasizing every word. At first he didn't understand what he was reading. Yanek speaks Ukrainian like a Ukrainian, but it was hard for him to read the language.

After he mastered the reading, he was amazed: the verses of the psalm were simple and understandable, but still wrapped in secrecy. Grandpa Sergei says that a verse like, "Praise the Lord, for He is Good, and His mercy endures forever," was quarried from a soul that knew how to pray. Prayer flows from the heart. Some people say that not every hour is appropriate for prayer. "From experience in the flesh I know that someone who ignores his mood and stands up to pray is a true believer."

Dwelling in the forest was different from camping in a field. In the forest, the shadows cover you, and the silence is great. You can hear every sound. It occurred to Yanek to ask Grandpa Sergei whether he should look for berries. Grandpa Sergei said yes, but he asked, "Don't go far away. It's easy to get lost in a forest."

Yanek is attentive and alert every time he's in a new

place. This time he didn't have to go far, because two hundred yards from where they had settled a cherry tree rose up, full of black cherries. Yanek didn't hesitate. He climbed up and stood in the midst of the tree and filled his hat with cherries. He climbed down the tree and rushed to Grandpa Sergei to show him the treasure. Grandpa Sergei touched the cherries, and his forehead filled with light. "These are marvelous cherries. Where did you find them?"

"Right nearby."

In the afternoon Yanek went out to look for berries and he also found some not far from where they had settled. They were little raspberries, wonderfully red.

For a long while they sat and ate. After the meal, Grandpa said, "Please read me another psalm from the Book of Psalms. Since you read to me, I feel that the verses you read throb more strongly within me."

Yanek didn't ask which psalm to read. He opened the Bible and recited Psalm number one. After he finished reading it, Grandpa Sergei asked him to read it again. Then Grandpa sank into himself and said nothing.

Grandpa Sergei was a soldier in every limb of his body. Sometimes it seemed to Yanek that the soldier within him stood out more when he was asleep, maybe because of the high boots and the leggings. But there were days when the soldier within him disappeared, and he was totally immersed in himself. Yanek tried not to disturb him on those days. Instead Yanek retreated behind the packs and bundles and observed the sights of the forest.

When Grandpa Sergei roused himself from his self-absorption he asked Yanek, "What do you see?"

"Two wagons full of clover."

"Is the driver young or old?"

"Old," Yanek answered.

"I like old wagon drivers. They suffer from their age and from their children, who don't respect them. But some of them are strong and bold, and they don't forfeit their honor. From them you can learn how to stand tall."

"How do you preserve your honor?" Yanek asked cautiously.

"By not complaining, not becoming bitter, being quiet when you don't have anything to say, and if you have something to say, saying it briefly. Not getting angry. Knowing that human beings are guests in this world, and not being arrogant. It seems to me that I have listed the main things for you."

"Thank you, Grandpa."

"You're an excellent trainee. If all trainees were like you, the world would be more merciful."

25

That night Yanek heard voices talking to him: "Yanek, you and Grandpa Sergei are fighting on a difficult front. This is a war of the few against the many. Evil has taken over the world, and it swarms in every grove of trees and forest, in cities and in the country. Even those who have some compassion keep out of the fray and don't raise their voices.

"Protection doesn't last forever. Grandpa Sergei has prepared you well. What you've done so far is praiseworthy, and in the future you'll do wonders. Weakness, even the slightest, is forbidden these days. The wicked have taken over the world, and we are commanded to do what we can, not just stand on the sidelines."

Yanek woke up. The voices he had heard filled him, not just his ears. He felt them in his arms and legs. They seeped the length of his body. It was cold, and he tried to warm his legs by jumping. The cold still bothered him.

Grandpa Sergei woke up, and he was glad the campfire was burning. Yanek brought him water so he could wash his hands and face. He wanted to tell him about the voice he had heard in his sleep, but he didn't dare. But in the end he overcame that obstacle and told him.

Grandpa Sergei listened and said, "What we hear in our sleep are the most important instructions in life."

"Who spoke to me?" asked Yanek.

"I don't know, but it's clear to me that you have to listen to those voices and think about them."

"Did someone from above speak to me? That's the second time I've heard voices."

"You have to be patient, to preserve the voices you heard and not tell anyone about them."

Yanek cooked cornmeal porridge and embellished it with raspberries. Grandpa Sergei tasted it and said, "Very tasty, and different from what we've been eating up to now." For a long while they sat and ate.

"It's a good thing my friend Kiril provided us with cornmeal. Otherwise we'd have to go from door to door and beg for alms. Let's bless him together and say: God, bless Kiril and restore him to strength."

As soon as they had said that blessing, Yanek saw Kiril before his eyes, sitting on the wicker chair where his late wife had sat.

While they were eating, a tall man emerged from the forest. The hair on his head was long, his face was gray, and his clothes were tattered.

Grandpa Sergei asked, "Who are you, and what are you doing in the forest?"

The man replied to the question with simplicity: "I live in the forest."

"And how do you provide for yourself?"

"Mainly with mushrooms and berries."

"Can I offer you a cup of tea?"

"With pleasure."

They sat and drank tea. The man apparently hadn't

spoken for many days, because he spoke in a torrent. "I've been living in the forest for years. There's nothing better than the forest. It keeps you away from people and their wickedness. But, to my regret, they even come here. They cut down the trees cruelly. It's hard to witness that murder. It's good I have a hut far from here. I flee to it so I won't hear the trees' screams."

"Won't you go back and live among people?" asked Grandpa Sergei calmly.

"No. People are evil. They hate quiet people."

"We don't have a house either," Grandpa Sergei said, trying to draw closer to him.

"Do you walk from village to village and ask for mercy?"

"No. On Sundays we stand at the church door and expect people to give to us out of the goodness of their hearts," Grandpa Sergei spoke with surprising openness.

"Why don't you go into the church?"

"They don't allow wanderers, cripples, and lepers to go into the church. Not only that: who would keep on eye on our bundles?"

"Are you the kind of wanderers who want to purify themselves and draw closer to God?"

"Let's not talk about that," said Grandpa Sergei.

"I don't need a thing. I have no complaints about any-one or about God. I'm with myself. Just with myself. The trees and an occasional dog are my friends. I have no need for anything more. In any event, thanks for the good tea. I'll be on my way. Maybe we'll meet again someday."

After the man went away, Grandpa Sergei sank into his thoughts, and when he roused, he turned to Yanek and said, "I have a request of you, Yanek, but promise me you won't be frightened by what I'm going to tell you. You're a soldier, and a soldier isn't easily frightened.

"I'll start right away: no one knows when his day will come. Today he's here, and tomorrow he's in the world of truth. Please, Yanek, do this act of mercy for me. Don't bury me in the village where I die. Ask the local priest to bury me in the village of my birth, next to my parents."

"What's the matter, Grandpa Sergei?" Yanek was fearful.

"Nothing's the matter. Because a person doesn't know when his day will come, and I'm no longer young, I wanted to tell you what I want. The Bible teaches us: when a person dies, he is gathered up with his ancestors. I wish to be gathered up with my ancestors, who are buried in the village where I was born. Excuse me if I've alarmed you. I assume I'll live till I return you to your parents. And also, I still have to strengthen your inner self. The path is long yet."

"Grandpa Sergei, it still frightens me."

"You mustn't be afraid. I'm not talking about now, but about the future. I, in any event, pray that I won't leave this world before I finish training you and return you safely to your parents."

"Grandpa Sergei," said Yanek, almost about to burst into tears.

"Yanek, my friend, patience, silence, and restraint—that's what's demanded of every soldier in a special unit. He accepts the good and the bad without raising his voice."

"Let me cry a little, Grandpa," Yanek surprised him. "I'm not weeping in despair, but in joy that you'll be with me."

"Just this once, and no more, my friend."

That night they heard thunder on the horizon. Grandpa Sergei stated: the Red Army has broken through the front and it's advancing.

"Will it liberate my parents and grandparents?" Yanek asked.

"Certainly."

He was going to say, Thank you, Grandpa, for staying with me, but he didn't say it.

26

The following days were tense. Yanek trained every day, adding exercises, and he was in condition. Grandpa Sergei spoke little. In the end he said, "The forest isn't a secure place. People you can't understand and criminals make their home there. Let's stock up on cherries and raspberries and get going. What we have will last until Sunday. On Sunday we'll go to a church." Yanek understood Grandpa Sergei's words, and after he finished his run and prepared breakfast, once they had eaten their meal, he went out to pick cherries and raspberries. From the top of the tree he could see Grandpa Sergei: turned inward, either a knight or a hermit.

When he returned, laden with cherries and raspberries, he took a handful out of the bag and offered it to Grandpa.

"Did you take some for yourself?"

"I ate while I was on the tree."

"Fruit that you've just picked brings you a message from the world of beauty," Grandpa Sergei remarked.

After they ate, Grandpa asked Yanek to light his pipe, and he said, "Yanek, my friend, please read Psalm 117. I believe that's the shortest psalm in the book."

"'Praise the Lord, all you peoples: praise him, all you nations, because his mercy is great for us, and the truth of God is forever. Halleluia.'"

Yanek read it and repeated it. Clearly, Grandpa Sergei was slowly absorbing the verses, and they filled him with delight. Yanek was surprised: the Book of Psalms was full of obscure verses, but Grandpa Sergei drank it down like vodka, and they fired his thoughts for many hours.

Then Grandpa raised his head and called out loud, "And the truth of God is forever."

After lunch they started off toward a village named Vasilovka, a quiet village. They didn't hate wanderers openly, maybe because not a lot of them visited the village, which was far from the main road and nestled in a valley. Yanek had been there before, and he remembered the tree and the stream nearby.

They reached Vasilovka toward evening. They immediately settled next to the tree in whose shade they had once stayed. Unfortunately for them, it started to rain. Yanek took the two tarpaulins out of the bundle. They covered the bundles with one and wrapped themselves in the other. Rain, which is a blessing for the fields, is sometimes a disaster for wanderers.

It rained all night, a thin rain. In the morning, when they woke up, Yanek saw that the rain had gotten into their packs. He immediately pulled the clothes out of the packs and hung them on trees. The cornmeal wasn't wet.

Yanek recovered from the wet night and went out for a run. When he returned, he made cornmeal porridge and embellished it with raspberries. They finished with a cup of tea.

The smell of morning arose from the houses, the fragrance of bread fresh out of the oven, mixed with vapor from warm milk. Yanek remembered the summer rain, the wet grass, and the sparkling droplets of water on the trees, his father and mother looking at the beauty. His mother used to say, "I love the rain at night, and the light the next morning. There's nothing like summer rain. It not only brings beauty, but also quiet joy." In every sentence his mother spoke, there was always at least one word or expression taken from her soul.

In the afternoon, Yanek asked, "Should I go to Olga's to buy supplies?"

"We don't have any money. We'll borrow from the money your father left us. Open the bundle and take out a fifty-mark bill. You should know that I'm not doing this with a light heart," said Grandpa Sergei in an embarrassed way.

Yanek immediately set out at a run. He remembered Olga from their earlier visit: not a tall woman, plump, smiley, who sold wares at a fair price. When he left, she had asked, "When will you come back here?"

"In some time," Yanek had answered.

"Don't forget to come and visit me."

"I'll come," he answered, and went away.

Strange, that short conversation, which had been held moderately and comfortably, was both disturbing and pleasant.

"Don't forget to come and visit me." That sentence remained stuck in his mind for a long time, but in their wandering it had faded.

Now he stood at the gate of her house, and to his

surprise it was open. He stood on the threshold and called out, "Olga?"

She appeared right away. She left her house, shaded her eyes, and surveyed him from head to toe, saying, "You've grown since I last saw you. How has the wandering been?"

"Fine."

"And now you've come to me to buy vegetables and dairy products?"

"Yes," answered Yanek.

"I'll bring you what I have in the garden right away, and I'll show you what I have in the kitchen. Come in. Why are you standing at the door?"

Before long she returned with a basket on her arm. She announced, "Here are vegetables straight from the earth."

"Thanks," said Yanek.

"Come into the kitchen with me, and we'll see what I can give you."

She took bread down from a shelf and took a jug of yogurt and a piece of cheese from the pantry.

When he was about to pay her, she approached him and said, "You're a sweet boy. There aren't many like you. Come to me, and I'll give you a kiss. How old are you?"

"Eleven."

"You're still a puppy. In a few months you'll be a man. Don't forget to come to me on your next visit."

Yanek gathered up the groceries and hurried out. When he got to the tree, he told Grandpa what had happened to him. Grandpa chuckled and said, "There's a woman like that in every village."

"A witch?" asked Yanek.

"More or less."

What had happened to Yanek seemed to amuse Grandpa Sergei. At last he said, "Every village has a woman who helps boys grow up. It's not a bad thing. Sometimes it's useful, and sometimes it's harmful, but not too bad."

Yanek wondered why Grandpa was amused, but he didn't dare ask.

The time passed without their noticing, maybe because nothing happened. Yanek ran, exercised, climbed trees, picked up logs, and practiced boxing.

An old peasant, who was on his way to work, lingered and asked Grandpa Sergei, "Where are you from, and where are you heading?"

"We're on a pilgrimage to the monastery of the Virgin Mary."

"You took a wrong turn."

"No matter. We'll get back on course in a day or two," said Grandpa Sergei. "What's going on in the village?"

"The Red Army broke through the front and is advancing."

"Are the people glad?" asked Grandpa Sergei.

"They're apprehensive," said the old man, and all his doubt showed on his face.

The clothes on the tree dried out. Yanek folded them and put them in the backpacks.

Saturday night is laden with disquiet. The men go to the tavern. In the summer they sit in the garden. At first gaiety fills the men as they sit, but very soon, after a few jugs of beer, it becomes boisterous. The boisterousness increases, and threatening words rise in the air. The fight ensues immediately.

This time there was no gaiety. The men talked about the war. Some of them believed that the Russians could never stop the German army. The Germans were going to conquer the world. But others thought that the winter would vanquish the Germans the way it had subdued Napoleon.

They dispersed before midnight. Though there were shouts, there were not threats.

The night was quiet and pleasant. They slept till dawn rose. Yanek lit the campfire and arranged the packs and bundles for the road. Grandpa woke up and was pleased by the fire's warmth.

"What's ahead of us?" Yanek asked.

"Struggles, my friend."

They finished breakfast and went to the church. On the way they passed by a barn. A boy stuck his head out of the barn window and provoked them, "Thieving tramps!" Grandpa Sergei gritted his teeth and didn't allow Yanek to hit him.

They reached the church before the services had begun, and they sat on the ground. Two other wanderers sat near them, as well a man with leprosy.

The worshippers came one after the other. No one put anything in Yanek's hat. Now they were waiting for them to leave.

Meanwhile the two village policemen appeared. A wanderer with his hands cuffed walked in front of them. The wanderer, a man of about fifty, with a pack on his back, took small steps without complaining or asking for mercy.

"What did he do?" someone on his way to church asked.

"He's a thief," answered the policeman.

"Faster!" The policeman raised his voice.

When the wanderer didn't do what the policeman wanted, he swung his whip at him. The wanderer fell down. The angry policeman kept hitting him.

People looked from their houses, but no one made a sound. Yanek wanted to get up and rescue the beaten man from the policeman, but Grandpa Sergei whispered to him, "Not now."

The way to the detention cell took a long time. The policemen spoke to each other and answered the questions of passersby. In the end the older policeman told the people who had gathered around what the wanderer's sin was: he had been caught in a garden, picking up fruit that had fallen from the trees. When the owner of the orchard ordered him to leave, the wanderer claimed that the fallen fruit belonged to the poor. Finally the owner of the orchard had to drag him out. He kept muttering, claiming he was within his rights. He was dragged to the police station, and there, too, he claimed that the fruit he had gathered had fallen. The policemen ordered him to shut up, confess to his crime, and pay a fine. The man refused to admit he was a thief. There was no choice but to take him to the detention cell. The policeman spoke in a businesslike way, like someone who was doing his duty, and his conscience was clear.

Grandpa Sergei listened and said, "That wanderer is a warrior, born and bred. If we had a lot of men like him, we could form a regiment."

28

They continued on the way to the village of Saint Mary, which was named after the nearby monastery, which was around twelve miles from the village.

They climbed up a mountain. Broad green fields and gardens spread out at the foot of the mountain, and their colors were beautiful. Marvelous tranquility lay upon them.

Yanek told Grandpa Sergei what his eyes saw. Grandpa Sergei remembered the place and said, "I loved to come here with my soldiers and train them. After training we would sit and listen to the silence that rose from the fields and gardens. Now I'm blind and I only see what I once saw."

While Yanek was contemplating that beauty, he saw two young boys attacking a wanderer. They knocked him down, kicked him, and spat at him. Yanek, without asking Grandpa Sergei's permission, leaped out, grabbed them by their coats, and threw them down.

"Why are you attacking a helpless man?"

"He's a tramp."

"Tramps are also people."

"They steal."

"How do you know?"

"They always steal."

"Now go down on your knees and ask forgiveness from this man."

They were astonished by that command and said, "Why should we ask forgiveness?"

"Because you kicked him and spat at him. If you don't ask forgiveness, I'll do to you exactly what you did to him."

"What should we say?"

"Say: We ask forgiveness of you for kicking you and spitting at you."

"We ask for forgiveness."

"That's not enough. I'll say what I said, and you'll repeat after me."

They repeated after him word for word, and when they finished asking forgiveness, Yanek said to them, "Don't forget that you swore to God. God sees everything and hears everything."

"We won't forget," they answered together.

"I'd better not see you hitting a helpless man again. I'll beat you till you bleed."

The wanderer was astonished by Yanek's courage. He stood next to his pack without saying a word. "Don't be afraid," said Yanek, touching his shoulder. In the end the wanderer recovered his wits and asked, "Who are you?"

"I'm Grandpa Sergei's grandson. He was a soldier in a special unit."

"Do you help wanderers?"

"If someone attacks them."

"I've never seen anything like that," the wanderer spoke with a tremor in his voice.

"It's just a bit of help," said Yanek.

This time, too, Grandpa Sergei was pleased with Yanek's conduct, and he said, "Hero. You also spoke excellently."

But for some reason Yanek's spirits fell. He didn't understand where he had gotten the strength to attack. If he had to do it again, he wouldn't know how.

He shared his feeling with Grandpa Sergei. Grandpa Sergei, after thinking about it, said, "If a person sticks to a just mission, his movements and his strength are doubled. You have to pray that God will be with you at hard moments."

"Does a fighter for justice have to train all his life?" Yanek asked.

"Certainly. He has to be strong. A weak body can't carry out great missions. Only a strong body and a sturdy spirit can do the impossible. You have to fortify your body every day with training, and at the same time pray that God won't abandon us."

"Thank you, Grandpa Sergei," said Yanek, and tears welled up in his eyes.

That night the thunder on the horizon grew louder. Grandpa Sergei said softly, in his special way, "The Red Army is advancing. It won't be long before it reaches us, and the wicked will beg for their lives, and all the innocent people who were sent to camps will come back home."

That night Grandpa Sergei seemed to be a head taller, as though he was about to rise from his bed and put on his uniform. His blindness left his face, and he looked like a commander about to set out at the head of his soldiers.

"Immunity doesn't last forever," Grandpa Sergei repeated several times. "In the end the wicked fall into the abyss. But until victory comes, we can expect severe trials. Yanek, you have to be in perfect shape to counter all local violence. We, in the end, are not wanted here. It's impossible to know what bad men are plotting. We have to be awake and alert, and pray that God will be with us."

They both folded their sacks and lay their heads on them.

"Good night, Yanek."

"Good night, Grandpa."

29

Without delay they headed toward the village of Saint Mary. On the way they stopped near a well. Yanek pulled up a bucket of water, and they quenched their thirst.

Grandpa Sergei said, "We say, 'the water of life,' because there's no life without water. God gave us this foundation of life in abundance as a gift. There's a pond, a well, or a river in every corner. We have to learn to say a blessing for the water."

Without going far off Yanek saw a poplar tree suitable for camping that night. It was still very light out. Yanek was weary, but he wasn't lazy about making the campfire. Grandpa Sergei said, "Brave boy."

Yanek made cornmeal porridge and sprinkled raspberries on it. He served a full plate to Grandpa Sergei and a little less to himself. After the meal he prepared a cup of tea and lit his pipe for him. After washing the dishes he said, "Good night, Grandpa Sergei. I'm going to sleep."

"Happy dreams," said Grandpa Sergei.

As soon as he lay his head on the sack, he fell asleep. He slept without interruption and got up early. The fire was still dormant, and Yanek added a few branches and revived it.

Grandpa Sergei woke up, washed his hands and face, and said, "I dreamed that I was in my parents' house. My parents came back from the field, and my mother was making lunch. The good smell of a cornmeal pie full of cherries rose from the oven. The crust was turning brown, and soon everyone would get a portion. The pie tin was large, and everyone would get seconds. Meanwhile Father put a bowl of cream on the table, and next to it a plate of cheese, and a hunk of yellow butter.

"Father turned to me and asked: 'Where have you been?'

"'In the army,' I answered.

"'Are you still in service?'

"'Yes,' I answer.

"'It seemed to me you'd already been released.'

"'You don't get released from the army,' I answered, wondering to myself why I had spoken that way.

"But amazingly, my vision returned to me, and I could see my father and mother with great clarity. I hesitate as to whether I should tell them that I'd been blind for years, and now my vision had returned to me. I told Father: 'You mustn't take things for granted.'

"'What do you mean?' Father asked.

"'For example, our vision. It's not self-evident. Today you see, and tomorrow you're blind.'

"'Is that what the army teaches?' Father asks.

"'Correct.'

"'If that's what it teachers, bless it. How is service?' Father goes on to ask me.

"'I do my duty.'

"'Will you always be in the army and never have a wife or a house?'

"'A soldier is allowed to marry,' I answer, 'but the leaves are short, just once a month. And if there's an alert, leaves are canceled. When I finish with the army, I'll get married.'

"When they hear my answer, Father and Mother laughed.

"I was glad to see my parents and the house. They had gotten old, but they were still living their lives in silence and moderation. I was careful not to make them sad. True, I didn't always understand them, and they didn't always understand me. Now, it seems to me, the bumps had been smoothed out. Every time I see them in a dream, I'm glad all day long. My mother's food melts in my mouth, and Father has wisdom about life that he inherited from past generations. Before their death, they suffered a lot, but they retained the image of God." Sergei summed up and immediately sank into silence.

The village of Saint Mary is pretty, with tasteful houses and well-tended gardens. With the money they'd collected, they'd buy food for a few days, but where can you buy here?

Grandpa Sergei rose to his feet and asked a passerby where to buy dairy products and bread.

"Not far from here, in the grocery store."

"God bless you."

"And you, too."

Yanek didn't delay but went out to shop. There were no customers in the grocery store, and the woman who owned it asked Yanek, "What do you want?"

"A loaf of bread."

"Anything else?"

"A piece of cheese and a jug of milk, vegetables and potatoes."

"I'll take care of everything right away. Where are you from?"

"I'm here with Grandpa Sergei. We're going to visit his sister in the village of Zhadovitse."

Before long the groceries he had asked for were lying on the counter.

"How much to pay?"

"Fifty marks."

Yanek was glad he hadn't spent more money than usual.

After he told Grandpa what he had bought and how much he'd paid, he admitted that he'd told a lie.

"How's that?" Grandpa Sergei was surprised.

"When I was asked what I was doing and where I was heading, I told the owner of the store: Grandpa and I are going to visit his sister."

"That's not a lie, that's a deception. That's how you deceive the enemy," said Grandpa, and they both laughed.

That night was clear and chilly. The campfire gave off pleasant warmth. Grandpa Sergei told him that if everything went well, they would also go to the monastery of Saint Mary. "A lot of pilgrims gather in the monastery in this season, and if fortune shines upon us, we'll get contributions for the next season."

"Will we go into the monastery?"

"The monastery is very well kept up, surrounded by gardens. There's a courtyard at its gate, and that's where wanderers and sick people of various kinds gather. Sometimes they allow the wanderers to enter without their bundles. It's very crowded, and you have to watch over your bundles with great vigilance. Twice I got fine contributions there. Once I wrestled with three ruffians and in the end they stole my bundle, and I was left without any equipment."

"Do we have to go there?" asked Yanek.

"A person has to take care of himself before he asks from God."

"Maybe the Red Army will come and liberate us?"

"Let's pray and wait for its arrival."

30

Yanek prepared supper. Grandpa Sergei praised the bread and vegetables, and he added what he occasionally used to say, "A person isn't alone in the world."

Yanek was frightened. Since he wrestled with the boys, he feared that his strength would fail him in the next trial. Grandpa Sergei says that everything flows from within. If the mission is clear and just, a person's strength is redoubled, and God adds to it.

Grandpa Sergei drank his tea and puffed on his pipe for a long time, and at last he said, "Yanek, my dear, please read me the first psalm in the Book of Psalms. But please be gracious and read it very slowly, so that I can absorb the words and the melody."

"Grandpa Sergei, don't you understand the words of the psalms?"

"I've already told you that I don't understand. There's no reason to understand prayer. You just have to pray."

Yanek doesn't stop training. His body had filled out in the last month, and he looked older than his age. In his dreams he's at home, next to his father and mother. Sometimes it seems to him that his parents haven't changed. Only he has changed. They observe him and are surprised by the change that has taken place in him.

"What did Grandpa Sergei do for you so that you changed so much?"

"I trained, and I keep training," Yanek answered.

"What else do you do?"

"I make meals for Grandpa and myself."

"Where do you sleep?"

"Most of the time outdoors."

The astonishment in his parents' eyes grew, and finally his father said: "We must get used to this. We were in camps, and we underwent difficult trials. It's impossible to talk about them now. Maybe it's forbidden to speak about them."

"Strange, I can't see it in you," says Yanek.

"Maybe we didn't change outwardly, but we're different inside."

"I have to go back to where I was, Father," Yanek says and stands up.

"Don't go. Don't leave us," a strong voice left his father's lips and shook him.

Yanek woke up.

The night passed without any difficulties. Yanek added branches to the dormant campfire, and the branches caught fire. A campfire burning during the cold morning hours imbues you with vigor that you feel throughout the day.

While he was getting ready to go on a run, a dog came, a puppy, and it sat among the bundles and packs. Yanek was surprised. He went over to it and patted it and then brought it to Grandpa Sergei.

Grandpa Sergei felt it with his hands and said, "He's barely half a year old. He's still a puppy. He won't be an adult dog for another three months."

The puppy sensed that they liked him and expressed his satisfaction with little barks.

"Where did you come to us from?" Grandpa Sergei spoke to him in a calm voice. "We'll watch over you, and you'll watch over us. We'll be hungry together and full together." So they adopted it.

The puppy changed their life. Yanek talked about him on the very first day. When Yanek went out to train, Grandpa Sergei stroked it and said, "As long as you're a puppy, we won't train you. But the day will come when we'll make a strong, proud dog out of you."

In two days Sunday will come. Despite the open and hidden threats, Grandpa Sergei decided to stay where they were, and on Sunday they would stand at the door of the church. "God knows how I hate standing there in that contemptible way, but there's no choice. We'll do it like soldiers carrying out an order."

Afterward Grandpa Sergei wondered what name to give the puppy. "We can't keep it with us without a name. A dog without a name is a blemished creature. It has no individuality. Yanek, can you think of a name?"

"Noble," said Yanek.

"Maybe he'll be noble when he matures. It's hard to call a soft puppy Noble now. The heart won't accept it."

"Maybe we can call him Prince," suggested Yanek.

"That's softer, more acceptable. Once I had a dog that I called Prince, but he died young," said Grandpa Sergei with a soft voice.

Since Prince's arrival, Grandpa Sergei's silences have gotten shorter. He sits and pats Prince and sometimes talks to him. "The problem is: we don't have food for Prince, just a saucer of milk, and now we don't even have that. If we don't find some sausage, we'll let him go. We can't starve him."

"Too bad," the words escaped Yanek's lips.

Meanwhile, the rumbling on the horizon grew stronger. Grandpa Sergei keeps saying they're close to us. "Collaborators, in their frustration, are liable to attack the weak. The weak are always scapegoats."

"Will Mother and Father and my grandparents come back from the camps?"

"Most likely," said Grandpa Sergei before folding the sack and laying his head on it.

Yanek remained on his feet for a long while. The thought that his parents would return from the camps soon excited him, but he didn't allow himself to be happy. Who knew what we could expect?

On Sunday Yanek woke up early, went out for his morning run, climbed trees, and did boxing exercises. When he returned Grandpa Sergei was awake, and Prince was in his arms. Grandpa Sergei had a very high opinion of Prince. "We'll train him easily."

Yanek prepared breakfast: bread, vegetables, and cheese. Were it not for the thought that in an hour they'd stand at the entrance to the church and wait for the worshipers' generosity, the meal would have made them happier.

Grandpa Sergei, after sipping the tea and puffing on his pipe, said, "We have no choice. We have to go. We'll do it like soldiers obeying an order they don't understand."

At the door of the church there were neither wanderers nor sick people. The worshipers hurried to the prayers and ignored them. For a long while they sat and looked around them: Sunday restfulness lay upon the houses and gardens. When the prayers were over, the worshipers left the church, and some of them left a small contribution in Yanek's hat.

After the worshipers had gone, Grandpa Sergei raised his head and said, "Thank God for this mercy." Yanek didn't count the money. He put the bills in a handkerchief, tied it, and gave it to Grandpa Sergei.

In the mountains the villages are smaller. The churches are low, and the houses are roofed with red tiles.

"Where are we heading?" asked Yanek.

"The time has come to taste mountain air and to prepare for the ascent to the monastery of Saint Mary."

While they were advancing, a short woman emerged from one of the houses, turned to Grandpa Sergei, and asked, "Where are you from, brothers, and where are you going?"

Grandpa Sergei was surprised by that warm greeting and said, "To the monastery of Saint Mary."

"May God bless you."

"May He bless you, too."

"Wouldn't you like to taste the soup I just cooked?"

"With pleasure," Grandpa Sergei replied.

The house was small, the inside walls were decorated with icons and flowers. The woman seated them at the table and said, "I'll go to get soup for the guests that God sent me."

Before long she brought two wooden bowls full of steaming soup as well as brown bread, and she said, "May God abide in your meal."

"Thank you," said Grandpa Sergei.

The soup was hot, and all the garden vegetables were in it.

When they finished eating, their host asked them, "Would you like some more?"

"By your grace," answered Grandpa Sergei.

"Where are you from?"

"Originally I'm from the village of Ivanov. I served in the army for many years. After my service I lived in the city and married. God took my wife from me when she was only twenty-eight. Only later did I understand what God had taken from me, and I started wandering to atone for my sins. And what's your name, if I may ask."

"Magda," she said, immediately adding, "For years I was a servant with the Jews. When I turned fifty I decided to return to my parents' house."

"And how are your parents?"

"They've passed away."

"May they rest in peace."

"I have some meatballs. May I serve them to you?"

"Willingly," said Grandpa Sergei.

Yanek looked around him: he'd never seen a house like that or a woman like that. The thought occurred to him that maybe she was an exalted angel who had been sent to help and nourish them. But her face and hands were like those of a woman who loves to serve and was pleased when people ate her food. There were no evident signs that she was an angel.

Grandpa Sergei asked, "Was it good for you with the Jews?"

"They appreciated my work and were fond of me."

"And where are they now?"

"God knows."

They rose to their feet, and Grandpa Sergei said, "May God bless you for this charity."

"May God bless your path," she said with her head inclined.

So they set out.

Yanek was curious to hear Grandpa Sergei's opinion about that special woman, but apparently Grandpa Sergei hadn't yet formed an opinion.

After walking for an hour, when they sat at the foot of an oak tree, he said, "It's good to meet a woman like Magda."

"Is she a messenger from God?" Yanek dared to ask.

"Her deeds testify that she preserves the image of God."

"You can't see that she's different from other people."

"You mustn't depend on your eyes. They don't always see the truth."

Yanek made a fire, prepared a cup of tea for Grandpa Sergei, and lit his pipe, and he remembered that Magda had asked, "Where are you from, brothers, and where are you going?"

"No one in our long wanderings has ever called us 'brothers,'" said Yanek.

"That's another sign that we're not alone here," said Grandpa Sergei. "We'll sleep here tonight, and tomorrow we'll figure out what to do. Many years ago I used to wander among these villages. I was a young soldier, ambitious and outstanding. One night, when we were tired after training and far from the base, we entered the monastery and asked if we could buy bread and cheese from the monks. The monks greeted us graciously, spread cloths on the long wooden tables, served us everything they had in the pantry, and they finished by bringing us good coffee, whose taste I can feel in my mouth to this day.

"After the meal, the abbot of the monastery said: 'Good, loyal soldiers. You protect us from robbers and trespassers, and this is an opportunity to thank you. Whenever you're hungry, come to us. We'll give you everything we have. You're going out tonight to guard our fields and orchards. May God protect you.'

"Then we were like young horses. We didn't know what life was yet. We leaped and ran and competed with each other: who can run faster, who can lift heavier weights, who risks his life with the greatest daring. Our bodies celebrated their youth, but our souls were still soft. I remembered the prayers in my parents' church. I remembered my father and mother kneeling in prayer. While I was living in my parents' house, I went to pray with them. The moment I joined the army, the training and forced marches filled me up. After basic training we were already like trained dogs. It's dangerous to run into them.

"That's how my first years in the army went. Afterward reality showed its face: my friends died in the line of duty, there were funerals, meetings with bereaved parents, and pains and grief. I looked for God, but I didn't see Him. I lost my way for many years. It wasn't till my Dorka was snatched away from me that the words of the prayers began to rise up on my lips.

"I have to add: your grandfather, Michael, also helped me to escape the morass. He was a true servant of God, and I made a point of observing the way he moved. His whole being spoke of the brotherhood of God. You bear his name, and I pray in my heart that he will watch over you and raise you up."

Hardly had the words left Grandpa Sergei's mouth before tears burst from Yanek's eyes.

Grandpa Sergei heard the weeping and said, "We're in good hands."

Without saying anything, Yanek curled up with Prince and lay his head on the sack.

Yanek woke up early and went out for his morning run. When he returned, he revived the campfire, made a cup of tea for Grandpa Sergei, and lit his pipe for him, and at the same time he also told him the truth: "We only have a little cornmeal."

"Thank God for that, too. There were days when we didn't even have a crumb." Grandpa Sergei's faith was firm, and it constantly grew.

Meanwhile a peasant passed by, and Grandpa Sergei asked him, "Where's the village grocery store?"

"To your right, not far from here. What do you want to buy?"

"Food."

"Are you a wanderer?"

"I'm a man, and my name is Sergei."

The peasant fixed his gaze on him and, without saying another word, went on his way.

Grandpa Sergei sank into his thoughts, and Yanek made porridge. After they ate and were silent together, Grandpa Sergei said, "Let's take a fifty-mark bill from the money your father left with us. Go to the grocery store and buy food."

Yanek didn't delay and set out.

There were no customers in the grocery store, and

Yanek asked for bread and cheese.

"How will you pay?" asked the woman at the counter.

"I have fifty marks."

"We don't accept German occupation money anymore," she said.

"Why not?"

"The Germans are retreating."

"So how can I buy?"

"With new clothes and valuables."

Stunned, Yanek returned to Grandpa Sergei. Grandpa Sergei listened and then said, "That's good news. Your parents and grandparents will return from exile."

Then Yanek said, "I have an idea: I'll take one of my sweaters, and in return I'll buy food."

"And what will you wear on cold nights?"

"I have another sweater."

When Yanek went back to the store, Grandpa Sergei didn't tell him, "bargain." He knew. Yanek stood up for himself. He wasn't easily cheated.

Yanek showed his sweater to the owner of the grocery store and asked, "What will you give me for it?"

"Where did you get that sweater?"

"Grandpa knitted it for me."

"You didn't steal it?"

"No. It's forbidden to steal."

She picked the sweater up again, examined it, and said, "I'll give you a loaf of bread and a piece of cheese for it."

"Is that all?"

"I'll add a sack of potatoes."

"I'm not asking for meat, but won't you add some vegetables?"

"I'll give you some, but don't ask for any more," she said and it was clear that she liked the sweater.

She placed the supplies on the counter.

Before putting the groceries in his basket, he said, "Could you please give me a little salt?"

She gave him some grudgingly.

They celebrated at lunchtime. Grandpa Sergei was amused, saying, "Sometimes God sends us Magda, and sometimes your sweater saves us."

While they were sitting, relaxed, under the tree, they heard the screams of a helpless person. Yanek ran to see:

on the slope, on the dirt road, stood a tall wanderer, and boys were throwing stones at him and cursing him. Yanek watched that horrible scene, stored up anger, and with a great rush he went down. The boys immediately sensed what they could expect and ran off. Yanek was going to run after them, but he preferred to see what they had done to the miserable wanderer.

The wanderer was on his knees. His face and hands were bleeding. With difficulty he managed to get some words out, just muttering: "They threw stones at me."

"Come with me. I'll wash your face and give you something to eat."

"No need. I'll be on my way. I'm used to it."

"Come," Yanek repeated. "My grandpa and I are sitting under the tree. We won't take anything from you."

"Leave me alone," he said, wiping his face with his sleeve. That gesture, which was meant to wipe off the blood, only opened the wounds again.

"Come to us. We have iodine," Yanek said.

"I'll be on my way," said the wanderer, without any signs of courtesy.

Yanek left him and retraced his steps.

As he drew near the tree he heard a voice calling, "Wait a minute."

"What do you want?" asked Yanek.

"I'll come to you," said the wanderer and started to climb up.

When he was standing near the tree, his face was covered with blood, and he breathed with difficulty. Yanek didn't delay. He washed the man's face with a thin cloth and spread iodine on his wounds.

The man recovered, looked around him, and asked, "Who are you?"

"Wanderers like you," answered Grandpa Sergei.

"Do they throw stones at you?"

"They do."

"So what to you do?"

"I'm blind, but my grandson, Yanek, is brave and teaches them a lesson."

"If only I had the strength to run after them."

"Where are you heading?" asked Grandpa Sergei.

"To the monastery of Saint Mary. I committed a grave sin against my father. I ignored his sickness and old age, and he died all alone. That heavy sin won't give me any rest. Thank you for taking me in and treating my wounds. I'm going on my way. They say that in a day or a day and a half you can get to the monastery. I have just one desire: to stay in the monastery for two or three days and die in the courtyard."

The man rose to his feet and went on his way. His height and his face remained for a while before they disappeared.

The nights are cold in the mountains at this season. Yanek wears a sweater and long underwear, but the cold still penetrates his bones. Grandpa Sergei doesn't complain. He sleeps on the plain and in the mountains, and he knows that in the early winter the winds in the mountains are sharp, and only a canvas army jacket keeps it out.

Yanek attends to a mission he set for himself: from where they stopped, he overlooks the roads. If boys attack wanderers, he lunges toward them and drives them away. Sometimes he catches one of them, slaps his face, and forces him to ask forgiveness from the wanderer he was tormenting.

One of the wanderers called out, "No one ever ran to rescue me before. Take this scarf, to protect you from the cold."

"Thanks," said Yanek, but he didn't take it.

"Who are you?" he asked Yanek.

"I'm Grandpa Sergei's grandson."

The wanderer was stunned by his answer, asked nothing more, and went on his way.

After returning to the tree and to Grandpa Sergei, he went to the nearby glade to gather mushrooms. Once he had gone to the woods with his mother to gather mushrooms. She had taught him to distinguish toadstools from edible mushrooms. They stepped cautiously on the moist earth, and suddenly a small swarm of mushrooms peeked out of the brown fallen leaves. His mother would kneel down and put them in a straw basket one by one.

The memory made him dizzy, and he halted his legs.

Yanek found an abundance of mushrooms. When he had filled the bag he ran back to Grandpa Sergei and told him about the treasure he had found. Grandpa Sergei heard and said, "Today we'll eat like kings."

Later Yanek asked, "Where will we go now?"

"We'll go to the Monastery of Saint Mary. Lots of pilgrims climb up to it in this season. I assume that they won't let us into the sanctuary with our bundles."

"Are we rejected?" asked Yanek.

"God loves wanderers. Satisfied, arrogant people aren't desired by Him. God brings near those who are in pain."

"Is that how it always was?"

"I believe so."

Later, with a smile, Grandpa Sergei added, "In the army you learn not to ask too much, but to act. Action comes before questions. Instead of asking about justice, it's better to do justice."

In his heart Yanek knew that Grandpa Sergei wanted to strengthen him to do justice. Every humble wanderer, for whom a helpful hand comes from somewhere, is fortified in his faith in humanity, and in a difficult hour he himself will extend a hand to one of his wanderer brethren.

Every day more wanderers gather, cripples and people with skin disease, making their way to the Monastery of

Saint Mary. Respectable pilgrims also walk alongside the miserable ones. This silent procession, which advances slowly and heavily, captivated Yanek's eyes and for a long time he stood still and observed it.

"A lot of wanderers are going up to Saint Mary," he told Grandpa Sergei.

"This is the pilgrimage season."

The pilgrims walked silently, without violence.

"Are they talking about the war?" asked Grandpa Sergei.

"I didn't hear them talk."

But at night they hear dull, heavy sounds. Grandpa Sergei has no doubt, the Red Army is approaching them. Yanek knows, Grandpa Sergei doesn't spread conjectures or fictions. He only says what he knows or believes. No wonder the soldiers in his unit followed him through fire and water.

That night Grandpa Sergei spoke a lot about the soldiers in his unit and about the power they projected. The moment the signal was given, they mounted their horses and set off at a gallop. Forty horses were a mighty force. The earth trembled beneath them.

People would cheer for them from far and near. Everybody know they were setting out on a rescue mission.

Once a flour mill bust into flames, and the unit arrived and immediately stormed the building. A lot of people were trapped in it. The unit broke down the doors. Some of them put out the fire with water, some of them scattered sand, and some of them made their way through the smoke and took out the people who were trapped. The medics tried to save lives, and indeed they did save quite a few people. At the end of the operation, seven corpses lay on the ground, including a well-liked soldier, Peter, a courageous fighter who was always the first to take risks.

Those who were saved — and many people were saved — hugged the soldiers and wept in their arms. Everyone cheered them: "Because of soldiers like these, there's a reason to live. Because of them, we know how to love."

"We wrapped our beloved Peter in the flag of the unit and put him one one of the horses, returning to the base in a funeral march. We performed dozens of missions like that," Grandpa Sergei finished and immediately sank into himself.

34

At night the voices spoke to Yanek: "Yanek, Grandpa Sergei trained you to be a warrior. Tomorrow you will receive the pistol. From now on, you will have to lead the campaign: one against the many. This is a noble war. The masses mustn't infect you with fear. The masses have no face, they're a herd. In the coming days you'll have to protect many wanderers, lost people, in pain. Don't be afraid. Your parents are with you. Your grandparents are with you, and the God of justice is on your side. You will raise the helpless up from the dust. This will make Grandpa Sergei's heart proud, along with all those in whose hearts the candle of God is lit."

Yanek woke up. Those clear words still floated before his eyes, and, amazingly, he remembered them. In his heart he know that a great mission had been entrusted to him, maybe one beyond his ability. For a moment he was alarmed, but he recovered immediately, approached Grandpa Sergei and told him about the dream. Grandpa Sergei listened and said, "May God be with you." He said nothing more.

That very morning some boys gathered and threw stones at the wanderers. Yanek, fortified by the night's dream, went down and fell upon them. They sensed his determined wrath and fled. But one of them, in his flight, threw a stone that hit Yanek on the shoulder. Yanek didn't back off. He ran after them until he caught one of them, slapped his face, and forced him to say, "I'm a criminal. I sinned before God and before the wanderer."

The boy repeated after Yanek, word for word. His lips trembled, and his body twitched. In the end he was forced to add, "There is a God in heaven, and He will judge me when the time comes."

"Now get out of here. Don't be seen again."

Not until he reached the tree did he realize that a lot of blood was flowing from his shoulder. He took off his shirt, wiped the clotted blood, and spread iodine on the wound.

Grandpa Sergei didn't leave his side.

"How much blood did you lose?" asked Grandpa Sergei.

"My shirt's a little red."

"Does it hurt?"

"No."

"In any case you have to rest for at least a day, to drink water, and to eat well."

"I wanted to cook mushrooms."

"You'll cook them in the evening, not now. A real soldier knows he has to rest when he's wounded. Rest is no less important than effort. Don't think, clear your head of thoughts, concentrate on getting better, because that's the main thing now."

Grandpa Sergei's words had an immediate effect. Yanek closed his eyes and fell asleep. His sleep was deep. Again he saw Christina standing in front of the class, summoning her classmates to leave the room and go out into the schoolyard to protest against Yanek's expulsion from school. The boys giggled and didn't move from their seats. Christina raised her voice. She didn't stop screaming even when the teacher came into the room. The teacher called the school nurse and the janitor, and they took Christina out of the classroom. She continued to shout in the corridor. No wonder she got sick, and now she's hospitalized in a sanatorium.

While he was dreaming, the booming of cannons shook his ears, and he woke up.

Grandpa Sergei was awake and asked, "Do you feel better?"

"Much better."

That night they heard shouts of pain. Boys had attacked one of the wanderers and stolen from him. Grandpa Sergei wouldn't allow Yanek to go down. "You're wounded, and your wound has to heal. A soldier is a warrior, but he's not suicidal," Grandpa Sergei spoke like a commander.

After sipping tea and puffing on his pipe, he showed Yanek how to take the pistol apart and reassemble it. He showed him twice. Yanek observed every detail and tried to do it the way Grandpa did. He didn't succeed the first time, but the second time he was precise and did it right.

"Take the pistol with the holster and put it on. Start getting used to it. It has to be with you day and night."

"Thank you, Grandpa Sergei," he said with emotion.

That night Grandpa Sergei's spirit was relaxed, and he

told Yanek more about his village, about his parents, and about his sister Irena. His parents were peasants in every respect, except they were different in one way: they didn't slaughter animals or eat their meat. Because of that they were labeled "vegetarians," a way of indicating that they had strayed from the ways of the majority.

His father was an honest man, severe with himself, giving alms to the poor and condemning hypocrites and cheaters. Because of these traits, his family wasn't popular in the village. Though some families did like them, most people called them "the vegetarians" and never invited them to their homes.

"Did you suffer from that, Grandpa Sergei?" asked Yanek.

"I suffered. But I didn't let that insult darken my spirit. Anyone who made fun of me and called me a 'vegetarian' got a smack from me. Gradually they stopped pestering me."

"Did you want to be a combat soldier even when you were young?"

"No. I wanted to be a priest. Our priest liked my father and mother. He was a tall, strong man who chopped wood and fixed gutters, and if a roof collapsed under the snow, he would rebuild it with his own hands. No one dared to flout him. Everyone respected him, even when he ordered them to take in wanderers during the winter and give them a hot meal."

"Did you want to be like him?"

"Yes."

"What happened?"

"I was drafted, and the army won my heart. Fortunately, I was sent to the special unit, which was sent on rescue missions both for the army and for the civilian population. I saw a lot of sorrow and pain during my service, but I also saw a lot of moments of exaltation. When a head suddenly peers out at you from a house that has collapsed, and you can save someone – that's the moment to act decisively. Everything depends on your movements. A careless movement, and you won't forgive yourself all your life."

Meanwhile Prince had disappeared. Yanek went out to look for him and wandered among the houses for a long time.

"What can we do?" he asked Grandpa Sergei.

"Maybe our Prince went back to his original home. Our food apparently wasn't nourishing enough for him."

"Will he come back to us?"

"We'll wait and see."

When Grandpa Sergei says "wait and see" in his special tone, Yanek feels that he's relating to life as to a secret whose ways we can't always figure out.

Yanek was sad, and a tear fell from his eye. When Prince was with them, he brought warmth and love. What could be done? It was hard for wanderers to take care of pets.

"Will he come back to us?" Yanek couldn't restrain himself.

Yanek forgot that Grandpa Sergei never answers the same question twice.

35

The next day Yanek had a lot of work on his hands. The wanderers on the dirt road to the monastery of Saint Mary were prey to boys who hit them and stole from them. Yanek would leap out like a young panther, fall upon one of them, and give him a drubbing. The wanderers crossed themselves at the sight of their young savior.

One of them stopped him and asked, "Who are you?"

"I'm Grandpa Sergei's grandson."

"May God bless you."

One of them handed him a warm coat and said, "Better it should belong to you than to the robbers."

Yanek refused it. "I'm not helping for the sake of money or an expensive garment."

"So why do you do it?"

"Because God commanded us to aid the helpless."

"And that's what you do?"

"Only that," Yanek said and went on his way.

Grandpa Sergei taught Yanek how to be silent, but he also taught him to say a word or two with clear content.

While the struggle continued, it began to rain. Yanek covered the packs and bundles with the big tarpaulin and took out Grandpa Sergei's raincoat for him, the coat that was left to him from his military service. He wrapped himself in the small tarpaulin. It rained hard, but Grandpa Sergei didn't lose his presence of mind. He spoke to a peasant who was running home and asked, "Is there an inn here?"

"No."

"So where can we find shelter?"

"There's an abandoned house not far from here. I think it still has a roof."

"Thanks for the advice, may God bless you."

Without delay, Yanek went out to look for the abandoned house. It still had a roof, but no doors or windows. Yanek returned to Grandpa Sergei and reported on what he had found. They immediately gathered up their bundles and packs and set out.

Luckily for them the fireplace in the abandoned house was whole. Yanek ran to the woods to bring branches, lit the fire, and, amazingly, the chimney drew well, and the fireplace gave them light and heat.

"There are miracles," said Grandpa Sergei.

Yanek wasn't idle. He went out and came back with two piles of twigs. "Now we'll also have couches to lie on," Yanek said happily. Then he cooked cornmeal porridge, added some cheese, and put sacks down on the twigs, spread a cloth for the meal, and they sat down to eat.

That night loud thundering was heard on the horizon. Grandpa Sergei's senses told him that the Germans were retreating, and in a few days the Red Army would appear.

"Will my parents and grandparents come back?" asked Yanek.

"Let's pray that they will."

The rain kept falling, and Yanek went out to see whether there were any wanderers on the road. No wanderers were to be seen, but several covered and ornate wagons full of respectable pilgrims were slowly advancing. Yanek went back and told Grandpa Sergei what he had seen.

Grandpa Sergei said, "The world stands upon those who suffer and who are in pain, not on those who are satisfied and arrogant."

"What do you mean by 'the world stands?'" asked Yanek.

"Those who suffer and are in pain know what a miracle is. They don't take anything as self-evident. They always cry out to God, and for that reason they are close to Him. People who are satisfied and arrogant have nothing in their world except themselves. Even if they go to church, they're far from God."

Meanwhile the fireplace was warming them. Even though the abandoned house was open to the winds, it wasn't cold. Yanek looked at the fire and felt that his father and mother were standing by him, and his heart twinged with longing.

Then Grandpa Sergei asked Yanek whether there was a mezuza on the doorpost.

"What's a mezuza?" asked Yanek.

"It's a tube with some verses from the Bible written on parchment, and Jewish people put them in a slot on their doorposts. Your house had one. You just don't remember. Check if there's a thick slot on the doorpost."

"There is, Grandpa."

Grandpa Sergei responded quickly: "They banished the Jews from here, too."

Yanek wanted to ask for more information, but he didn't. Grandpa Sergei's silence was sometimes so solid, that he couldn't bring himself to disturb him. Once Grandpa Sergei said to him that it's best to be silent about things about which we have nothing to say.

Every hour or so Yanek went out to see whether there were wanderers on the roads. Suddenly he heard the sound of bitter weeping. A wanderer was sitting under a tree, completely wet. His backpack and bundle were also wet.

"What's the matter?" asked Yanek.

"I'm in despair. I hoped to get to Saint Mary and pray for forgiveness. In the end I'm stuck here, completely wet, and my bundles are also wet, and it's hard for me to pick them up. This is the end of me."

"Come to us. We're also wanderers. We found shelter in an abandoned house with a roof," Yanek offered.

"I won't go into an abandoned house. It belonged to Jews."

"Why not?"

"Ghosts and evil spirits lie there. Once I went in and they bit me. I swore I'd never go into an abandoned Jewish house again."

"We've been living there for a week."

"That makes no difference. They bit me."

Yanek didn't know what to say. Talking about the Jews, ghosts, and evil spirits put life in the wanderer's face. "That's what the Jews left for us," he added. "People shouldn't be allowed to go near those abandoned houses."

That miserable man, who had been crying bitterly a few minutes before, now spoke with self-confidence.

Yanek went back and told Grandpa Sergei what had happened to him.

Grandpa responded, "There's no limit to superstition. For now the abandoned house is protecting us. The fireplace, burning day and night, gives off pleasant heat, and the mildew on the walls no longer gives off such an unpleasant smell."

Outside it was cold and wet. Had it not been for the abandoned house, they would have been dragged to the monastery of Saint Mary with the wanderers.

Yanek practices taking the pistol apart and putting it back together every day, and he shoots at targets only late at night, so that he'll be ready when the fateful day comes.

Grandpa Sergei keeps repeating: "Not to shoot, except in an emergency. And then, only in the air. If you shoot and hit someone, we'll arouse the whole village against us."

Yanek understands these instructions very well, and he hopes that his hands will stand him in good stead, and he won't need the pistol. It's too bad that his hidden strength only comes out of hiding in times of danger. During the day, sometimes weakness afflicts him, and he wonders: how can I overcome five or six opponents? They're my height, older than me, and no less strong.

At night the voices speak to him again: "Don't be afraid, Yanek. God is with you. God gives a lot of strength to those who fight the wicked. Quantity won't determine the outcome. You mustn't underestimate the strength of the loyal and dedicated few. They can do the impossible. And you, Yanek, will be among them."

Yanek woke up. The darkness outside was thick, but the fireplace glowed and gave off light and heat. Grandpa Sergei was sleeping in his clothes, like a soldier. Yanek sat on the twig couch, and the voices that had spoke in him still murmured in his head. He was at full strength, but after drinking a cup of tea he saw his mother before him, and she said to him: "My dear, it's good that I'm seeing you, and you, me."

He grew stronger immediately.

36

Meanwhile the thundering in the sky grows stronger. Grandpa Sergei asked a peasant whether the Germans were retreating.

"So they say."

"And are there signs of it?"

"The railroad station is full of wounded soldiers being returned to the rear."

"God bless you."

Grandpa won't skip washing his face and upper body in the stream. This is a habit from his army days. Though the water is cold, washing is necessary to be alert and clean. Yanek does as he does. A dirty body isn't ready for the struggle.

From day to day there are more wanderers on the roads. Sometimes, in great irritation and with frazzled nerves, a wanderer attacks a companion walking at his side, and they fight with each other till they're bleeding. Yanek separates them and says, "Wanderers shouldn't fight. You're sons of God. You have to behave patiently. Help each other in these difficult times."

They are so given over to the heat of the fight that Yanek's words only incite their anger, and in the end, having no choice, Yanek draws the pistol and threatens:

"If you don't stop this fight immediately, I'll shoot." They're astonished by his determined look and by the pistol. They shoulder their packs and flee from him.

In the evening Yanek wanted to say that the struggle was discouraging. But he restrained himself and didn't say it. He knows that the word "discouraging" was distasteful to Grandpa Sergei. So he said, "The wanderers and the helpless people don't know how to defend themselves. In the end they fight with each other."

Grandpa Sergei listened, heard his sentence, and said, "Those poor people have been so humiliated, they're so helpless, in so much pain, that they've forgotten that God created them in His image. They have to do their utmost just to stand on their feet, to curse, and to fight."

"What must I do?" asked Yanek.

"Awaken human pride and the divine spark in them."

"Will that help?"

"Even if it doesn't help, we have to do it."

They were running out of food. Yanek took a woolen scarf out of his pack and said to Grandpa Sergei, "I'll go buy food in the grocery store."

"What will you give them?"

"I have a new woolen scarf."

"Take my scarf. I have two."

"Sorry, Grandpa, you're older than me and you need to preserve your body heat."

"But you're a warrior, and you're exposed to strong winds."

Yanek found a compromise: "This time I'll take mine, and the next time I'll take yours." Grandpa chuckled: "A true Jewish soul."

Yanek ran to the grocery store. He showed the scarf to the owner of the store right away and asked her, "What will you give me for it?"

"A loaf of bread and a piece of fresh butter."

"What about potatoes, too?"

"I'll give you some, but no more than a kilogram."

While standing at the door of the shop, he saw her picking up the scarf and whispering, "New." When he heard her say "new," Yanek's heart twinged. His mother knit it for him a month before he left the house.

Yanek woke early and saw Prince before his eyes. In the few days the dog was with him, his heart had become attached to the sweet creature. He showered him with affection so he'd eat something. He turned up his nose at cornmeal porridge, refused to touch fruit or potatoes, and just tasted some cheese. He was apparently hungry and ran away to the peasants. With them there was always meat.

"In the army they say 'an army marches on its stomach,'" Grandpa Sergei tried to amuse Yanek, but this time his words didn't console him. More and more he felt that part of him had left with Prince. He kept looking for him in vain.

For a while the abandoned house protected them, but evil voices had begun to surround them in the past few days. At night Grandpa Sergei woke up and heard someone's steps. The intruders didn't speak, but it was clear they were plotting to kick them out or beat them.

That very night Grandpa Sergei decided that the next

day they'd leave the abandoned house and get moving. They ate breakfast, Grandpa drank tea and puffed on his pipe. When Yanek asked to go down to help one of the wanderers, Grandpa Sergei wouldn't allow it: "We have to be on the alert."

In the afternoon Yanek filled the backpacks and wrapped the bundles, and they parted from the abandoned house. Before going out, Grandpa Sergei said, "Yanek, go to the doorpost and kiss the mezuza. That's what the Jews do before they leave home." Yanek walked over to the mezuza and kissed it. For a moment they stood at the door of the abandoned house with their packs, and then they set out.

"The abandoned house was good. It preserved us for quite a few days," said Grandpa Sergei.

Yanek knew that Grandpa Sergei felt closeness to plants and animals. Now he felt that he also conversed with inanimate things. But when they were at a distance from the abandoned house Yanek felt that his lips, which had kissed the slot in the doorpost, had linked him to some riddle. What it was, he didn't know. He wanted to ask Grandpa Sergei, but didn't. Maybe it would become clear to him as they walked. Maybe he would ask at their next camp.

Grandpa Sergei said, "Every journey is a new encounter with yourself. Among other things, you see what you saw, you hear what you heard, and if you have a friend like Yanek, who tells you everything he sees — your life expands, and you're glad you're not detached from the world."

The cannons thunder. The stream of wanderers on the way to Saint Mary does not cease.

"What should we do? How can we help? You make things easier for one of them, and dozens pass by alongside you, injured and wounded."

Grandpa Sergei believes that a true warrior's strength flourishes and grows when all seems to be lost.

"Grandpa Sergei, I don't always feel strong." Yanek didn't hide his apprehension.

"Because we're not connected to God all the time. The moment God plants the feeling of justice in it, our strength increases. 'Fear not and be not afraid,' God says to Joshua, and so says He to all fighters for justice."

Usually Grandpa Sergei is turned inward, but on some days his speech is as strong as his silence.

The sky is cloudy, but no rain is falling. Yanek, in any event, is prepared for any trouble that might come. Meanwhile he found a thick tree whose branches are spread densely, and they sat beneath it. Dry branches were not lacking in the forest. Yanek gathered them and made a fire. The fire immediately gives a feeling of a place you can return to.

Yanek doesn't take his eyes off the main trail leading to Saint Mary. The bullies recognize him from far away, and when he goes down and approaches the trail, they flee. Yanek doesn't run after them. He sits and surveys the area. Most of the pilgrims to the monastery are wanderers. Some of them are also householders who are making a pilgrimage to the monastery of Saint Mary to pray and ask forgiveness for their sins.

Suddenly Prince is standing before Yanek's eyes, and the pain of his disappearance returns to him. The few days he was with them are stored up in his body. Since he disappeared, Yanek has been yearning for him.

When he returned from the driving off the bullies, he found Grandpa Sergei covered with blood. Once again two ruffians had attacked him Grandpa Sergei wrestled with them, knocked them down, but before he did that, they managed to scratch him. Yanek washed his face with a cloth and put iodine on the scratches.

Grandpa Sergei didn't complain. He just said, "They took advantage of my blindness, and they'll give an accounting to God for that."

Suddenly a boy of about seven approached them, looked at them, and asked, "Who are you?"

"My name is Yanek."

"And what do you do?"

"I punish the bullies who attack wanderers, cripples, and lepers."

"Do you do that by yourself?"

"No by myself, with God's help."

"Can I join you?"

"Not now. When you grow up."

For a long time he stood there, stunned with surprise, and then he went away.

Yanek feels that the coming days will be difficult. He feels it in his arms and legs. His thoughts don't disturb him. He has cut himself off from them.

The following day they left the big tree with the wide top and approached an outlook from which they could see the path to the monastery of Saint Mary.

"What do you see?" asked Grandpa Sergei.

"People walking slowly."

"A lot of them?"

"Not so many. Most of them are wanderers."

"Is anyone attacking them?"

"Some bullies are falling upon them and robbing their bundles."

Yanek tensed up. Grandpa also grew tense, but he gives no orders. Yanek looks around him quietly, chooses the target, and falls upon it quickly and with great strength. This time he knocked down two large boys. They begged him not to hit them. In the end he ordered them to kneel and ask forgiveness of the wanderers.

"We ask forgiveness," they called out together.

"Not that way."

In the end they said, "We ask forgiveness from the people we harmed and from God who ordered us to love every human being."

They got mixed up. They didn't say exactly what Yanek told them to say. Yanek looked at them with contempt and ordered them to repeat the words he had dictated. In the end, when they didn't manage to do it, he asked them,

"Who is the king of the universe?" After a hesitation one of them said, "God."

"Correct, and what did He command us to do?"

"Not to hit and plunder the wanderers."

"And now, together: not to hit and plunder the wanderers. Now get out of here slowly and think about what you've sworn. And think about what you've taken upon yourselves."

38

The next day he again looked at the path leading to the monastery of Saint Mary. The wanderers advanced haphazardly, dragging their feet and pulling their bundles after them. Boys stood on the hills and threw stones at them. In vain the miserable people tried to shield their heads with their coats. The stones hit every part of their body. Yanek dove down and pounced on the ruffians. He managed to slap some of the boys in the face and recover the bundles from them. That day he went down several times. Every time he went down, he understood that his efforts were just a drop in the bucket. The boys were insolent, and the wanderers didn't even have the strength to flee.

Yanek understood the situation thoroughly. He went back to Grandpa Sergei, told him the facts, and asked for his advice. Grandpa Sergei wasn't quick to offer advice. He withdrew into himself, and in the evening he said: "The ways of God are hidden, but we shall do what we are capable of doing."

In his sleep, Yanek saw his mother, with a backpack on her shoulders, and she could barely walk. Alongside her was his father, carrying a heavier backpack. Yanek leaped and forced his way through the crowd. He immediately took off their backpacks, removed them from the crowd, took them up the hill, and sat them down next to Grandpa Sergei.

When he woke up the dream was still clear before his eyes. It was cold, and Yanek quickly lit the campfire. The strength that had built up in him hadn't faded, and he felt that soon he would do something worthy. What would it be? He couldn't guess. Enthusiasm such as he had never known throbbed within him. Again he looked at the trail rising to Saint Mary. From the way the wanderers were walking, you could see that they were mustering all their strength to climb up, but this section of the trail was steep and muddy.

Just then the sun came out, and the sky brightened.

"What do you see, Yanek?" asked Grandpa Sergei.

"The wanderers have left their shelters and are climbing up the trail to Saint Mary."

"Is anyone throwing stones at them and grabbing their bundles?" asked Grandpa Sergei.

"They are throwing stones. I'll go and send them packing," he said and fell upon the stone throwers.

His eyes saw a scene clearly: masses of wanderers were on the exposed trail. Gangs of thugs were throwing stones at them. One of them grabbed a wanderer's pack. The wanderer tried with all his might to save his few belongings, but his efforts were in vain. For a long time he lay on the ground, but the other wanderers walked past him without saying a word. Finally one of them addressed him, saying "Get up. What was seized from you won't be returned. There's no point in lying on the ground." The wanderer didn't listen to that advice. He stayed prostrate on the ground. Finally he raised his upper body, looked at the indifferent brethren around him and said, "Everyone

is concerned only with himself. No one will help you up. When I die, they'll throw me into a ditch. They won't bury me." Thus he sat and muttered to himself. Despair dripped from every word that left his mouth. In the end a wanderer passed by him and said, "Get up. There's no point in sitting in the middle of the path."

"Thugs stole everything from me. I have nothing."

"If you sit on the path, will that get it back for you?"

"I'm amazed by my life, which is on the verge of the abyss. From now on, there's nothing but death."

The other wanderer looked at him and said, "You can also be amazed while you're standing."

Yanek understood: from now on he also had to struggle against the indifference of the wanderers, who had lost the image of God in their wandering.

39

That day, as we have said, he went down to confront the young men several times. At the end of the day, he was so exhausted that he could barely stand up. Hardly had he sat next to Grandpa Sergei than his eyes closed and he fell asleep.

In his sleep the voices spoke to him again: "Yanek, don't despair. Grandpa Sergei trained you for courageous deeds. For the possible and the impossible. You saw your brothers, the wanderers, and they were stricken, plundered, and downcast. You must restore the image of God for them. Without the image, they cannot rise up."

"What must I do?"

"You must do what your heart commands you to do."

"I'm exhausted."

"So it seems to you. Great powers are stored up within you."

When he awoke, dawn had already risen. Grandpa Sergei was still sleeping. Yanek stirred up the campfire, buried a few potatoes in it, and put a kettle of water on the coals.

When Grandpa Sergei had woken up and washed his face, Yanek gave him a cup of tea and lit his pipe. He wanted to tell him what the voices had said, but he didn't dare. In the end he took courage and said, "Grandpa, the voices spoke to me again last night."

"What did they say?"

"That I had to restore the lost image of God to the wanderers."

"And what did you say?"

"I didn't say anything."

"Keep those words in your heart. Dreams don't speak in vain."

Yanek gave Grandpa Sergei a roasted potato and a piece of cheese, washed the dishes, arranged the packs and bundles, and at last he said, "Grandpa, I'm going on my way."

"May God preserve you."

Yanek went out. He didn't know what the day would bring. He marched empty-handed, but with the vigor of someone who had engaged in physical training for a long time. On the way he saw a piece of metal on the ground: a fragment of a pot or basin. He picked it up and examined it, and it immediately occurred to him to round it into a megaphone. He continued on his way without hurrying. He felt that strength was gathering in the muscles of his arms and shoulders. Those feelings didn't distract him.

He advanced slowly. It was noon, and wanderers were moving on the trail, including some cripples on crutches. Boys had gathered on the hills across from them. They weren't throwing stones. They were chatting, pushing each other, and laughing. That sight made him angry. He approached the trail. Without sensing what he was about to do, he picked up the megaphone he had made, put it to his lips, and shouted, "This is Yanek speaking, the grandson of Grandpa Sergei, a master sergeant in the special unit, who was given medals after many battles. He has authorized me to tell you: there is a limit to humiliation; you must preserve the image of God that has been given to you; do not fear. Fear is our great enemy. It strikes us, and not the stones that ruffians throw. Leave behind the fear that you're imprisoned in. You're going up to the holy monastery of Saint Mary, and you mustn't fear thugs."

"Who are you?" called a voice from the crowd.

"I'm Grandpa Sergei's grandson."

"Who appointed you to preach to us?"

"I'm not preaching. I want to help you leave the prison where you're trapped."

The boys on the hill, who heard his words, began to throw stones in every direction, hitting several people. Yanek didn't lose his presence of mind. He swooped down on the boys and knocked down two of them. The others ran off.

This time he bound the hands of one of the bullies and turned to the wanderers, saying, "You see how easy it is to chase them away. They're not heroes, just petty robbers. They draw upon pollution. Every wind of justice will knock them over."

"Who are you?" The same skeptical voice was heard from the crowd.

Yanek didn't get angry. He answered softly, saying, "I'm the grandson of Grandpa Sergei, a warrior experienced in battle.

"Where did you learn to attack?"

"From Grandpa Sergei."

Now the thunder of the cannons was replaced by the rumble of tank treads. The front was close by, but the mighty movement of steel, didn't stop the boys from attacking the wanderers again and robbing their bundles.

Yanek leaped out, hit them with great force, and returned the packs to their owners.

When he returned from the pursuit, the tone of the wanderers' voices changed. They raised their eyes to Yanek and asked, "What are we to do?"

"Arm yourselves with knives and forks or broken glasses. If anyone tries to steal from you, hit them and wound them."

This did not put an end to their struggles that day. At night the boys tried once again to hit the wanderers and steal from them. Yanek ambushed them and fell upon them.

Failure didn't weaken the bullies' resolve. They kept climbing up and grabbing bundles and packs.

Yanek ambushed them again, slapped their faces, and rolled them down.

This went on for most of the night. The rumble of the tank treads grew closer and closer, and Yanek called out on his megaphone, "You must be patient. The army of rescue is close to us."

But, as though out of spite, the engines suddenly fell silent.

"Where are the saviors? Why aren't they coming?" A voice was heard from the crowd.

"They've come a long way. Now they're resting," Yanek answered.

Yanek didn't shut his eyes that night. He helped give water to thirsty people, and for those who were hungry, he asked those who had something to contribute a little bread.

The people obeyed him. They asked his advice and didn't conceal from him that they were very frightened about what the next day would bring. Yanek's advice was: "You have to equip yourself with something sharp. Don't be afraid. Fear only weakens you. The evildoer senses fear and is bolder."

Some of the people wept and wanted to die. Yanek held their hands and their shoulders and said, "You have to be strong now. The Red Army is close to us. They know how to deal with hooligans. They have tanks and cannons."

One of the cripples, a man with one leg, said, "For years I've prayed to reach the monastery of Saint Mary and ask to be cured. I guess I won't get there."

"You mustn't be discouraged," Yanek said to him. "Your father and mother are waiting to see you."

"They're sure I was killed in the great bombing," said the cripple weakly.

"Think of them, think of their happiness when they see you alive."

40

Then heavy rain began to fall. They were exposed, and no shelter was visible. Yanek went to look for a place to hide from the rain. He looked for a long time and finally found an abandoned house with half a roof.

He immediately went back to Grandpa Sergei, took the bundles, and they started off. Grandpa Sergei praised his quickness and alertness. "Even my soldiers wouldn't have done better than you."

The abandoned house was exposed, without windows or a door, but luckily the fireplace was intact. Yanek, without delay, went out to gather firewood. Then he came back and lit the fire. Only now did they see how badly the house was damaged, but the fireplace gave off pleasant heat. Yanek didn't rest. He came back with many branches.

In the end he collapsed on the pile of branches, in convulsions. Grandpa Sergei called out, "Yanek, what's the matter with you?" He knelt next to Yanek and felt his forehead and pulse. The convulsions kept shaking him.

Grandpa Sergei tried in vain to feed him a spoonful of tea. "Drink, dear, it will do you good." In the end he wrapped him in his army winter coat and kept urging him to open his mouth and sip some tea.

Grandpa Sergei remembered there was aspirin in Yanek's pack. He groped in it and found a small metal box, took out a pill, and put it in Yanek's mouth.

The fireplace gave off heat. Grandpa Sergei didn't move from his place. He held Yanek's hand and whispered to him: "The war is over. You'll go back home, to your parents. They're certainly expecting you. Drink, please. It will make you stronger."

Yanek didn't react. From time to time he uttered a word or a fragment of a sentence. Grandpa Sergei didn't try to rouse him. He knew that Yanek needed that sleep, but apparently it was sowing bad dreams in him.

The sleep lasted too long. Grandpa Sergei added some sugar to the tee. Yanek licked his lips. Grandpa Sergei kept talking to him. "Don't let the dreams frighten you. Sometimes monsters steal into them. Don't be afraid. Grandpa Sergei is watching over you."

Grandpa Sergei watches over his sleep, gives him tea to drink, dries his clothes. From time to time he asks how Yanek is and keeps repeating, "The war is over. Your parents are expecting you."

This lasted four days. Yanek didn't wake up, so Grandpa Sergei decided to speak to him clearly: "You've been immersed in a deep sleep for four days already. I don't know what's happening to you. Please, dear, come out of the darkness. You know how limited I am. I can't do anything without you. Both of us will perish in this cold, exposed ruin."

Not until the next morning did Yanek open his eyes and ask, "Where am I?"

"You're here with me," Grandpa Sergei answered quickly.

"I guess I was asleep," said Yanek, without knowing what he was saying.

"You slept a lot, four days in a row. I spoke to you. I wanted to know what was happening to you, but you didn't answer. Your sleep was very quiet, and that also worried me."

"Sorry, Grandpa."

"It didn't depend on you. Sleep knocked you down. How do you feel now? In a little while I'll make you a cup of tea. You're thirsty, dear. Where were you in your sleep?"

"I was asleep," said Yanek, and it was clear that he hadn't woken up completely.

"You slept deeply."

Hardly had the words left Grandpa Sergei's mouth when Yanek plunged into sleep again. Grandpa Sergei tried in vain to stop him from sinking, but this time the sleep was short, just a few hours.

Yanek woke up and rose to his feet, asking, "Should I make cornmeal porridge?"

"No need. You should rest."

"I'm absolutely fine."

After finishing the porridge, Yanek said, "I'll go and get some branches."

"I won't let you go by yourself. I'll go with you."

Yanek gathered branches, and together they brought them back to the ruin.

"What happened to me?" asked Yanek.

"You were exhausted from running and from the heavy wet weather. We won't set out today. I think that by now your parents will be coming home, and we'll help them fix up the house. Rest, my dear. Don't be ashamed to rest. In the past few days you fought like a lion."

41

The following days were quiet. The war moved away from that place, and, though shots were heard now and then, they felt safe in the ruin. Grandpa Sergei didn't neglect Yanek for a moment and sometimes reminded him about the people they had met on their way: the peasants and the former soldiers, and the children. "If you met someone on the way, that's a sign that he's a messenger. You have to remember him and think about what he was trying to convey to you." Grandpa Sergei spoke at length about his former soldier, Kiril, who had suffered so much in his life. "He was a hero, and in his last war he surpassed himself."

Suddenly he addressed Yanek and said, "You've seen a lot of things in our journey. We've received a lot of gifts. We didn't always know how to appreciate them properly. When you go back home to your parents, and all the trials we've undergone are behind you, you'll certainly ask yourself: what did Grandpa Sergei give me?"

Yanek was alarmed and said, "Grandpa Sergei, I know your every movement and gesture. Everything you said to me in the morning, the afternoon, and the evening. Don't worry, Grandpa, I retain your words in my heart."

"Pardon me. I had no doubt," said Grandpa with a slight laugh.

The daily routine didn't change, but Grandpa Sergei's face changed. He often sank into thought, recalled his sister, his late wife Dorka, his youthful love, Tanya, his soldiers, with whom he had gone a long way in life. He asked Yanek to remember Kiril's generosity, for giving them a quarter of a sack of cornmeal, which had nourished them for many days, and to visit him. It would be a very good deed to visit him. He has lost everything, and people probably ignore him. "Tell your father about him. Your father will certainly give you money to bring to him."

"Grandpa Sergei," Yanek was alarmed again. "You'll be with me, and we'll do it together."

"Certainly I'll be with you."

The war moved away from them. Grandpa Sergei seemed to be roused from slumber and said, "We mustn't delay. We have to go back home."

"When?" asked Yanek.

"Tomorrow," Grandpa Sergei's answer came without delay.

Yanek asked for permission to go to the store, and Grandpa Sergei allowed it. Yanek took a shirt out of his pack, which still showed signs of ironing, and he said, "It's small on me now. I can't wear it."

"Keep it. Take a piece of my clothing. Your mother will decide what to do with it."

"Please, Grandpa, the shirt is small on me. All my clothes are small on me."

"Take my scarf," Grandpa decreed, removing it from his neck.

Yanek set out. He was still weak, and his legs barely carried him. The thought that he was going to sell Grandpa Sergei's scarf disturbed him, and he went back the way he had come.

"I can't sell your scarf."

Grandpa Sergei heard him and responded immediately, "Clothes wear out in the end."

"I like your scarf," said Yanek, bursting into tears.

"My intention was," Grandpa Sergei's voice grew softer, "to return you to your home with all your clothes and with the valuables your father left with us."

Yanek couldn't stop crying, and he murmured, "Not the scarf, not the scarf."

"It's not fitting for a combat soldier to cry," Grandpa Sergei's commanding voice returned to him.

After recovering, Yanek asked permission to look for mushrooms. Grandpa Sergei allowed it. He looked for a long time and in the end he found a cluster of mushrooms. He immediately picked them and put them in his hat.

Without delay he returned to the ruin and told Grandpa Sergei about his find.

Their lunch included cornmeal porridge, mushrooms, and berries. Grandpa Sergei was content and repeated a proverb he liked, "Who is rich? He who is happy with his lot."

Afterward he recalled his late wife's face and spoke about Dorka's beauty and modesty and her ability to listen to people. "Women, relatives, used to come to speak with her. After a conversation they would hug and kiss her. I didn't deserve her."

42

While Grandpa Sergei went on to talk about his life, Yanek fell asleep.

In his dream, he and Grandpa Sergei were sitting in a wagon on their way home. Only now did he grasp what he had undergone since his father left him with Grandpa Sergei. The broad fields, the encampments in the shade of sheltering trees, the cool taste of the water he drew from dark wells, the streams they had bathed and washed their clothes in, walking to a village and the joy upon finally reaching the tree at the entrance to the village.

While he was immersed in those sights, the driver stopped the wagon and said, "The rain isn't letting up. The road is full of potholes, the horses are tired. The wagon's wheels won't stand up to this pounding. Get off. I'm going back home."

"You're making us get off in the middle of fields, with a heavy rain? Don't you have mercy in your heart?" Yanek spoke to him mildly.

"No," he answered curtly, in one word.

"You've gone more than a third of the way. In an hour and a half we'll be in the city. Why won't you finish the job, so that you'll get the wristwatch we promised you?"

"I don't care. I'm going home," he said dryly.

"God has given you an opportunity to do a good deed and also get paid for it. You started the good deed — finish it," Yanek spoke quietly to him.

"Get off right away, or I'll throw you off."

Yanek, without delay, jumped off the wagon and spoke firmly, "The days of bullying and lawlessness are finished. Take us to the city immediately." To give credibility to his words, he drew the pistol from his belt and fired a shot in the air. He got back onto the wagon and said, "Drive on now, without arguments and threats."

The wagon driver said nothing and whipped the horses. All the way to the city, Yanek didn't put the pistol back in his belt.

Many thoughts raced around in his head, but not one was clear. When they reached the city, Yanek directed him to his house. It was morning, and there was light in the windows of the houses. Not in Yanek's house.

"Even though you drove with a wicked heart and you forgot that there's a God in the world, I'm giving you the watch I promised."

Upon hearing Yanek's words, the man got down from his seat and said: "Look, two wheels are broken, and it's lucky I had wheels to replace them with. I haven't forgotten that there's a God. I just wanted to spare the wagon."

"And why didn't you want to spare us?"

"I spared you, but I had no choice."

"Was the wagon more important to you than two people with no roof over their heads in the rain and wind?"

"Why argue? What happened happened."

"And you feel no remorse?"

43

While the war was moving farther away, the wanderers were fleeing to the monastery, and there was no bad omen in the sky but a stray bullet struck Grandpa Sergei in the forehead. It happened all of a sudden, almost without a sound, and, had it not been for the shock that moved his upper body slightly, his death wouldn't have been noticeable.

Very little blood flowed from his forehead. His position didn't indicate pain.

Yanek knelt and the words, "Grandpa Sergei" escaped his lips, as though to say: what happened to you?

There was absolute silence all around. Here and there a horse, mule, and calf. "Grandpa Sergei," he called again, and this time in a choked voice, looking at his bent head, he wondered why there was no answer. Grandpa Sergei didn't always answer his questions. Quite often he sank into himself and delayed his answers, and for a moment it sounded like one of those silences when he didn't answer.

Grandpa Sergei didn't move. The moderation that restrained him seemed to have grown stronger, and for a moment it seemed to Yanek that it wasn't death that had silenced him, but that marvelous moderation that conquered him every time he thought or sank into reflections.

Where were the thugs? Where were the wanderers?

Where were they? Yanek woke up, but he immediately grasped: the wanderers had pressed in through the iron gate of the monastery with great force. Grandpa Sergei and Yanek had accompanied them, but they hadn't gone in.

As he was his habit, Yanek lit the campfire and put the kettle on the coals. The full flame brought to his eyes the way they would sit next to the fire. For most of their days together, the fire sheltered them. The thought that Grandpa Sergei wasn't among the living floated from his body, but even after it arose, it went out immediately. Only when one of the local madmen attacked him and called him a stinking tramp, Yanek grabbed him and threw him to the ground. He squirmed with his arms and legs. The squirming brought Grandpa Sergei's death before Yanek's eyes, and he let the madman go away without anger.

When he returned to the campfire he saw Grandpa Sergei lying in a position of thoughtfulness. "Grandpa Sergei," he called out loud. He straightened his head and put it on the sack where he used to rest.

Then he poured himself a cup of tea. Drinking tea was part of their conversation, or, rather, their silences.

Once Grandpa said to him, "I'm silent because I don't know what to say."

Once, in a moment of great enthusiasm, he said, "I'm silent because I have more words than necessary."

At the time, as we have said, Yanek didn't understand most of the words and terms that Grandpa Sergei had used, but in the past months some of them had become clear to him.

Now he burst into sobbing, deep sobbing that broke out from within him. Grandpa Sergei forbade crying. He used to say, "Weeping is weakness. True wanderers don't allow themselves such a surrender."

Suddenly a cold wind blew, and Yanek quickly covered Grandpa in his winter army coat.

"Grandpa, are you asleep? Once you told me that our sleep is attached to the night, to the great sleep, from which it draws glowing sights and words of truth."

"What do you have to sell?" the peasants sometimes asked him.

"I have nothing to sell you. I'm devoid of possessions," he would answer.

They smiled at you, as if you were trying to cheat them. Their opinion of you was foolish. They didn't imagine to themselves, couldn't imagine to themselves, that you were wandering in order to be close to God.

"What do you have hidden?" they kept asking. "We'll pay you with horses and a wagon. You can wander wherever you please."

In vain he told them, "I don't have a penny, and I don't need money either."

Because of their disbelief, they would attack at night.

Then reality came and showed Yanek its face. An old peasant approached them and seeing Grandpa Sergei lying without moving, he asked, "Who's that man lying on the ground?"

"He's my grandfather, Grandpa Sergei," Yanek answered.

"When did he pass away?"

"An hour or two ago. A bullet penetrated his forehead."

"Where will you bury him?"

"I'll take him to his home village, to Ivanov, so he'll be gathered with his ancestors."

"That's good. When will you set out?" he kept asking.

"Soon. It should be known to you, sir, that my grandfather was an officer in the rescue unit, one of the famous units. Everyone who served in his unit respected him even after he finished his service."

"I'm sure that they will receive him with joy in heaven, and you will be blessed in this world."

The old man, who seemed to be a wise man, removed the cloth of fog from Yanek's eyes and showed him what his duty was at this time.

44

While he worried about what to do and how to do it, he
saw a cart lying on the ground, a cart that had been used
to transport potatoes and watermelons from the field. In
their great haste, the wanderers had abandoned it.

He went over to it right away and turned it back upon
onto its two wheels, gripped the shafts, and rolled it to
the tree.

After he lowered the shafts to the ground he was
alarmed, because this was a device that would serve death.

He stood for a long time without doing anything.
Grandpa Sergei's face was calm. No pain was visible on
it. The hole in his forehead, through which the bullet had
penetrated, had widened slightly, and the flesh was red.

"What must I do"? he asked himself, as though he
were facing an impossible task. But as he stood and
wondered, a practical idea arose in his mind: first he
would place the corpse on the cart. Alongside it and at
its feet, he would place the clothing and the objects that
had served them. But meanwhile he understood that if he
wanted to honor Grandpa Sergei, he couldn't pick him
up by himself.

While he was standing there, half frozen, he saw two
peasants approaching.

"Dear uncles," he spoke to them. "I need your help

urgently. My grandfather, Grandpa Sergei, was shot a few hours ago by a stray bullet, and I intend to bring him to be buried with his ancestors. My grandfather was a respected man, a famous commander and a lover of humanity."

"How can we help you?" asked one of the peasants.

"You can help me place the body on the cart in a respectable manner."

"We'll do it," they said together.

For a moment they stood next to the body and crossed themselves. Yanek spread a blanket on the floor of the cart and placed a folded sack for Grandpa Sergei's head. After delaying for a moment, looking at the body and estimating its weight, they picked it up, and Yanek helped them place it slowly on the floor.

"Thank you from the bottom of my heart, uncles. Your deed will make an impression in heaven," said Yanek.

"What's the name of the deceased?" asked one of them.

"Sergei Ivanovich," Yanek answered quickly.

"The famous master sergeant Sergei Ivanovich?" the man was stunned.

"Yes. Where are you from?" Yanek asked, suddenly feeling excited.

"We grew up in the same region."

"In Ivanov?"

"Yes, yes, in Ivanov."

"What a childhood, what youth, what a life. Only Sergei knew how to profit from the muscles of his arms and legs and from his height. We were also tall and thin and quick, but not like him. Right from the first days in the army, Sergei stood out. Even then his commanders admired him. Too bad he didn't study in high school. If it hadn't been for that obstacle, he would have finished his service as a great general. Now he's lying in this miserable cart. That's life. They tell us we mustn't complain. We won't complain. Go, friend, and bring our dear comrade to his eternal rest. Don't cover his face. A man like him deserves to go to the grave with his face exposed."

After they went away, Yanek placed the packs and bundles in the cart, and when there was
nothing else, tears came to his eyes, and he sat and wept. Grandpa Sergei, where have you disappeared to? How can I find you? What can we do in this world without you? The questions rolled around in his head, and he couldn't stop them. In his heart Yanek knew that Grandpa Sergei didn't like questions that had no answers. He promised himself that someday he would correct this fault and stop asking.

Without further delay, he took up the shafts and set out.

The cart was heavy, and Yanek could barely drag it.

Grandpa Sergei had led a whole platoon behind him. A commander has to be at the head. That was his way, and not only in the army. No wonder he was awarded the imperial blue medal and many other medals, but he never boasted about those medals. He often said: a soldier is flesh and blood, he learns service and discipline in the army, so that he can serve God when the time comes.

While Yanek was pulling the cart, he heard a voice: "Yanek, I haven't parted from you, nor from your father or your grandfather. We were bound together in this world, and we will be bound together in the world to come. Don't be sad. The path to the infinite is long, but this is the start of the path."

Yanek heard Grandpa Sergei's voice, stopped the cart, and said, "Grandpa Sergei, speak, your grandson is listening."

As soon as Yanek stopped the cart, Grandpa Sergei's voice was silenced, as sometimes happened, and Yanek knew that by the evening Grandpa Sergei wouldn't speak to him anymore.

45

While Yanek was pulling the cart, the chilly evening fell. Grandpa Sergei's face didn't change, but it grew paler, as when he sank into himself.

Yanek was thirsty and went to light a fire. It seemed to him that the smell of the campfire would arouse the desire to speak in Grandpa. For a long time he awaited his voice, but not a syllable came from his lips.

Yanek poured a cup of tea for himself. He took a piece of bread out of his pack, dipped it in the boiling tea, and the good flavors he knew from this wanderings returned to him and filled his mouth.

"Grandpa," he spoke to Grandpa Sergei without raising his head. "We won't see each other next to the campfire anymore? Won't you tell me about your other life anymore? Won't you tell me about my father and mother and grandfather anymore? If they don't want to receive you in your village, I'll take you with me, and you'll be with me until you come back to life."

He waited for an answer for a long time. When none came, he lowered his face to the ground and fell asleep.

In the last watch of the night, Yanek woke up, and to his surprise a tall, thin wanderer was standing next to him, and he asked, "Who are you?"

"I'm Grandpa Sergei's grandson."

"Where is he?"

"Yesterday he was shot in the forehead. Soon I'll take him to his native village in this cart, and there he'll be gathered with his ancestors."

"Was he a wanderer?"

"He was a wanderer heart and soul. All his life he wanted to purify himself. What little he had he wanted to give to charity."

"May God preserve him in heaven," the wanderer blessed him and turned to go.

"Why are you leaving me?" Yanek was choked with tears.

"I'm going to my fate."

"Why won't you stay for a moment?"

"My friend, I would sit with you, but I have to go. My father is very sick, and I haven't seen him for many years. These are the last days when I can see him. Everyone bears a burden of guilt on his shoulders, and this is my burden now."

Yanek didn't move. He was amazed by the man and his way of standing, by his laconic speech and his parting. A difficult mission, Yanek said to himself.

Then he recovered, put his belongings back on the cart, grasped the shafts, and set out.

The sky was bright and his head was free of thoughts. He was harnessed tightly to the cart and pulled it at a steady pace.

Suddenly a road sign appeared: "Ivanov – twenty kilometers." All during their wanderings, they had paid no attention to signs. Suddenly here was a clear one: Ivanov. Grandpa Sergei didn't pronounce the name of his native village often, but every time he said it, his voice trembled. Now Yanek heard that trembling.

He raised his eyes. The village in all its green splendor appeared to him, extending over a kilometer. This was Grandpa Sergei's world. Here he knew every clod of earth and grove of trees. In his childhood he had run in the fields, helped his parents to pick fruit in the orchards, gone to school early in the morning and done his homework in the afternoon, and then he had gone swimming in the river with Tanya, his beloved. In just twenty kilometers, Grandpa Sergei would be home again.

All during his wanderings with Yanek, he had regretted that he hadn't returned to his native village after his army service, that he had broken his promise and not gone to visit his father in his old age, and he hadn't taken care of his sister when she was ill. That sadness narrowed his soul, and instead of being connected with many people, he had restricted his world ever more.

Grandpa Sergei's mother kept saying, "Sergei has a great soul, but he narrowed it. The day will come when he will rouse from his apparent slumber and be the one he is supposed to be."

46

In another twenty kilometers: Ivanov. If I make an effort, I'll reach the village tomorrow.

Grandpa Sergei used to say, "Everyone will return to his village some day, to his father and mother, and they will gather him up with them." But in his lifetime he hadn't been able to return. It seems he was very close to it several times, but he hadn't dared to enter.

A few months ago, after they lit the campfire in the morning, Grandpa Sergei told him that he was thinking of returning to his native village. Yanek was stunned and asked whether it was far from there.

"No," he answered with just one word.

"Am I allowed to go with you?"

"Allowed."

"I won't get in the way?"

"No."

Since that conversation, Grandpa Sergei hadn't spoken about his native village. Sometimes it seemed to Yanek that Grandpa Sergei had lost the key to his dear ones and to his ancestors, and he was waiting for a miracle so he could go in among his loved ones without the key.

For a moment he thought he would sit down where he was, but he realized immediately that he was forbidden to sit down at that time. He had to deliver Grandpa Sergei's body to the elders of the village so they could prepare it for the upper world.

While he was about to harness himself to the shafts, he saw a man approaching him. He appeared to be a soldier, but without uniform or a weapon.

"What are you doing here?" he spoke to Yanek in a friendly way.

"I'm taking my grandfather, Grandpa Sergei, for burial," Yanek answered.

"Where are your father and mother?"

"In the war."

"Are you a Jew?" the stranger asked.

Yanek held his breath and finally said, "No."

"Don't be afraid. The war is over."

"I'm not afraid. Grandpa Sergei taught me not to be afraid."

"I wanted to tell you, the war is over. You can go home. What's tying you to the man in the cart?"

"I want to watch over him and accompany him to his village."

"I understand you. Do what your heart tells you to do. Just don't be afraid to go home."

"I'm not afraid. But now I'm burdened with this obligation."

The man disappeared, and Yanek harnessed himself to the shafts and set out. First it was hard for him. It seemed to him that Grandpa Sergei was opposed to being transported. "Grandpa Sergei," Yanek spoke to him. "Am I doing something you don't approve of?"

Grandpa Sergei didn't answer. His face became more and more closed.

While pulling the cart, Yanek felt that the burden was getting lighter.

"Grandpa Sergei, I want to talk with you. During our wanderings, we had a special language. You were the only one I spoke to in that language. You were the only one who understood me, and I understood you. Actually, we didn't speak a lot, but I never had the feeling of not speaking or of emptiness. During the long summer nights, you would sometimes ask me about the color of the sky, about the trees, and about the houses and the people in them. You were surprised by people's empty talk. You used to say: 'I pray that what you tell me and describe for me will abide with me forever.'" Without noticing it, he grew tired, pulled the cart under a tree, and decided to light a campfire right there. If he had come upon a grocery store or a fruit and vegetable stand, he would have taken a scarf or shirt and traded it for bread and a piece of cheese, fruit, and vegetables.

"A month ago you asked me whether I remembered that I'm a Jew. I didn't know how to answer, and I finally said, 'Very little.'"

"'How is that?' you wondered.

"'A few days before we left the house on our way to you, my father asked me to forget I was a Jew. It was a new way of speaking, and a new determination, that I hadn't heard from him before. I didn't understand what he meant. In the end he said, 'You have to learn from

Grandpa Sergei. He is a commander and a marvelous teacher. He'll teach you to be a villager, but, no less important, to be a soldier. Grandpa Sergei was an important commander. He knows the ways of nature and the ways of the army.'

"'And what will become of me?' I asked.

"'You'll change.'

"'I don't want to change,' I said and started crying.

"'My dear, you have to change. With Grandpa Sergei you'll change easily.'

"'Father, I don't want to change,' I repeated stubbornly.

"'If you don't change, you'll suffer a lot.'

"Those were my father's last words to me. He frightened me so much that at night I dreamed that Grandpa Sergei, in his desire to change me, pierced my ear.

"For many days I couldn't remember how I parted from my father."

47

Night was falling, and Yanek slowed his steps. He heard and saw the peasants returning from the fields, the carts loaded with green and red cabbage. Yanek was familiar with this emergence of the evening, and he loved it.

Suddenly a drunken song broke through that beauty. A tall peasant headed the band of drunks, singing a muddle of melodies. The songs fell away, and only a march remained. Rather, scraps of a march, and this is what they sang:

"The Jews are gone. The Jews are smoke.

"You won't even find them in a cloud."

At first the drunken crew responded and repeated after him, word for word, but a short drunkard cast doubt on that march and composed other words, singing:

"The Jews are alive, the Jews are alive.

"They're found in every hiding place.

"In every garbage heap they swarm.

"They're alive. They're alive."

The tall drunk didn't accept the march of the short drunk, and he shouted at him, "They're gone, they're gone, not even in a cloud."

Yanek stood there. He didn't understand that competition. He grasped the cart's shafts and moved on. Only after he had gone some distance did he know that he had done something that was forbidden: flight wasn't proper for a person who had been Grandpa Sergei's pupil.

Yanek remembered how Grandpa Sergei had fought against drunks, crazy people, proud people, who had approached him as if he weren't a man but a shadow. In times of danger, Grandpa had filled with silence. His alertness was restrained, immobile. At the right moment he would grab his opponent and throw him down.

Once he had pinned down a gigantic peasant. The giant was so embarrassed and ashamed that he called to him, "How did you do that? You should be ashamed of yourself. Next time I won't let you touch me."

While he could see Grandpa Sergei in his full, alert silence, he lay the shafts on the ground and ran over to the short drunkard, and with a voice that was not his own he shouted: "Why are you happy at the misfortune of other people?"

"It's allowed to be happy at the misfortune of wicked sons of the devil," said the drunk.

"People should be judged as individuals."

"Sons of the devil are judged together."

"People are created in the image of God."

"Damn you!" The short drunkard cursed him.

The other drunks tried to get close, but seeing Yanek and how angry he was, they realized they should keep their distance. The short peasant didn't stop provoking Yanek, who didn't respond to the provocations. He just said with huge contempt, "Shut your mouth."

Every minute one of them would pull himself up and

threaten to hit Yanek, but that was just in appearance. They could barely stand up on their rubbery legs, and the more they shouted and cursed, the weaker they got, till they finally slumped down and fell asleep.

Yanek looked them over from close up and let them be. When he returned to the cart he felt great closeness to Grandpa Sergei. Grandpa Sergei's face had changed. Death had left its mark on it: it was gray, but all his goodness of heart remained intact.

Suddenly he felt uncomfortable because he was about to deliver Grandpa Sergei to the elders of the village. It wasn't for nothing that Grandpa Sergei hadn't returned to his native village. If he had wanted to return, he would have returned. His relatives and the people of the village had something against him. Who knew whether they'd want to accept him, to forgive him.

He pulled the cart under a tree and sat down. Hardly had he sat down when he heard Grandpa Sergei's voice: "Don't hesitate, my friend. Take me to my native village. Talk to the priest. He's a decent man. He'll recognize me easily. He'll take care of my body and return me to my ancestors. It's forbidden to leave a person unburied too long. The body has to return to the dust. Don't hesitate. Eat and drink something, and slowly, but without hesitation, make your way to the village."

48

From here on the road was paved. The sun shone between the clouds, and Yanek pulled the cart with ease. He felt he would reach the village soon. It occurred to him that Grandpa Sergei's soul had long since gone up to heaven, and now his body had to be returned to the earth from which it was taken.

In the evening Grandpa Sergei would sometimes forget he was blind. He would open his blind eyes and lean his body toward the breeze, trying to touch it. He used to say that in the evening a person's soul expanded, and it wants to rise up.

In the army, from your first day in basic training, they try to narrow your life, to command you what to do and what not to do. Not even the nights are your own. But, amazingly, Grandpa Sergei liked that severe restriction just as he loved to take flight in his mind and plunge into a broad world that was entirely clean.

The army taught him to be stingy with words. Everything he did or asked his soldiers to do was marked by that restraint. Yanek felt, perhaps even more than before, that Grandpa Sergei had planted the roots of restraint in him. It was just too bad that he hadn't managed to teach him the melodies he remembered from his time in the village.

Once he asked Grandpa Sergei, "Did your mother sing

you lullabies and shepherd's songs?"

"She did. They were planted in me like fruit trees. Unfortunately I've lost my singing voice. Lullabies and shepherd's songs pacify the soul and restore it to its first home."

Still Yanek had tried several times to listen to Grandpa Sergei's voice. Perhaps he would catch a song that his mother had sung to him in his childhood.

From where he was he could see the approaches to the village of Ivanov. Grandpa Sergei used to pronounce that name with sweet emphasis and always with a tremor. It was clear that he was connected to every piece of furniture in the village, to every bench in a yard and to every tree and flowerbed in front of the houses. Not to mention the fields, the stream.

Up to now it had seemed to him that Grandpa Sergei was with him. That's why he spoke to him as when he was alive. Yanek was sure that he didn't answer only because he was sunk into himself. Now, when the gates of the village opened to him, he knew that he had to leave Grandpa and stop bothering him with questions. He was sorry about their separation. He had often dreamed that when the war was over he would return to his home with Grandpa Sergei, and his former life, which had sunk inside him, would be restored.

Once he asked Grandpa Sergei, "When will I be a Jew again?"

"When you return home."

"And now where am I?"

"You're wandering with me."

Just then a calf came out of a grove of trees and stood

in the middle of the road. Yanek put the cart shafts down on the ground and looked at it. For some reason it seemed to him that he was about to be slaughtered for someone's dinner, and Yanek shouted, "Run away, run away." But the calf was a friendly creature and wasn't alarmed by Yanek's shouts. It didn't move. Yanek raised his voice and shouted louder, and the calf ran for its life.

From then on he didn't stop the cart. The first houses peaked out from the shrubbery. An elderly woman walked to the dairy. It was clear that the road was taking him to the center of the village. An old man leaning on a cane came out of one of the courtyards.

"Good evening, Grandpa. Where does the priest live?" asked Yanek.

"Go straight, and people will tell you."

Without putting down the shafts, he kept moving forward. Now the evening was full. Bluish smoke curled up from the chimneys of the houses. Housewives were preparing suppers, the men were coming back from the fields and stabling the horses. Yanek knew these sights very well, but he had always seen them from a distance. They had never tried to cross a village with their bundles and packs, not even in times when no one raised their voice against a stranger.

A boy showed him the priest's house.

"Thank you," said Yanek.

The boy stood there and was surprised: you don't have to thank someone for something like that. The longer he stood, the more the surprise showed on his face.

Yanek knocked on the door. The priest shuffled in his

slippers and appeared in the doorway: a tall man whose back was bent by the years, and his long hair had thinned.

"What do you want, my lad?" He spoke cordially to Yanek.

"My name is Yanek. I was Sergei Ivanovich's errand boy."

"Our Sergei Ivanovich? What happened to him?" The priest's hands shook.

"The day before yesterday a stray bullet hit him and killed him on the spot."

Upon hearing that news, the priest's watery eyes opened, and he called out, "Vera, Vera." Immediately a tall woman appeared, took him by the arm and shoulder, and sat him down in a wicker chair.

When he had recovered, he spoke to the woman and said, "Did you hear? Our Sergei has been hurt. A stray bullet hit him."

"Where is he?" asked the woman, as though she had been awakened from sleep.

"He's here in the cart," said Yanek and removed the coat he had placed over Grandpa Sergei's face.

His face had changed a lot. It was gray, but its features were still lively.

"Our Sergei. Look what happened to our Sergei," said the priest with a weak, almost choked voice.

"We have to cleanse him and dress him," Vera spoke in a frighteningly practical tone.

"Don't hurry. Give us a moment to look at him," he said and immediately spoke to Yanek. "Sergei went blind. He was wandering among the villages and was a wanderer of God. So I was told by a woman who met him."

"That's true, sir," Yanek confirmed.

The priest looked at Grandpa Sergei's face for a long time, and he wanted to be told about everything that had happened to him after leaving the village.

In the end, without moving his face, he said to Vera, "Call the novice priests and tell them to bring a stretcher."

"Should we tell the family?" asked Vera.

"No. Not until we've cleansed the body and dressed it. Then we'll call the family. In any case, the funeral will be tomorrow morning."

Meanwhile two novices appeared, dressed in clerical robes, and bearing a stretcher. Without asking anything, they stepped over to the cart, looked around it and in it, lifted up the body, and placed it on the stretcher. Then they took it away.

The old priest sighed, as though he had done his duty. From now on everything was in the hands of heaven.

It was silent. Yanek was hungry and tired and could barely stand up.

Suddenly the priest spoke to Vera and said, "Get a bowl of soup for the boy. What's your name?"

"Yanek."

In a few minutes Vera served him a bowl of soup and some vegetables.

"Give him a slice of bread, too," said the priest.

After doing what the priests had asked of her, Vera closed the door and blew out the lantern.

Yanek finished the soup and the bread. With his mind emptied of thought, he got into the cart, curled up in Grandpa Sergei's military winter coat and fell asleep right away.

49

At midnight the cold woke him up. The house was shut, and searing cold already prevailed in the large courtyard. Yanek hopped and rubbed his hands. Finally, when the efforts to warm up were fruitless, he lit a campfire. Luckily for him, nobody woke up. He stood and warmed himself, and he had some tea.

Early in the morning some people gathered in the courtyard. They were dressed in work clothes and were apparently on the way to work. After waiting for a while, a man went and knocked on the door.

"Who's there?" a woman's voice was heard.

"We came for Sergei's funeral."

"Funerals aren't held at dawn," the same voice answered.

Afterward the family gathered. Two brothers were somewhat similar to Sergei, but their children looked different.

"How many years has it been since you saw Sergei?" An old man approached them and asked.

"Many years," answered one of the brothers.

"When did he die?"

"The day before yesterday."

Those simple, straightforward words sounded clear in the cold air of the morning. They kept repeating: "We came from darkness and we'll go into darkness. There's no point in asking."

Then the priest appeared, wearing his ceremonial robes. He raised his two white hands and called out loud, "Welcome."

The two young novices approached him, and the priest whispered something in their ears.

People kept gathering, and the courtyard filled up.

Then the two novices brought the coffin and set it on a platform. At the sight of the coffin, there was movement among the people. Grandpa Sergei lay there with makeup on his face, dressed in a black jacket and a white shirt, and wearing a green necktie. His formal appearance and the perfume they had sprayed on him did away with all the signs of his recent life. It was clear — he no longer belonged to here.

One of his brothers, seeing the well-dressed body, was moved and said, "Just the way he was."

The second brother didn't stop crying.

Suddenly one of the villagers raised his voice and said, "Sergei, you were our hero. Our children spoke about you before they went to sleep. We missed you. We expected you would return one day. But we didn't want you to return this way," he said and burst into tears.

Meanwhile many other people gathered and stood next to the fence. All of them wanted to see his face in the coffin, but there was no pushing.

Suddenly a woman's voice was heard. All the women had been in love with him. Every time he came back home from the army, there was a celebration. All the girls envied Tanya, his girlfriend.

An old man pointed at Yanek and said, "This boy brought him. Look at him."

No one approached him, as if he were a detail without value in Sergei's journey.

Now everyone was waiting for the priest's words. The priest straightened his clothes and his hair, took a few steps forward, and began: "Since your childhood, Sergei, since I baptized you into the faith, you have been with us. We saw you grow up, study in school, with in the fields with your parents. You were devoted to your parents and to the church. You never missed a service. When the day came for you to enlist, you joined the army, and there, too, you met with praise. You rose higher and higher, and in time you became the commander of a unit for special missions. Your heart didn't swell, and your eyes weren't haughty. On leaves, when you returned home, you would put on work clothes and go to work in the fields and the dairy. Your parents weren't the only ones who were proud of you. The whole village looked up to you. When you finished your long tour of duty, decorated with medals for excellence, everyone expected you to come home. Your girlfriend expected you to marry her, but you put off returning. People saw you in bars, in gambling houses, in coffee houses, and at the movies. I heard, and I was sorry for your soul. I loved you. I knew how much goodness was in you. I gathered my strength and wrote you a letter. I hate to write sermonizing letters. It's better for someone to come back to himself from within himself, without reminding him of his sins. You didn't answer me. In time I learned that you found a

decent woman and married her. I was glad. I hoped that
one day you would come back to us. Then your young
wife died, and you became a widower. The Jews who
had taken you under their wing went bankrupt, and you
began to wander. From time to time I received a brief
greeting from you. They told me that you had adopted
the ways of the wanderers, who seek their way to God.
Several times I wanted to go and visit you, but I didn't
manage. There were understandable delays and incomprehensible ones. You didn't wait for me to come. You
went to your final rest in the place where God chose to
take you to Him. It appears that the young Sergei and the
grown man, Sergei, were loyal servants of God.

"Now your journey is done. Now we are accompany-
ing you to your final rest. In the name of your ancestors,
who have been buried here for generations, and in all
of our names, we ask your pardon if we haven't acted
properly toward you. You are dear to us and will remain
dear," the priest finished his eulogy, and there was a lot
of weeping.

The two novices covered the coffin and bore it to the
cemetery. From then on there were no more speeches,
just prayers. Even after the coffin was buried in the earth,
the people didn't disperse. The weeping and fragments
of talk continued. The priest removed his sacred robes,
and all the splendor that had enveloped him departed.
He looked like one of the old peasants: short, bent over,
leaning on his staff, and cautious in his old age.

50

Once the people departed, Yanek dared to approach the priest and introduce himself again. "My name is Yanek. I brought Grandpa Sergei here."

"How long were you with Sergei?" the priest asked with dry objectivity.

"About a year and a half, your holiness. My father brought me to him and asked him to watch over me."

"Are you a Jew?"

"Yes I am, your holiness."

"How did he watch over you?"

"He taught me to be a Ukrainian. I knew how to talk a little Ukrainian, but Grandpa Sergei taught me to speak correctly, to pronounce all the words right, and to act like a Ukrainian."

"Did you go to church?"

"They don't allow lepers, people with mental illnesses, and wanderers into the church. Among other things, Grandpa Sergei taught me to speak sparingly and to be satisfied with little."

Upon hearing Yanek's words, the priest bowed his head.

After a pause he roused himself and asked, "What are you going to do?"

"I'm going out on the road to look for my parents and grandparents."

"Where were you born, and where did you live before the war?"

Yanek told him the name of his small city.

Suddenly, with no warning, the priest turned his head to the back door of the church and called out with a thin voice, "Vera, come to me." Vera arrived, and the priests instructed her: "This lad is going out on the road. Make him a basket with bread, cheese, hardboiled eggs, and pickled cucumbers."

"I'll do it right away."

"Go in peace. By virtue of the mercy you showed to Sergei, may God preserve you and return you to your dear ones."

Again he was by himself. It occurred to him that if it rained, he could go into one of the huts used to store firewood, and he would see again everything that was shown to him at Grandpa Sergei's funeral. Rain didn't fall, and he stopped next to a tall plane tree and said to himself, "This is how we used to stop after a period of wandering."

Grandpa Sergei often said, "A wanderer who doesn't exert his legs isn't worthy of being called a wanderer, just an idle passerby."

In their long journey, they had met quite a few wanderers. Most of them had forgotten their destination. They were lazy, drowsing by the side of the road and in the entrances to bars, dragging along trails to peasant houses to ask for charity. To tell the truth they were beggars, not wanderers. A true wanderer is poor, but his poverty doesn't degrade him.

Now Yanek remembered the wanderers who had tried to flee to the monastery of Saint Mary. They had been close to the monastery, and with some effort they could have gotten there. But the will to struggle had died out in them. The young peasants robbed them of their packs and bundles, and they also kicked them.

Grandpa Sergei called out in encouragement, but, as always, most of the wanderers faltered and lay down on the ground.

Memory of being together with Grandpa Sergei filled him with longing. Grandpa Sergei had strength that he never expressed by using high words or raising his voice. Injustices and coarseness made him angry, but he never allowed anger to take control over him. All his movements were restrained, and he himself inspired silence.

Only now did understanding begin to seep into Yanek, that he remained to preserve Grandpa Sergei's treasures. Neither the priest nor his brothers understood him. But Yanek would have to work hard to collect his clear words, the implicit sentences, those that were spoken in melody or silence.

Once, when they were sitting at the entrance to a church, they heard the priest's sermon. Grandpa Sergei listened hard and finally said, "Spread with honey."

Yanek already knew that this insight was the essence of Grandpa Sergei's conception: speak simply, clearly, in a few chosen words. Anyone who speaks at length and piles up words is suspect of deceit.

51

It was evening again, and Yanek lit a fire. The supplies that the priest's housekeeper had given him were fresh, and he quickly prepared them, as he had done while Grandpa Sergei was alive.

Since Grandpa Sergei's departure, he makes a point of doing everything exactly the same as before. Sometimes he feels that he's more attentive.

Sometimes it seems to Yanek that Grandpa Sergei had a doctrine that could be taught, but how does one learn a doctrine that is mainly silence?

Once when Yanek brought him a small package of apples, he took an apple in his hand, and, after touching it and smelling it, he said: "God, I love your apples."

On cold nights, when the campfire didn't warm him, he would get up, rub his hands together, add wood to the fire, put a potato in it, and whisper: "God, what would we do without you? We are so narrow-minded that we take most of your gifts as self-evident."

When melancholy gripped him, he would ask Yanek for the brandy bottle and say, "God sometimes allows us to sin so we can recover the lost image of God."

Once Yanek asked him whether God dwelled in the church. He didn't answer with words, but he raised his hands and made a sign – no, and he immediately pointed at his chest as the dwelling place of God. Yanek loved his movements, the way he rose and sat, the way he curled his body before falling asleep. Every movement of his had power, but also humility.

Without noticing, Yanek closed his eyes and fell asleep. In his dream he saw his beloved uncle Joseph sitting on the ground. His hair had turned gray, and his two large, burning eyes were dulled, but he kept looking. Yanek recognized him, knelt, and called out, "Uncle Joseph." Uncle Joseph opened his large eyes and, with a weak voice, he said, "I'm tired."

"I'll make you a cup of tea," Yanek offered.

"No need. I'm tired."

Yanek didn't give up. He brought him a cup of tea and put a spoonful to his lips. His uncle sipped, raised his eyes, and he seemed to recognize Yanek, who kept spooning tea.

"Where were you, Uncle Joseph?"

"In a place it's impossible to talk about," he said and leaned his head against a tree trunk.

Yanek woke from the dream. It was morning.

52

After that there was silence, as after every war. Cows and horses were scattered on the fields. Here and there a farmer was estimating the damage of the war. Far off on the horizon a man was walking on crutches.

At this season the family used to gather on Grandpa Jacob's farm. At the last gathering, Yanek was nine. Grandma Sara was no longer among the living, but her two daughters continued to run the household and take care of Grandpa.

Among those who came to these gatherings was his beloved Uncle Joseph, dressed well and smiling to everyone. Uncle Joseph was the beacon of the family. His talents were already evident when he was in high school. He was accepted in the university at sixteen, and there, too, he never ceased surprising people, but women were his undoing. He married twice and divorced twice. The family also stood by him when he stumbled. After a while he recovered, and his research once again produced marvelous results.

At the last gathering Uncle Joseph had sat next to his sister, Yanek's mother. His sister looked like him, but her temperament was different. She married a prosperous merchant and led an ordinary life. Uncle Joseph loved her, and every time he got into trouble, or his spirits fell, he would come to be with her and hear her advice.

A few days before the gathering, bad dreams had disturbed Yanek. He wanted to talk to his mother, but for some reason he didn't dare. In the end, when he did dare, her mind wasn't open to him. She said, over and over, "Not now."

Though there were no inauspicious signs, the people spoke about the imminent war as if it were an established fact: the trains weren't on time in arrivals or departures, people returned to their parents in the villages, the streets were full of abandoned animals. But aside from those bad signs, that it was also possible to interpret differently, there were no visible signs. Business went on as usual, the streets were swept and washed in the morning, and the shop windows were lit at night. The coffee houses were crowded with people, and couples walked arm in arm on the promenade.

Yanek was still in school. Surprise quizzes and examinations oppressed him, but the grades he brought home were excellent. His parents were content.

At last the gloom left his mother's face, and she said, not without an apology, "Come, dear, let's sit and talk. The time is available."

Yanek wanted to tell her about the dreams that frightened him, but the words, or rather the clear pictures that scared him, passed from his eyes in daylight, and he didn't know why he had been so panicked.

"Tell me, my dear," his mother asked him again, but the more she asked, the more the words shrank and went silent.

Yanek was pained by that block. He promised his mother that soon he would tell her everything.

But meanwhile the preparations for the gathering at his grandfather's farm were over.

Early in the morning a carriage came and gathered them. Yanek was excited. He hadn't shut his eyes all night long, and now, when he was sitting next to his mother in the carriage, he only wanted to sleep in her lap.

He slept for half the trip, and the remnants of his dreams drifted off as if they had never existed.

The road up to the Carpathians, which Yanek knew very well, was lit up. Hardly had two hours passed before they were at the gates of the farm.

Two Labrador retrievers greeted them with barks of joy. The yard man, who knew them well, came out to greet them.

"Here we are," his father called out. He helped his wife out of the carriage.

Grandpa Jacob had changed since his wife's death. His back bent. His gaze softened. The presence of that tall, broad-shouldered man was diminished in the courtyard. Yanek's mother, who loved her father dearly, fell into his arms and wept. Her father stroked her head as in her childhood.

Jennie, his mother's sister, who was also tall, came, dressed in pleasant autumn clothes. She had taken a degree in pharmacy and was about to open a pharmacy. She had gone to the big city to study on her own, and she had graduated with honors. She hugged and kissed the arrivals, and when they praised her achievements she said, "You can't imagine how stupid the other students were, especially the women. You should know that wisdom does not dwell in the pharmacy school."

"Would you choose a different profession?"

"Certainly. But the medical school doesn't let Jews in.

The Jews are forced to study — if they insist on studying — just pharmacy and dentistry, and even that with restrictions. The thought that every day I'd have to hurt people, just that thought, deterred me from studying dentistry."

Hardly had she spoken when her face went pale, and her heart felt faint. His two younger sisters quickly brought her some pear conserves and a cup of water. Jennie sipped, tasted the conserves, and her face recovered. "The passage from the flat city to the mountains made me dizzy," she said, and added, "Nothing can be done."

"What's the matter, Jennie?" they surrounded her.

"Nothing, just some dizziness," she said, and everyone laughed.

The return to the farm was always exciting. Some people turned pale, some shed a tear, and some broke into a flood of speech. Even in ordinary times the return to the farm was exciting. No one arrived there indifferent.

True, since Grandma Sara's death, the look of the farm, and especially Grandpa Jacob himself, had changed. Life here was full of non-speech. His children knew about Grandpa's distress, and everyone came to the gathering.

During the gathering the conversations and meals calmed everyone's mind slightly. Grandpa repeatedly told about times past, about the farm's days of greatness, about Grandma Sara's doings, about the sorrow and joys. They celebrated the holidays here in full splendor. Especially Passover and Shavuot. Hanukkah and Purim also raised their spirits. Grandpa Sara had made every holiday into a celebration.

53

Everyone loved to return to the farm. While Grandma Sara was alive, it was, of course, different. On Friday evening she would light candles and bless them, and Grandpa would say the kiddush blessing on the wine, and childhood days would once again light the house.

Now the members of the household sit and converse, recall memories. As though on their own, resentments and insults from long ago rise to the surface.

Surprisingly, Uncle Joseph announces that he has great love for the farm. Every time he returns, his life is renewed. Separation from the farm caused him quite a bit of depression. It was too bad he hadn't understood that earlier — life was more important than the scientific research he was engaged in. It sucked up your marrow and dried your bones.

Everyone listened to him. Grandpa sat in the wicker chair and didn't utter a word. Once he used to be an active participant in these discussions. Now he just sat, as though to say, we've already discussed that. I've seen too many contradictions in my life. To my regret, they can't be resolved.

The two sisters, who had never been away from the farm for long, prepared lunch as in times past. Grandpa recovered. He sat at the head of the table next to his eldest daughter, Yanek's mother.

Vegetable soup was served, and it gave off a thick

vapor, and after it there came a great awakening.

Yanek's mother sank into conversation with her brother Joseph. Yanek suddenly felt alone. At first it seemed to him that the gathering would be happy, because his birthday was approaching. The family used to give presents early. But this time no one offered him a present, and that darkened his mood.

It was good that Aunt Jennie approached him, hugged him, gave him a kiss, and asked, "How are you, my dear? Why is your face sad?"

"I have bad dreams at night," Yanek told her.

"Did you tell about them to Mother?"

"No."

"Why not?"

"Mother has been busy recently, and I didn't want to bother her. When I decided to tell her, she said, 'Not now.'"

"When it's a matter of dreams, of this sensitive and painful expression, you mustn't be polite. You say: 'Mother, I want to tell you my dream. It's urgent.'"

"I told her in my own words."

"I'm ready to listen," said Aunt Jenny in a decisive way.

Yanek was surprised. He hadn't expected to be understood so easily.

"Aunt Jennie, at this moment, I can't find the words to tell you. Maybe tomorrow I'll be able to tell you," Yanek spoke in a voice that wasn't his own.

"Strange," said Aunt Jenny. This time she was also surprised. But, to her credit, she didn't press him.

Yanek went outside to look at the farm. At this season, early spring, most of the trees were still bare. Here and there an almond tree bloomed. Grandpa loved his

243

orchards. With his own hands he pruned them and took care of diseases and the fallen branches. He didn't manage to convey his love for the fields and orchards or his love for the tradition to all his children, though most of his children were drawn to the holidays. On the holidays they went up to the farm and stayed there for two or three days.

When he met Aunt Jennie in the living room, she hugged him and asked, "Now do you have the words to tell me your dreams? I won't tell anyone. It'll be a secret between us."

Yanek smiled and said, "Why should I make you sad?"

"It's not right to leave you with dreams like that."

"This evening, before I go to sleep, I'll tell you."

Meanwhile Grandpa woke from his doze and everyone surrounded him. He spoke about his longings for Grandma. They had been together for most of their lives. She had been sixteen when they married. They had improved the farm and raised their children with their own hands.

Uncle Joseph took the floor again. "Father, we're always with you. We love you. The farm is precious to us. You dwell in every one of your children. You gave each of your children a portion of yourself. Mother was no different from you. Her generous heart is planted in all of us. It was easy to love her. She always had some food or drink with her, not to mention a comforting word. The folk songs she used to sing to us before we went to sleep are still stored up within us like a sweet secret, and on the long summer nights she used to tell us folk tales. True, each of us has gone in a different direction, but we have remained close to you and Mother."

After Uncle Joseph spoke, it seemed that a lot of people in the living wanted to add something, but that was wrong. His emotional words stunned them. For some time the living room remained wordless.

After that Yanek's mother dressed him for the night and kissed his forehead. Hardly had she left his bedroom when Aunt Jennie appeared, "May I sit next to you? Do you want to tell me about a dream or two?"

"In a little while."

"I promise I won't tell anyone about them."

Yanek began to speak, "Father, Mother, and I were standing in a field and looking at the sunset. Suddenly big horses came out of the horizon, horses such as I've never seen. There was fierce desire in their whinnying, and it was clear that we wouldn't escape alive from their galloping. 'Lie down,' Father called out in a horrible voice. Mother and I did lie down."

"And what happened?" asked Jennie.

"Apparently the horses jumped over us, but the fear remained.

"The next day I had another dream. This time we were on a lawn. The big horses were grazing quietly. I wondered how the anger and desire had disappeared from their eyes. I looked at them. Their eyes said, 'You're wrong: the anger and desire are within us. We are nourishing them in secret, and when the time comes, you'll see them.'

"Every night the horses come back. I have no doubt that they want to gobble us up. But for some reason they haven't done so yet. Will they gobble us up?"

"Horses don't gobble people up," Aunt Jennie replied.

"But these are wild horses."

"They're not wild horses. Just big ones."

That last sentence remained in Yanek's mind before he sank into a deep sleep.

54

Early the next morning Uncle Joseph and Aunt Jennie left the farm. Yanek's grandfather and his mother sat in the dining room and drank coffee. They spoke slowly and with pauses, and they were clearly close to one another. Yanek's father sat outdoors, sunk in thought. Yanek usually didn't disturb him, but this time he violated that principle and approached him.

"Father, good morning."

"Good morning, dear."

A year had passed since his business had collapsed. True, every month Grandpa sent him some money to live on, but that assistance didn't make him happy. The thought that he was needy darkened his spirit.

"Why did you get up early, dear?" his father wondered.

"The light here woke me up."

"Too bad. Morning sleep is the best sleep."

"Father, why didn't you go in to drink coffee?"

"In a little while."

Suddenly Yanek realized something he hadn't grasped before. His father's big lumberyard had been seized. Now the doors were locked with chains and sealed with wax. No one entered or left. His father spent most of the day at home, pacing about from room to room, and when his mother asked him something, he stood there in silence.

He didn't speak with anyone. Uncle Joseph, whom he loved dearly, also failed to get a word out of his mouth.

"There's no reason to blame yourself. The conditions changed. Logic has been lost. Everything is chaotic. Once the storm has passed, life will get back to normal," Uncle Joseph kept whispering.

His father didn't answer. His gaze showed clearly that he didn't agree. His father usually didn't argue with his brother-in-law. Uncle Joseph was a master of language, and he always won arguments, but
Yanek's father had the power of silence, which he got from his life experience. He had worked for years in forests and sawmills. The various workers, the porters, were men without words. The sounds they emitted from their mouths were like the sounds of tall trees and the voices of animals. His father understood them, and they obeyed him. Now not only was the lumberyard closed. His father's whole being was trapped. No one, except the family, dared to approach him.

For lunch the sisters made borscht with sour cream, blintzes, and a fruit salad for dessert. Without Uncle Joseph and Aunt Jennie, the house was silent. Yanek's father sat and drank the red borscht with the haste of an unfortunate man. The simple, pretty house, that the sisters kept tidy with devotion, the house where generations have lived, suddenly seemed exposed to danger.

Grandpa approached Yanek and asked, "What are you doing these days?"

Yanek was alarmed by the question and said, "I'm attending school."

"Are you a good student?" he asked with a smile.

"I do the best I can," Yanek answered, knowing that his grandfather would be pleased by his answer.

Then one of the younger sisters burst into bitter tears. Grandpa knelt, hugged her, and spoke softly to her, saying, "No disaster happened. The world is open before you. You can go wherever you want. You're only twenty-three."

Yanek's mother also came to console her, but the younger sister wasn't consoled. She sobbed with the voice of a persecuted person who refuses to be consoled. "Everything is closing up. Where will I go? I'll never be able to get to Herbert."

When all the words of consolation were in vain, Yanek's mother hugged her and took her out to the gardens, to the soft light of the afternoon, and she said, "Come to me, my dear. It's quieter in our house. Here threatening ghosts roam. There's no point in sitting and listening to them. Here everything is laden with the past. It's stifling. You have to live in the city, to walk on sidewalks, to dawdle and look in shop windows. To sit in coffee houses. Herbert was an episode. He happened to cross your path and went back to where he came from. Who knows who he was and what he carries within him. How many times did you meet him?"

"Twice."

"We must say, as they did in past generations: it's all for the best."

Her words fell on deaf ears. She was stubborn. "Everything is closing up. There's no opening. I'm choking," she spoke and fainted, and only when the old Ukrainian housekeeper spoke to her in Ukrainian did she open her eyes and ask, "Who's here? Why have you all gathered together?"

The housekeeper answered, "You had a bad dream and thought it was reality. We came to take you out of the dream, and we're all here to greet you."

The gentile housekeeper, who had served in that house for generations, hugged her like a hurt child and gathered her to her breast.

In the evening a carriage came to collect them. Grandpa, the two young sisters, and the Ukrainian housekeeper stood at the gate. Grandpa hugged and kissed those who were departing. The housekeeper hugged Yanek's mother and said, "May God preserve you. He is the only one you can depend on. Come back to us as soon as you can."

His mother hugged her sisters and tears flowed on her face.

That was the last gathering at the farm. No one imagined that it would be the last.

Yanek was tired. The short time at the farm filled him with sights. It was hard for him to think about them. He closed his eyes and fell asleep.

55

When Yanek awoke from a long sleep, it was morning. Rain had fallen at night, but Yanek wasn't wet. He had slept in Grandpa Sergei's army coat, and he had wrapped his head in a tarpaulin.

The long dream was still within him, but it wasn't clear to him. He knew it was a dream of many places and much talking, some of them in the farmhouse, and some in the gardens. He had met many people, but the morning erased them from his mind. Before his eyes stood the tree and the cart.

Just then he felt remorse, because he hadn't left Grandpa Sergei's clothes with the priest, so they could be buried next to his grave.

Without his noticing it, the remorse raised up sights from Grandpa Sergei's funeral: the priest, the two novices who had taken care of all the preparations before the burial.

Grandpa Sergei had a low opinion of the churches that didn't allow the mentally ill, lepers, and wanderers to enter their gates. But when he was lying in the coffin, wearing a black jacket and a green necktie, he seemed peaceful, so as to say: we all die. We all will be lain in a coffin. All the ceremonies are false, but, what can be done? People need this child's game.

Yanek was thirsty and lit a campfire. He placed the kettle on the burning branches. Before long, he was holding a cup of tea. While drinking it he realized that the long dream that twisted in his mind was still a tangle and couldn't be unsnarled.

Meanwhile, in the grove before him, wounded soldiers gathered, men who had been demobilized and were making their way back home. They were lost refugees, wanderers missing arms and legs. The sun came out from behind the clouds and lit up the grove and the men, and for a moment it seemed to Yanek that in a little while a village holy man would appear before them, would speak to them with soft words, and instruct them to go to a place where there was hot water for showers.

No holy man appeared, but a truck full of food arrived. Two soldiers from the Red Army stood in the door and handed out bread and tins of sardines. The men crowded the sides of the truck, but there wasn't a riot. Yanek approached and received a loaf of bread and a can of sardines.

A man who was sitting under a plane tree stared at Yanek. Finally he approached him and asked, "Do you speak Yiddish?"

Yanek hesitated and in the end said, "My mother tongue is German, but I understand Yiddish."

"The war is over. You can take the wooden cross off your neck," the man spoke clearly.

"Soon," Yanek said.

"Why not now? It will remove you from fear and loosen the shackles you put around your neck."

"I still have some obligations before I do that," said Yanek, feeling that he was speaking the truth.

"Obligations to whom?" the man jumped up.

"Don't worry. I am faithful to our God," said Yanek.

"Do you come from an orthodox Jewish home?"

"No," Yanek answered promptly.

"Sorry. I have just one more thing to tell you: not far from here they're giving out used clothing."

Yanek didn't know what to say. Finally he just said "thank you," harnessed himself to the cart, and set out. He walked for a long time. At least he stopped beneath a broad oak tree.

It was on a hill from which he could see the fields and orchards, and they were entirely green. Here, too, soldiers who had just been demobilized were walking in long lines. Refugees and cripples, though they were walking together, each one looked lost.

Hardly had he set the shafts down on the ground when thirst assailed him again. He went to gather firewood, and with every movement that he made until he lit the campfire, he saw Grandpa Sergei before his eyes. His features hadn't changed. The cry, "Grandpa Sergei," escaped his lips.

Flames rose from the twigs, and in a few minutes a cup of tea was in his hands.

After the funeral it had seemed to him that Grandpa Sergei had sailed off into the expanses of heaven, and he would never see him again. But there were hours when Grandpa Sergei appeared to be tangible, and every part of his body was full of vitality. It occurred to him that now he should bring Grandpa's clothing to their final rest.

Once a week they used to stop next to a river, bathe, and wash their clothes. Grandpa Sergei would say, "You have to honor clothes. They're close to our skin and they gather up everything that the body conveys to them."

56

Meanwhile Yanek changed his mind: maybe it would be better to go down and observe the people who were swarming on the dirt roads. Maybe he would find someone he knew.

The time he had spent with Grandpa Sergei had cut him off from his home and his parents. But not completely. There were days when he saw them in waking dreams or met them in dreams at night. All the meetings were like in a lake of fog. Nevertheless that distant closeness would move him and in the depth of his heart he looked forward to it.

If he met his parents, where would they go? To their house or to Grandpa Jacob's farm? His mother often said, "Let's go to Grandpa Jacob's. I need rest like air to breathe."

The short vacations at Grandpa Jacob's were stored up in him very well. At the farm his mother would return to herself and talk to Grandpa in Yiddish.

While he was wrapped in sights from home he saw a woman walking on the road who was very similar to his mother. The more he looked at her, the more the lines of similarity came together. "Mother," he called out. As soon as the sound came from his mouth, it was clear to him beyond any doubt that she wasn't his mother. He bowed his head and covered his face with his hands. Disappointment filled him, and he stood where he was for a long time, and when he was roused from the void that surrounded him, he harnessed himself to the cart and set out.

The cart was light, and he pulled it without feeling it.

For a long time he pulled the cart. Finally he realized: it was light because it was without Grandpa Sergei.

Then he camped under an oak tree with broad branches. Grandpa Sergei always asked about the thickness of the trunk and about the boughs of the tree, and whether its roots were exposed. When a tree was to his satisfaction, they would lay down their bundles and sit under it.

He was tired and about to curl up in the cart and go to sleep, but he remembered Grandpa Sergei's command: you shouldn't go to sleep without eating.

There were plenty of dry branches here. He lit a campfire, and in a short time the water was boiling in the kettle. He liked this hour. In fact, he loved every hour with Grandpa Sergei. Grandpa Sergei would grasp the cup and sip the tea. The skin of his fingers was cracked like that of tillers of the soil, but at the same time as delicate as a city-dweller.

Yanek ate the bread and cheese. The food that the priest's housekeeper gave him was fresh and tasty. He felt Grandpa Sergei's presence growing stronger. It was as powerful as if he were sitting next to him.

"Grandpa Sergei, are you here?" the words broke from Yanek's lips.

"What do you want?" the answer was prompt.

"Nothing. I just wanted to know whether you will always be with me."

"Always."

That word brought a smile to Yanek's face.

Now he knew that he would bury Grandpa Sergei's clothes in that place.

Without delay he brought Grandpa Sergei's army shovel from the cart and began to dig. The earth was damp and loose. Within a short time the pit, about a meter square, was ready. He straightened the sides and said to himself: this is a pretty place, high, visible but not conspicuous.

Yanek added some twigs to the fire, poured himself a cup of tea, and felt Grandpa Sergei's exposed presence.

He wanted to ask whether the place and the tree seemed good to him, but he didn't ask.

He sat and remembered the trees at whose feet Grandpa Sergei had also sat, and it seemed like a long journey with short pauses. Grandpa Sergei chose the trees, and there was a reason for his choice. Usually it was a tall tree with broad branches, that would protect them from rain and also hide them from the eyes of evildoers. The tree didn't always fulfill Grandpa's expectations. But the silence of every tree was inscribed in Yanek's memory. Grandpa Sergei used to say, "It's a fine thing to pray next to a tree and to hear prayer."

Without preparations, he fell asleep on the edge of the pit.

57

Early in the morning he woke up and immediately added branches to the dormant fire. He asked himself whether he should boil water in the kettle on the fire or start the work of burial. Yanek felt that it wasn't right to drink tea before burying Grandpa Sergei's clothes.

At night, in his sleep, he planned the order of burial. First he would put in the boots. Grandpa Sergei had two pairs, which he cleaned from time to time and spread oil on them. "Solid boots are the secret of correct walking. A torn boot, with the big toe sticking out of it, is a miserable boot, and you're better off walking barefoot. A bare foot is an honorable foot," he used to repeat.

Yanek went to get them, and before placing them on the bottom of the pit, he looked at them. A good army boot that wraps the ankle well, the thought went through his mind.

Before putting them on, Grandpa Sergei used to feel the leather.

Once he said, "My feet have shaped the boots. Now they fit my foot, and they're comfortable."

Then Yanek brought the socks. There were three pairs of socks, and he was careful to wash and darn them. Whenever he came home on leave, Grandpa Sergei's mother used to give him a pair of woolen socks she had knit herself. Of all the socks that he had and wore out, there remained three of his mother's pairs. Yanek put them on the boots.

Not until he placed the shirts — two army shirts and one civilian shirt — did his hands begin to tremble. Now he wasn't sure whether the order was correct.

He looked for the Bible in Grandpa Sergei's bundle and read the verse: "And God said to Abram: Get thee from thy country and thy homeland, and from the house of thy father, to the land I will show thee." Grandpa Sergei loved that verse. He knew it by heart, but he used to ask Yanek to read it out loud to him.

For a moment he stood in front of the open grave. His mouth opened, and he spoke: "Grandpa Sergei, the day before yesterday you were gathered among your ancestors. Today I'm burying your clothes and your belongings. I didn't want to abandon them. I pray in my heart that what I'm doing is according to your will. I know, you didn't give much importance to material things and possessions. But your clothes were always clean and fit your body. As you used to say: 'the honor of the body is the honor of its appearance.'"

The pit filled with clothes. All that remained of Grandpa Sergei's bundle were the kettle, the plate, the cup, the knife, the bag of tea, the brandy, the pistol, box of sugar, and the valuables that his father had left with Grandpa Sergei. A thought occurred to Yanek: maybe it would be better to burn the garments than to bury them, in case they're uncovered. But he immediately changed his mind. To burn them would be a violent action.

Only after he closed the grave did he feel that now Grandpa Sergei had been taken from him. He wanted to take a sip of brandy that would spin him around and throw him to the earth. Often, when Grandpa Sergei saw that Yanek was depressed, he would say, "Yanek, take a sip of brandy. It will spin you around and remove you from depression."

"Now we'll fire three shots in honor of Grandpa Sergei," he said, without planning it. He removed the pistol from the holster and fired three shots, the way Grandpa Sergei had taught him to shoot.

He lit the fire and placed the kettle on the burning branches, sat down, and looked at the fire.

Those were the most beautiful hours of his journey with Grandpa Sergei.

He poured himself a cup of tea, and the sadness that had threatened to take possession of him since he arranged the clothing gripped him more strongly.

"I believed we would both go to greet my parents," he said, and tears welled up in his eyes.

Without thinking of it, he removed the cross from his neck and lay it in the cart. Then he took off the peasant shirt and the linen trousers and tried to put on the clothes that his mother had put in his backpack. But, unfortunately, time had done its work: the clothes had become small on him, and he decided to loosen the seams. That worked, and he managed to put on the clothes.

Now, in his ragged clothes, he looked like a refugee. Before setting out he stood next to the grave and said, "Farewell, Grandpa Sergei. I'm leaving you. You will always be with me. I expect to hear your voice and see your face. I'm going to look for my parents, and I pray I'll find them. I'm not afraid. You taught me not to fear."

58

He immediately hoisted the pack to his back and set out. It was cold, but he was pleased he had decided to take Grandpa Sergei's military jacket. In the past days he hadn't taken it off by day or by night.

Fields and groves of trees surrounded him with silence on every side. He marched without stopping.

Everything that had happened to him in the past days was as if erased from his mind. He was void of sensations and emotions, and it was good that his half-frozen feet were willing to march and to bear him.

After an hour of walking he wondered: where were the demobilized soldiers, and where were the refugees? Nothing could be seen or heard.

The peasants he had met during the journey with Grandpa Sergei didn't conceal from them what they had done to the Jews. Their expression was a mixture of indifference and sadistic pleasure.

Grandpa Sergei would scold them and say, "You mustn't take pleasure in other people's misfortune."

Yanek heard and didn't hear their words. In any event, he didn't ask much, and Grandpa Sergei didn't tell a lot.

Suddenly a group of refugees emerged from the tall weeds. They marched energetically, and it seemed like they knew where they were going. Yanek joined them and noticed that they didn't talk a lot. After walking for

an hour they stopped and sat at the side of the road.

A woman who was sitting next to him raised her head and asked, "What camp are you from?"

"I wasn't in a camp."

The woman was astonished and asked, "How come?"

"I was with Grandpa Sergei."

"In his house?"

"No. We wandered from village to village," Yanek said, feeling as though he was divulging a secret.

"Do you call him 'Grandpa Sergei' because of his age?"

"No. He was a grown man, but not an old one."

Only now could he see the refugees' faces, familiar faces, like those of his parents, grandparents, uncles, aunts, and cousins. It seemed to him that if he looked at them carefully, he would find his relatives.

"Take a slice of bread and some sausage," the woman offered.

"I don't eat meat."

"Why not?"

"Because Grandpa Sergei didn't eat meat."

"Have some bread and cheese."

"Thanks."

Yanek looked at the people again. They were so familiar, as if he had seen them in his house, or in the lumberyard.

"You wandered with Grandpa Sergei during the whole war?" The woman went on to ask. "Weren't you afraid?"

"With Grandpa Sergei, you aren't afraid," Yanek said and he was glad he had found the right words.

"What city are you from?"

Yanek named the city.

"Not far from here. What's your family name?"

"Wiener."

"Wiener of the big lumberyard?"

"Yes."

"I knew your father and mother. Who didn't know them? Everyone in the city and the surroundings needed wood. In the Wiener lumberyard you could find all kinds of wood: wood for heating, boards for furniture, beams for houses, wood for wagons, and hoops for barrels.

"It was a whole world. Next to the lumberyard there was a coffee house that was decorated tastefully. People used to go there before buying or afterward, or they came to eat soup. Young couples would meet on dates there. The coffee house was always full, but never crowded.

"Near the lumberyard there was a shop where all the toys were made of wood: children, clowns, dogs and cats, big wooden blocks, houses of various sizes, some for pennies, some for a lot of money.

"What can I say? It was a whole world. You probably don't remember me, but I remember you very well. You used to stand next to your father and eat ice cream. Now we're going back to emptiness, to the empty roads, to the empty houses. Everyone is a remnant of a family."

Suddenly she hugged Yanek and in a soft voice she said, "You have to be strong and not let your spirits sink," and for a long time she kept talking about the lumberyard and everything it gave to the city, and while she was talking, she fainted and fell to the ground, but she managed to say, "Watch over this boy. He's a precious boy. He has no one in the world."